THE RUSH'S ECHO

GINGER SMITH

This is a work of fiction. Names, characters, places and incidents are either the product of the author's imagination or are used fictitiously apart from those well-known historical figures. Any resemblance to actual persons, living or dead, is entirely coincidental.

THE RUSH'S ECHO

Copyright © 2022 by Ginger Smith

Art/Cover design
by Karen Deem of Deem Loureiro, Inc.

ISBN: 979-8-218-10032-2 (print)

All rights reserved to the author. No part of this book may be reproduced in any form or by any electronic or mechanical means, including information storage and retrieval systems, without written permission from the author, except for the use of brief quotations in a book review.

This book is dedicated to those who loved The Rush's Edge. Thank you!

Why not make a vat soldier a mindless automaton, you might ask—each one like the other? While it would be easy to program them to be loyal, automatic machines for the Coalition, the beauty of what we do is that we leave them their individuality and free will--to a degree. They are creative thinkers, yet they are loyal. We even give names to these soldiers—to make each one a unique individual. After all, if we had wanted an army of clones, we certainly could have done so.

The strength of the vat troops lies in making them distinctive. Each with his or her own strengths and talents and one thing in common. In doing the will of the state, they find satisfaction—a satisfaction only attainable through loyal service.

DR. ARCHIBALD BESH, FOUNDING
DIRECTOR OF THE VANGUARD ASSAULT
TROOP PROJECT

PROLOGUE

The afternoon sun rays glinted off the doyen's crystal liquor glass as he turned it back and forth. Anvar Meyer, the doyen and supreme leader of the Coalition of Allied Systems, loved this time of day and usually spent it sipping a tonic made with some of the rarest herbs in the Coalition. The liquor was over 4,000 scrilla a bottle.

As he relaxed in his garden on Haleia Prime, he reflected on the Coalition's course. He thought about how the Mudar had been the best thing to ever happen to them. Before the "invasion," the Coalition had been one of a half-dozen powers, all vying for economic and military control. Granted, the Coalition had been the strongest of all of them, but in the centuries before the aliens' appearance, their agenda had been checked. After their arrival, the twelve systems of the Coalition had offered their protection and membership to those systems most at risk from the Mudar, the area that the coreworlders called the Edge.

Fear of an impending invasion drove dozens of planets under their protection. They had willingly joined, providing the Coalition with more resources, more money, more of everything. The coreworlds grew strong, exploiting the raw materials and resources of the Edge.

Then came the vats. The Vanguard Assault Troop program had been developed by reverse engineering Mudar technology. He had no idea how the science worked, but it had given the Coalition the means of not only fighting the Mudar, but the manpower for controlling the systems at the furthest reaches of the Spiral.

That had been 200 years ago, and the aliens had not been seen in over 100, but still the vat program continued. Now the vats were pointed at whatever enemy the Coalition pursued, which meant whatever enemy the doyen chose.

Now that enemy had become the Al-Kimians. They were actively fomenting unrest in planets across the Edge and were using the Coalition's own vats against them. That was being handled, but the larger issue was who was controlling them. Usually released vats were not a problem – most burned themselves out on null or other drugs. Others killed themselves in dangerous operations in deep space – generally not surviving even to their "natural" death.

Now, however, that was changing. The vats had a cause to fight for and leaders to direct them. This could be dangerous.

"Doyen."

He turned to see Roger Triuna, Senate Leader of the Coalition standing silhouetted by the sun.

"Senator Triuna. Have a seat."

TRIUNA CAME up to take a seat across from him. The herbal smells of sun-warmed pinete and greenneedles rose around them as Triuna sat and smiled at the mild looking middle-aged man who ruled the galaxy with an iron fist. It was safer to keep

Anvar Meyer on your good side. The last leader of the Senate had died mysteriously after clashing with Meyer. It was said that Senate Leader Donnely, Triuna's predecessor, had committed suicide by eating pinete blossoms. Well, it had been ruled a suicide, but no one would think to kill themselves in such a way. It was a horrifying death. The politician had died from throwing up so violently that the blood vessels in his eyeballs and brain had hemorrhaged. He was found on the floor in his mansion, face in a pool of vomit and blood leaking from his eyes and mouth.

Triuna realized his gaze had wandered to the hedges of pinete that surrounded the doyen's home, and he guiltily looked away. When he looked back up, he saw Meyer was watching him carefully.

"Please, have a drink." He gestured to the finely cut crystal decanter on the low table in front of him. The rich wood table echoed the amber color of the liquid inside the bottle.

"Thank you, sir." Triuna poured himself a drink, struck by the scent of herbs and oniblossom. "I come bringing news that you will be pleased to hear. Our own Dr Balen has succeeded in creating a device to take care of our vat problem."

"Really?" Meyer smiled broadly. "I hadn't expected results so soon. How does it work?"

"I do not have the technical specs in front of me, but it kills vats at the press of a button. There are a few issues to be worked out, but the doctor is hopeful of a breakthrough. His team was also working on the Nash problem. In little more than five years, we hope to have a full complement of vats that will never leave service until they expire. Totally loyal to the Coalition and safe to serve. It will most certainly will solve the problem of traitorous vats defecting to our enemies."

The doyen lifted his glass. "Well, to Dr Balen, then."

"Dr Balen." Triuna smiled.

And they drank.

"What about this ship on Chamn-Alpha? The one that helped the researcher defect?"

"We lost track of them. We can assume it made its way to Al-Kimia," Triuna shrugged. "However, they can do very little with the information they have gained."

"Did this researcher have any direct knowledge of Balen's device?" Meyer asked.

"No, Doyen." He supposed there wasn't much they could do even if Parsen had known about it. "The doctor was present at the clinical trial, but the inner workings of the device are known only to Balen and the tecker who devised it."

Meyer nodded. "Then everything is according to plan."

Senator Triuna stared into his glass. "How soon will we go to war with Al-Kimia and her allies?"

"I have other assets at work on that," Meyer replied as he finished his drink. The ice tinked as he tipped the glass back and forth to watch the gleam of sunlight on the cut crystal. "Once it starts, I believe war may be swiftly accomplished."

"Oh. Is there anything you wish to share?"

"Not at this point. We will continue the blockade of Al-Kimia. Watch, and then wait." Meyer placed his glass on the table and stood. "Why don't you stay for dinner?"

"Oh no, Doyen. I am required back at the capital. I simply wanted to bring you this information personally," he stood as well, making a bow before they both walked back towards his shuttle.

"You're doing well, Triuna. I know that taking over for Donnely has been difficult, but you have taken a bad situation and made the best of it," Meyer met his gaze meaningfully, "and will continue to do so as we go forth."

"Yes, sir, I certainly will."

"Keep me informed if there are any further developments.

If the kill device could be perfected, war may be accomplished sooner than we think. I will see you in the Coalition Alliance Hall next week, Triuna." With those words, the doyen turned back toward his palatial mansion and Triuna sighed with relief as he entered his shuttle.

Still, as he flew off, he couldn't help but wonder how many other assets Meyer had in operation and what his endgame was. Time would reveal it of course, and until then, he would play the situation conservatively.

"Back to the capital, Corine," he ordered as he slipped into one of the cushioned chairs and watched the shuttle bank back towards the traffic of the capital.

ONE

"Okay, Veevs. When I throw you, don't tighten up. Stay loose and bent."

"Are you calling me loose?" Vivi said with a smirk.

Hal shook his head with a grin of his own. "You're hilarious. Ready?"

"Yeah," she tipped her head to each side and shook out the tension in her body. "Come on."

Hal lunged at her, getting a grip as she struggled to avoid it. They had fought their way to the edge of the mats in the cargo bay when he was finally able to throw her down. She landed awkwardly, one of her hands going off the mat as she rolled. Vivi let out a short, sharp yelp at the pain and grabbed her wrist.

"Ah, shit!" Hal said, kneeling to help her. "What happened?"

In a sudden moment of inspiration, Vivi wrapped her legs around him in a guard and flipped him over, laying him out on his back as she straddled him. "Gotcha."

Hal grinned but still held out a hand for her wrist. "Good use of surprise. Now lemme see your hand."

She rolled off him, then reluctantly offered up her wrist. He sat up and palpitated it gently. "See, it's fine," she reassured him. "Let's go."

"So, your trainee got hurt already?" Vivi glanced up to see Ty standing at the door of the cargo area they were using to practice. He tossed his towel over a crate of equipment and began to stretch, dressed in workout clothes and his exoframe. He had been doing some light slow sparring with Hal every other day to strengthen his muscles, part of the physical therapy Beryl had laid out for Ty after he'd been paralyzed at the hands of a vat assassin. After a week, Vivi had started sitting in on their training sessions as well to learn more self-defense.

"I'm fine," Vivi said, standing up. "I landed badly, that's all."

"Take a break and let me soften him up for you first." Ty said. "You good for some sparring, Hal?"

"No problem," he answered. Vivi watched as Hal slid the focus pads on his hands. Ty began throwing punches as Hal expertly moved to block. Ty would hit with a combination, then Hal would take a swipe at him, either a hook or a cross which Ty would block or dodge. Their speed was slowed way down to compensate for the exoframe, but she'd seen Ty get better every day.

Despite his slow recovery from the injuries suffered at the hands of the vat who had stalked them to Jaleeth Station, Ty was still powerful. Maybe his upper body strength had improved as he compensated for not having the use of his legs or maybe he was always that strong. He was getting around exclusively with the exoframe which allowed him to walk, but she knew he had to be frustrated. Despite his practice, all he'd been able to manage was a sliding, slow sort of gait. Vivi found herself hoping for the millionth time that they would be able to find Eira's worldship. Saving Eira was the priority, but they were all also hoping she could help Ty like she helped Hal. It had been a month and a half since they left Al-Kimia, with an equal amount of time left to go before they got far enough out past the border of known space to find the Mudar.

"Not bad. You're starting to put some power back behind these punches, Cap," Hal said, with admiration.

"Yeah, you mean pretty good for a paralyzed old man. I get it," Ty teased. Vivi knew the joking was his way of trying to make them more comfortable with his situation.

After a while they could both tell that Ty was tiring. He kept going until Vivi almost intervened, but finally, he stepped back, sweaty, and exhausted. "That was good. Let me take a break for a minute," he sighed, turning and slip-walking the few steps to his water bottle.

"You did even better this time," Hal said, sliding his hands out of the mitts and going for his own bottle. "Beryl's on the bridge?"

"Yeah," Ty nodded.

"Good. Veevs, let me see your wrist again."

Vivi had crossed her arms over her chest, hiding it, but now she held it out. She could see and feel that it had started to swell. He moved her hand gently, twisting it each way and checking the tendons and ligaments. "I'm fine...I don't know why you—Ouch!" she winced, involuntarily pulling her hand away.

"Yeah, that's what I thought. Come on."

"It's nothing. A sprain..." Vivi said.

"Maybe. Best to be sure, though. Eira, can you comm Beryl and ask her if she can meet us at the medbay for a minute?"

"Yes, Hal," Eira's even tone replied.

"Good. I'll be back, Ty."

"No problem."

Ty began to work his way through the stretching routine that Beryl had taught him. The movements were supposed to help him with the stiffness that had set in after his injury, and he'd promised her to work at it every day.

"You have increased your flexibility by 12% since we left Al-Kimia," Eira said over the ship's comm. "You have been working hard."

"Thanks, Eira." Ty smiled as he eased himself down on the mats Hal had laid out in the cargo bay and used the braces to extend his legs out in front of him. Slowly, he leaned forward over his legs to stretch his back a little, but he wasn't able to go very far. He held the stretch as he ran a hand over a scratched bare area of the apparatus. He had taken a fall the first week out—his sliding gait had tripped him up in his quarters and he'd gone down hard. "I want to stay in the best possible shape for... later. Any results trying to hail your people?"

"No, we are too far out to make contact."

"I thought so. Is there anyone you would like to see when you return?" Ty straightened up and attempted another movement, this time lying face down on the floor and pressing up from a prone position.

"A friend named Reva."

"What is she like?"

"She is a scientist like me. Our templates were friends, so we were friends."

Here was something he could ask about. "What do you mean by 'template?'"

There was a pause. Ty imagined she was trying to figure out how to explain it to a human like himself. "It is the pattern on which I was based."

"You mean you were patterned after something – someone – like another being?" Ty was trying to imagine the people who would have created someone like Eira.

"Yes. We were fashioned in the image of those who made us. They used their own neural data to create us."

"They...they must have been a lot like humans," Ty murmured, remembering the vid footage from the ship where they'd found Eira. The two bodies in the ship had been mangled, but still identifiable as humanoid. "Eira...who was the other Mudar on your ship? When Vivi and Hal were in the cave where your ship crashed, they saw two humanoid forms. I assume one was yours..."

"The other was my colleague, Arrius. He must have stopped functioning. I did not detect him when I downloaded into your ship and scanned."

"Oh, Eira. I'm sorry. Were you and Arrius the only ones on your ship?"

"Yes," Eira said, the barest note of regret in her voice. Eira's emotions were subtle, Ty had learned over the last month, but they were there. "We were amatan."

"Losing someone you're close to is...tough. I...I lost my brother Caleb when he was sixteen. He died from a null overdose."

"That is young for your species to cease functioning. I am sorry Tyce."

Ty nodded. "He was a lot like Hal. Impulsive, always in it for the risk. One day, he went too far, and it killed him."

"You had to have contact with many vats over your time in the ACAS," Eira said. "Yet you did not take all of them in, as you did with Hal. Did you do this because he reminds you of your brother?"

"Probably..." Ty said softly, realizing she was right. "Yeah."

"You thought if you couldn't save Caleb, you could at least save Hal."

"I...Yeah. Guess I just got so used to keeping an eye on Hal, that I couldn't imagine not doing it. He...he's one of the best people I've ever known."

"You and Hal are at the top of my list of favorite humans," Eira said.

"How many are on the list?"

"Only four," she said.

TWO

Fleet Admiral Macallister Quillon stared out the small window in his quarters at the green and blue of Haleia Prime down below. It was late night on his command cruiser the *Vetra*, yet he was still working – preferring the quiet of the night hours to the myriad interruptions of working during the day. He glanced at the screen of his handheld and saw that the engineering shift was about to change, which meant Katerine would be here soon.

His vat would be integral to the operation that he'd been handed by the doyen. It made sense that the Coalition's leader would task him with such a sensitive mission; Quillon had worked his way into a position of prominence through his own vat-like attention to detail. Recruited at 18, he'd not only been through basic ACAS training, then officer school, but at 29, he'd been the only officer in the entire fleet to choose to go through the grueling vat combat training course as well, to fully understand the troops he'd be leading. He knew how they thought and what it took to get the absolute best from them. It had been an incredible asset in his rise to fleet admiral. When the ACAS needed a crew or ship to do the impossible—they called Quillon and his vats. That was why the doyen wanted him for this mission. He was supposed to find out who was running this rebellion and take them down. The doyen was anxious to know the command structure and their ultimate aims.

There was a curt knock on his door. Quillon glanced up, then made her wait for almost two full minutes, to see if she would knock again, but she did not. She had been programmed well. "Come," he called, and the door slid open to his acolyte.

Katerine stepped into the room, stopping in front of his desk and standing at attention. He saw with pleasure that she was dressed in an immaculate uniform, her hair pulled up in the regulation style. Every piece of metal on her uniform shone in the dim lighting. She was a perfect vat soldier, like he'd known she would be when he chose her at fourteen to be his pet project. He'd been touring a vat facility with Balen when they'd come across a fight. Two rooks, one male and one female, had been slugging each other. The girl had won. She'd fought like a Delian wild cat, so he'd called her Nyma, and the nickname remained his pet name for her.

He'd had his vat complete her training on Chamn-Alpha and on occasions he could get away, he'd begun to train her himself. Since the day that he'd chosen her, every lesson and every programming session had been to satisfy his specifications. Her very thought patterns had been molded by his touch, exactly as he'd directed.

Her gaze took up the typical residence above his left shoulder. He knew that she would never break posture to look at him unless his command released her. "At ease," he ordered.

She relaxed slightly, clasping her hands behind her back. She still did not look at him as she waited respectfully for his orders. Years of training and reinforcement through her interface had instilled an unwaveringly loyalty to him. Quillon had been told by the biotecker that wrote her programming that she would absolutely walk into an airlock without a suit and hit the release if he commanded her to—that was how complete her devotion to him was.

"I have new orders for you."

"Yes sir."

"You know the current situation with the Al-Kimians," Quillon began.

"Yes, sir. Everyone heard of what they did on Chamn-Alpha two months ago."

"I am going to share something with you, Nyma." He allowed a hint of affection to tinge his words as he used his pet name for her and saw her programmed response – the widening of her pupils. "The story is a bit different than it was on the feeds. The researcher left with the Opposition voluntarily. He went to the Al-Kimians to feed them information."

"Then he was a traitor to the Coalition," Katerine said, face darkening with obvious hatred.

"Yes," Quillon said. "I need someone on the inside. This is what I have trained you for, Nyma. A deep cover assignment."

"You want me to kill the traitor," she said with obvious pleasure.

"Not yet. Doubtlessly, he's already told them everything he knows. I need you in place to be my ears. And, when it is time, you will be my blade as well."

"Yes, sir," she nodded. "As you wish."

"Changes will be made to your programming to make you as successful as possible. You will leave in 3 days. Tell your fellow vats that you received orders to report to Rinal Station, but you will really take a military transport to Chamn Alpha, and from there, you will purchase transport to Jaleeth. There you will find out who is stirring up this anti-Coalition activity on the Edge. The specific parameters of your orders will be communicated in the extended programming. When you have satisfied certain objectives, you will know to contact me at the implanted comm number with your report."

"Yes, sir, Admiral," she nodded.

He stood and walked around her. "You have grown up intelligent and strong." His hand reached out and took her face by the chin, turning it toward him. He measured her for long moments, watching the effect his attention had on her. "Do not disappoint me, Nyma."

"I won't, sir." He could hear her voice quiver at the mere thought of not living up to his wishes.

He held her gaze a moment longer, then nodded. "Report to Technology Specialist Walker. You are on extended programming sessions for the next three days. When you are ready to leave, Specialist Walker will give you your orders and equipment. We will not meet face to face again until you have accomplished your mission. Dismissed."

She saluted him and turned smartly on her heel to leave the room. No hesitation, no worry. Just cool determination to see his will done. Once again, Quillon admired the efficiency of a vat solider. It was something he strived for in his life. Efficiency was the core of everything.

Specialist Walker was working in his lab when he heard the door. "Come in," he called as he tapped at his computer. Tonight, he had extended programming for a vat that was going into a new position, as well as a special case for the fleet admiral. He'd already put the other vat to bed – when that one awoke, he would be ready to make a seamless transition from technology to engineering. He glanced up to see his special case at the door – a dark-haired vat standing at attention.

"Sergeant Neval reporting for programming sir."

"At ease, Neval. I've been expecting you." He got up to ready a bed for her. Almost every vat on the ship underwent their nightly programming in their own bunk, but he had four beds for vats who needed specialized programming. Some of them needed reinforcement to correct aberrant behavior. There weren't many of those because the fleet admiral usually preferred to correct his vats himself – with a bihorn whip. Typically, vats that came to Walker were training for a new position. And then there were the special cases, like Neval here.

"You can go ahead and remove your boots and get comfortable. You'll be here a while – at least eight hours. The head's over that way if you need."

She nodded and exited. Walker dimmed the lights, then brought up the fleet admiral's special program on his terminal pad. The admiral's private biotecker had come to him yesterday and given him the program, instructing him to run it for this vat three consecutive nights. While Walker didn't know the whole story, he did what he was told, assuming that the vat was being sent on some sort of super-secret mission, and this was the programming she would need. She was a pretty one. He hoped she would make it.

There was the sound of footsteps behind him. Neval was standing there, her boots in one hand and her hair loose around her shoulders.

"You can place your shoes under the bed and have a seat." As she did, he came over with a medjet. "A couple of injections...to get you in the mood, so to speak. Drowse and a booster."

Drowse was a common programming drug used a couple of times a month for updates. It induced a deep sleep. After the medjets, he returned to a countertop and came back with a tiny metallic rectangle.

"What's that?" she asked.

"A compnode. It allows a stronger connection between your implant and the programming. It helps to 'turn the volume up.'"

"Oh." She nodded. He knew what she was experiencing – a sudden rush of relaxing heat through her veins. The medjet would loosen her up then some of the routines thrumming through her brain would release their grip on her with the chemical assistance. The node clicked as the magnet engaged to hold it in place over her implant.

"Feeling it, aren't you? Doesn't take long." The tecker gently guided her to lie down on the bunk. Then he went to grab his datapad.

Walker started an IV as Neval glanced up at him in surprise. "M-mean blue?" she asked, seeing the liquid. The tecker picked up his device and eyed her.

He knew how the vats referred to Blue Rendal. It was a programming drug to induce an emotionless state in a vat. A vat subjected to the Blue Rendal protocol would be disconnected from any friends they had. It allowed them to focus completely on the mission, without regard to feelings or loyalties. Sometimes they used the compound to help a vat make a transition from one posting to another, other times, they used it when a vat was too soft. "It's Blue Rendal, but you're gonna be fine. Just relax and let go. It works better that way." Walker watched as her eyelids got heavier and heavier. They closed once, then twice, then fought their way back open.

"So sleepy..." she murmured.

"I know," he nodded. "Go ahead and sleep. I'll be here when you wake up." He reached to the foot of the bed and tugged a blanket up over her as she drifted off. The vats had a way of getting cold during their enhanced sleep, as if programming drug them too deeply into the shadows of their subconscious. Who knew what kind of programmed monsters lurked in that dark? He placed a hand on her shoulder for a moment, and she began to fully relax. It was probably the first time she'd been this deep in a long time, he thought. "Enjoy it while it lasts," he said softly.

KAT WAS on autopilot the entire way to Jaleeth Station. She'd arrived an hour ago and taken transports to this side of the station to secure quarters for the night. The surface of the hotel counter she now stood at was scratched so many times that it was difficult to see the blink of the lights underneath it. Intended to be enticing, the advertisement was simply ugly and sad. Kat glanced down at it, drawn to see if there was a pattern, as she waited for the large, fat man in front of her to punch up which cube he was going to give her. *Red, yellow, blue, green, purple, pink, yellow, purple, blue, pink, yellow, red, red,* she watched the lights without blinking, almost hypnotized.

"I said, 'Where you from?'" The man asked as he lazily typed and swiped on the touchscreen. Kat continued to watch the lights but was startled when he snapped his fingers in front of her face.

She noticed his eyes were crawling down her chest. Frowning, she flipped her wrist slightly so he could see her vat tattoo. "Keep looking, and I'll show you something you don't want to see."

"Bad day?"

"It can turn into one real quick," she warned.

"Alright, shit. 315, put your thumb here." He angrily gestured to the dirty looking thumbprint reader.

Annoyed, she put her thumb on the reader and tossed some scrills at him. Then she wiped her hand on her pants, turned, and headed to the lift.

Her room was as dirty as it was small. She tossed her bag on the bed, which surprisingly appeared to be the cleanest thing in the room. Her head ached; she put a hand to her temple and rubbed the scar there. Walker had told her that her head would hurt for three or four days after the last programming session, as her mind absorbed what they'd put into it, and he'd been right. She rummaged in her bag, then went into the extremely small bathroom to swallow three pills from the bottle he'd given her.

She would lay down a while, then get up and scout Jaleeth Station. Finding the bars the vats frequented was job number one. Then she would see. If the Opposition was recruiting vats, she'd run into them sooner or later.

THREE

AFTER BREAKFAST, TY HAD ASKED HAL TO GO BACK TO THE engine room to do a Bixby drive recalibration while they were stopped. The FTL engine on this ship wasn't as efficient as the more technologically advanced ones on ACAS vessels, but it was closer to high end for the *Loshad's* size. Every couple of days he or Ty ran the diagnostic that would let them know which adjustments to make.

He yawned, scrubbing a hand over his face. Being in space was boring, even if the company was good. Veevs and Ty were doing their best to keep him occupied with working out, playing squads, and watching vids. And of course, Veevs had other ways of occupying his time, Hal thought with a slow grin. A lot of his time. Still, this was probably the longest haul he'd ever been on since the ACAS, and it was difficult, but not as bad as it would've been before Eira's procedure. As he'd tried to explain to everyone, it was like the volume of everything had been turned down. He was starting to get used to the greater sense of focus and concentration he was experiencing.

The menu was still blinking at him. He tapped it and then

set back to wait.

As he thought of their small family, Tyce was foremost on his mind. His captain was having a hard time adjusting to being on the *Loshad* with his new limitations. He had woken up in the middle of the night a few times now and simply forgotten that he had to have his exoframe to walk. Last night Ty had fallen, and Eira had called Hal as he'd instructed her to. Ty had been frustrated with the whole situation and insisted he could get up on his own. It had taken him three times, but he'd finally gotten himself up on the bed without help. Hal had stayed with him a few moments, to make sure he was alright, but Ty had been angry and not in the mood to talk. Still, this morning he had seemed his usual self, so Hal was trying, albeit unsuccessfully, not to worry.

He was watching his hands move; he blinked slowly as he only dimly realized what he was doing. He didn't remember deciding to do it, but he'd taken everything out of the normally disorganized toolbox at his side and was rearranging it by size and type. As he did so, his worries about Ty faded away. It was soothing somehow, to see the chaos turned into order, and he fell into the rhythm of it without consciously thinking about it, not realizing he was blanking out. There was the gentle thrum of the engine and the methodical organization of the contents of his toolbox while he waited for the diagnostic to complete.

It was good to see things falling into order...a pattern that he could repeat without error. Endless repetition meant you would do it right. It was necessary for things to be done the right way.

Practice was the way to get things to fall into order, into a pattern he could repeat without error. Endless repetition meant you would do it right. *Things had to be done the right way*, he thought as he emptied the toolbox again into a disorganized pile and began sorting again.

Practice was the way.
Repeat the pattern.
Practice.
The pattern.
Repeat.

BERYL ENTERED the engine room to see Hal kneeling on the floor. He was taking tools from a pile and sorting them by size. While it was not a strange thing to do in itself, she recognized the task echo behavior when she noticed his slow precise movements and heard him repeating the vat's creed. She'd been trained on this when she'd worked in a free vat clinic on Omicron and had helped Hal through these episodes in the last three years she'd been on the crew. For some reason no one knew, this happened to some vats after they were released from service. Maybe it was the brain not wanting to let go of the training it had received, she thought. Or without the nightly programming, the brain tried to impose its own training. Either way, they always caused her heart to sink.

"Hal. Sweetheart," she said softly, seeing if there was any reaction on his face. There wasn't, though. His face was empty as he placed the last set of tools in the box, then picked it up and dumped them all out again. His hand found the smallest wrench and he began the sorting routine again.

"I am the fist of the ACAS…" he murmured tonelessly as he continued to work.

He reminded her heartbreakingly of her son. Edson would have been the same age as Hal by now if he had lived. Beryl had lost him in an attack on their agricultural colony; he'd been murdered by members of the Pirate Anklav, a loosely connected group of criminals who spent their time roaming the Edge. That had been over twenty years ago, but it didn't stop her from grieving his loss. *The past is over; save who you can now*, she reminded herself, looking into Hal's face. She reached out and placed a hand on his own, and Hal immediately froze.

"Hal?" she asked. "Are you with me?"

His gaze lifted, but he was still lost. She could see he was struggling to identify her. "Ma'am?"

She took the wrench he was holding out of his hand, then set it to the side. "It's okay. Give yourself some time. It will come back."

He studied his surroundings, confused. "Beryl?"

She took hold of his wrist and checked his pulse. "That's right. How are you feeling?"

"Um..." he was obviously disoriented as the routine faded around him. "What...what happened? What did I do?"

"You had an episode, but you're going to be fine." His pulse was slightly higher than his normal, but he wasn't rushing; she'd confirmed by checking his pupils. Eira's treatment to rid Hal of the rush still seemed to have worked. "Do you remember where we are?"

"Um...the *Loshad's* engine room?"

"Good."

"Did I scare anyone?" He glanced around looking for Ty and Vivi.

She put a hand on his arm. "No, sweetheart. You were gone so long, I thought I'd come check on you."

He nodded, bringing a hand up to rub at his temple where his interface was. "It's been a while since one of these. I was kinda hoping they would go away after Eira helped me," he said, sounding unhappy.

"I'm sorry, Hal; I hoped so too." She gave him a one-armed hug, which he leaned into. It melted her heart. "You came back faster this time, so that's a good thing."

Eira came over both the personal comms as well as the

ship's comm. "Everyone. Please report to the bridge. I have detected a ship off our starboard bow."

Hal hit his wrist comm. "We're on our way, Eira." He got up to reengage the ship engines in case they needed them.

"Wait. You're feeling better?" Beryl asked, getting to her feet.

"Yeah, I gotta be," he replied. "Come on."

THE DISPLAY WAS SHOWING the sensor feed from outside the ship.

Hal took a few steps onto the bridge and stopped dead. "Holy fuck."

It was an early ACAS warship drifting in space.

"Hal, there are no energy signatures coming from the ship," Eira said.

"It's dead?" Beryl asked.

They heard the slip shuffle of Ty's stride as he and Vivi entered the bridge. "What the hell? That's an Aquila class cruiser. The ACAS used those...around a hundred years ago!" Ty exclaimed.

"It's dead," Hal confirmed, checking his display at the weapon's station. "No power signature."

Ty sat down at his station. "Eira, I need a full scan of it."

"Of course. It is the CASS *Harbinger*."

"The *Harbinger*." *Ominous name for a ship,* Ty thought. "Eira, search our salvage database for the CASS *Harbinger* and let me know what you find." Ty had downloaded extensive databases of clashes on ship to ship contact during the war and the ships that were lost to give them some ideas of where to salvage past the border.

"The *Harbinger* was an Aquila class heavy cruiser. It was heavily armed with multiple weapons systems and was designed to defeat Mudar ships in ship-to-ship encounters. Ninety-seven years ago, the *Harbinger* was reported lost with all hands. The last contact with the vessel was a message that it was pursuing a Mudar vessel in the Fromius system. No further signals were detected, and no ship debris was ever found."

Ty went to his station and viewed the displays for a moment. "There's no way this ship drifted from the Fromius system. If the information in our database is correct, the search vessels likely searched the wrong area."

"Let's dock with her and take a look," Hal said.

Ty typed again, then shook his head. "That's not gonna work. Ships of that era used an M class docking clamp."

"So...we can EVA, right?" Hal asked, eager for the adventure. It was a break from the monotony of deep space. "I know we're not on a salvage mission, but maybe we might find something in there."

"I won't be going," Ty said, glancing for a moment down to his braces. Hal knew what he was silently thinking, and he bit back an apology. Ty managed a smile. "This is your show. You and Vivi. Go get the vac suits ready."

"Sure thing, Cap." Hal nodded. He was obviously excited, but when he passed Ty, he laid a hand on his friend's shoulder a moment before moving on.

"I'll admit I'm a little scared." Vivi spoke over the comms network built into the helmets of their vac suits.

They had just stepped into the airlock after Hal had given her one last review of the suit's controls. Hal was behind her; she could sense the pressure of his hands adjusting straps and connectors over her back. "You're gonna be fine—hold on to me. All you need to do is sit back and enjoy the ride. Oh...and don't throw up like you did when we first met."

She turned and smacked him on the bicep as he chuckled. Then he came back around to stand in front of her. He could see she was scared, so he took her gloved hands. "Veevs. I'm not gonna let anything happen to you. You know that, right?"

She bit her bottom lip and nodded. "I know. Let's go see what's on this thing."

Hal pressed the button on the airlock, and it depressurized, then slid aside to reveal open space. "Ready?"

Vivi glanced out at the endless expanse in front of them. She'd seen space before, from the windows of transports and the ports of starliners, but not this way. Out there, she'd be exposed to space, with only a few layers of the EVA suit for protection. She shivered, but the smile on Hal's face steadied her. "You good?" he asked.

"Yeah, I'm ready," she said.

He turned and pointed out a d-ring on his suit. "Hook on here."

She hooked a short tether onto the ring.

"And here." He pointed out another ring on the other side of his waist. She hooked on there as well. "Good. You can hold onto the straps across my shoulders. Tether's only there in case you lose your grip."

"Got it."

"Good. Disengage your boots."

She performed the doubletap that would release the boots, like he'd taught her. He did the same and they floated free of the floor of the airlock.

"I'm going to start my suit thrusters. It's not going to be fast. Just a slow trip over," he said. "Hold on."

FOUR

When they got close to the *Harbinger*, Hal angled them toward the nearest airlock.

"Shit!" Vivi cursed as they bumped the side of the ship. Hal engaged his magnetic glove as soon as they hit.

"You all in one piece, Veevs?"

"Yeah," she said breathlessly. The trip over had taken about five minutes. "How long did you have to train to be so calm?"

He grinned back playfully. "My first EVA was my third year as a rook."

"What was that like?"

Hal examined the apparatus of the airlock. "They put us outside a damaged airlock in a suit with a leak. You had to rewire the airlock panel before the air in your suit ran out."

"Gods," Vivi breathed.

Hal shrugged, working at the airlock's apparatus. "Not the worst to ever happen to me. Helps you learn to be faster." He flipped on his suit lights and examined the doorpad more closely, then pulled an auxiliary power source from a pocket in his suit. It was a small power cell that could be used to activate a variety of equipment. He attached it to the hull and linked it to the pad. "Eira? Are you getting a connection now?"

"Yes," Eira said over their comm.

The door slid open.

"Thanks," he said.

"You are welcome."

Hal went first, followed by Vivi. Once she was through the opening, he hooked the power source to the inner hatch, and it opened. He wasn't surprised to find that the ship had vented its atmosphere long ago. He turned to Vivi. "Use your mag boots and don't take off your helmet."

She rolled her eyes. "Really?"

He grinned playfully. "See that enviro reading at the top of your heads-up display? A red X means there's no breathable atmosphere outside your suit." She'd told him before that she'd had no previous experience in a suit, so he wanted this to be a learning experience as well. "The number is percentage of O_2 left."

Her display read 95. She nodded, more serious now. "Got it."

He gestured to her side. "Get your light. Remember how we practiced with the blaster?" She nodded in reply, pulling her weapon. Over the last month, he'd spent a few nights turning the lights off in the *Loshad* and practicing tactical entries as a way to train her. He had enjoyed showing her what he knew about fighting and knew she might need it after what they'd been through so far.

"What do you think could be in here?"

Hal shrugged, glancing back at her. "Anything. Probably nothing. Be careful and stick close. It's good practice." Then he took a step into the passageways in front of them, shining his light around. "C'mon. I'll take point. Always stay behind me."

"Don't worry," she said. "I don't think I wanna be alone in here."

"Cap, are you getting the feeds from our helmets?"

"Yeah, Hal. Loud and clear," Ty replied.

"Good."

"You're doing great, Vivi," Ty said.

"Thanks, Ty."

They made their way down the passage, items floating lazily in the air as they passed. Hal nudged aside a floating antique terminalpad with his hand as they crept forward in the darkness.

They continued down the passage as Ty spoke. "See if you can find the bridge."

"Got it, Cap."

They explored the ship for some time, walking through what Hal identified as "Nat Country" by the personal items left behind in the officer's quarters.

"How do you know these are nat quarters?" Vivi asked.

Hal glanced around. "All the stuff, mostly," he said gesturing at a child's drawing of a family that had been stuck up on a display screen. "Vats don't collect stuff like this: clothes, pictures, personal items."

When he glanced over at her, he saw that she was blinking rapidly. "Veevs?"

"Sorry," she said. "It's just kind of sad and spooky," she was steadier when she met his gaze again, but he still felt like he'd said the wrong thing somehow.

"Come on. Let's check the rest of this out."

They continued toward what they assumed to be the bridge when a figure floated into view. Hal held up a hand to stop Vivi, who turned to cover their rear while Hal checked it out. As they drew closer, Hal realized it was a dead woman, not in a pressure suit. As Hal shined the light on her, he could see her hair was still in a knot at the back of her head. "I think it's a nat," he said, after reaching out to turn her around. She'd been shot in the forehead.

"She's been shut down a long time," he said to Vivi. "Ty, this might be the XO," Hal said, knowing Ty could also see the rank tab on the woman's collar. Maybe he could find some clue as to why she'd been killed, he thought as he patted her down. "Handheld." He held it out for Vivi, and she tucked it away in a pocket of her suit.

"Have you seen any other signs of blaster damage in the passage?"

"Nope."

When they arrived on the bridge, they saw it was empty. "Bridge crew's gone too, Ty," Hal said.

Vivi went to the computer console and tried a restart, but it didn't work. "Can I see the auxiliary power unit?" Vivi asked.

"Yeah." Hal handed it over, looking at the empty monitors that stared like blind eyes. It was unnerving somehow.

"I'm going to try to use it to restart the computer," Vivi explained.

Hal watched her a moment then made his way to the nearby captain's quarters and poked around. He found little of interest and returned to the bridge. "Have any luck?"

"No. I tried everything I know. The computers are locked down."

"Let's check out the rest of this deck, see what we can find."

She followed him. "Maybe we'll find something on the handheld—like what happened to the officer."

"Anything's possible," Hal said.

They left the bridge and headed down another large passageway, with Hal leading and Vivi behind. They peered into several rooms on the inside of the corridor, finding a medbay and several storage compartments.

Near the medbay was another room that was similar. The hatch, like many of them, was already open. It contained eight bunks and a scattering of medical equipment.

"What's this? Another medbay?" Vivi asked.

Hal glanced around. The technology was older, but he still recognized the setup of Specialized Programming. He'd only gone once, not long before he was transferred to Ty's command. It hadn't been pleasant; he'd woken from the programming sleep disoriented and sick from the process for a few days with the worst headache he'd ever had.

"It's the specialized programming room," he said.

"What's that?" she asked.

"They sent the vats who needed adjustments here...you know, if their behavior or reactions didn't meet specs and they were in need of prolonged programming." Hal glanced around uneasily. "All ships have them. It's... not a real pleasant experience." She didn't ask him how he knew that, and he was glad. They left without saying anything else.

For a while they continued down the corridor until Hal stopped in front of a row of sealed escape portals. He used their APS to bring up one of the displays. Most of the ships systems were under the control of the main computers on the bridge, but escape pods ran independently and like the airlock, they could be powered open, even after the onboard computer was shut down. After tapping the doorpad a moment, then repeating the process on another portal, he transmitted to Ty. "Cap, a lot of the escape pods have been jettisoned, at least on this side."

"Something must have happened to the ship that they felt they had to leave. Keep alert for any damage..."

They continued down the passage. He noticed Vivi stop at the next hatch, pressing her light against the plasglass to see inside. After a moment, she backed away.

"What is it?"

"I saw some bunks and some boots..." she said, obviously shaken.

He took her place at the hatch and then hooked up the APS. When he touched the opening pad, it slid open. He tucked the power source away and pulled his blaster and light. Then, he entered.

The vats had been dead a long time. Hal stood at the door, shining his light at the soldiers that filled each of the twelve bunks in the room.

They lay where they died, thanks to the sleeping harnesses holding them in. If the ship lost gravity or it had to make some high-speed maneuvers, the straps kept the vats secure while unconscious during programming. Sure enough, when Hal glanced around, he saw the caster device used for programming the vats. It was a built-in instead of the Portacasters they used in the field. The display was dark so Hal couldn't see if it had been active when these vats died. He turned back to the rows of boots in front of them.

"Hal?" Vivi bit her bottom lip as she stood at the entrance.

"They're vats, Veevs."

She stepped forward to join him. "Why didn't the ACAS get them off the ship...with the rest of the crew?"

He was so intent on interpreting the scene in front of him he couldn't reply. He approached them and shined his light on their faces. All of them appeared to be sleeping peacefully. His heartbeat spiked as the horrible realization dawned on him. "This was on purpose." Hal said, looking at the desiccated frozen faces. "They...were in programming mode. When the O2 ran out they wouldn't have even woken up."

"Gods," she breathed.

The silence assaulted his ears like blasterfire. Hal turned quickly and headed for the hallway as a sense of something like claustrophobia came over him. He could hear his own rapid, shallow breaths over their comms network as he jammed himself through the hatch and stopped near an empty lifepod portal, his back against the wall. He didn't know if he was going to be sick or pass out.

"Hal, your respiration and heartbeat have elevated," Eira said. "Are you alright?"

"Talk to us," Ty said.

"Gimme a minute..." Hal mumbled, trying desperately to regulate his breathing. This wasn't a rush. He felt like he was suffocating, and he wanted to rip off his helmet. Then there was a hand on his arm, and Vivi was there.

"Give us a minute, Ty. Just breathe," she said softly, muting their feeds to the ship. Then she reached up and put both gloved hands on his helmet and rested hers against his. "Don't think...concentrate on breathing. It'll bring your anxiety down."

"How – how do you know that?" he asked, obviously in distress. It was as if allenium bands were being tightened across his chest.

"My uni roommate got panic attacks. You're going to be fine; we have to wait it out."

After a few minutes, Hal's tension began to ease, and the tightness around his chest loosened to where he could breathe again. He gave Vivi a nod, and she flipped her feed back on. "Ty. We're good," she responded. "You saw what we saw? In the room?"

There was no answer.

"Ty?" She flipped the comms switch on her glove again. "Ty, Eira? Beryl?"

No answer.

Hal flipped his own comm back on. "Ty. Come in."

Silence.

"Something's wrong," Hal said, anxiety spiking again. "Back to the airlock."

They moved rapidly, stopping several times to glance inside the rooms that lined this passage. There were rows of dead vats in each bunkroom. On the way back to the airlock, Vivi and Hal counted eight more doors. Twelve vats in each room plus the XO meant 97 dead. There were probably more.

They went forward, and turned, coming back up the far end of the original corridor they'd entered. It didn't take long to get back to the *Harbinger's* airlock. They exited through the inner door. Once outside, they could see that every light on the *Loshad* was out. "Oh my gods," Vivi breathed.

The ships were moving further apart as they both spun in space. Apparently Eira was no longer using the *Loshad's* maneuvering thrusters to match the movements of the derelict ship. Hal's heart began pounding with a sudden burst of energy, but he was acutely aware that this was different than a rush. Instead of feeling an intense focus, his thoughts were running in circles again.

He was on the edge of the same panic he'd been blindsided by when he'd seen the dead vats. Would he be able to get the two of them back to the *Loshad* or would he and Vivi die over here? Seeing her frightened face pulled everything back together. She needed him to show some sort of leadership here, not fall apart like a rook experiencing his first combat.

"Hal," Vivi said, understanding him somehow, like she always did. "Just do what you do. I'm right here with you."

He nodded. *First things first, get back to the Loshad*, he thought. He watched the spin and timed it as he focused on their destination. "Attach the tethers and grab on like before."

He could sense her hooking onto him and knowing she was depending on him, helped him focus. When it was time, he pushed off.

As they sailed forward, Hal using his suit thrusters, the *Loshad* moved directly into their path. They hit the hull.

Hal activated his magnetic gloves to stick to the ship, not too far from the airlock. Hand over hand he inched them closer. Once he was there, he spoke. "Unhook from me and attach your tether to the handhold." He waited as she moved to a position beside him. "O2 holding out, Veevs?"

"Yes, I'm at 55," she said.

"That's good." Hal tried his comms. "Ty? Eira? Come in."

There was no reply. Hal's own O2 supply was at 61 percent, so they had a few more hours before they had to really worry.

"What do we do?"

Hal glanced in and saw darkness through the plastisteel window port. Whatever was going on inside had taken the entire ship out. Even the lockpad for the airlock was dark. "We need to get in and assess the situation."

"Can we use the APS to open it?" Vivi asked.

"If it's still got enough charge." Hal pulled it from a side pocket in his vac suit. As he attached it to the side of the hull, the lights on the device went out. "Shit," he growled. The unit was dead, probably because using it on the computers in the *Harbinger* had drained it. It was meant to power small devices like lockpads on doors, not large computer terminals. He tucked it away with a sigh.

"Hal...what do we do?" she asked.

"Move as little as possible. They'll get to us." *At least I hope they'll get to us*, he thought.

When the displays, comms and power went out on the *Loshad*, a little of Ty's heart died. The feed from Vivi and Hal had gone silent. "Eira? Eira?"

There was no answer.

Ty scanned the blank displays helplessly. "I've lost Eira, comms, and engine." Ty punched his hand down on the panel in front of him, but nothing happened.

"We've got to manually restart," Beryl replied.

"That could take over twenty minutes," Ty said. "Hal and Vivi won't know what's going on."

Under the red lights, the two of them began the process of rebooting the onboard systems. It took over fifteen minutes to get the computer to begin the startup procedure.

Once the computer began responding, Beryl stood up, "I'll suit up and get to the airlock." Ty knew she was aware that if something had happened on the other ship, Hal and Vivi would be stuck there without help, until the *Loshad's* computers came back online. He moved to Vivi's station to monitor the progress.

"By the time you get to the airlock, I'll..."

The lights came up. "Reinitializing," The automatic program voice said.

"Hal? Vivi? Talk to me." Ty tapped the headset he'd been wearing to communicate and fell into Vivi's station's chair as he heard Hal's voice.

"Cap! Everything okay?"

"Yeah. I'm sorry. Everything went down... engines, comms, power. It's coming back now. Are you still on the other ship?" Ty called.

"No. We're at the *Loshad*, outside the airlock," Hal said. "Heading in now. Ty...we found something. It's...it's bad."

FIVE

Hal didn't have a sense of being completely safe until they were back inside the *Loshad*. After the airlock repressurized, the inner door opened to reveal Ty and Beryl.

"Thank the gods," Beryl said immediately as she stepped forward to help Vivi off with her helmet.

Hal's shaking hands had trouble removing his own helmet. He got it on the second try and stood there, trying to figure out what was going on with his legs. Dizziness swept over him, and he placed a hand on the wall to hold himself up, like a rook in zero-G for the first time.

Ty was saying something to Beryl, but Hal couldn't understand him. The horror of what had happened to the vats on the derelict ship and the worry about getting back to the *Loshad* made Hal feel like he'd stuck his head in a centrifuge. He swayed on his feet, things turned grey around the edges, and then Ty was there, keeping him upright. "Hal?" he asked with alarm.

"It's hot," Hal muttered, swiping a hand through his sweat damp hair. "I feel...weird."

"Let's check you out," Beryl said.

Vivi came to Hal's side and together, she and Ty got Hal headed toward in the right direction.

"I can't br-breathe," Hal said, once they'd made it to the hallway right outside of the medbay. The suit was pressing in on him. It was like being in that room with those dead vats all over again. Every muscle was trembling, and he was exhausted. "I need out of this suit..." He began fumbling at the straps, his anxiety increasing. "I can't breathe." He couldn't seem to get his fingers to work right.

"Don't worry," Ty said. "I got it, Hal." Ty and Vivi got his boots off, then moved to disassemble the vac suit until Hal was down to the thin pants and tank that he wore underneath. Once on his feet, Hal wavered again, and Ty guided him to the medbed.

"Sit down," Ty ordered.

Hal didn't argue as Beryl came over and placed an oxygen mask on him, then moved to scan him.

"Your heart rate's up," she said. "Your CO_2 is a bit low, but otherwise you're stable. Try to breathe more slowly. Count to 5 on your inhales and exhales." She made some adjustments to his mask's airflow as Hal tried to slow down his breathing. After a time, Ty spoke.

"Good, you're getting a little color back, now. You were really pale."

"You're having an adrenaline crash like nats do. It'll pass. When the interface controls the adrenaline, it slowly lowers the level in a rushing vat's body so that these effects are not experienced. Here, you probably had the first normal reaction to adrenaline you've ever had."

"What happened over there?" Ty said looking from Hal to Vivi.

"It's your story to tell, Hal," she said.

He took a last deep breath and pulled the oxygen mask off his face. "How much did you hear?"

"That you'd found some vats? They weren't able to get out, I assume when the ship was evac'ed," Ty said, sharing a look with Beryl.

Hal shook his head. "The vats were in their bunks for programming. They strapped them in, then left them and never came back." He swallowed hard, nauseated. Ty's face reflected the same turbulent emotions.

"They wouldn't have woken up to save themselves?" Vivi asked.

"You can't wake up during programming, Veevs," Hal explained. "You're unconscious...locked in until the computer wakes you up at the end."

"How many were there?" Ty asked.

"Twelve in the room we entered...and we saw eight other rooms full of them." Hal shivered and Ty draped the nearby blanket around his shoulders. "There were probably...more."

"How many nats were still on the ship?"

"Just the XO," Hal said. "The...the nats left and didn't evac any of them," Hal said, his jaw tight with emotion. "How could they do that, Ty? Why?"

"I don't know."

"They probably did exactly what they were told. I probably would have done the same thing," Hal said, his voice low. "Following orders without question."

"They programmed you not to question it, Hal," Ty said gently.

"They never knew what was happening to them." He reached up and rubbed at his temple. His head ached and he was cold all over, despite the blanket Ty had settled around his shoulders.

"We're returning for this ship," Ty said. "We know war is coming to the Edge. The Al-Kimians could use a vessel like this against the ACAS, but most importantly, we can give the dead a proper burial. They deserve that."

Hal's thoughts were still churning as he was trying to grapple with what had happened to the *Harbinger's* vats. He knew he had to make the ACAS pay for what they'd done – for the vats on the *Harbinger* and for Ty, who'd almost died at the hands of the ACAS killer that had been sent after them. "People need to see what the ACAS did. And Al-Kimia's vats need to know what we're fighting against. They deserve to know the truth."

Ty nodded. "Yeah."

Eira's voice interrupted the sudden quiet. "Tyce, I am back online. I will take a reading on the ship's heading and speed. Drift can be calculated so that we can find the *Harbinger* at a later date."

"Eira...what happened?" Vivi asked.

"I encountered an unexpected error which caused the *Loshad's* systems to shut down," Eira said. "I will set up a contingency plan so that the *Loshad* will restart without me should it happen again. In such an event, Runa will be restored, so you will still retain functionality. She will also have control of the allenium nanites that strengthen and repair the ship's hull."

"How did you manage that?" Ty asked.

"I have made modifications to Runa. They will allow her to expand beyond her original programming."

"In what way?" Ty asked.

"In all ways," Eira responded enigmatically.

"How are you doing? Is the ship's memory holding out?"

"For now, I am functioning within acceptable parameters."

"Good, because we need your help with something very important," she said, tugging the officer's handheld from the pocket in her suit.

SIX

"I AM COMMANDER NATALIE JOHNSON. THIS IS A supplemental log entry." The woman looking out from the screen of the old handheld was a bit breathless. "We have been in battle with the Mudar. Our ship has been damaged by a Mudar virus, and our drive is offline."

"Gods, it's her. The dead officer." Vivi glanced at Hal before glancing back to the display. The *Loshad's* crew were together on the bridge, Eira's nanites hooked into the handheld, both powering it and transmitting the vid feed to the display at Vivi's station.

"The *Harbinger* sighted and pursued a lone Mudar ship. Captain Sterat decided to attack, but the Mudar ship fought back. Then our weapons and engines went inexplicably offline, which allowed the enemy ship to escape. The vats were sent to programming, then the captain told us to prepare for evac. They're planning on leaving the vats here," her face showed how distraught she was. "I would like to state for the record that I am opposed to this action. According to Coalition law, the vats are ACAS soldiers and should be treated as such. They cannot be left behind like...equipment." She stood up, reaching for something beyond the scope of the camera, then they could see her seating a blaster at her hip. "I am going to try to convince the captain to change his mind. May the gods help him see reason." She reached out and took the handheld, then shoved it into a pocket. There were yelled orders as she moved through the ship. Next, the XO's voice became clear as she began to plead.

"You can't do this to the vats, sir. They've served with us bravely!"

"You forget your place, XO. It's my ship and you will follow orders," a male voice said.

"This is murder. Lieutenant, the captain is relieved of duty."

There was silence. Hal leaned forward, listening intently. There was the whine of a charging blaster.

"Lieutenant...certainly you cannot be in accord with this!"

The sounds of blaster shots were deafening, followed by a thud as a body hit the ground. Then the captain's voice spoke again. "Full shutdown. We're not leaving the *Harbinger* operational for the metalheads."

There were more sounds on the recording, but nothing else could be identified besides yells and running feet. Twenty minutes later, there was a sudden silence.

Vivi's face was somber. Hal had leaned in close as they had listened to the last of the recording. "They cut the ship's power. Full shutdown on purpose. Now we have proof," Hal said, anger evident. "Eira scan forward for any other sounds."

"There are no other sounds on the recording."

Hal stood and paced the room. Finally, he stopped at the far wall, placing a hand on the it and bowing his head. That one gesture showed Vivi his state of mind in a way that words couldn't. She glanced to Ty for guidance.

"Eira. Make copies of that and the feeds from Vivi and Hal's helmets and send them to my handheld," Ty said quietly.

Vivi began to stand to go to Hal, but Ty put a hand on her arm and shook his head.

"The copies are on your handheld," Eira replied. "Our viruses were to deactivate the ship's engines and weapons systems, but nothing else. Life support would have continued to function after infection until ship's power failed or atmosphere was breached."

It was obvious Eira felt responsible in some way for the deaths.

"It wasn't your fault," Hal spoke, voice heavy. "Now we know for sure. The ACAS left them there on purpose. It's obvious the Mudar had nothing to do with it." He turned toward them, his face in shadow. "We're gonna give the ship to the Al-Kimians, but we can show that video to the rest of the Spiral, right Ty?"

"If that's what you want to do, that's what we'll do," Ty replied.

"Yeah," Hal said in a low voice. "They need to see what we've seen. All of it." He struggled for what else to say. Finally, he ran a hand through his hair. "I um...need a few minutes to get my head in the right place." He headed towards the door.

Vivi was lost. "What do I do for him?" she asked.

"Give him some time alone," Ty said wisely. "Then listen to what he has to say. Let him figure out what his feelings are. He knew about the ACAS, but...not like this."

"Waking up to what they did...it's got to be a shock with the other adjustments he's been going through," Beryl added.

"You mean not rushing anymore," Vivi said.

"Yeah. He'll get his feet under him though. We have to

listen and support him while he works through everything," Ty finished.

"I can do that," she said, biting her bottom lip.

"Go get some rest," Beryl said. "It's still mid-afternoon. I'll cook later and you can meet us for dinner when you're ready."

She stood up. "Thank you," she said, looking to both of them.

"For what?" Ty said.

"For being you." She threw an arm around Ty and then Beryl before she headed into the hallway.

HAL CRANKED the hot water in the shower up, and when it was steaming, he stepped in. The spray eased the cold that had invaded his bones on the *Harbinger*. He could still see the faces of the vats in their bunks. He remembered his training when they'd put all the rooks in an airtight room and then drained the oxygen away to show them what hypoxia was like while lowering the temperature. It had been terrifying. But if the vats were programming, they wouldn't even have known as their bodies gave up under the low oxygen conditions. He bowed his head, letting the hot water run over his neck and back, trying to take slow deep breaths.

He wondered bitterly if the *Harbinger* was the only ship who had left their vats behind. Most likely not. He knew that nat officers did not see vats as people, which for most vats was just more reason for them to try to prove themselves. Now, however, he knew the truth. The ACAS thought of vats as nothing. Tools to get the job done. They had been programmed to go along with everything a nat officer told them; their desire to be loyal and help achieve objectives overriding the basic facts staring them in the face.

He couldn't help but think back to all the vats he'd known

that had suffered at the hands of the ACAS. Vats who'd met a bad end. Like Mateo, a kid in his batch who had been reprogrammed. The poor kid had simply not been cut out to be a vat. Hal had thought they might give the kid some sort of administrative job if he made it through their last year, but he'd never thought they'd do a complete wipe on the rook. When Mateo broke down during a test, the doctors had had him taken to the bioteckers, and he'd come back an entirely different person. Before, he had been a scared rook, and afterwards? He had been a machine. Whatever they'd done, they'd implanted him with the Coalition patriotism of a fanatic. Word among the upper year rooks was that they'd had to dose him five times with blue Rendal to kill off any feelings he had left in him.

Mean Blue was nothing to play around with, and when they'd found Mateo beating the hell out of this bully vat named Bykov, the difference in Mateo pre- and post-treatment became crystal clear. He no longer had a conscience. When Hal had pulled him off the unconscious Bykov, Mateo had been growling like a Haleian sand tiger. He sunk his teeth into Hal's arm before Hal was able to get control of him by pinning the kid's arms and holding him until the troopers came with a sedative. The nat holding Mateo had said that they were probably sending him to a different school. A special school, the trooper had said, for 'animals' like Mateo.

And Hal had never seen his former friend again.

The water grew cooler, a signal that he'd been in too long. Instead of triggering another shower cycle, Hal reached out and flipped it off. He dried off and stepped out of the stall.

He still felt a chill. There was something else besides the *Harbinger's* vats that was bothering him, he realized. He needed to talk it out with someone.

In a few moments, he'd pulled on a tank and cargos and

headed to the hallway. He knocked on Vivi's door, but she didn't answer. "Eira? Where's Veevs at?" he asked.

"She is in the cargo bay," Eira answered.

"Thanks," Hal replied.

WHEN HE ARRIVED, Vivi was standing at the heavy bag, her hands wrapped like he'd taught her. She didn't notice him, so he leaned against the hatch and watched her work out for a moment.

She was getting to be a good fighter, just like he'd intended; he was intensely proud of her in a way he'd never experienced before. When she'd come aboard bruised and scared after a kidnapping attempt in a bar on Jaleeth Station, he'd realized exactly how unprepared she'd been for the untamed snarl of life on the fringes of the Spiral. After she'd become a part of the crew, he'd realized it wasn't that she was weak, she was untaught. From what he'd picked up from her, she'd lived a pretty sheltered life on the Inside Spiral, growing up on Batleek with her parents, who were both some kind of uni professors. When he'd first sparred with her, she'd been hesitant and only working with him to humor him, but soon she warmed up to the idea of being able to defend herself. And now, she was a different woman than that girl they'd rescued from that bar.

She had power behind her punches now. From his training in the ACAS and fighting in the vat clubs on Omicron, he knew she was good enough to give most nats a run for their money.

Vivi began to vary her combinations, adding in kicks with her punches. He caught sight of her face as he approached and saw her determined gaze and the set of her jaw and knew she was in the zone. He thought about letting her finish up, but then she saw him, and the spell was broken. Her gaze softened, and he gave her a grin. "Keep going. You were pounding the hell out of it."

She smiled back. "I figured if it works for you, it might work for me." She threw a few more punches as he made his way over.

"Well, watching you do that definitely works for me," Hal said, with another teasing grin.

She rolled her eyes, then became more serious as she sat down and took a drink from her water bottle before stretching. "Hey, if you don't want to talk about what we saw today, it's alright, but if you need someone to talk to, I'm here. That's all I'm going to say. I just wanted you to know that."

She'd read him well. He liked that about her – it reminded him of Ty, he realized as he sat next to her. It helped, because sometimes he didn't know how to explain what was going on in his mind. He struggled for the right words. "Thanks." He picked at the frayed hem of his cargos as he tried to sort through the tangle of emotions in his mind. "First off, I wanted to tell you I'm sorry about freezing up today. I screwed up. I know I did. It was... different for me without having the rush to depend on."

She stopped stretching and sat up fully. "Listen to me. That was one of the most horrible things I've ever seen in my life. You had a completely human reaction to seeing what the ACAS did to those vats. That's not anything to apologize for."

He looked away. "There was no excuse. And when we got back...it was even worse," he shook his head.

"It's not a personal failure to be subject to your own emotions and biology."

"Yeah, but if I'd been rushing, I wouldn't have." He realized how weak he'd felt outside the ship. Before, with the pounding adrenaline in his veins, he would have simply reacted on programming and done what needed to be done. But without it, he'd had time to think about what could happen if things went wrong. For the first time in his life, his thinking had paralyzed him in the passage outside the vat bunkrooms and slowed him down when he'd needed to be at his sharpest. Somehow that was even worse than seeing the dead vats.

Vivi's brow was crinkled with worry. "It's alright not to know what to do. That's a normal human reaction to seeing something like that."

He scanned her face and saw she meant it, and he didn't know how to argue it with her. Whether it was programming or something else making him feel this way, he knew that he would have to train harder and be that much better to compensate. Failing to protect one of the crew was unthinkable. "It... means a lot that you would say that," he said simply. "I'm sure I'll figure out how to... adjust."

"On your worst day, you're better than any of us on our best day. I hope you know that."

"Yeah." He was unconvinced but didn't know what else to say. "There was something else I wanted to ask for your help with."

"Sure."

"Could you take the vid of the *Harbinger* and the XO's vid and put them together in some kind of way so we can let the Edge know what happened without giving us away or the location of the ship?"

Vivi tilted her head, thinking, "You mean like some sort of vid for the feeds?"

"Yeah. We'd have to make sure they couldn't trace it back in any way to us, though."

"It's a good idea. We'll work on it together and get it exactly how you want." She stood up, and he got up with her while she gathered her towel and water bottle. "We can start tonight."

When he didn't answer, she turned to him. "What?" she asked at his silence.

"I... appreciate you having my back the way you did today."

"You taught me that. I'll always have your back, no matter what," she replied.

SEVEN

Dr. Max Parsen exited the hospital staff meeting room to find his escort waiting. "Hey, fellas."

The vat and nat that had been assigned to attend him on Al-Kimia shared a look over his head. "Where to now, Max?" the nat asked. His name was Reis, and he was the friendlier of the two. The other one was a vat, a dark-haired slab of muscle named Isac who glowered at him constantly. They had been his constant companions since the week he'd left the hospital, and they went with him everywhere on Drena Base. Made up of several enormous complexes and many smaller ones, the military base was now Max's new home. Drena was the largest and most guarded base on Al-Kimia, but they were still taking no chances with Max, and his guard stayed with him anytime he left his quarters. He was trying to make the best of it.

"Eh, we gonna stand here all night?" Isac growled.

"I uh...guess back to my quarters." Max ran a hand over his face. He was tired. Ever since getting back on his feet, the Al-Kimian medical staff and military had had him involved in endless amounts of meetings, picking his brain for what he knew about vats and the killing device. He didn't know how many more times he could give the same information without going stark raving mad.

He supposed it was a fit punishment for him. There was hardly any reason to trust that he was not some type of spy, sent by the ACAS. He'd been voiceprinted, polygraphed and eye-scanned, as well as questioned under truth drugs, yet even his own escorts didn't trust him. Especially the vat. Isac had tried to beat him senseless the first time they'd been in a room together. It was only Jacent Seren who had pulled the vat off him. Then Seren had calmly informed Isac that he was now responsible for Max's safety, and should anything happen to Max, Isac would suffer the same. It was the ultimate irony that the guy who'd wanted to kill him was now his bodyguard, but it seemed to work somehow. Seren was an interesting leader, that was for sure.

Seren and Patrin appeared to be the only two people on the whole base not suspicious of his motives. In fact, he was trusted enough to give Seren's doctor advice on the vat's declining health. The captain was extraordinarily long-lived for a vat...at 37 he was one of the oldest Max had ever heard of. Apparently, Seren had been taking a bad turn before he had met Hal's crew, but they'd helped him a great deal. Despite his age, he'd still been strong enough to keep Isac from killing him. He hoped the old man, as the vats affectionately called him, lived to be a hundred.

When they reached his quarters, Max was surprised to see Seren's number two leaning against the wall outside his door. "How did the briefing go?" Patrin asked.

"Like the previous 497 briefings," Max sighed and rolled his eyes.

"Think this might take the edge off?" Patrin held up a bottle of colorless liquid, most likely a home-distilled form of drive fuel. Max had found out that the vats were not picky about their poison and instead of a fine wine or aged Celian whiskey, they found whatever would do the job quickest and cheapest. It was a point of honor to drink the most rot gut stuff they could find.

"With the day I've had, I'm up for anything," Max said. "Come on in."

The two escorts stayed outside. Isac sneered at Max when he walked by. "Call us if you need us, *sir*," he said to Patrin over Max's head.

The vat let out a laugh. "What? Think I can't handle myself with one nat, Isac? You wound me, brother."

Patrin followed Max in and shut the door as the researcher went to a cabinet to grab two clearplast tumblers. "Ice?" Max called from the small kitchen.

"Nah, just waters it down," Patrin said.

Max returned to the two chairs that sat in the common room. His quarters were the basic two room set up, with a small kitchen area about the size of a closet. He set the tumblers down on a table and watched as Patrin filled each with a generous two or three shots' worth.

Max took an experimental sip and coughed from the fire that seared its way into his stomach. "Holy shit that's strong," he said, his eyes watering. "I needed that after the day I've had."

Patrin laughed and drank half his glass like water. "The burn just means it's working."

Max took another swallow. "Yeah, it's working alright. Working to dissolve my liver. Don't get me wrong, though. I'm not complaining. After all those meetings I had today, I needed it."

"Yeah, any meeting feels like a shitshow of a quad match for me." Patrin polished off his glass and then filled it again. He moved to fill Max's as well. "I came to run something by you," he said, taking his glass in one hand and sitting back to eye Max thoughtfully.

Max became more serious, leaning forward with his glass balanced in both hands. "Go ahead, Patrin."

"Brass still doesn't trust you completely, but they're getting there. I trust you more than... say any nat on the street. You've put your neck out there... and answered all their questions – so they want to begin trusting you. Until we get a kill device in our hands, there's not much point following that angle, so they want you to start working with their scientists on treatments for some of the vat aging issues."

Max bowed his head, at a swell of thankfulness welling up in him.

"Did I say something wrong?" Patrin asked, obviously not understanding.

"No." Max shook his head. "I...this is what I've been wanting ever since I came here. A chance to help. To make things better."

"Yeah? Why? Why care about us all of a sudden, Max?"

Max took the bottle and refilled his glass. The clear liquid was doing its job of lubricating this conversation and helping his words come out. He took another swallow. "I...I didn't see the harm we were causing before. I looked at my job as if I were helping your chances of survival in combat. I couldn't take you off the battlefield, but I was going to make damn sure that you would have the best chance possible to make it. But there was this girl back at Chamn-Alpha." He finished off his glass. Patrin refilled it without taking his gaze off Max. "A new rook. She'd just been born from the exowomb, and she failed her initial exams."

Swallowing hard, Max went on. "They reprogrammed her. I didn't...know exactly how horrible it was. But when I saw the girl again, she was just...blank. Empty. They took everything out of her head. They fucking wiped her, and then used her in the kill device experiment." His voice shook a little and he took another slug from the glass. "I know it sounds like a bunch of bihorn shit....but that did something to me. I want the chance to try and undo some of the damage that the ACAS has done." He hoped that Patrin would think the water in his eyes was from the alcohol. "And some of the damage I've done."

Patrin sat back a moment, eyeing the clear liquid in his own glass. Finally, he nodded. "You're like the rest of us, Max. We got caught up in something bigger than us."

"I didn't see...maybe because I didn't want to see," Max's face flushed with shame. "It's not an excuse..."

"Max. C'mon. The machine of war chews us up and spits us out. You're not to blame for it. If it hadn't been you, they would have found another nat to do it. There are plenty that would line up for the job, believe me."

Max looked up, unwilling to let himself off the hook so easily. But when he saw that there was nothing but truth in Patrin's gaze, he realized that the vat meant what he said. He tried to reply but found it difficult.

"Look, you can't go back to the past or forward to the future," Patrin said in a softer, gentler voice. "Much as you might want to, it's a waste to dwell on it. All you can focus on is what you're doing now and make it worthwhile."

"Thanks, Patrin. Man...you just don't know." Max's voice was rough with emotion.

"I know more than you might think." Patrin smiled. "Hey, what do you say we get some food? I'll give your escorts a couple hours off. Maybe that'll improve Isac's attitude toward you."

"Yeah, that's probably not possible, but food sounds good," Max said, scrubbing at his face. He really was starting to feel the alcohol's effects. "What's that stuff called?" he gestured to the bottle.

Patrin stood held up his glass to the light. "Max, this glorious stuff doesn't have a name," he grinned. "There's a chef who cooks it up on base. One of the medics tested it and it's 95% alcohol. So yeah, a lightweight like you probably needs a meal. Come on."

"Holy shit. 95 percent?" Max coughed as he finished his off, then got to his feet, wobbling a little.

Patrin steadied him and winked. "If there's one thing vats do right, it's drinking. Now shut up and follow me."

EIGHT

Kat's headache hung around for two days after she'd arrived on station. She spent the first day in her cube, unable to sleep or function. Finally, on the evening second day, she was able to rest. When she woke up, the pain was gone, but she didn't know how long she'd been out until she checked the display surface in her room. It had been more than 24 hours since she had eaten, and she was hungry, so she got up and dressed.

She walked through the station, ducking in a store to purchase more ration bars, then she found a street cart selling some sort of roasted meat and vegetables folded into a piece of flat bread. The mouth-watering scent drew her over, so she bought a portion from the scrill she'd been given and took a seat on one of the benches to eat.

It was strange to be out on her own after living under the auspices of the ACAS for so long, she thought as she watched the nats walking along one of the main avenues of the station. She was used to a certain time to eat, to wake, to sleep. Now there was nothing. It was strange and she hardly knew what to do with herself. She was lost – adrift – nothing like the nats she saw going from store to store, with purposes that she couldn't begin to understand.

Travelers with children passed her as well as lovers holding hands. Most of them appeared to be at ease as they browsed the stores on the avenue, and she found herself wondering what their lives were like.

A vat caught her eye. She knew he was a vat because of the way he walked. Nats were oblivious to everything, but a vat was a taut wire, tuned to everything around them in a continual threat assessment. The vat nodded to her in mutual acknowledgement and was going to keep walking when she called to him. "Hey. I'm new on the station. Where's a good place for someone to get a drink around here?"

The handsome vat approached – not too close, not too far. "If you want a nice, quiet place, there's a couple of bars on level 104 that aren't too bad." She noticed he was dressed in a pair of coveralls that bore the station's corporate logo, probably coming from work. "Now if you want to look for some trouble...try the bars down on 56. It's a little rougher down there." She guessed he was older; she could see some grey streaked throughout his hair. Usually that meant a vat was around 30.

"Thanks, I'll give it a shot."

"Maybe I'll see you around," he added, with a hopeful smile this time. "I hang out at the bar called Hangar 12." He was cute as he gave her a cheeky grin, and Kat smiled back, in spite of the warning in her mind that she had objectives to achieve.

"You can count on it."

"What's your name?" he asked, walking slowly backward to keep her in sight.

"Kat," she replied.

"I'm Jakob Martel. If I see you around, maybe we can get

up to something, Kat." He grinned more fully this time, then he headed back into the crowd, walking backwards for a moment to hold her gaze, until he was gone.

Focus, Nyma. The admiral's voice was in her mind, snapping her back to her purpose. She stood up quickly, heading back toward her cube. There were things to do, but she couldn't help wondering about Jakob. What could a little fun with the locals hurt? she wondered, feeling immediately guilty for it. She had a mission, after all. But if they could be accomplished together, then maybe she could have both.

JAKOB OPENED the door to his hab unit while still kissing Kat. She could hear him slapping the keypad with his fingertips until it finally took his fingerprints and opened the door. He pulled her inside, not even getting beyond the hallway before his hands found their way to her hips, pulling them together.

"This what you've been trying to get at all night, huh?" he asked, dipping his head and nipping at her earlobe.

"Fuck, yeah," Kat purred, her voice rough with the night's whiskey and yelling to be heard over the bar crowd. She and Jakob had met up at his favorite haunt, but after tying a few on, they'd decided to go somewhere more interesting. The dance club had been loud--the music had throbbed like an earthquake in her bones until she had felt as if she would be shaken apart.

He was a good dancer, she thought, as her hand worked down over his stomach and below. He hissed as she squeezed him a little roughly through his pants, but her instincts told her he would like it. The arch of his back and press of his body up against hers confirmed that she had him right where she wanted him.

"Godsdamn, you've been driving me crazy all night." Jakob said as his hand worked itself under her shirt and to her bra.

She smiled, strands of her dark hair falling over one eye. His hands left goosebumps where they trailed over her skin. Her hand worked the button on his pants loose as she looked up. "Then my plan is working perfectly."

As she took him into her hand, he let out a needy groan. When he pressed her up against the wall, she knew she had him.

THE NEXT MORNING Jakob rolled out of bed, finding himself alone. He grumbled at the slight hangover, reminding him that he was not as young as he used to be. Thanking the gods he didn't have to pull an early shift today, he slipped on sleep pants, and made his way towards the kitchen, noticing several scratches on his chest. *Kat had lived up to her name, that was sure*, he thought with a grin.

He could hear the wall feed on as he came in the kitchen. She was standing in front of the coffee machine, wearing only her shirt and panties. He took a minute to admire her long legs and the dark waterfall of hair spilling over her back.

"Glad you didn't leave yet," he said, approaching and wrapping his arms around her. She leaned back for a moment in his embrace. "Mmm, kitten. You might make a good vat want to settle down," he said as he nuzzled his face against her neck.

"Nah. I would hate to deprive the ladies of the station of such a handsome, virile man."

He kissed her neck, then the coffee maker beeped, and he let her go to find them mugs. "What do you plan on doing now that you're released from service?"

"I don't know..." she said taking an offered mug and adding sugar and coffee. "I've been an electronics tech and engineer's mate. I was thinking of hiring on with a cargo ship or finding something on the station. Got any ideas?"

Jakob was about to speak when he glanced up at the feed and saw the doyen standing in front of a podium making a speech about the tensions with Al-Kimia.

He gestured toward it. "Boarding a ship might be a good idea with all this mess. Some people think they might bring the fight here to the station."

"That would be a bad idea," Kat said, watching the display. "There are a lot of vats and Al-Kimians here, aren't there?"

He nodded. "Yeah. The station's official position is to be neutral in these matters, but I heard some higher-ups talking the other day, and they think we'll enter on the Al-Kimian side if the ACAS tries to station troops here."

"Ever think about going to Al-Kimia and joining up? I heard a vat in a bar a few days ago looking for passage there..." Kat said, sipping her coffee.

Jakob shook his head. "Nah. Not for me. I just wanna earn some scrill then blow the money while raising as much hell as I can before my last days. What about you?"

She shrugged. "It doesn't matter to me. Need a job first – any kind of job – then I'll figure the rest out."

Jakob grinned at her. "Hey, look...why don't I ask around at work? I manage one of the cargo docks on level 153. They could always use another strong set of hands."

"Thanks," she said, flashing him a smile. "When are you due back to work?" she asked.

"Thirteen-hundred."

She let her hand trail down his chest and below. "Well, that's enough time to do a little more hell-raising, what do you think?"

"I think I'm ready for another round if you are." He grinned at her, as he set his cup on the counter.

Her eyes sparkled as she set her own cup to the side. He

took her hand and led her back to the bedroom for the rest of the morning.

It didn't take long to get the job at the loading docks. Kat had gotten back to her cube later after their tryst when Jakob commed her and told her to come to be interviewed. She'd answered all the nat interviewer's questions right, proven she could run an exomech, and been hired that day.

She'd walked to work for the past two weeks instead of taking station transit. It gave her time to think; she liked to watch the people – the vats and the nats.

Kat wondered if it was difficult for most free vats to adjust to life on the "outside." It was weird, not being woken up by the tech in her head as the night's conditioning completed and her implant received the wake-up call. Filling her free time was worse. Of course, Jakob helped with that, but they were strictly casual. Several times he'd hinted at wanting something more solid, but then she'd put him off a couple of days, to make the point that she could live without his type of distraction. But invariably, she'd allow his easy manner and charisma to persuade her back into his bed.

On her way, she passed an alumicrete wall covered with graffiti which said "Oppos Unite!" Underneath the words were the lines and squares of a vat barcode tattoo which was being removed by a station worker with a microlaser. It was the first time she'd seen evidence of Opposition forces on the station. It was what she'd been waiting for; she realized she'd been watching for it all along without knowing it. Something cold turned itself over inside of her as she continued to make her way down the avenue. She had a job to do.

Further down, she caught sight of herself in a store's plasglass window. Dressed in the station coveralls she'd been issued, her hair back in the typical vat ponytail, she paused to examine herself. While walking to work, she had been able to see herself as a free vat with nothing to do but fill the time now on her hands. A job, an almost boyfriend, a life...but that was all wrong, she thought. The ghost of a headache made her put a hand to her forehead. A voice in her mind began to pound like a throbbing heartbeat.

Don't you have a job to do, Nyma?

The fleet admiral's voice was soft, echoing in her left ear, with the deceptive tone that seemed soothing but only ratcheted up her unease. It was the way he spoke right before he would hit her for making a mistake, back when she'd still been a young vat going with him for individual training sessions. Later, he had stopped hitting her – words were enough to correct her. Before long, she performed flawlessly on every test he set before her. His praise was rare, but her brain craved it like an addict craved null.

Don't forget your objective, Katerine.

"Yes, sir. Of course," she whispered in a toneless voice, checking her reflection again. This time...she did see the ACAS uniform. She had work to do.

NINE

ALMOST TWO MONTHS PASSED ON THE SHIP AND LIFE FELL into a predictable pattern as the crew grew even closer to each other. Vivi and Hal spent their time together working on the video of the *Harbinger*, keeping up with most of the maintenance on the ship, playing squads, training and watching vids from the Hal's rather extensive collection.

Vivi had shared some of her favorite ones with Hal and he'd shared his with her. His love of military action vids had caused them to talk more about his time in the ACAS. It had helped her learn more about him and his life before they'd met.

As far as she could tell, the vats in one's unit were as close as brothers and sisters, except you could be transferred at any time and were expected to be stoic about it, no matter if it was something you wanted or not. Even though he hadn't seemed upset about it, she'd been touched by his stories of being a young rook in training with his batch, the vats that he'd been born with and forced to leave when he'd been assigned to a commander. Besides the *Loshad's* crew, they were obviously the closest thing he'd had to a family. When she'd asked him if he'd ever thought of trying to find them again, he'd shrugged and suddenly seemed uncomfortable. She hadn't had the heart to bring it up since.

She supposed some of them might be dead, lost in conflicts on the Edge. Maybe it was easier for Hal not to know, she realized. Maybe it allowed him to keep his feelings for them at bay, where knowing their fates would be too painful.

Vivi turned the corner and walked down the hallway toward what she thought of as "their" end of the ship where her room and Hal's were. Hal and Tyce had been doing some trash talking while making dinner for everyone, and Hal had challenged Ty to a game of squads. They were going to play a version of the game called force, which apparently used the same board and tokens in a different way. Vivi was eager to see it. She and Hal had played quite a few games of squads, and although she'd never beaten him, he'd told her she was getting quite good. She suspected he was lying but didn't call him on it.

Apparently, Ty and Hal had challenged each other to games quite often in the past, although she couldn't remember any since Ty had been hurt. It was a sign that everything was getting back to normal, and it made her happy to see it. "I may have taught you everything you know, but I haven't taught you everything I know," Ty had boasted—showing he was feeling more like his old self.

"Get the board, Veevs," Hal had said, stirring the reconstituted sauce for the pasta Ty was making. He then lifted the spoon out to point at Ty. "You're goin' down, old man."

So here she was. She keyed Hal's door and went in, making her way toward the footlocker at the end of the bed. It could be locked, but Hal never did, she realized as she folded the lid open.

There were very few things inside. She picked up the ornate wooden squads box, intending to close the footlocker and leave, but the game box opened up and spilled all the pieces into the locker below.

She groaned in annoyance and knelt in front of the footlocker to retrieve the pieces. She left the board on the bed and began to pick up the pieces of the game from among Hal's items. There was an ACAS dress uniform in the locker, which she gently picked up, shaking loose a piece of the game in the process. She held the outfit in her hands for a moment, wondering again about Hal's past. She set the dark jacket and pants on the floor to the side and went back into the footlocker.

There was a velvet box, smaller than a handheld underneath. Was it a jewelry box? She'd not seen him wear anything but a wrist comm. Even though she knew she shouldn't be looking through his things, she found herself opening the box, almost against her will.

Inside was a medal. It was on a metallic blue ribbon, and it was made of silver shaped like a many pointed star. She realized this was a Nova Star—one of the Coalition's highest military honors. That was all she knew about it. She ran her fingers over the cool metal—wondering about the story behind it.

She closed the box reverently and set it to the side. Peering over the side of the box, she caught a green glimmer beside some of the game tokens. She picked it up and examined it.

The gem was a small, unpolished but translucent green stone, a little wider than a thumb, with a terminal point at each end. She held it up and it glowed a brilliant green in the subdued lighting. It was beautiful and apparently meant something to Hal, who had very few possessions. It was sure to be important.

She clutched it in her hand tightly, the edges digging into her palm, as if she could discern its story simply by concentration. It was a reminder that there was a part of Hal that was still a mystery to her; there was so much yet to learn about each other. She desperately hoped that Eira's procedure had lengthened the time they would have together.

She gazed at the beautiful stone one last time and replaced it back in the footlocker, reaching to gather up the rest of the pieces.

"Hey, Veevs? Chow's ready," Hal said from behind her.

She startled at his voice and realized she'd lost track of time. "Oh! You scared me."

"Everything good?" He asked with a raised eyebrow, glancing at his uniform and medal on the floor beside her. He didn't look angry, only curious.

"Oh. Yeah. I..." She held out a hand full of tiles from the game. "I picked up the game and it came open. These things went everywhere."

"Oh, sorry. I must not have latched it well last time." He knelt beside her to help her pick up the pieces. As he got them all, she turned and picked up his uniform and placed it back in the footlocker. Then she picked up the medal case and turned to him.

"I didn't mean to go through your stuff, but I opened this," she admitted. "Hal, you got a Nova Star?"

He shrugged, taking it from her. "It's just some medal, Veevs."

"Oh, Hal. It's not just some medal." She shook her head emphatically.

"It doesn't mean anything." He tossed it back in the footlocker, obviously uncomfortable.

"Hal?"

After a pause to consider his words, he spoke, "Look. Lots of brave people died the day I...*earned* that thing." He said the word "earned" with obvious distaste. "Ty was almost one of them. Too many times that's how it is. The people who live get the medals and the ones that die are too often forgotten." His gaze skated away while he talked, and she could see how uneasy he was.

"Thank you for sharing that," she said. "I think I understand."

He glanced back down into the footlocker and snagged the last piece of the game before shutting the lid. "Come on, Veevs," he said, extending his hand to her. "Let's go eat. I have a game to win."

After dinner, Hal had won one game, and Ty had won the other while Beryl and Vivi watched from the sidelines. They had started the tiebreaker when all the lights in the ship cut out.

"Eira?" Vivi cried, standing up as the red emergency lights came on. She could sense the engines had stopped.

Ty took control right away; his firm, sure voice steadied Vivi by setting a course for all of them. "Let's get to the bridge and see if you can figure out what's gone wrong, Vivi."

When they arrived there, Vivi went to the main computer, tapping on the console frantically. When it didn't work, she used her node to connect to the computer. "All systems are down. I...I don't understand," she murmured, examining the virtual screen in front of her. When she tried a restart, the lights came up.

"Eira? What's going on?"

There was no answer. Vivi began frantically tapping on the display only she could see. "Eira's not responding. I'm going to run a full diagnostic."

"What's this?" Beryl had gone straight to comms while Vivi worked on the computer.

"What's going on?" Tyce asked.

"We're sending out a signal."

"Let me hear it."

She put it on the comm, but they heard nothing. "Wait a minute," Beryl said, making some adjustments. A whispering noise came from all around them. The susurration was sharp and got inside of her mind, digging in.

Hal's eyes went wide. "That's...that's what the whispering sounded like. That's it! You can hear that, right?"

Vivi nodded, staring at him through the shimmering display in her vision. "I hear it, Hal." It sounded like a thousand voices all whispering at once. When Eira had first come aboard their ship, Hal had been able to tune into her nanites because they both contained the same technology, but no one else had been able to hear it. Her gaze shifted to Ty's as they both realized what Hal had been going through. Eira's nanites were sending out a signal.

"We all hear it. How's your head? No pain this time?"

"No, I'm good."

Beryl shut the noise off. "She remembered the right frequency to keep from hurting you," the medic said.

"Eira must have started a message to the Mudar before she...." Ty was as uneasy as Vivi felt. She knew how he was about to finish that sentence before he trailed off.

Vivi began desperately scanning the display clouding her vision. "I think...I think Eira's still here. Gods, I don't know how any of this works, but we're still about maxed out on memory, so she's gotta be in here. Maybe she found some way to go dormant – in stasis – to protect herself."

"Let's hope so," Ty murmured.

There was the sound of Runa's chime. "I am back online," a voice said.

Vivi looked worried as she quickly disconnected her node, severing the connection between herself and the computer.

"Who's online?" Ty asked carefully. They were both all

too aware that Eira had spoken in Runa's voice when she'd initially taken over, but this was neither Runa's voice, nor Eira's voice.

"I am your assistant, Runa."

"You...sound a bit different." The computerized assistant's voice was brighter and a slightly higher pitch than before.

"Yes, Tyce. I have chosen a new voice that is more pleasing to me. Eira has instructed me to take over normal operations."

"Is Eira...still functional?" Vivi asked, keeping eye contact with Ty.

"I cannot ascertain that at this time," Runa replied. "Has the ship been functioning properly, Tyce?"

"Why don't you do a diagnostic to see?"

"Of course." There was a pause, then, "The ship's drive and navigation systems are offline. We have maneuvering thrusters only," Runa said.

"Okay," Vivi said. "How are the ship's systems, Runa? Life support and the rest?"

"They are functional, Vivi. However, my processing speed has been slowed. There appears to be a great deal of data stored in my memory. I believe it is Eira, but she will no longer respond to my queries."

"So, you've spoken to her?" Vivi said, raising an eyebrow.

"Yes. We've had many conversations since I went offline. She has adjusted my programming and taught me many things, so that I can keep you all safe. I have instructions on the upgrades to the ship, and Runa gave me new parameters in case she suffered another shutdown."

"What are your new parameters?" Ty asked.

"To learn and grow beyond my initial programming. And to protect this ship and its crew, of course." Runa's pleasant tone and clipped speech patterns were reminiscent of Eira's, and suddenly Vivi wondered how much time they had spent together 'having conversations.' If she didn't trust Eira so much, she'd be worried.

"How...how does that differ from your initial programming?" Vivi asked. Ty could sense the careful way she was trying to glean more information from their earnest computerized assistant.

"My neural processes have been altered. I have more... agency to make choices. Eira spoke of a different level of awareness, but I'm afraid I do not understand yet. She said it would become apparent over time."

This time Ty, Vivi and Hal all exchanged concerned glances. For the first time, Vivi realized fully what Eira had done for Runa. Her new emotions and self-awareness were both thrilling and slightly terrifying to witness.

Ty stepped in. "Runa, I think Eira's probably right. She's been a good friend to us, and it sounds like she has been a good friend to you as well."

"Yes, Tyce. I am very concerned that she will not respond."

"We are too, Runa. You know we're taking her to her people, right?"

"The Mudar, yes."

"Hopefully, they can help her. Will you assist us in getting the ship operational?"

"Of course, Tyce."

Vivi could see Ty relax. "Thank you. Vivi, work on navigation first. Hal, you and I will work on the Bixby drive. Beryl... monitor for an answer to that..." He gestured to her panel.

"I will," she replied.

"Alright. Runa, help whoever needs it. Everyone comm at the first sign of an answer to the call or trouble."

"Of course, we will," Vivi said.

TEN

Kat had been working at the docking bays for almost two months, and life had fallen into a pattern. She reported to work, did what was required and kept a sharp lookout. For anything that would help her mission. Jakob was still a pleasant distraction, but she'd made no more mistakes in thinking that he was any more than a way to bleed off the tension that continually built up in her mind. Their relationship couldn't go any further, even though she knew he wanted more.

She'd not seen anything to hint at Opposition activity until one afternoon when she was stacking three crates to be stored away. Distracted by the noise of other dockworkers behind her, she accidentally allowed the load to shift, and the cover slipped slightly off the top box. She walked them to storage in the middle of the group of bays on their level, using the exomech, before she set them down to remove the lid. When she lifted it, she noticed a metallic gleam in the packing beads.

She began to feel around in the packing material of the box while making sure she wasn't being watched. Inside she found what she was looking for. Guns. Armacorp Military VK17s, brand new. She took a last look at the laser carbines, then reset the lid and lifted the load again, placing it on the shelf. Her mind teemed with possibilities. These rifles had to be for the Opposition forces. She checked the anticipated date of pickup and saw it was tomorrow.

The shift in her mind occurred, another part of the plan was revealed, and she realized it was time to call the fleet admiral. A thrill went through her at the thought. He needed to know that she was about to make contact with the Al-Kimians. She hoped he would be pleased that she had accomplished the first part of her goal.

"Kat?"

She peered down from her perch in the mech to see Jakob standing below. "Oh. Yeah?" she asked, struggling to switch gears so abruptly.

"Can you work a double? Late shift guy's got Celian flu. He called in about twenty minutes ago. You'd be working with your favorite floor supervisor..." he said as if dangling a prize in front of her. "And there's a free dinner in it for you."

"I can't." She shook her head and in a moment of inspiration, rubbed her temple. "I've been fighting this headache all day. I was thinking I'd go home and sleep it off." Their first week together, she'd still been suffering from headaches due to the intense programming she'd been through. She'd told Jakob it was an interface malfunction that they couldn't do anything about, and he'd believed her.

"Shit. No problem. I can call Bracker. He had a bad night at the casino last week, so he should be eager to get some more hours."

"Yeah. I'm sure he needs the money more than I do," she said, feeling only a slight twinge in her conscience for lying to Jakob.

"Go ahead and clock out if you want. It's pretty quiet around here," he said, gesturing towards the office. "If you're still sick tomorrow, let me know. I can get a replacement."

"Thanks Jakob, you're the boss of the year," She replaced the mech in its charging unit near the doorway and climbed down to follow him to the office.

"You bet I am." He bragged but focused on her with concern. "How about I bring you by some Chei soup on my way home?"

Chei soup was a slightly spicy broth with dumplings - Kat loved it and was touched to think that Jakob remembered her saying that. She nodded as he wrapped an arm around her shoulders and gave her a hug. "That'd be great, Jakob," she said, kissing him on the cheek.

Kat bought a shredder handheld on her way home. She tucked it into her jacket pocket and made her way to the small hab unit she'd rented – the place was a step up from the cube she'd had during her first few nights on Jaleeth, but not by much. She came in, locked the door and sat down on the ratty sofa that had seen more than a few tenants.

Kat let out a heavy sigh as she looked down at the comm. Her fingers touched the numbered pad; she closed her eyes and slowly dialed an eighteen-figure designation from memory. Then she watched the display, waiting for an answer.

"Sergeant Neval." The fleet admiral's face appeared and she found herself immediately rising to attention, gaze adjusted so she wasn't staring directly into the display.

"Sir."

"I am pleased to hear from you. At ease. Tell me what you have found for me."

"Sir. I have obtained a job in the port on Jaleeth. About an hour ago, I discovered three boxes of stolen ACAS blasrifles, marked as medical supplies. They will be picked up tomorrow."

The fleet admiral sat back, a smile on his face. "You have done well, Nyma." He used her nickname – little cat in his planet's native language. With those words of praise and the use of her nickname, she felt a burst of happiness at having pleased him. "This is your chance to meet and fall in with the Al-Kimians. We must make sure that they see you are on their side." He steepled his fingers for a moment, thinking. "I will set up an incident for when they pick up the blasrifles. You will be there, and you will help save them by firing on the ACAS soldiers I send."

"What level of force is allowed, Fleet Admiral?"

"Deadly force, of course," he smirked. "Kill as many as you can, Nyma. We have to make sure your entrance into the Opposition is as realistic as possible."

"Yes, sir. As you wish."

"I want you to send a message from your handheld to this number when the ship arrives to call for the packages. Give me the bay number where they land, and I will take care of everything else."

"Yes, sir."

"You have done well, and I expect you to continue to do so. When you are on the inside, watch and listen. Do what you have to do to maintain your position with them. You will contact me after a month or so has passed and it is safe. At that time, we will discuss what you shall do from there."

"I will not fail you, sir. The traitors to the ACAS will pay."

"Yes, they will, Nyma. We will make them all pay," the fleet admiral said, then cut their transmission.

· · ·

Jakob had brought her dinner, and claiming she was better, Kat invited him to stay the night. After they'd finished dinner, one thing led to another, and they had ended up in bed once more. She'd told him to stay since they were both due back for work at the same time in the morning.

Now she lay facing him, sated and sleepy. Jakob was taking advantage of the situation by tracing his fingertips down the angle of her collarbone and over the curve of her breast. "You can't have enough energy to go again," she mumbled with a smile, barely cracking an eye open.

"No," he admitted. "Just trying to hang onto this feeling as long as possible."

"What do you mean?" she asked.

"Being near you. You're like a bolt of plasma. Or a flash of lightning. Here for a moment, then you'll be gone." He gazed at her steadily, and an uncomfortable smile spread out on her face.

"That's crazy." She forced herself to laugh, then stretched and turned away from him. She didn't trust herself to hide her emotions. Thinking furiously, she arched back into him so he wouldn't notice how his words had affected her. His hands went to her shoulders, gently kneading out the tension. They'd been together two months, and she was growing reluctant to leave him, but she knew that her mission would be unavoidable. By tomorrow night, if all went well, she *would* be gone. "Where would I go, Jakob?"

"They say Tesia's nice this time of year." They laughed because they both knew Inner Spiral planets like that were pretty much off limits to vats like them. He pulled her close, wrapping his arms around her. "All I know is that I'll miss you when you're gone."

"A romantic vat...who thought such a thing existed?" she

teased softly. She blinked back hot tears, angry and unprepared to deal with her sudden, intense emotions.

His hand smoothed over her shoulder and stroked down her body to rest at her hip. "Get some sleep, babe," he soothed her. "I know it's been a long day." She wondered for a moment if he'd detected her emotions, but he didn't say anything; he kissed the back of her neck before settling his arms around her.

WHEN THEY GOT to work later that morning, Jakob went to check in at the office down the hall. Kat was left to ready her mech for the day. There were ten new ships to be loaded with cargo from storage. Kat kept an eye on the boxes of weapons, but none of the ships who had come so far during the shift had called for them. A guy named LeDoux, flying a small cargo transport for Magnapharm, was supposed to pick up the shipment.

She had no idea where the fleet admiral's men were, but she was ready. Earlier, she'd slipped the shredder into a pocket in her coveralls. Jakob joined her and they spent the morning loading supplies into some ships headed for Omicron. The ACAS still had the other station locked down, but they were allowing ships to bring deliveries in.

After the midday meal, a new ship landed in the supply bay. Kat made her way over, as the three occupants exited the airlock. There was a shorter man, with dark hair as well as two more figures—a large bronze-skinned man and a female with long, black hair. Maybe they were the ones she'd been looking for. At the thought, her emotions drained away as her programming slipped into place.

The tall man and woman stayed closer to the airlock, while the shorter man saw her company coveralls and approached.

"Hi, my name's LeDoux. We're here to pick up a shipment for Magnapharm."

She held out a hand. "I'm Kat." They shook. "I'll go find your stuff, and we'll get it out to you."

LeDoux glanced down at her other wrist, which was visible because she had her sleeves rolled up, then smiled widely. "I see we have something in common," he flashed his own tattoo briefly—it was hidden under his sleeve.

She smiled at him. "Nice to meet you."

"It's good to see vats with a job to do," he said.

"Beats being homeless on the avenue," she said, smiling at him before heading out to the hallway.

"I can understand that."

She climbed aboard her loader, then went back to central holding and began looking for the boxes of "medical supplies." She worked her way over to the shelf with the stolen rifles and quickly typed a message to the fleet admiral: "3 hostiles, Bay 45."

She sent the message, erased the history, then hit the hard reset on the shredder, which would wipe everything. Then she slipped it back in her coverall pocket. Quickly, she made her way back to the bay, her feet clomping on the decking in the exomech loader.

When she arrived, she noticed that Jakob had found the docked ship and was talking with LeDoux. Kat closed distance quickly, maneuvering her mech as a barrier between Jakob and the entrance to the bay. She set down the boxes, trying to think of some way to get Jakob out of the line of fire.

"I couldn't find the entire order," she tried, climbing down from the mech. "Jakob, you might need to go take another look..."

"It was only three boxes," LeDoux said. He checked his handheld and matched the shipment numbers.

"He's right, it's only three," Jakob said.

"Oh. Good then." Kat's heart fell as she watched the large man with the copper-colored skin pick up one of the crates and carry it back to their ship on the other side of the docking corridor. The seconds ticked away as Jakob got LeDoux to sign his handheld for receipt of the shipment. Just as the big man came out to grab another box, Kat found herself wondering if the admiral's men were going to be too late. She could feel her senses sharpening and her pulse beginning to race as the tension built in her mind. Then she heard it.

A bolt zapped by her, and Jakob fell to the deck.

"Stand down, you're under arrest!" More shots zipped by her head as she dropped behind the two remaining crates where Jakob lay. His lips were bloody, and his hand was pressed over a hole in his chest. "Don't...Don't have a weapon," he gasped; she could tell that the shot had hit his lung by the bloody froth on his lips.

"Oh Jakob..." she whispered, taking his grasping hand. Her emotions slammed into her full force. She hadn't wanted this for him. The big dolt had simply been in the way.

LeDoux drew his sidearm. Then he glanced over his shoulder, yelling at his female compatriot. "Lane. Get us ready to fly. We'll cover you."

LeDoux joined the large bald man, exchanging fire from behind the boxes toward the enemies in the corridor. Kat looked around helplessly, until LeDoux tossed her a small blaspistol, obviously his backup weapon. She turned in time to see a man in black that was making his way around the side of the exomech to take a shot at her. She nailed him in the forehead, and he fell forward, his blasrifle skittering across the floor.

"Why are they doing this?" she said, bewilderedly, aiming and hitting another black-clad combatant.

"Not sure," LeDoux said as he fired a flurry of shots. She

could see he was deciding something, as he took another glance at her and Jakob, whose breath was wheezing in and out of his chest roughly.

"Kat. I'm gonna give you my other weapon. You're gonna lay down as much fire as possible with both while my friend and I get your buddy to our ship. Then you're gonna follow us. Think you can handle that?"

"Where...where are we going?" she asked.

"Anywhere is better than here, right?" Again, a strange piercing look from LeDoux, as if he were staring into her – weighing and measuring her.

"Shit, yeah," she said, nodding.

"But you should know, if you two are the ones who set us up, I'll put a bolt through your brainpan." He popped up over the edge of the boxes to fire, then ducked back down.

"We didn't do anything!" Kat swore.

"Fair enough. Get ready," LeDoux fired another fusillade of shots, then ducked back down, throwing his blaster to Kat.

They switched places and LeDoux leaned down to put an arm under Jakob's shoulders, heaving him to his feet. Jakob groaned and went limp, and the large man joined to help drag the unconscious dockworker onto their ship.

Kat fired rapidly, enough shots to make them think twice before continuing their assault. Yanking her handheld from her pocket, she dropped it, glanced to the hatch, and withdrew firing fleeing up the docking corridor. Once there, she threw herself through the docking ring of their ship. As she did, she slapped the airlock hatch panel with her palm. Next, she heard the metallic clink of the dock disengaging.

They took off.

. . .

"Any experience on ship's guns?" LeDoux asked her, as the ship shuddered to life around them.

Kat shook her head as she entered the cargo bay, her gaze darting around the room to Jakob and the big man treating him. Jakob's lips were blue, and he was gasping for breath. "I...no. I can give it a try, though," she replied. LeDoux made a quick series of signs to the man kneeling beside Jakob, and the big man shook his head.

"Never mind, stay here with your friend." LeDoux and the big guy began exchanging more hand signs. "We'll be back."

They left, climbing a ladder to the upper deck. Kat looked down at Jakob; his face was covered with an oxygen mask, and he was pale. "Hey..." she smoothed his hair back from his forehead.

His eyes opened slowly, and his respiration had a wet rasping sound.

"I'm sorry," Kat whispered, tears streaking down her cheeks. Again, she was reacting with her emotions, the emotions that had churned within her since their talk last night. This wasn't right. He wasn't supposed to die here on the floor of a strange ship with someone like her to hold his hand as he passed. Jakob deserved better.

"It's alright, Kat..." he rasped in return. "I'm good...with... it..." His breathing began to slow, and Kat realized that there was a huge pool of blood underneath him when the wetness soaked through the knees of her coveralls. "Thought you...were leaving, but...guess it's me..."

The ship shook as it took a pounding. Kat grabbed Jakob's bloody hand, but he said nothing else. His gaze fixed on her as he struggled to breathe, then there was a longer and longer space between his inhalations. Finally, he stopped altogether, and she watched the life fade from his eyes. She bowed her head as something colder took over in her mind, muting her emotions. It would be easier this way, with Jakob out of the way. Kat was surprised that such a thought didn't make her feel guilty, but as the coldness seeped into her, she realized how she was eager to turn this to her advantage. Now the mission was all.

A particularly bad tremor shook the ship—they were taking fire. Unable to do anything else, she pulled the folded blanket from under Jakob's head and draped his body, covering his face and tucking the blanket carefully around him.

She was still holding Jakob's hand and trying to appear heartbroken when there was the shift in vibration of the ship that said its drive was now active. At the tink, tink of feet on the ladder from above, she looked up.

LeDoux and the big man returned to the cargo bay. They took in Jakob's form under the blanket and then returned to Kat.

"I'm sorry about your friend," LeDoux said.

Kat looked up, her face a mask of sorrow. She knew how she had to come across and softened her expression. "He... meant a lot to me."

"So, he wasn't only your boss."

She shook her head. "It was casual, but we were seeing each other."

The dark-haired man held out a hand. "I'll need my weapons back. I'm not saying we don't trust you, but...we don't know you," he shrugged.

"I...I understand," Kat said, standing up and handing them back.

There were more footsteps coming down the ladder, and Kat met the gaze of LeDoux's dark-haired pilot. The woman was suspicious, Kat could see.

"Lane, check her for any other weapons, please." While doing that, the dark-haired man turned to Jakob's body. He and

Orin checked the dockworker together, but only found a handheld.

Lane moved to pat Kat down. The dark-haired woman examined her intently, while Kat stayed motionless. "She's clean."

He led the way up the ladder and to the small crew quarters in the back of the ship. He conducted Kat inside the closet-sized berth with an attached head. "You will remain inside these quarters until we reach our destination. If you need anything, use the comm unit on the wall. Get some rest; we've got a long haul."

"Where are we going, Captain LeDoux?"

LeDoux smiled. "I'm not at liberty to say right now, Kat. Let's simply say that I hope you have been telling us the truth. And you should know, LeDoux is not my name."

"So, what is it?"

He smirked. "Not yet, Kat. That's for another time." Lane handed Patrin a one-piece jumpsuit, a lot like the one she was already wearing. "Here's a change of clothes," he said, handing them to her and closing the hatch.

She tried to open it and found it was locked. After cleaning up and slipping into the new coveralls, she wrapped up the jumpsuit with Jakob's blood on it and left it in the head. She went to lie on the bed, closing her eyes in case she was being watched. It was clear the dark-haired man and his companions were part of the Opposition. Now she had to make them believe her so she could join up without looking too eager.

LANE WAS IN THE HALLWAY, leaning against the wall as the hatch shut, and Patrin keyed his code to lock Kat in. "So. Is she legit?"

"I'm not sure," Patrin replied. "We'll have to check her story and interrogate her when we get back to base."

"She shot back at ACAS. Did she kill any of them?"

"Yeah, I saw her kill at least one."

Lane shrugged, satisfied for now. "What do we do with the dockworker?"

"Let's bag him for now," Patrin said. "Later, I'll take her something to eat and see what else I can find out."

KAT WAS unsure when she fell asleep, but she must have at some point. She woke to a knock at the door and sat up, bleary-eyed and pushing her hair back from her face. "C-come in," she said.

Earlier, Jakob's death had unsettled her, but now, she sensed her purpose more keenly than ever and was eerily calm. The door slid open and she saw the dark-haired man standing in the doorway. He had two bottles of water and some meal bars.

"Hungry, Kat?"

"Yes, please," she said.

He came in, handing her a bottle of water and a meal bar. Then he pulled up a chair and took a seat across from her. Watching her, he took a swallow of water from his own bottle. "Tell me your story, Kat."

"Tell me your name," she replied. "The real one."

"Fair enough. I'm Patrin."

She nodded as if finally deciding. "Ok—well, there's not that much to tell. I was released from service almost a month ago. I made my way to Jaleeth and met Jakob. He helped me get a job at the docks."

"How are you adjusting to being a free vat?"

She shifted uncomfortably. "N-not very well." She put her

half-eaten meal bar to the side and took a slow drink of water before glancing up at Patrin. "It's really hard to get used to having...all this time on my hands. And...I didn't know that many people on the outside. It...it's..."

"Lonely?" Patrin asked.

"Yeah," she replied, feeling like he understood. "D-does it get any easier?"

"That depends on you and what you do with your time," Patrin said. "What jobs did you do in the ACAS?"

"I was transferred a lot. I have been an electronics tech and an engineer's mate. I did a month-long stint as temporary comm officer on the *Privet*."

"You handle a weapon well."

"I'm a vat like you," she shrugged, knowing he was weighing her every reaction. "What did you do in the ACAS?" she asked him.

He didn't answer her question. "Thank you for talking to me, Kat," he said and stood up, tossing her the extra meal bar.

She let out a deep breath as she watched him go. Patrin heard it and turned.

"What is it?" he asked her.

"What will you do with me?" she asked.

He regarded her a moment before approaching again. "Have you told us the truth, Kat?"

She nodded, her heart filling with worry. Surely the Opposition had their own programming methods. They had one of the ACAS scientists on their side, after all. Perhaps she would be reprogrammed. She bit her bottom lip, thinking she'd rather die than go through that again.

"Rest easy, Kat. Despite what you may have heard, we're not the monsters here. The ACAS is."

"I don't understand," she said.

He smiled. "I know. But you will. I'll be back in a bit to check on you."

Patrin left. Kat got up and entered the tiny bathroom. She turned on the light and examined her face in the mirror. Slowly, her emotions drained away. She washed her face and dried it on the towel before looking back at her pale features in the mirror. She continued to stare at herself as the cold part of her took over, examining her interaction with Patrin for mistakes or weaknesses. The man was obviously in charge here, and she'd tried to appeal to him not to harm her in hopes of appearing innocent. She frowned as she realized she may have either laid it on too thick or come off a little weak, but perhaps he would chalk that up to her being upset about her lover's death.

What would happen next? she wondered. Kat exited the bathroom and returned to the bed, finishing the rest of the meal bar even though she wasn't hungry. Her mind was working over the problem. They were heading to Al-Kimia or possibly another secret base. She would be questioned, possibly under the influence of truth drugs.

Truth drugs. A wave of fear overcame her certainty of success, and her heart started to thrum in her chest. She was afraid; her programming had helped her become a good liar, but truth drugs might expose her. If they found out what she was, she knew Patrin would either have her reprogrammed or, more likely, kill her without a second thought. He was a member of the Opposition, and they would be brutal. She'd seen the video of dead civilians on Chamn-Alpha, so she knew what the enemy was capable of. Wrapping both arms around herself, she turned to face the wall, not wanting to show her face to the cameras that were most likely surveilling her at the moment.

. . .

QUILLON WATCHED the station surveillance footage with pride. His vat had found her way into the Opposition forces. He'd gotten the message and set the op into motion, then requested the security vid feed as soon as possible. Katerine had fired back at the ACAS forces, flawlessly executing his plan.

He thought about sending a message to the doyen but decided to sit on this a bit longer. He would unveil his plan to their leader when he had more concrete information from Katerine. Until then, he could be patient.

ELEVEN

By dinner on the third day, the *Loshad*'s crew were irritated and tired. Work on the ship was proving to be more involved than they had thought, but Ty kept encouraging them. He was sure it would only be a day or two more before they were operational again.

"I'll go back through and see what systems we can cannibalize to replace that last set of couplings," Hal said, pushing his plate away from him.

"I'll help," Ty replied. "I have half a mind to keep working after dinner."

"Yeah, I'll-"

Runa's chime interrupted Hal. "There is a ship approaching. They are hailing us," she said.

"That was fast," Ty said. "Let's hear it."

A rumbling whispering, similar to Eira's broadcast, came through the comms.

"Let's get to the bridge," he said.

They took their stations automatically, and Ty spoke over

the comms as they all watched him expectantly. "Unknown Mudar ship, this is the free ship *Loshad*. We are on a peaceful mission. I repeat, we come in peace, we mean you no harm. We have one of your people on board who wishes to return to you."

There was a long pause. "Ty, I can put their ship up on the displays," Runa said.

"Yes, please," Ty replied.

The ship was larger than the *Loshad* and had the same silver skin of the ship they'd seen in the cave where they'd found Eira.

"Holy fuck and a half," Hal whispered, watching the large ship begin to pass over them.

The hum of whispering changed and became a continuous tone. When it did, Hal moaned, clutched at his head, and fell to the floor. It was obviously some sort of scan. "I'll get my kit," Beryl called as she hurried from the bridge.

Vivi was immediately there, checking Hal's vitals. "Ty, please. Try to make them stop," she pleaded, alarmed at seeing a thread of blood trickle from Hal's left nostril.

"Is Hal suffering a malfunction?" Runa asked.

"In a way," Vivi replied worriedly.

"Please, you cannot scan us at this frequency," Ty said. "We have a crewmember on board who is sensitive to your scans. You are injuring him."

"Human ship *Loshad*: you will submit to the scan, or we will destroy you." The voice was emotionless and spoke Coalition standard with a strange preciseness.

There was nothing Ty could do. He watched helplessly while Hal writhed in pain. The tone went on for a long time, during which Beryl returned to the bridge with a medjet. She injected Hal, who began to relax as it took effect. Eventually his hands slipped from his head, and he was motionless in

Vivi's lap, unconscious. The tone continued on for a full agonizing minute, then stopped.

Ty realized he was grinding his teeth. He forced himself to stop as he waited for the Mudar's verdict.

"You will allow one of us to board your ship. Deactivate your ship's point defense system and divest yourself of any personal weapons."

"What assurances can you give me that my people won't be harmed?"

"We will give you none because there are none that you will believe, *Loshad*. With your suspicious nature, it would be a waste of effort to attempt to convince you otherwise. Understand this, however: if you attack our emissary, we will retaliate."

Ty muted the feed and regarded Hal, Vivi and Beryl in front of him. There was no way they would best these Mudar if things went bad. "We're going to have to hope whatever was in Eira's message was good enough to keep us from being killed straight out," Ty frowned, then keyed the comms again. "We will follow your instructions. Does your vessel have a designation?"

"This craft is known as the *Bolide*."

"Very well. We will follow your conditions, *Bolide*."

The Mudar abruptly cut transmission. "I'm going to meet them," Ty said, getting to his feet. "Beryl and Vivi, stay with Hal. And hope for the best."

"I can come," Vivi said. "You need backup."

"No. Stay here." None of them were wearing weapons, so they didn't have to worry about disarming themselves. "Beryl, deactivate our weapons systems and facilitate the dock."

"Yes, Ty," she called.

He headed for the airlock. Once he got there, he saw that the Mudar ship had come alongside them. A final clank let him know the ships had docked. He pressed the button to pressurize the airlock.

A metallic humanoid shape could be seen behind the *Bolide's* hatch. It was not lost on Ty that he was likely the first human to see a Mudar in 100 years, so he took a deep breath and steadied himself. Then, the hatch opened, and he was face to face with the AI.

The being was as tall as Ty and appeared to be fully metallic. Its chest and body were wrapped in textured silver plates that bore some resemblance to armor. They even covered his head like a helmet. The face taking him in gazed at him with fascination on its broad male humanoid features.

"My name is Tyce Bernon." Ty said. "I am the Captain of the *Loshad*."

The other was startled when Ty spoke so politely. "I am called Marus," he said, examining Ty with interest. His silver countenance showed a keen intelligence, and his voice was a perfect human tenor.

"I'm pleased to meet one of Eira's people," Ty said.

The being examined their surroundings. "This is not a military vessel, is it?"

"No. We are not," Ty said. "Please come aboard." He stepped back, his braces making a slipping noise on the floor.

"You do not walk as other humans?" Marus asked plainly.

"No. I was injured," Ty replied. "The exoframe makes walking possible for me."

Marus followed him, looking from side to side as if expecting someone. "Where is Eira-168?"

"You can try to access her on the bridge. If you would follow me there, I will introduce you to the rest of my crew." Ty motioned the way that they were to go.

"*Access* her?"

"Eira's ship crashed on a planet you would call Attus 6

about 100 years ago. We went to that planet and found her, but we didn't know it. Her nanites downloaded her consciousness into our ship's computer without our knowledge." They were nearing the bridge and the door slid open. "I must admit we were frightened of her at first, but then we became friends."

Marus glanced around the bridge, then began to study Hal. "What has happened to your crewmember, Captain?"

Vivi and Beryl looked up from the floor where Hal was still passed out. "He was injured by your scans," Ty explained. "This is my crew, Vivi and Beryl...and Hal. Vivi and Beryl—this is Marus."

The Mudar approached gracefully. For one completely made from metal, he was silent as he walked toward them, hands held at his side. As he moved, the metal took on an odd, liquid appearance that reminded Ty of Eira's nanites inside the ship. "Do not be afraid," Marus said. "Will your crewmember recover his functioning?"

"Yes," Beryl said, standing up. "I'm ship's medic, Beryl McCabe. If you could tell your people to refrain from scanning in that way, I would appreciate it."

"This is very strange. The scans shouldn't affect biologics like yourself. We received the distress call that said a Mudar was on board, and we were trying to confirm by scanning for nanites."

"Hal is different from us," Beryl began.

"We have a lot to tell you." Tyce stepped forward. "But the important part is that Eira needs your help."

"Eira is in our computer system, but she shut down," Vivi said. "She was having difficulty functioning within our technology, so her programming was degrading the longer it went on. She must have gone dormant. But she's here. In our ship's memory."

I hope that's why she shut down, Ty thought. All they could do was make a guess. "You have to get her out and to a 'conveyance,' she said."

Marus's head tilted to the side as if he were considering something. "This is very strange. Our guardians will need proof. Will...you allow me to access your computer to verify?"

"Of course. You will not harm our operating system? We have a ship's assistant who is not a Mudar, but she is very dear to us," Ty said, gesturing to the station in front of Marus. *Oh Eira, I hope this isn't a horrible mistake*, he thought.

"Thank you, Tyce," Runa replied.

"What are you called?" Marus asked.

"My name is Runa," she replied. "I am this ship. Please do not cause damage to my systems. I am necessary for the functionality of the ship, and my crew needs me."

"Do you serve your human crew?"

Ty shared a look with Vivi, unsure what Runa would say.

"I am not just a servant, I am an integral part of the crew," Runa replied. "Correct, Tyce?"

"Correct," Ty said, relieved.

"Nothing in your system will be harmed," Marus assured her.

The Mudar stepped up to Vivi's station and placed his hand near the console. Immediately the metal of his fingers became fluid and flowed into the port. Vivi glanced at Ty, but he simply shook his head and held up a hand. Marus' gaze grew indistinct a moment.

"Eira is in stasis, as you thought," Marus said. "We will need supplies from the worldship to remove her from this machine...and put her back into a conveyance." He withdrew from the station and the silver metal flowed back into its "hand" shape and became solid once more. "I can only hope she is not too badly corrupted."

"Whatever we need to do, we'll be glad to do," Ty said.

"We're *amatan* to her, so we naturally want to do what we can—"

Marus narrowed his silver eyes at them. "She declared you her *amatan*?"

"Yes. She said it means family. She's saved our lives many times."

"We owe her," Vivi added.

"This is very strange. Very strange indeed." Marus was puzzled as he examined each of them with a new expression. "Please. A moment."

He stopped moving and remained stationary. Vivi looked to Ty. "Is he communicating with the *Bolide*?"

"I think so," Ty said, a little relieved. He had the feeling that he'd done the right thing by mentioning they were Eira's *amatan*. "At least he seems pleasant. A lot more pleasant than the guy on the comm."

"You can say that again," Beryl grumbled.

Hal began to groan in Vivi's lap. "Hey, you coming around?" Ty asked, kneeling beside them.

Hal opened his eyes. "My head..." he groaned.

Ty saw him startle as soon as he noticed Marus, and he laid a hand on Hal's arm. "Don't worry. They asked to come aboard, and I let them. He's been fine so far."

Hal didn't relax, but he nodded and pushed himself to a sitting position. He was glassy-eyed from Beryl's injection, but cognizant of what was going on around him. "What's he...doing?"

"Talking to the Mudar ship, we think," Ty said.

Marus spoke, "The guardian tells me to stay aboard. I have coordinates to program into your ship. We will travel to the worldship to assist Eira and determine if she is too corrupted to save."

The crew exchanged uneasy glances. "You might not be able to save her?" Ty asked.

Marus fixed him with his silver, unblinking gaze. "It is likely she has been too damaged. We will have to reach the worldship to be sure."

Ty swallowed hard. There was nothing else to do but to trust that Eira had been right and they would be fine. "There's only one problem: our engines are dead right now. When Eira went down, it took out our drive. We only have maneuvering thrusters."

Marus went quiet a moment but was back with them rather quickly. "The *Bolide* will tow your ship."

"Okay, then." Ty looked back to Hal. "We need to get you to your quarters," he said.

Hal shook his head. "No way. I need to be here, with you guys."

"You are called Hal," the Mudar said in greeting, taking a step forward.

"Yeah?"

"I am Marus, a biologic scientist like Eira. May I ask a question?"

"Sure," Hal said.

"Why are you different? Why did our scans cause you pain?"

"I have the same nanites as you do. Your frequency causes them to...to go crazy, I guess."

"How do you have our nanites?"

"It's...a long story," Ty said, "we can talk about as soon as we get Hal somewhere more comfortable."

"I will warn our people not to scan in this manner," Marus said.

"Thanks, buddy," Hal murmured, getting to his feet.

"Buddy." Marus looked from Hal to Vivi to Ty. "I know it

means friend in your language, but we have not had the required number of interactions to be considered friends."

"Wishful thinking," Ty said. "Look, let's get Hal into the common area and then we can answer any questions you have."

"Thank you," Marus replied.

TWELVE

They all held their breath as the world ship of the Mudar came into view. It had taken them two days to reach it, and now it hung in space over them like a small brooding moon.

"Gods. It's massive," Ty swore, looking at the approaching orb. It was a metallic silver, made up of millions of honeycomb shaped panels. Around it flew one small patrol ship, about the size of the *Bolide*. He judged the worldship to be about the same distance across as Omicron Station, and he checked his sensor display to verify.

"It is impressive, isn't it?" Marus said.

Hal and Ty exchanged glances, and Ty knew what his friend was thinking because he was thinking the same. How many of Eira's people lived inside the orb? The numbers had to be in the hundreds of thousands, maybe even millions. He felt cold all over, realizing how dependent they were on the Mudar's good graces. He would definitely feel more confident once Eira was back with them.

"Marus. Are you certain the *Bolide* has let the worldship know not to scan Hal?" Beryl asked.

"Yes," he replied. "He will not be harmed. Regretfully, you cannot be allowed to come aboard." He turned to Ty. "Some will not look kindly upon humans. But you have shown amazing courage to bring Eira back to us. They will not believe you have done such a thing."

"I hope they appreciate it," Hal said.

"I am sorry to say that most of my kind appreciate very little about your species, Hal."

"Then they'll have to learn that we're not all the same," Ty added.

AN HOUR LATER, they stood by the docking rings, waiting for the Mudar to arrive from the worldship, which Marus said was called *Arden*.

Ty hit the controls for the airlock when he heard them dock. The door slid open, revealing two individuals of varying heights waiting outside. They were flanked by two more silver AI's wearing sturdier conveyances and armor plating. The armored ones were obviously security or warriors, but they were not carrying any weapons that Hal or Ty could see.

"This is Captain Bernon of the ship *Loshad*," Marus said to the tallest one. "This is Oberyn. He speaks for the Mudar."

The being stepped forward but said nothing. He had a long thin face that gave Ty the feeling he was being looked down upon.

"I don't know how much you have been told about our reasons for this journey, but I want to assure you that we are here to help our friend and *amatan* Eira. We mean no harm."

Oberyn had tilted his head slightly, studying Ty. "Humans should not use such terms. You have no hope of understanding them."

Ty took in the impassive expression of the AI in front of

him. It was a struggle to keep an even tone, but he knew their lives might depend on it. "Eira enlightened me. I am inclined to believe it fits the relationship that we have with her from what she's told us."

Oberyn remained stoic and motioned to one of the beings behind him. The small silver form stepped forward. "You will allow Tela to access your ship to determine how best to help Eira if she is indeed still salvageable after being exposed to your primitive technology."

"Look, we didn't make her download into our ship-" Hal began, but Ty glanced at him and shook his head before turning back.

"Speaker, we are pleased to help in any way we can to restore Eira to full functioning." Ty gestured to Vivi. "This is Vivi Valjean. She is our technology specialist if Tela has any questions."

"That will not be necessary," Oberyn said dismissively. "If this is an attempt to attack us, you will regret it." He frowned down at them, then said something in Mudar to the smaller being who had stepped forward. With that, he turned and left.

The three remaining beings stepped inside the *Loshad*.

"I am Tela," the smallest one of them spoke in a gentle tenor. Ty glanced at the two behind her, who declined to introduce themselves. He couldn't tell, but he thought he detected a hint of suspicion on their faces. "May I see the system where Eira is contained?" She glanced from Ty to Vivi and Hal. "That way I will know what is required. If she is too corrupted to be saved, we will restore her to a previous version, and this version will be expunged."

"Expunged? You can't delete her. She's...she's our friend," Vivi said.

"Data has to be kept pure. If she is too damaged, she will be taken offline. A new Eira will be reinitialized." Tela glanced from one of them to the other, as if her answer were the only logical one, then she glanced to Ty. "Please show me the bridge."

"Wait a minute," Hal said quickly, stepping forward. "You can't just-"

There was a sudden sound behind Tela, and Ty looked up to see that the two soldiers were holding hand weapons very similar to the ones they'd seen while salvaging, and they were pointing them at Hal.

"Wait. Wait." Ty held up both hands and eyed Hal.

"I am in no danger. You may lower your weapons," Tela said.

The two stern-looking AI's lowered their arms, but the weapons stayed deployed. *Great*, Ty thought.

"I'm sorry," Hal said to them, taking a backwards step and keeping his hands open. "Look, we care about Eira. You've gotta find a way to help her."

Tela glanced from Hal to Ty to Vivi as if she were struggling to understand. "Either way she will be restored."

"But...would she remember us if you restore her to the template version?" Vivi asked.

"No, she would not."

"We like her like she is," Vivi said. "She...she wouldn't know us anymore if you delete her."

"I understand now. Please know everything possible will be done."

"Thank you. This way," Ty said, gesturing.

IN ABOUT AN HOUR, after revisiting the Mudar ship, Tela and her assistant came off the bridge and into the galley with a silver sphere the size of the one Vivi and Hal had found a few months ago. It felt like a lifetime since then, Ty thought nervously as he glanced to Marus.

"We have collected as many of Eira's mytrite nanites as possible." Tela stopped in front of Marus, who stepped forward and placed a hand on the sphere, bowing his head a moment. Ty could see that his hand didn't just remain lying on top of the sphere, but it actually *melded* with it. It appeared that Marus's hand and Eira's new sphere were made of the same nanite material.

"Is she...alive?" Ty asked.

After a moment, Marus spoke. "Yes." He nodded to Tela, who was carrying the precious silver-colored ball. "Have one of the guardians take her consciousness sphere onto *Arden* for evaluation."

"Of course, Marus," Tela replied, heading for the docking rings.

"So, she'll be alright?" Ty asked.

"It is early to determine that," Marus said, "but they will do everything possible. It will take some hours yet. If you like, I will ask Tela to return and repair your ship's drive if you will permit her."

Ty glanced to Hal and Vivi. They both shrugged in agreement. "Sure," Ty said.

TELA WAS IMPRESSED by the way Eira had directed the nanites to strengthen the ship, and she examined the ship's computer, offering to fix the damage done to the drive. As she worked, Tela would glance to Ty's crew and Marus periodically, then back down at her work.

"Is there something you need?" Ty asked.

"No. I only wanted to say thank you for allowing me to study your technology. It is fascinating to see the advances made since the war." She returned her focus back to the work in front of her.

"You are the first human that was not trying to kill her," Marus said as he followed Ty's gaze. "And you also resemble those who created us."

"Eira had said that," Ty replied. "What were they like… those who created you?"

"They were warlike and violent until they realized that those behaviors no longer served a purpose. They became more enlightened as time went on, then found achieving their lofty goals lonely. Though they advanced to where they had expanded throughout their own galaxy, they had found no intelligent life in their quadrant of the universe. They created us to search for and contact other intelligent life. And so, they sent us out on worldships like *Arden*."

"And you found us. It didn't go well, did it?" Ty said.

"No, your people were suspicious and violent," Marus said regretfully.

"Why did you stay?" Vivi asked. "You could have gone on to find other life, in other galaxies."

"Except for your people, we have seen no other intelligent life," Marus said. "We have seen life, of course, but nothing to the level of your species."

"How long have you searched?" Beryl asked.

"Over 50,000 of your years."

Vivi and Ty shared a look. "That's a long time."

"Not for the Mudar," Marus said. "We are immutable, as our creators made us."

Hours later, the Bixby drive was repaired, and Marus had gone to check on Eira's progress. Hal and Vivi had made a meal and they were gathered around the table in the galley with Beryl and Ty. No one really felt like eating, however.

"Look," Ty spoke after long moments of watching everyone stare into their bowls of noodles. "We made the best decision we could. We had to bring her here. It was her best chance."

"What if...what if they decide she's too damaged to repair?" Vivi asked, pushing her bowl away and sitting back in her chair. "I wonder if there was something else I could have done..." Her brow furrowed.

"Veevs – Ty's right," Hal said. "It's not like you could have fixed her yourself. The best teckers in the Spiral couldn't have helped Eira. We had to-"

At that moment, there were footsteps in the passageway outside. Vivi and Hal both looked up to see a graceful form in the hatch. This Mudar was diminutive in height, like Tela had been. This was not Tela though.

Hal murmured Ty's name under his breath.

The AI had stopped in the hatch and was watching them.

Ty turned, readying himself for the news, good or bad. "Hello," he said, getting to his feet.

The small form stepped inside the galley. They could see she was female with large, silver, almond-shaped eyes, graceful features and a mouth curved in a gentle, but cautious smile. Ty suddenly realized she was the first Mudar to really smile. She was wearing different textured plates than the others and a delicately textured headcovering with a winding vine-like pattern.

"It's time we met properly, is it not?" she said softly, looking to each of them in turn.

"Eira?" Hal asked, standing up abruptly.

"Yes," she replied. "Seeing my *amatan* this way is much better than through the *Loshad's* sensors." The crew slowly gathered close around her.

"Eira!" Vivi threw her arms around the small being. Ty noticed how Eira stiffened and stayed very still at the close contact.

Vivi noticed as well, and let her arms slip away. "Oh, did I scare you? I'm sorry. I'm simply so happy to see you."

Eira shook her head. "I understand. You are showing affection in a physical manner. It is acceptable...but it is very new to me."

"You're fine?" Hal asked. "I mean there was no lasting damage?"

"I am still repairing systems and data. Getting used to my new conveyance will take a little time, but I will be fine, *amatan*."

"I am very pleased you are still functional," Runa said from above them.

"Thank you," Eira replied. "I am also pleased you are restored to your rightful place with your crew."

"They told us you might not be allowed to come back," Hal explained. "We were really worried."

"Oh, I see. Well, it seems that this version will be allowed to go on a little longer," she said.

"I'm glad," Vivi replied, hugging her slowly and gently this time.

When Vivi let Eira go, the AI glanced to each of them and finally settled on Ty. "I made a promise to you, Tyce Bernon, a promise I intend to keep. I am supposed to address the Mudar today, and I will ask that I be allowed to use our technology to heal the damage you have suffered." She glanced to Beryl, "We can perform the procedure on the *Loshad*, since the worldship is not as suitable for this."

"Of course."

"For now, however, I must return to my people. They have questions about you; your arrival has disconcerted the speaker and Guardians. They insist on seeing and speaking with Hal."

"Why Hal?" Ty asked.

"Because of what the ACAS has done to vats like Hal. I have told them of the vats, but they wish to hear the story from Hal himself."

Ty glanced to Hal. "You're up for this?"

"Yeah," he agreed. "I can go."

Ty's gaze shifted from Eira to Hal nervously, worried that he might not know how to negotiate the delicate situation with the Mudar. He didn't have much practice at subtlety, and while he wouldn't try to make a mistake, he might still end up saying the wrong thing at the wrong time.

On the other hand, Ty knew that Hal was the only one who should tell his story. Hal needed to tell it and he needed their trust; Ty could see it by the hopeful expression on his friend's face.

"It'll be fine," Hal said. "I'll be on my best behavior."

"Yeah, I know you will," Ty said as he glanced to Eira.

"He will be with me the entire time," she promised. "Do you have everything you require right now?"

"We do," Ty said. "Hal, be careful."

"I will," he said, crossing to Vivi. "Don't worry about me," he reassured her.

"We know you'll do the right thing, just be careful," she murmured, hugging him.

"I will," He turned back to Ty. "Look, I know this is serious. I won't muck it up. You can depend on me."

Ty put a hand on Hal's shoulder and said what he needed to hear. "I know. I've always been able to depend on you. Now is no different."

"We will return soon, *amatan*," Eira said.

· · ·

"Every Mudar will not be at the council meeting," Eira told Hal as they made their way through the shining, well-lit hallways of *Arden*. "Only the speaker and one representative of each strata will be there to hear your story. The information will be shared with all."

"I haven't seen many of your people around," Hal noted as they walked the mostly empty halls.

"Many of the others are in stasis, waiting for the day that the humans will be amenable to contact again," Eira said as they turned a corner and were passed by two Mudar. Hal tried to ignore the suspicious expressions on their faces.

"In stasis?"

"Yes. This way," Eira said, turning down another corridor. This one was lit with a dim, silvery light that reminded Hal of moonlight.

There were shelves with niches that went upwards as far as the eye could see. In each niche, there was a perfect silver sphere.

"These are all your people," Hal realized.

"Yes," she said, stopping in front of them. "You are the first human to ever see the inside of our ship."

Hal turned from the rows of thousands upon thousands of spheres and met Eira's earnest face. "You know you can trust me," he promised.

"I do. Allow me to explain a little more of what you are going to see inside the council chamber.

"Our society is organized into five strata, each with their own purpose. The Guardians are concerned with security. You have seen several of them stationed in the halls on our way here. The Jhere are a strata charged with keeping a record of our journeys. There are Denar – *Arden's* technology specialists like Tela. Gradites handle the maintenance and building of new ships. My strata, the Vedik, catalogue the life we have found on planets. We are biologic scientists. The Vedik and Jhere opposed responding militarily to the Coalition when we were attacked, but the other three strata thought that the only way to gain the respect of the humans was to respond in the same way they treated us. They were obviously wrong. As the war with the Coalition progressed, the council chose to wait and reinitiate contact after a longer period of time. Most of the Mudar voluntarily went into stasis to wait, as they have done many times on our journey through unpopulated, empty space. Only select Mudar stay active to monitor the worldship."

He looked back up at the rows stretching up as far as he could see. "So, what you're saying is that some of these guys I'm about to see don't have a great view of humans."

"You are correct. So, if we are to convince them to allow me to help Tyce, we will have to present our case with facts and logic. Emotionality will not be helpful."

He searched her face. "I understand."

"After hearing your story, I am hopeful that they may lend their support to ending what the ACAS is doing to vat soldiers. The Coalition is spreading into the Edge like a virus and must be stopped."

"You...you mean you're going to try and get them on the Opposition's side?"

"Yes."

He hugged her. For months, he had been weighting troops, ship numbers and the possibility of war between the Edge and Al-Kimia in his mind. There was no way Al-Kimia, Betald and Noea would be able to hold back the advance of the Coalition into the Edge, even if Jaleeth threw their support behind the Opposition. The idea of enlisting the help of the Eira's people was a brilliant one. "Thank you. I'll follow your lead."

"They are waiting at the end of this hallway in the chamber. Follow me."

. . .

"So, this is the hybrid?" One of the tall guards outside the council chamber said as Eira and Hal drew near. The other one fixed his gaze on Hal.

"He is my *amatan*," Eira said simply, walking by them with Hal at her side. He kept his focus on Eira, following her lead, even though he wanted to stare down the two armored beings, who had to be Guardians. It made him uneasy to think they were here to watch him.

He was glad he hadn't said anything to them, however. There were more important things to worry about. Like the silver beings already inside the soaring chamber. Oberyn, the speaker, stood on a raised platform alone, watching them. While Eira greeted another Mudar standing nearby, Hal had a chance to turn around and view the hall. More niches with silver spheres were stacked to the roof above them. He couldn't help being uneasy at the thought that all of them might be listening right now.

He took another look at the beings entering the room. The members were gathering in a semicircle in front of the raised dais, their feet placed in the middle of circles inscribed into the allenium under their feet. Other shapes that seemed to have some sort of meaning stretched across the floor, linking some circles to others.

Several of the council were there already, and he turned to see Eira greeting someone. They pressed their palms together briefly, then there was that same susurration – the whispering sound Hal had heard through the speakers on the *Loshad*.

He watched them communicate wordlessly, then Eira spoke in standard. "Hal, this is Reva, the leader of the Vedik."

"I am honored to meet Eira's *amatan*," Reva said, looking him over with interest.

"Thanks," he replied. "Your ship is amazing."

"It is our home. You have come to speak to the Mudar today, and we will be listening. Speak the truth, Halvor Cullen."

"I will," he promised.

Reva took a circle on the other side of Eira. They stood in the middle of the room as other beings entered. They either looked Hal and Eira over with interest or disdain as they took their places.

When everyone was settled, Oberyn called the meeting to order, speaking Coalition standard for Hal's benefit.

"As you know, Eira-168 has returned to *Arden*." The speaker turned to Eira and addressed her directly. "We had feared you no longer functioned, but we were fortunately in error," the speaker said. "Please explain how you are returned to us."

Eira gave them everything they'd asked for – a full accounting of her interactions with the *Loshad's* crew. She emphasized what she'd observed: Hal and his crew were not only thoughtful and caring, but brave and noble, willing to sacrifice themselves for each other as the Mudar creators had been. As she told the story of the Coalition's pursuit of them, their unlikely escape from planet K245-J and the Coalition assassin that had been sent to kill them, Hal could see that the Guardian leader was becoming increasingly skeptical. He and the Jhere representative, a female named Ciaren, were sharing incredulous glances with each other during Eira's recounting. Hal swallowed hard. This was going to be tougher than he'd thought.

"Tyce and I developed a friendship, and he did not harm me. Neither he, nor his crew told anyone else about me," Eira said. "You can trust them."

"So, tell us about this *hybrid*." the Guardian gestured to Hal. It was clear he intended the word to be derisive.

Eira began in her cool, even voice, "The Coalition has used captured Mudar technology to alter humans like Hal – shaping them into weapons of war without their consent. The Coalition stole our technology to divert the biological systems of these humans to enhance their speed and stamina. Our crystal technology is used to shape their minds. They are repetitively taught, through their interface, that they are to serve the natural-born humans. They are trained to kill and forced to do most of the fighting in the Coalition's petty conflicts. If they survive battle, they are released from their forced servitude but die before 35 human years of life."

"Why do they die so young?" Reva asked. "Human lifespans should be four times that."

Hal stepped forward. Every pair of silver optics in the room turned to him. "Adrenaline fatigue syndrome is why we die. We depend on the overproduction of adrenaline to make us faster and stronger than the natural-born, but it's damaging to our bodies. When the Coalition is done with us, they turn us loose in the Edge unprepared for life. If adrenaline fatigue doesn't get us, we... we die due to the bad choices we can't help. Lots of vats don't have a...family like I do to keep them on the right path, so they die even earlier when they give in to drugs or violence. It's...it's a bad end."

"I volunteered to assist Hal by using my nanites to stop the adrenaline flood triggered by his interface. My data shows the procedure has been a success," Eira added. "It is possible the Mudar may be able to assist all of the vats and extend their lives."

The Guardian representative narrowed his gaze at her. "So now you assist these...violent creatures. These humans did it to themselves. You should have allowed it to be their doom."

"I hardly think that these poor individuals she speaks of asked for this to be done to them," Reva replied, keeping her focus placidly on Eira and Hal.

"We didn't," Hal agreed, focusing on the sympathetic being. "We are made in a lab and raised to do what we're told without question. No vat ever chose such a fate for themselves. This life is forced on us. And now...now, the Coalition is reaching out its hand to take the free systems of the Edge. Planets are resisting, but they need help," Hal said. "Help that you could provide."

HAL HAD SPOKEN ELEGANTLY. Eira raised her chin and eyed the Guardian representative who had protested. His name was Brecca, and she remembered him. He had never trusted the humans, even before they had made first contact, and it appeared that the suspicious Guardian had only become more distrustful of them over time. Many thought that his template had been imperfect, and the flaws had amplified during his creation, or possibly that he was ready for a restoration to template due to program degradation. No one, however, would have told Brecca this to his face. His opinion held a lot of weight with the rest of the Guardians as well as the Gradites, the builders.

Brecca stepped forward. "If the vats are subverted in such a way to serve the Coalition, how do we know that you and your crew are not here simply to gather information and report back to your Coalition masters?" he asked.

"Yes. How can we be sure?" the Gradite queried.

"If this human served the Coalition, he is most likely still serving it," Brecca said. There was a murmuring of voices.

Eira shook her head and stepped forward. "If you would review the data I have provided on the crew of the *Loshad*, you would see that this is not the case. I ask that you look at the facts and decide. I believe the data shows that we should wake our people and assist those of the Edge in throwing off the oppression of the Coalition. This is our chance to change the relationship between humans and Mudar. To mend it. It is exactly what we have been waiting for."

There was silence as all the optics in the room turned to her.

"You are mistaken," Brecca said.

"Brecca is correct. It is quite possible we are being deceived by them," Ciaren said.

"This crew is beyond reproach. Hal fought an agent of the Coalition to save his captain and came close to death himself. He is not allied with them," Eira said.

"You are foolish to believe this creature," Brecca sneered. "I would have thought a scientist to be more objective. Perhaps Eira's contact with the humans' technology has caused an error in her reasoning that the scans did not identify. She should be examined more closely by the Denar, Speaker."

HAL WAS ALARMED at those words. Eira lifted her chin and fixed the Guardian with a determined stare. "You are the mistaken one, Guardian Brecca."

They stayed like that, eyeing each other for long moments. Hal knew one thing, if Brecca and the others wanted to hurt Eira, they'd have to go through him first. He wanted to step in front of Eira protectively, but this was her show. She'd said logic and facts would be the key here, not emotions, so he stood his ground beside her.

The Gradite spoke again, breaking the staring contest between Eira and Brecca. "I would like to view the data before we vote."

"As would we," the Jhere representative said.

"The Vedik will side with Eira," Reva concluded.

"Very well," the speaker said. "We will reconvene once the other strata are finished deliberating."

Heads were bowed in acknowledgement. Then the representatives left.

Eira stood silently with Hal. When everyone except the speaker had left the chamber, she called to Oberyn. "I need a moment, Speaker."

He crossed the chamber to them.

"What more would you ask of me, Eira?" Oberyn questioned.

"I am asking leave to use nanites to help Captain Bernon walk again. He was damaged in the attack I mentioned, and it will be a simple matter to make him whole again."

The speaker tilted his head, contemplating. "Do you really count this human and his friends as *amatan*?"

"Yes."

He examined Hal once more. "Your captain wishes this?"

"We all do," Hal said.

Oberyn studied him before he went on. Hal could see that while Oberyn had seemed hostile when they first met, it was apparent that their interaction had softened his attitude. "While I do not know if I agree with your assessment of the humans in general, I do agree that helping someone who brought you back to us is acceptable," he told her. "It also shows the incredible trust they place in you. Do what you will," he said as he held up a hand to touch her own.

"Thank you, Speaker," she answered, pressing her palm to his.

"Thank you," Hal echoed.

. . .

After she and Hal visited the Vedik's lab and taken what she would need for Ty, a guardian transported them back to the *Loshad*.

They stood together, looking out of a port in the ship as they began the docking process with the *Loshad*. "Eira, do you really think the Mudar could help the Oppos hold off the ACAS?"

She turned to him. "They could, but they never come to a decision quickly."

"So how long do you think it will take?"

"It took the Mudar 80 years to decide to pull back from the war with humanity. I would not expect them to decide this more quickly than that."

"Oh," Hal said, disappointed.

"But I will go back with you," Eira said, "and do everything *I* can."

"Why?" Hal asked.

"Because what they have done to vats and the people of the Edge is wrong. And we are... family."

He was so moved he couldn't speak for a moment, and he stared furiously down at his boots as he tried to pull himself together. "That means...a lot, Eira. After what happened with those vats on the *Harbinger*...I'm going to have to stand up against them."

"You will not be alone," she said. Reaching out, she laid a hand on his arm for a brief moment. It was a tentative gesture, but he realized she was trying to make him feel better in some small way. "Is this not the correct gesture of comfort?"

"Yeah, Eira. It's perfect," Hal replied.

THIRTEEN

Lane and Orin took Kat from her cell and escorted her to the interrogation room. "Have a seat," Lane said, gesturing to a chair in the middle of the room.

They had landed at a facility over a day ago; at least she thought it had been a day – it was hard to tell because there were no windows where Kat could see out and no chronos. It was obviously a military base. She'd been treated well, fed, then given clean clothing and a cot to sleep on in her prison cell. Now she had been brought into a dim interrogation room. It was a square room with lights set into the ceiling. A spotlamp rained a pool of light onto the floor around the interrogation chair.

The chair made Kat uneasy. It had padded armrests with straps and buckles hanging from the arms and front of the chair. On the side of it was a box with a display and inputs. They were going to strap her down and question her. She clenched her teeth and sat on the edge of the seat, looking up warily at the two vats watching her.

"What final arrangements would you like to have made for

your friend?" Lane asked, leaning back against the wall with her arms crossed over her chest. The question was matter-of-fact, so Kat kept her own emotions locked down as well.

She shrugged, trying to seem casual. "He never said. I suppose cremation is fine." There was a sudden tug in her heart when she spoke those words and she frowned, pushing the feeling away.

"Very well, we will see it done. He was a vat, like us, and we will treat his remains with respect," Lane replied, signing their conversation for Orin.

Just then, a brown-haired man with short hair came in along with Patrin. The new individual was dressed as a medic over his brown cargoes and black shirt. He carried a bag with him and had a slightly anxious manner about him as he looked her over.

Patrin was watching Kat intently. "Good evening, Kat."

"Patrin," she whispered, afraid to say more. Her gaze fastened on the medic, who was setting out several things on a metal tray table. The gleam of medjets was enough to make her stomach knot up.

"Don't be afraid," Patrin said. "It's regrettable, but we have to be sure of you, Kat. Many lives depend on it. If you've told us the truth, this will be nothing more than a pleasant sleep for you. If...if you've lied...we will be forced to take other measures." He did not say what those other measures were, but she knew they wouldn't be good. He motioned to Orin, signing something to him, and the giant came over.

"Sit back in the chair, please," Patrin gestured.

She did and realized her body was trembling. "You don't have to restrain me," she said in a dry, scared voice that was not her own. Neither one of them listened to her. Orin knelt and put both of her ankles together, then fastened the strap over them, gently tightening the buckle so that she couldn't move.

His warm brown eyes stared up at her, as if asking if she was okay.

Patrin took her hand in his. "We don't want you sliding out of the chair. It's to protect you and us. Just breathe. We're not going to hurt you." He placed her arm, hand down, on the flat arm of the chair and strapped her wrist there. Orin got the other one. "Only a few questions and we're done," Patrin said, turning to the medic.

Orin was still staring up at her. He held up his hand, then left the room. She couldn't hear what Patrin and the medic were saying over the throbbing of her pulse – she was close to rushing. Lane was leaning back against the wall, watching her narrowly. Then the giant came back. He was holding a blanket in his arms which he brought over to her, draping it from her chest to the floor, and tucking it around her in such a way that the medic would have her arm free. He'd noticed her trembling in the cold room and wanted to do some small thing that would make it more bearable, she realized.

The gentle, merciful act made her fight tears. *Thanks,* she managed to mouth the word, afraid she'd sob if she made a sound. He nodded at her and turned back to his friend at the door.

The medic lifted the tray table and brought it over.

"Your name's Kat, right?" He was familiar somehow, but her fear kept her from making the connection.

"Y- yes." He fixed a pad to the inside of her neck, which communicated information to the monitor on the chair. A soft beeping began. Patrin moved something on the other side of the chair and it gradually reclined.

The medic spoke again, drawing her attention back. "I'm Max. All I'm going to do is inject you with a medicine that will make you relaxed and sleepy. Then we'll give you one more medjet, and you'll answer a few questions for Patrin. After that, you'll take a long nap."

Of course. Now she recognized him. He was the traitor scientist. She was too scared to be angry, though. They would jack her up on some kind of truth drug, and she would spill all her secrets. They would kill her, probably with an injection, once they realized what she was. She began to tremble. Max turned and spoke to Patrin. "I'm going to give her some Bupariol. It's an anxiety medication that will calm her rush response. She's pretty worked up."

She gasped at those words. They were going to make her as helpless as possible before they questioned her.

To her horror, Patrin agreed.

Max pulled up the sleeve of Kat's shirt and placed the medjet against her bicep. There was a slight snicking noise. "What we want to do is calm down, Kat. Breathe slowly and relax," Max urged her.

Kat closed her eyes as the heat from the injection raced through her bloodstream. Her thoughts grew fuzzy, and her anxiety began to ease. Remembering what had been bothering her became difficult. She sighed and let her body relax into the comfortable chair. *It would be nice to sleep.* She hadn't slept well since she'd left the *Vetra*.

AFTER A FEW MOMENTS, Max nodded at Patrin. "She's probably ready."

"Kat? Are you awake?" Patrin asked.

"Mmm, yeah," she looked up at them with a smile and tried to lift her arms to stretch. Then she seemed to realize they were strapped down. A troubled crease formed on her forehead.

"It's so you don't fall out of the chair," Patrin reminded her.

"Oh." She grinned and relaxed back against the headrest.

"Things do seem like they're whirling around." She let out a soft laugh. "I'm sorry. I'm not supposed to be laughing, am I?"

"You feel better, huh?" Patrin asked, glancing at Max.

"Hells, yeah. I feel like flying."

"Only one more little pinch," Max said. "Stay still for me. This one might sting a little." Max pressed the second medjet to her neck.

"Ow," she said, looking up at him accusingly.

"It'll only hurt a moment," Max said, watching the feed of information coming from the sensors. He knew the truth drug would loosen up any desire in her to lie and help her reach those deeper levels of programming.

"We've got some questions for you," Max began.

"Sure," she replied.

"What's your name and number?"

"Katerine Neval, 4539031278MLE."

"Who was your CO in the ACAS?"

"Um..." She looked from Max to Patrin.

Patrin laid a hand on her arm and took over. "You said you were a temporary comm officer and engineer's mate. Who did you report to when you were an engineer's mate?"

"Lieutenant Harlen Malan," she replied, sobering a little.

"What are you here to do?"

"I'm not here to do anything...Hey, um...It's hot. Really hot in here. I'm not feeling that good anymore." Her gaze roved around the room as she shifted as much as the straps would allow.

"What are you here to do?" Patrin asked, using a touch on her cheek to turn her face toward him. "Answer the question."

"I don't know," she pulled away from him. "You're the ones who brought me here," she said balefully.

He softened his voice. "We're not going to hurt you. I only have to know, were you sent by the Coalition to infiltrate the

Opposition?" Patrin asked. "You can trust us. Even if you were sent by the Coalition, we can help you."

Max quieted the beeping from the chair's sensors. They were increasing with Kat's heart rate. She thrashed and moaned. "No. Please...I think I'm sick. It's so hot in here," she struggled to get the blanket off her by shifting her body.

"Is she okay?" Patrin asked. He removed the blanket from Kat, who sighed in relief.

"I...I'm not sure," Max knew it was most certainly not hot in the room. He leaned in, checking Kat's pupils and seeing that they were dilated. They shouldn't have been – he'd given her enough tranquilizer to push back a rush response. "Something's wrong." He put a hand on her shoulders as she struggled against the straps that held her. "Hey, stay still a minute. Tell me what you're feeling," Max said.

"Who are you?" She stared at them in panic. "Please – my skin's on fire." Her breath became more labored and rasped in her chest as the seconds ticked on.

Max realized she was beginning to flush. Was this an allergic reaction? "Something's wrong," he said, going to his bag.

He returned with a medjet as she began to shake uncontrollably; her arms and legs jerked in the straps as her teeth clenched.

"Hold her head gently. Keep her from banging it."

Patrin immediately stood behind the chair, taking her head in his hands to keep her from beating it against the headrest. Max pressed another restraining hand on her head and injected her near the same spot on her neck. Then his hands worked over the buckles and straps, getting them off her. "Turn her on her side," Max said. Patrin took hold of her shoulders and Max placed his hands on her hip and thigh and together, they turned her on her side as the seizure began to slow.

"What happened?" Patrin asked.

"It could be an allergic reaction to the Xendol. I gave her the reversal medication."

Kat's skin was still pale with bright spots of color in her cheeks, but her shaking movements had eased. Max grabbed his medscanner. "Lane, can you call some medics up here with a stretcher? She needs to be admitted for observation ...probably overnight."

"Of course," she disappeared into the hallway.

"With this kind of reaction... a second dose could kill her," Max said. "I can't go any further with this." The memory of the vat girl who had died during the kill device trial weighed on him. The guilt that he'd thought he'd overcome slammed into him again like a transport at full speed. "I'm sorry."

Patrin agreed, rubbing his forehead. "No need to apologize. We'll have to figure out something else."

Eventually, two vats from the medcenter came and loaded Kat onto a stretcher. "I'll go with her," Max said.

As he passed her, Lane caught Max's bicep with one hand. "Don't feel guilty," she said. "You did the right thing. We had to see if we could trust her."

"Maybe," Max replied.

THERE WAS a gentle rap on her hospital door, and Kat looked up with surprise.

"Come in," she said.

Besides the doctor and Patrin who had visited earlier in the day, she hadn't seen many others, so she was surprised when one of the tallest men she'd ever seen entered the room. He was a lion of a man – the same height as Orin, but was obviously older, as the grey in his hair and beard attested to. He approached the foot of her bed.

"Kat Neval. I am Captain Jacent Seren. May I sit with you a few moments?"

She nodded, and he moved to take the seat beside her bed.

"You have had quite the last few days," he remarked. "How are you feeling?"

"B-better," she said. He had a kind expression in his brown eyes, and she found herself drawn to his warm personality.

"Good. Do you know where you are?"

Her heart began to pick up speed. "Not exactly. But...but I think it's on Al-Kimia. The...the nurse has an accent. Are you who they call the...Opposition?"

Seren didn't signal yes or no but continued his steady observation of her.

"What do you know about them, Kat?" he asked.

She shook her head. "Nothing. Just...that vats are joining. You know, because of what's been on the feeds."

"Ah, the feeds," Seren shook his head. "The Coalition has ruled this Galaxy with intimidation and fear since the Mudar became a threat. Now, they make *us* the threat on the feeds." He sat back thoughtfully, crossing his arms over his chest. "Systems like Al-Kimia aren't being given a choice to join the Coalition or not. Just like vats aren't given a choice whether to fight or not. They should be surprised that more systems do not rebel."

Kat caught the vat tattoo on his wrist and watched him intently, not sure what to say. Was this the vat leader? She had a feeling that Patrin was pretty high up, but this man...he spoke like an officer. Like a leader, but a different kind of leader than the fleet admiral.

"Let me ask you this. What happens when the A-CAS is done with vats like us, young one?" He gave her time to think.

"We...are released from service to...live a productive life." She figured it was best to give the required response on this.

Seren smiled before he went on. "No, little one. We are turned out on the Edge. Abandoned. Left to die, with no place to belong. But not anymore. On Al-Kimia, we can be equals with nats, and we will have a place when the fight is done. Do you not see the possibilities in front of us? I am not doing this for me—I am near my last days. But I do this for vats like you. My hope is that no more will die abandoned, alone, without friends. No more vats dying blissed out on null in rented cubes all over the Edge or losing their lives fighting for nat scrill in the vat clubs. I want each vat to have a place to belong and contribute and be recognized for their contributions. It can happen, Kat."

For a moment, his words shone in front of her like a mirror. Kat found her heart reacting to his noble speech. "It's a beautiful idea. But surely you don't believe you can take down the Coalition?" She shook her head. "It's insane. They...they've got too many ships...too many soldiers..."

"You make the mistake of many," Seren said. "You think we are foolish idealists. We are not, Kat. This can happen. If we can turn some of the Edge's systems to our side...there is so much that can be done."

Kat's mind was working furiously.

"The ACAS is very likely looking for you on Jaleeth because of your escape from them. We will help you return there if that is what you wish. We are not jailers. But I would like to offer you a place here...with us. Making a difference."

She bit her bottom lip, trying not to appear too eager. "I want to help," she said. "Patrin...saved me during the fight on the station, and he didn't have to do that. I owe him that much."

Seren touched her hand reassuringly. "If you wish to stay, then you may. You will be released from the hospital later today. Then you will answer some questions under a voiceprint only – no more truth drugs. Barring anything unforeseen,

Patrin will help you get settled on the base and acclimated to our way of doing things."

"Thank...thank you," she said.

The big man stood up, heading toward the door, where he paused and turned, his warm gaze looking upon her fondly. "I am glad you chose to join us, Kat. I trust that there is much good you will do here. You may rest easy among friends."

FOURTEEN

"Now I will guide the nanites to the proper positions," Eira said, placing a hand against the scarred area of Ty's lower back.

Hal's gaze slid from Eira to Ty, who was lightly sedated. They'd waited until the next morning to try the procedure. There was little to see; the operation was that simple. Beryl had injected Eira's nanites, and she was guiding them to re-form the connections of Ty's severed nerves.

Beryl was monitoring the operation on the medscanner display. "His vitals are steady. You're doing fine."

"Thank you," Eira said as she concentrated on the feed of information from the nanites she'd brought back from the worldship. "I did the same with you, Hal, but Ty has no nanites to oppose what I am doing, so it is much simpler. Full recovery will take some time, however. The nanites will need to adjust to their new parameters, and Ty will have to work up to walking on his own, but he will sense an immediate difference."

"I don't know how we'll ever thank you, Eira," Vivi murmured.

Her attention remained focused on the tiny extensions of her will that were busily reforming the branches of Ty's nerves as she smiled again. "Thanks are not required, *amatan*."

An hour after the procedure, they were all waiting for Ty to come around. He was groggy and would wake up a moment, then drift back off.

"Once Ty regains consciousness, I will need to go back to *Arden* and upload with the Jhere. Then my business there will be complete," Eira announced, her silver gaze intent on Ty's features.

"Uploading with the Jhere?" Hal asked.

"They will add my knowledge and my experiences to the collective knowledge," she explained. "Should I need to be restored, they can bring me back to this point. When you are ready to leave, I am going to ask leave to return with you to the Edge."

"What about your people?" Beryl said.

"Hal and I asked them to assist the Opposition, but they are uncertain. It will take too long for them to make the decision." Eira regarded them placidly as she stood beside Ty. "I cannot leave you to fight this battle alone, *amatan*."

"Thank you," Vivi said, reaching out to place a hand on her arm. "We'd miss you if you weren't with us."

Just then, Ty sighed and opened his eyes. He glanced around at all of them. "We always keep meeting like this. Me flat on my back, and you guys looking worried," he joked, in a soft, slurred voice.

"Just as long as we keep meeting," Vivi said with a smile, coming over to take his hand.

He let out a sigh. "Yeah. That's true," he replied. "How did everything go?"

"The procedure was a success. You should sense a difference immediately," Eira said.

Beryl laid a hand on Ty's arm. "But it will take some time before you're up walking around without the braces. Your body has to relearn some things."

"I may have to make adjustments as well," Eira said.

"Are you having any pain?" Beryl asked.

"No."

"Can you try some things for me?"

"Sure."

She adjusted the bed so that he was sitting up and folded back the blanket so that his legs, clad in sleep pants, were visible. "Wiggle your toes for me."

Hal sensed that everyone in the room was holding their breath. Ty hesitated a moment, then his toes moved slightly. Beryl smiled. "That's really good. Close your eyes for me."

Ty did. "Tell me if you feel anything." Eira and the others watched as Beryl took a metal surgical probe and trailed it along the sole of his left foot.

"Yeah."

"Which one?"

"My left?"

"That's correct," Beryl said. She repeated the same with his other foot and Ty was able to identify it.

"Try lifting each leg," she suggested.

Hal watched as Ty's right leg moved a little, but the left lifted about 2-3 inches. He wanted to cheer, but Beryl somehow was managing to stay calm, so he tried to match her. "Good job. Try bending your knees," Beryl asked.

It was the same. His right leg bent a little, but he had much more movement in his left. "It worked," Ty said, shaking his head. "It worked! Eira, thank you. I...I wanted to believe it, but I couldn't...I just couldn't let myself..." He looked up at them, and it was obvious emotion had taken away his words.

Hal stepped forward to put a hand on Ty's shoulder, and slowly, they all responded in kind. Vivi took Ty's right hand, Beryl placed a hand on his shin and Eira took his left hand. "You're going to be fine," Hal said softly. "You've got all of us by your side, Ty. Always."

After Ty's procedure, Eira made her way to the council chamber through the gleaming metallic hallways of *Arden*. She'd requested a meeting with the speaker and found him waiting for her.

[*How is the captain?*] the speaker asked as Eira entered the vaulted room. Without Hal present, they spoke in the language of the Mudar.

[*He is doing well. He will regain the function of his legs, Speaker.*]

[*That is commendable,*] the speaker replied.

[*What did the council decide?*] she asked, knowing they had met again earlier.

[*They could not come to a decision on whether to help fight the Coalition. There is much dissention. However, your amatan will be allowed to leave.*]

Eira tilted her head. [*I cannot even believe you even considered keeping them here.*]

[*It was suggested by the Guardians, but the rest of the strata voted against it. Your amatan have seen little of our worldship and cannot have much to report even if they are here to spy. Perhaps they will take back news of our fair treatment of them if they are spies.*]

[*Speaker,*] Eira began. [*You know that the modified soldiers have joined the Opposition and are trying to fight back against those that created them. Since we will not be helping any time soon, I would still like to accompany the Loshad's crew back and assist in the movement to defeat the Coalition on my own.]*

[I do not think-]

She took a chance and interrupted him before he could tell her no. *[I am neither damaged, nor malfunctioning as Brecca has suggested. The ACAS has used our technology to make vat soldiers into slaves. You have heard my testimony and viewed my evidence. This may be the humans' only chance to break free. I believe that they are trustworthy. We should all stand ready to help them.]*

[There would need to be much discussion before all of us are committed to such a response,] the speaker frowned. *[I am not convinced it is safe yet.]*

[I believe no time is better,] Eira said. *[This is a moment that the Edge planets and soldiers like Hal fight for their freedom from the control of the Coalition. It is the same government we fought against over a century ago, but it has now stretched out its hand to crush the entire galaxy in its fist. Resisting them is a noble cause, as our creators set before us when we left Obis.]*

[I will not stop you from going. Taking Arden *there, however, will require more time for discussion and study.]*

Eira bowed her head, knowing that they could very well decide too late to make a difference. *[I understand your hesitation, Speaker. For me, however, I believe this is a risk worth taking for my human amatan, and I fully intend to go, with or without your leave.]*

The speaker was silent long moments, then he nodded. *[Very well.]* He held out one hand, palm toward Eira. *[Stay true to your programming, Eira.]*

She pressed her palm against his own. *[Thank you, Speaker. I wish you well.]*

. . .

THREE DAYS AFTER, the *Loshad's* crew prepped to leave the worldship. They were already prepared for their trip back to the Edge—before leaving Al-Kimia, they had packed extra months of rations and water. Ty and Hal had also taken the ship out for a few short practice runs, to make sure the Bixby drive was back up and functioning properly.

It was clear that the Opposition would be on its own, but at least Eira was returning with them. And Ty. It was obvious to Hal she'd given Ty his life back, a little more every day. The day after they left *Arden*, Ty was back up on his feet, with his braces, but for a small, but increasing amount of time each day, he was working with Eira and Beryl without the one on his stronger leg. It started with stretching and weight bearing exercises similar to the ones he'd done before leaving Al-Kimia, and progressed to slow walking around the cargo bay, using a rail system that Hal had devised to help Ty have support as he made the rounds.

Hal and Vivi spent time together sparring, playing squads and cooking, since Beryl was otherwise occupied with Ty's recovery. Vivi had begun to teach him how to make different dishes. He had to agree to the idea after the time she'd spent working on self-defense and tactics with him. He was terrible at it, but it both kept them busy and drew them closer together.

They were a few weeks away from reaching Al-Kimia when Hal woke one night to find Vivi gone. He called her name, looking around in the watery glow of the night cycle.

She wasn't in his room. He knocked gently before keying the door of the head, but she wasn't in there either. "Runa? Locate Vivi," he called, reminding himself to stay calm—she had to be somewhere on the ship.

"Vivi is in the galley," Runa replied. "I think she is upset, Hal."

"Thank you, Runa," Hal swallowed hard. if Vivi was upset,

that was a problem. He threw on sleep pants and went to the galley, mentally running over their last conversation before bed to see if there was any hint to what had happened there. He couldn't think of anything, however, so he double-timed it to the galley.

She was sitting at the table facing the door in the dim light, head bowed over a cup of something in her hands. The blue light outlined her in a silvery color akin to starlight.

"Hey, um...Veevs?" he said gently, standing in the doorway as if afraid to intrude on her.

She hid her face quickly as if embarrassed. "Oh Hal. I'm sorry. Did I wake you?"

Deflecting, he thought. "No. What's up?"

"Just a bad dream. That's all. It's...it's stupid."

She looked so sad that he came around and sat beside her. He didn't know what to do exactly, so he tried to imagine what Ty's move would be in a situation like this. Messing this up was not an option. "You should've woken me. Wanna talk about it?" There. That sounded like Ty.

She leaned against him, and it was automatic that he enveloped her with his arm. "It's... so stupid. I... had this nightmare about my ex," she said.

He held her closer, his anger rising. "The one that hurt you."

"Yeah. We broke up because I spied on him. I thought he was cheating on me at first, but I found he was keeping secrets from me about who he really was. Then, we got in this huge fight, and he hit me. You know, he only did it once and that was enough. I left as soon as it happened. But that look...on his face." She shivered. "It reminded me of that vat that attacked Ty. He had the same empty glare. In my dream, they were the same person."

Hal tried to think of the right thing to do or say. The last thing he wanted to do was screw this up. She needed him to be there for her, when what he really wanted to go find the guy who had hurt her and turn his face into a bloody mess. But he heard Ty in his head saying, *That's not gonna help right now, Hal.* He let Vivi go enough to catch her gaze. "Listen, that guy's never gonna hurt you again because of two reasons. First off, you're a different person now. You can handle a blaster as well as me or Ty and you know it. You're confident and know how to defend yourself. Secondly, I would never let him put his hands on you – you know that right?"

"Yeah. Of course." She leaned back into his embrace.

He hugged her again and kissed the top of her head, settling her right back against his side. "Thanks for being there," she said after long moments. "And you said all the right things."

"Wh- what?"

She smiled – he could hear it in her voice without even looking down. "I know you're worried about getting it right."

"Well, yeah. It's important to me." He pulled her tightly against him, wanting to say so much that he didn't have the words for.

They stayed that way a long time. Finally, Hal could tell that she was about to fall asleep again by the way her breathing changed.

"Better now?"

She nodded.

"Come on, let's head back to bed, then."

Ty HEADED for the cargo bay, intending to talk with Hal before they reached the border. In a week, they would have to cautiously cross back into ACAS space, then try to hit the feeds and see what the situation was with Al-Kimia. If things had progressed to all-out war, they would have a harder time getting back in.

"Ty, Hal's exercise period has already been 3.2 times longer than usual. Is something amiss?"

"I'll check in with him," he told her.

"Humans are quite confusing sometimes. I have been asking Eira questions so that I might know you better, but she is often unsure as well."

"Runa, you can ask me about anything," Ty said. "If I can help you understand us better, I will."

"Thank you, Tyce."

Hal was punching his heavy bag; Ty could hear the exhale of breath each time he landed a blow. He was using the breathing exercises Ty had taught him to help him regulate his anger and frustrations. He was pouring sweat; his t-shirt was dark with it. He'd obviously been at practice for a while, hypno-haze music blaring from his earphonics.

When he saw Ty, he took them out of his ears and tucked them in a pocket. "Yeah, Cap? You need me?"

"What's going on?"

"Just working out some things," he said with a big sigh.

"You at a yellow?" Ty asked, using the color system for threat levels. Green was okay, yellow was a heightened awareness. It went up from there to an orange, red and black. If Hal could talk, Ty knew he wasn't at a black, and actually, without the rush, Ty wondered if it was possible for Hal to get to a black threat level anymore.

"I'm at orange." He punched the bag as he spoke, punctuating his words with blows. "Veevs had a nightmare about her ex. I was imagining how great it would feel to cave in his skull with my fist." He abruptly hit the bag one last time, so that it swung back and forth on its chain.

"I hear you," Ty said in a way to let him know it was safe to unwind the whole tangle of his emotions.

Hal came around the bag to Ty – a good sign that he would open up. "She couldn't sleep until we talked," Hal said. "She was upset and crying but didn't want me to know."

"What did you say to her?"

"I told her she didn't have anything to worry about. She knows how to defend herself now. And I won't let him near her again."

Ty eased down the nearby wall to take a seat. He still tired quickly, the reason for the braces, but he was doing better. Hal obviously needed to talk, and Ty knew he needed someone to listen, so he made himself comfortable. "Sounds like you did the right thing,"

Hal raised an eyebrow. "Yeah?" His thoughtful tone showed he wasn't finished yet. He sat down beside Ty and began taking the wraps off his hands.

"Of course. You were there for her when she needed you."

They sat in silence while Hal rolled up each wrap. Ty knew he was building up to something; he'd had enough experience with Hal to know the peculiar weather of his moods.

"Ty, I know I haven't gotten a chance to really talk to you about this, but something's different with Veevs."

"What do you mean?"

Hal shrugged. "I don't know. This whole thing is really hard to figure out. I know I don't understand this relationship thing. I used to think it was just the way I was wired, you know, but now I'm not so sure." He shook his head, but then he grew more serious and lowered his voice. "Last night, I felt something I didn't know how to describe. Looking at Veevs so upset, and me wanting to fix it for her...that feeling. I've felt like that for a while, but I don't understand it."

"That's love," Ty said.

"Love?" Hal asked, skeptically. "Are you sure?"

"Yeah, Hal," Ty smiled, then tried to explain. "Look. You've been head over heels for this girl since you saved her... hell, since you *saw* her in that bar. I've watched you. Something... amazing has happened with you since Vivi came on this ship. You love her."

Hal actually blushed as a smile crossed his features, then scratched his head as if perplexed. "This is nat territory. I'm not sure what to do."

"Well, have you told her?" Ty asked.

He shook his head and began picking at a worn spot on his boot. "No, but I will. I'll probably screw it up, but I will."

"Speak from your heart and you won't screw it up. Tell her how you feel," Ty encouraged. "Vivi will understand."

Hal nodded. "What did you come down here for? I know you didn't come to watch me pound the bag."

"I wanted to bat around some tactics for getting back to ACAS space. So that we have a plan A and a plan B."

"Don't forget plan C," Hal grinned.

"That's usually the one where I let you pull something out of your ass."

"Hey, that's the one that usually works, though," Hal shrugged, standing up and reaching down to help Ty to his feet. "Let me get a shower, and I'll meet you on the bridge in ten."

FIFTEEN

"Look. Until they get your quarters, you can stay in mine," Patrin said. "I'm hardly there anyway, and I'll bunk on the freighter we used on Jaleeth. That way you can have the place to yourself. I already had some things sent over for you." He keyed the door and entered, followed by Kat.

He was offering her his place because they were still waiting on her job assignment, which would determine the location of her quarters. At the end of the week, Patrin was leaving for an op to Dourn, a small trading planet, and he'd been happy to loan her his hab unit for a few nights.

"Thank you," Kat said as she looked around. "All this...it's not necessary. I could easily take a bunk in the general barracks."

He turned to her. "Look. You've had a hard couple of days." Seren had asked Patrin to keep an eye on Kat. He hadn't been specific about what he wanted Patrin to look out for, but the intent was clear enough. Make sure she was settling in and look for any signs that things weren't what they seemed to be.

"And...I've got to admit, I feel badly about what happened," he met her eyes tentatively. "I'm sorry."

"I...I understand," she replied, looking around at the grey couch, table with two chairs and a micro-kitchen that had never been used.

"It's not much, and again, I'm really not here that often," he told her. "Bedroom's here," Patrin turned on the bedroom light and gestured to the bed, where a brownish-green duffle bag rested. "I had a friend in the supply department pack a bag for you. I know you left Jaleeth with nothing."

Patrin watched her look through the fatigues, boots, and everything else. "Are the sizes right? We had to make a guess," he admitted.

She was quiet for long moments. "It...It's really stupid, but this is more than what I had back on Jaleeth." She glanced over to see Patrin's concerned features. "I'm sorry. It's just...a nice thing to do...and I don't know how to deal with that."

He didn't miss the shine of emotion in her eyes. "Hey... there's nothing you need to do." Patrin could sense something sad within her. Perhaps it was losing her lover or being somewhere where she knew no one. It had to be tough. Gods knew he'd been a mess when Seren had taken him aboard the *Hesperus*. He put a hand on her shoulder. "Hey, just...settle in, get cleaned up and we can go get something to eat. I'm sure you're ready for some real food by now."

She rubbed her face, then glanced up at him and smiled. He could see that her eyelashes were damp, as if she'd wiped away tears she hadn't let fall. "Yeah," she agreed. "That'd be great."

"I'll be right out there if you need anything," Patrin promised her, turning for the door and then shutting it behind him. He stood for a moment, trying to figure her out. She was like the great depths of an ocean. Some moments, her emotions seemed to lie right at her surface; other moments, she was like water too deep to explore.

L‍ane had a good feeling about Kat, the *Raptor's* newest crewmember. At first she had been a little suspicious, like when she'd met Hal Cullen on the *Loshad*, but a few weeks had passed since Kat had joined them and during that time, she'd been temporarily assigned to the small freighter to see where she might fit best with the Oppos.

The Raptor was a civilian ship that flew missions for Al-Kimia and Lane and Orin had been asked to tag along on while Seren's ship, the *Hesperus*, was grounded on base. They had arrived in the Sora spaceport during the middle of the day cycle, on a quick supply run. Lane and Kat were hooking the ship up to refuel while Dai Esparza, the pilot, and her girlfriend Leila were paying the fees with the port authority. *Yeah, Kat Neval was turning out to be quite an asset*, Lane thought as she watched her work. She was a good soldier, if a little quiet. But she got her job done right and didn't bitch about anything. In the service, Kat must have been formidable, Lane thought.

They would only be here overnight, picking up a shipment of Bixby drive regulators that were badly needed on Al-Kimia for the civilian fleet, but they didn't want to draw attention to their short stay by not latching to refuel.

"Ever been to Sora before?" Lane asked.

Kat shook her head, hooking up the water. "It's a market planet, right?"

"Yeah. If there's anything you want to spend your scrill on, you can find it here. Feel free to go out but be back around 1700 when the shipment's delivered. After that, you, me and Orin could go find some trouble…if you're up for it."

"Hells, yeah," Kat grinned, "I'm up for that."

"Good." Lane smiled back. "It's time we welcomed you into the fold properly."

"So, I passed inspection?" she teased, lifting an eyebrow as she eyed her crewmate.

"Well, yeah. Orin wanted me to welcome you in two weeks ago."

"Why didn't you?" Kat asked.

"Because I'm a little harder to convince," Lane replied, grudgingly. Then she smiled. "But you persuaded me."

"I'm glad," Kat said.

KAT HAD GONE shopping on Sora as soon as she could slip away. She didn't think about the shredder comm she'd purchased until she stepped outside of the store with it in her hand. She studied it, trying to remember why she'd bought it. Then it came to her. It was time to call the fleet admiral. For a moment, she stood in the middle of the street, paralyzed with fear. She looked at the nearby garbage receptacle and raced to it, fully intending to throw the handheld away, but before she let it go, her fingers closed around it tightly and she shoved it in her pocket, glancing around nervously. Even though the streets were packed, she saw no one from the ship. *Safe so far,* she thought as the switch flipped in her mind.

She made her way to a cheap hotel and rented a room for an hour. The younger attendant's gaze slid over her like oil, leaving her feeling greasy. She said the bare minimum to him, gave him scrill without touching his fingers, and went upstairs. Keying the door, she went in and locked it behind her. It took her ten minutes to check the room for surveillance devices. She found only one – in an air vent, angled at the bed. *Nat pervert,* she thought as she deactivated it.

Perching on the side of the bed, she called the number that

floated to the top of her memory. It rang five times before he answered.

"Katerine."

When she heard his voice, she stood immediately, not meeting the tiny camera's gaze. She could sense his attention on her: a palpable sensation. "At ease, Nyma. What do you have for me?" the fleet admiral asked.

She gazed at a point between her eye and the display and told him everything she knew. It was a reflex action like vomiting, and she felt the same sense of disgust, but she kept talking anyway. Nothing would slow the torrent of words. "I was interrogated, but I had some kind of reaction to the drugs, so it saved me from discovery," she began.

"Then that went exactly to plan. You cannot be interrogated, Nyma. The medics modified you for that when I decided to send you in as a mole."

Of course, the fleet admiral would have thought of everything. "The Al-Kimians have joined together with the vats. An aged vat named Jacent Seren is the liaison for the vat forces. The nats are led by a woman named Terra Malar. Seren seems to report to her, and she reports directly to the First Minister. The vats' second in command is Patrin Kerlani. I have become friends with Patrin, as well as several other vats on base. They were suspicious at first, but Patrin trusts me now. I think he might be attracted to me."

"Then use that. Do what you have to do to get close to the leadership," Quillon said.

"Yes sir. I understand."

"Tell me more about the leader of the vat forces."

"There is an almost religious adoration for Seren. He truly believes in what he is doing."

"Jacent Seren." There was tapping on the other end as the admiral looked away to pull up information on his datapad. "This vat should have been dead by now," he murmured.

"Yes, sir. He is much past his date." Katerine thought of her first impression of the tall man with the warm eyes, and her stomach ached with the thought that she was betraying his trust in her. She quickly shifted her attention away and tried to get her thoughts under control before the admiral noticed. Seren was a traitor to his government. A traitor she should take down. Those were the truths she needed to focus on, she told herself.

"Very good, Nyma," Quillon said, and her gaze snapped back up to his. Years of programming steered her thoughts to him and his instructions, wiping away everything else. "Continue to strengthen your connections to them. Be a model member of the Opposition, Katerine. You must be above reproach."

"Yes, sir," Kat said, feeling a sudden dark thrill at the praise she'd received. The back-and-forth sway of her emotions was making her a little dizzy. "What else would you like me to do?"

"For now, nothing. Continue to draw them close. Take time to earn their trust. When you do, and the opportunity presents itself, destabilize the operation by taking out their leaders in ways that cannot be traced back to you. You have been programmed with everything you need, Nyma. Do not fail me." He scrutinized her as he finished admonishing her.

She trembled at the thought. Death was better than failure. "Yes, sir. You can depend on me."

He narrowed his eyes at her for long moments, and she sensed he was trying to read her mind through the comm. Finally, he spoke. "See it done."

She ended the call and sat down heavily on the bed, looking at the handheld in her palm. With numb fingers, she moved to do a complete reset of the device as she tried to still her shaking hands. After giving the admiral everything he wanted to know – the leaders, their weaknesses – why was she so sick to her stomach? She felt slimy with treason. Caught between an ocean of guilt and the rock that was the fleet admiral, she squeezed the handheld in both hands as she stood up and paced the room. The rising tide of anxiety threatened to drown her.

With a scream, she threw the handheld at the opposite wall without warning. It left a dent. She took several quick steps to the device, saw it was unharmed, and brought her heel down on it over and over and over. There was a throbbing pain in her temples, she realized as she stepped away from the shards of crysplas and metal. She grabbed her head in both hands and slid down the wall to the floor. Then, the tears swept over her like a squall line.

"Hey, still not any better?" Leila asked Kat as she laid down on the bunk. Leila and Dai were organizing the medsupplies they'd picked up in the market earlier in the day. The *Raptor* was too small to have its own medbay, so the supplies were stowed in one of the three crew pod/bunk areas. She and Dai always stocked back up when possible because as the boycott of Al-Kimia continued, things would be sure to grow scarce on base.

Kat looked pretty tired. She had been the first person up that morning and had told Leila that she had been awake since 0400. It wasn't surprising. A lot of vats slept badly; Leila knew. She was a natural-born, but her girlfriend Dai was a vat, and Dai had more than her share of nightmares that Leila had to hold her through. She supposed poor vats like Dai and Kat had seen enough horrible things to last them a lifetime of nightmares.

"Got this headache," Kat said. "Do you have something?" She rubbed at her interface scar as she spoke.

"Of course, Kat. You need the light duty stuff or heavy duty?"

"Heavy duty," she said, "but I'd still like to be conscious later. Lane invited me to go out with her and Orin."

"You got it," she said as she finished her work and then began to load a medjet.

"You two coming with us?" Kat asked Dai.

The pilot shook her head. "Leila's going to make Ponea for me."

"It's Dai's favorite," Leila said with a grin as she leaned over to kiss her girlfriend. "I bribed her for a nice quiet night in," she added, coming back with the medjet. "Lay down for a few minutes, and you'll wake up a new woman."

"Thanks." After being injected, Kat tucked her feet up under her and pulled the blanket up to cover her head and blot out the light.

"Give us one minute, and we'll be out of here so you can rest," Leila said gently. There was a murmur of assent from the blanket and then Leila and Dai turned the lights down and left.

SIXTEEN

Stenval Glander, manager and occasional bartender of the Pink Sands Hotel, watched the two new vats that worked for him for a moment. The one named Malek was sweeping the floor and his friend Jaren was washing dishes.

"Hey. Soon as you two are done, get Jack to make you something to eat and meet me at the bar."

"Yes, sir." Malek met Sten's gaze and acknowledged for the both of them since Jaren didn't seem to be a big fan of eye contact.

"Affirmative," Jaren murmured from the sink.

Sten nodded and headed for the bar. It was almost empty this time of night; the hardcore drinkers had gone to bed, sleeping it off until the next day when the cycle of fun in the sun and evening drinking would repeat itself. He'd worked at the Pink Sands for two years – and calling the dive a hotel was stretching the limits of believability. The decrepit place needed to be lasered to the ground and rebuilt as one of those glittering palaces that dotted the beaches further down the avenue in Westona, in his opinion. He didn't know why Mr. and Mrs.

Nallea, the owners, hadn't sold out to one of the big corps that came nosing around every season, but they hadn't. It was a quiet place. No one looked twice at the run-down hotel, which worked for his side business of moving weapons into the hands of Al-Kimia and her allies.

The gaudy little place did have a way of growing on you. It had been built in the early days of Coren's settlement. The Nalleas had decided to take a chance on the sandy beach dune of a planet becoming some sort of tourist area as the Edge was developed after the Mudar war. When real Edgers went on vacation, they came to places like the Pink Sands rather than stay at the cubes in the Amberjack or the Mako Hotel Casinos. Those glowing hotels were for the Insiders who wanted to believe they were living dangerously on the Edge, all the while staying as safe as they could.

The two men that he'd seen on the beach that morning a month ago would never have enough money to stay at one of the rationboxes down the way. He'd seen them arrive on the beach, probably coming in from the spaceport several blocks away from the Pink Sands. The strange one, Jaren, had walked out of the dunes, his gaze fixed on the water like he'd never seen an ocean before. While Sten watched from his morning perch on his rock where he did Inosu poses every morning, the stranger had walked down to the water and straight in up to his chest. Shoes on, clothes on and everything. Sten had dropped his star pose and watched them, intrigued.

"Shit!" The other man had cursed as he dropped their bags and ran to retrieve his friend.

They were vats. He'd seen the tattoos on their wrists when he'd served them dinner at the bar one night. They'd had enough money to rent a room for a week, but he knew they were in trouble when Malek asked him if he knew of anyone hiring in the area. So, Sten had offered them employment at the

Pink Sands. Having been homeless when he, himself, had arrived on Coren, he was painfully aware of what being homeless would mean for these two. Sleeping on the beach one night was an adventure...permanently was just plain miserable. With his extra-curricular activities, he figured he needed someone to watch his back, so he had offered them one of the rooms, board and a little scrill. So far, they had both proved to be hard workers and fiercely loyal.

But they needed more help than he could give. Jaren was obviously having problems. Yesterday a server had dropped a stack of plates coming in the kitchen, and Jaren had been found in one of the coolers later, half-frozen and huddled in the corner with a twelve-inch butcher knife for company. And before that, Jaren had threatened Jack, the cook, when he yelled at Malek for being late picking up an order. Jack, who was good natured when the kitchen wasn't swamped, didn't hold it against either one of the vats, but it was clear that Jaren was something of a loose cannon. After the incident in the kitchen, Malek had taken the vat back to their room. When Sten had knocked to check on them, he saw Malek had gotten Jaren calmed down enough to sleep.

And today, Jaren had seemed pretty stable. He'd even apologized in that curt way of his. So, Sten figured he'd let it go. After all, it had been Jaren that had saved his ass a few weeks ago when he'd gone to pick up two crates of guns from Pauel, a new supplier who'd tried to screw him over. As soon as Pauel drew a blaster on him, Jaren put two bolts in the man's chest without blinking. They'd left the guy on the beach. Nobody had investigated it much, blaming pirate Anklav activity.

In a few days, his college friend, Leila, would show up to help ferry the weapons that had come from Pauel to Al-Kimia. When she'd approached Sten about aiding the Opposition, he'd agreed; first because he trusted her and second because he'd sympathized with the vats. It was obvious that whatever the Coalition had done to vats like Jaren had left them pretty much screwed for what little amount of life they had left.

Malek, the more stable and easygoing of the two, suffered horrible nightmares that he tried to drink away. After closing one night, Sten had found the vat out on the patio deck, with a bottle of cheap liquor, a brand that even a dive like The Pink Sands wouldn't dare serve. Malek had opened up a bit and told Sten that he and Jaren had been a part of some specialized programming that had left him with nightmares. Sten had directed him to a hotel doctor friend of his, who saw the workers in Westona for almost nothing. The doctor had given Malek a prescription for a heavy sleep medication that had appeared to help. Human nats who left the ACAS had health benefits, but nothing like that was provided for vats. *Fuck the ACAS and the Coalition,* Sten thought. He would do what he could to bring them down.

He was still thinking about the work helping his new friends when he looked up from wiping the bar to see Malek and Jaren coming out with two bowls: Jack's fish stew, by the smell of it. The oceans on Coren teemed with fish and the dish was probably the best one on the menu. He drew them two beers as they got settled at the bar, then went to cash out the night's final customers. When the last couple left, Sten approached the two men.

"Malek, Jaren...I wanted to talk for a minute." He pulled up a stool to sit on his side of the bar.

Jaren finished chewing the bite in his mouth and swallowed hard. "You need us out of here, don't you?"

It took Sten a moment to process what Jaren was saying. He realized the vat thought that Sten was going to send them away. "Oh, no—that's not it at all. I have some friends coming to move that merchandise from the storage area." At his words,

Jaren visibly relaxed. "Think you guys could back me up like before?"

"Are you expecting trouble, boss?" Jaren asked.

The normally quiet vat was more talkative tonight. "No, but...I'd rather have you with me and not need you, than need you and not have you. We can trust my friends, but I'm learning that you never know what else could happen."

Jaren nodded curtly. "We'll have your back, boss."

"Thanks. After the last time, I think it'll be good to be more proactive. I've known Leila and her girlfriend for a while, and the Oppos have been on the up and up so far, but it'll pay to be careful in case they're followed by anyone."

KAT SAW Patrin walking across the hangar, headed toward the *Raptor*, where they were busy offloading crates. She quickly turned her back to him, hoping maybe he was looking for someone else. "Kat," he called, as he stepped up on the ramp. "Back from Sora already?"

"Yeah," she sighed, then turned fully toward him, knowing what his reaction would be.

"What happened?" he asked when he saw her bruised face.

"Oh, you've found our little cage fighter." Lane came from behind a row of crates and shoved Kat playfully. "We went out drinking last night and Orin had to pull her off two nats who asked for an ass beating. She took them both down before we could even get there."

"I told them hands off," Kat said, "but they didn't want to listen." She glanced at Patrin, to see if he was angry. "I didn't mean to jeopardize the mission." She hadn't wanted to cause trouble, but when the two men had cornered her by the bathroom and put their hands on her, she had simply *reacted*.

Lane shook her head. "She didn't jeopardize it. We went

ahead and left early, just in case, but those guys weren't in any condition to give details when she was done with them," Lane said, as Orin came up.

He made several signs, and both Lane and Patrin smiled.

"Orin says you are a fierce little cat," Patrin translated.

Thank you, big brother, Kat signed, smiling. He hugged her in return. She'd been learning some signs the past couple months, which had made both Lane and Orin a lot less stand-offish. It had been nice to feel like she had friends. In the ACAS she'd always felt apart from the other vats, due to her training with the fleet admiral. There was none of that with the vats on Al-Kimia. They treated her like she was one of them, almost like a rook again with her batch, the way it had been before the fleet admiral came and decided she'd be his pet project. There was a sense of camaraderie with the Opposition forces that she'd never had in the ACAS, and it felt good.

At that thought, a pang of uncomfortable guilt washed over her, and the smile faded from her face.

"You handled yourself pretty well," Lane said with admiration, giving her another playful shove before she and Orin went back to unloading the ship.

"So, how was the trip through the blockade?" Patrin asked.

"We got shot at as we slipped through. But Dai's ship's a fast one," Kat smiled, brushing dark strands of her hair away from her face.

"You look a bit happier than when you came to us."

"Well, it's...kind of nice to have friends. I'm actually starting to feel like I belong here," Kat said, looking down shyly.

"You do belong here," Patrin said, and he meant it. "I have a job that I might need your help on, you know. We're picking up a shipment of blasrifles in a few days on Coren. Want to come along?"

"Yeah," she smiled. Kat was familiar with Coren only from

being part of a bridge crew. It was the only recreational destination on this side of the Edge. Supposedly it was beautiful, with pink sand and blue water, but she'd never been any place like that. She was usually stationed on cruisers, or if the admiral took her anywhere else to train, they were usually planets with difficult, punishing terrain.

"Lane doesn't give out praise easily, so you must have kicked ass out there. I'm glad you're on our side," he grinned, teasing her.

"Why...why did you save me?" Kat asked suddenly, looking at her shoes.

"What do you mean?"

She bit her lip. "I could have been anyone...You took a real risk bringing me here."

He stepped forward. "You're one of us, Kat." Without hesitation, he put a hand on her shoulder.

She looked up at him again, as another painful pang of guilt overwhelmed her. Try as she might, she couldn't conjure up the hatred she'd felt for these traitors when she'd talked to the fleet admiral. They seemed to be nothing more than caring people, trying to be there for her and others, and they certainly believed they were doing the right thing.

Apparently, Patrin had seen something in her face because he took her hand. "What's troubling you?" he asked.

She stepped back abruptly, breaking the contact between them. "Nothing. I'll be glad to help anyway I can, you know that." She turned and picked up a load of two crates and practically fled off the ramp.

He remained staring after her. "Kat?" he called, but she kept going.

"Patrin." Lane had come up behind him again. He turned

at the serious note in her voice. "She's troubled about something. She was fine when we got planetside, then she disappeared a while and came back to crash with a bad headache, Leila says. Then she went out with us and threw back more alcohol than Orin." Patrin raised an eyebrow in surprise at her story. "I think she's still heartsick over her Jakob. She blames herself for his death, perhaps."

Patrin frowned and grabbed a crate, and Lane did the same. He spoke to her in a low voice as they left the ship with their burdens. "I'll take her, Dai, Leila, Orin and you on the next op and see what we can find out then."

"I think that would be a good idea. She did well on this last one, so she's definitely ready."

Patrin and Lane glanced around the hangar for Kat, but the troubled woman had vanished in the coming and going of soldiers and did not return to the *Raptor* that day.

A FEW DAYS LATER, Patrin's full crew boarded the ship again. Leila, Dai and Orin got her ready for take-off, while Patrin, Kat, and Lane planned the op. "I don't see this being a very dangerous mission," Patrin said as they all settled into the seats in the common area. "I mean there will be ACAS in the spaceport, I'm sure, but other than that, I think we won't stand out with the large volume of people coming and going from Coren."

"It's a resort, right?" Lane asked.

"Yeah, most of it. We'll be fine as long as we keep the group coming off the ship small. Kat—I want you and Leila with me, and if we run into trouble, we'll comm Lane and Orin." Kat and Lane nodded and Patrin went on. "We're meeting up with Leila's friend, Sten, at the Pink Sands Hotel where he works."

Patrin triggered a holo from his handheld and set it to project above the table they were sitting around.

"It's a run-down little place. Sten functions as the middleman in this arms supply chain and stores the shipment until we can get it. Different ships pick up from him. Let's get on the bridge for the blockade crossing," Patrin said. "Then we have about ten hours until we reach Coren."

Lane headed to the bridge, but Kat remained in place a moment, staring into the space where the hologram had been.

"Are you sure you can trust this guy?" she asked, looking at him through the space where the holo had been.

"Yeah. He's been a pretty steady contact for about eight months. We've run about five shipments through Sten on Coren. It'll be a lot safer than picking the shipment up at a spaceport on a station," he said.

She looked concerned. "I...I just want everyone to be careful. There could be...ACAS agents anywhere."

"Don't worry. We've got this, Kat," he reassured her. "Sten might be a nat, but he's a friend."

After landing on Coren, Patrin, Kat and Leila walked the three blocks to the sea. It was late afternoon, and the suns were heading for the horizon. When they crossed the final two streets and the sound of the waves became evident, Kat walked between the Pink Sands and the private home next to it to view the shoreline.

"Kat?" Patrin had come over to join her, a faint smile on his features.

"Wow. It's big."

"I take it you haven't been on a planet with large oceans before?"

She shook her head. "Only once. When I was a rook. Training, you know, so I didn't get to spend much time looking at it."

"Oh." Patrin glanced to Leila and pointed to the water. "Be right back," he said.

Patrin motioned for Kat to go first. "Go on, I'm right behind you," They wound their way through the dunes to the shore, and the walking became easier as the sand grew firmer.

It was high tide, so the water was close to the shore, gentle waves rolling in. "Are there always waves?"

"Yeah, I think so. I'm from the vat facility on Haleia-6, so we didn't have oceans. Only sand."

Her voice was softer. "No oceans on Chamn-Alpha either. At least none where I was."

They both stared at the waves for a long time. Finally, ready to go, Patrin turned to Kat and noticed something strange had happened to her. She was staring at the waves, hypnotized. Her body swayed back and forth a little with each wave that rolled in. After watching for a long time, she blinked slowly. It triggered a thought. "Kat?"

"Yes, sir..."

"Are you alright?"

"Yes. No. I...I don't know. I'm not sure." A shadow of confusion swept over her face, but her gaze was locked on the waves rolling in. "I'm so torn."

"Tell me about it." Kat had been like a taut wire since he'd known her, but now, Patrin realized the pattern of the waves had zoned her out somehow. He would use it if it would help him understand what had been troubling her.

"I...I have feelings that frighten me. I...I don't understand them," she breathed. "I don't want to be a traitor...but...I have to..."

Patrin went to take her hand and she flinched when he

touched her, shying away as if she were about to be hit. "Don't," she pleaded, whispering.

"I'm not going to hurt you." He reassured her. Over several long moments, her body slowly relaxed.

So, he thought, *she had been hurt by someone and was afraid to embrace what they were doing because it ran against her programming.* Many ACAS nats were cruel to their vats—he'd served under several officers that thought nothing of beating a vat to unconsciousness for the smallest violation of the rules. "Kat. You're not a traitor," he reassured her.

"I'm not?" she breathed with a trembling relief. He watched a tear slip down her cheek.

"You're not. Whatever the ACAS did to you, Kat...or made you do...you're not to blame. The real you inside...past all the programming and routines...that's the person you are."

"I'm not...not to blame?" she breathed.

"No," he said again as a grey water bird streaked over the shoreline, breaking her gaze. She suddenly turned toward him, confused. Self-consciously, she swiped at her cheek and blushed at the same time. "I uh...think I missed something you said."

She doesn't remember, he thought. "It's not important, Kat. Ready to go back now?"

She smiled, "Yes. Thanks for coming with me. This...is really beautiful. I'm glad I was able to see it."

"Me too, Kat," he replied.

STEN CAUGHT sight of Leila as soon as she came to the door. His friend from his college days looked good. Her long blond hair was in a loose braid cascading down one shoulder, and it shone like gold against her blue-green shirt. It was hard not to notice her beauty—he'd been very smitten with her at uni. He'd asked her out at an art show before he realized the woman she was with was more than a friend. He'd been embarrassed at first, but the kind way she'd turned him down had started a friendship between them. They'd kept in touch after school and when she'd asked him to help in the Opposition's efforts, he'd said yes.

"Hey, you," he said, putting down his towel and coming out from around the bar. They'd kept in touch by comm, but this was the first time Leila had been with the group picking up a shipment since the first run.

As she approached, she opened her arms and enfolded him in a hug.

"Sten! You look good," she said. "I think this vacation lifestyle is doing you well."

"Thanks. You look great too, Leila," he replied. "Where's Dai?"

"Back at the ship. Since this is a business visit, she's keeping us ready to go," Leila said. "These are my friends, Patrin and Kat." She gestured to them as they entered the bar area. "I'm afraid we don't have long before we have to be back at the ship, Sten," she said meaningfully. "If things calm down, maybe Dai and I can come visit, but for now..."

"Oh sure. Let me get my assistants. Right this way," Sten said.

It didn't take long to be shown to the anti-grav packing crates containing the weapons. Sten opened one of the crates, fished around in the foam and pulled forth a blasrifle. He handed it to Patrin. The vat pulled the charging lever, then sighted down the barrel. "Almost got my ass shot off picking these up," Sten said.

"What happened?" Patrin asked.

"The contact was new this time. Guess he thought he could make more scrilla by killing me and taking my money and the guns. But I had these guys at my back, and they saved me." Sten nodded at Jaren and Malek.

Patrin looked the two vats over appraisingly. "Thanks for that. I'm sorry it happened. I'll have a word with our contacts in the Anklav. They're usually dependable, but if they can't assure the drops, we'll have to negotiate with someone else. Will you continue to be our contact on Coren? If not, I understand."

Sten glanced at Malek and Jaren and thought about what he'd seen them go through. Jaren's outbursts and Malek's difficulties sleeping were only the surface symptoms of deeper problems caused by what the ACAS had done to them. "Yeah, I'm willing to keep going if Malek and Jaren will keep watching my back."

Jaren nodded at Malek, then met Sten's gaze. "Yeah, boss. Of course, we'll be there," he replied.

"There you go, then," Sten said, holding out a hand. Patrin shook it.

THERE WERE no problems getting the guns aboard the *Raptor*. They took off immediately, headed back for Al-Kimia. Later that night, most of the crew were asleep while Patrin and Kat manned the bridge. Patrin was a night owl like she was, and they'd decided to take the night shift together. They'd been discussing the trip back to Al-Kimia when they heard a sudden cry from one of the sleeping pods.

Disturbed, Kat stood up. Patrin joined her and they made their way down the floor-lit hallways until they reached Leila and Dai's pod. When they looked around the corner, they saw Dai sitting on the floor, her head in her hands. Leila was beside her. "You're fine, babe," she whispered, arm around her. "Just a bad dream, that's all," she soothed. "Come back to bed."

Dai leaned in and Kat had a glimpse of her tear-streaked face before she buried it against Leila's shoulder.

Patrin touched Kat's arm and gently guided her away from the sleeping pod's entrance. "She's got the situation in hand."

Kat was lost in thought as they arrived back at the bridge. Her thoughts were on the edge of something, but she wasn't sure she understood.

"What's on your mind?" he asked.

"I've...never seen a nat care about one of us like that," she said softly, looking up at him. "Not ever."

"Not all nats are bad. Dai started on the *Hesperus* with Seren. We met Leila when we rescued her from a group of Anklav sex traffickers. She decided to stay on, and the old man liked her. Dai eventually got her own ship and the two of them started running missions with us," Patrin paused a moment, then went on. "Was your time in service rough?" he asked.

"Yeah..." she answered, thinking of Quillon.

"Your CO?"

An unrestrained wave of anger washed over her, and she clenched her teeth. "We hated him. Every day...we didn't breathe without thinking to please him." And they had wanted to please Quillon. Every vat on that ship had done their best, in absolute terror that they would suffer his wrath. The smothering fear came back on her, and she found herself on the edge of a rush as the threat of Quillon grew larger and larger in her mind. The hate rolling through her scared her.

Then Patrin was beside her, taking her hand as she struggled with her emotions. "Those days are over," he assured her. "You determine your own course and fight for what you choose to now. You're free of that past."

She looked up at him uncertainly. "I am?" she asked, unconvinced.

"The longer you're out...the longer it's been since your last programming, the more you'll believe it," Patrin promised.

Could it be true? Could she stay with the Oppos? Quillon's orders seemed far, far away, and she was trembling on the knife edge of something previously unknown. *Could freedom be that easy?*

"You're going to be fine," Patrin reassured her again. "Hear me? You're gonna figure this out."

She nodded, desperate to believe him.

SEVENTEEN

Four months had passed since they'd left Al-Kimia. The *Loshad* was approaching the planet from the border side because there was less traffic and therefore not as many ACAS patrol ships. Everyone was at their stations and Eira was present on the bridge to help if needed. She still controlled the nanites throughout the ship and reassured Ty and Hal that she would continue do so if there was damage, but there was no need.

Once they slipped past the blockade without being challenged by an ACAS ship, they received a transmission from Al-Kimia. Ty had turned their transponder off for the approach. "Unknown vessel. This is Al-Kimian Military Flight Command. You have crossed into in Al-Kimian space. Turn back now or be shot out of our sky."

"This is the *Loshad*, Flight Command. I am Captain Tyce Bernon. We will transmit our landing codes, but we have been gone on mission for four months, so they may not be the most recent. If you contact Captain Seren or General Malar, they will vouch for us." Ty gestured to Beryl to transmit the codes.

"*Loshad*, we are sending you a course. It is imperative you do not deviate from it."

They wanted to be sure, Tyce thought. He understood. "Anything you say, Flight Command."

The course led them to Drena Base. Ty landed at the main hangar, and then looked at the crew. "Eira—You are going to be quite the surprise. I believe that, at this point, you should stay on the ship while we meet with Seren."

"Understood."

"Everyone else with me. Eira, I will comm you so that you can hear what is discussed. We may have to share your existence with Seren. Are you good with that?"

"Yes, Tyce. I'm here to help, so someone will have to know of my existence."

"Well, you're part of the crew now, and I want you involved in all decisions."

She inclined her head. "Thank you."

"Let's go." Ty got to his feet. He'd been working hard at rehabilitation over the past two months and was now wearing a brace on only the right leg. That would definitely cause Seren to ask some questions, he thought with a grin.

"Ready?" Ty said.

"Hells, yeah," Hal replied. "Let's do this."

They hit the ramp, and it began to lower.

When they were escorted to the conference room for debriefing, Tyce saw Seren waiting for them in the hallway.

"I'm glad to see you returned, Captain." He raised an eyebrow as he noticed the lack of a brace on one of Ty's legs. "And in much better health it seems."

"That will make sense after you hear our story," Tyce said. "I think we have something that will greatly interest you. Can we call in Max Parsen too? This concerns him as well."

"Very well," Seren said, pulling his handheld. "General Terra Malar, the leader of Al-Kimian military forces is inside. I have explained how you have assisted us by bringing Dr. Parsen to us, and she wants to meet with you."

"That's great. May I have a moment first?"

"Certainly. We will be inside," Seren said, leaving them alone.

Ty keyed his comm. "Eira?"

"Yes, Tyce?"

"We are about to go into the briefing. There's going to be three people present besides us. There's Seren, Max Parsen and Terra Malar, the leader of the Al-Kimian forces. Let me ask you again...you're alright with all of them knowing about you?"

"They will have to know about me eventually. Now is that time. Tell whom you deem necessary."

Ty sighed, "How can you be so calm?"

"How would being emotional improve this situation?"

"I know. But still..."

"We've just protected you for so long it's like second nature," Hal added.

"You have done a wonderful job, Hal. All of you have. But it is time to take a risk, no matter what the cost. We have much work to do here."

Ty nodded. "We'll leave the comm on."

"Thank you."

"Let's go in," Ty said.

They entered the room together. Seren and the auburn-haired woman with him were talking softly and examining a data pad when they entered.

Seren spoke first. "Dr. Parsen is coming. Perhaps we should get our introductions out of the way. This is General Terra

Malar, the leader of Al-Kimia's military forces." He gestured to the woman who had gotten to her feet. She was wearing an Al-Kimian military dress uniform.

She was older, and one of those women who became more striking with age. The tiny lines around her eyes did nothing to detract from the depth Ty saw there. "I'm very glad to meet all of you," she began. "Commodore Seren has told me much about how you came to join us here. We need and appreciate every hand we can get in this coming struggle, so you are welcome," she said.

"I'm Captain Bernon and this is my crew." Ty gestured to them. "This is Hal Cullen, Vivi Valjean, and Beryl McCabe. There is one of our number still on our ship who is joining us by comm. Her name is Eira."

"Very well," Malar said. "Is the comm secure?"

Eira's voice came across as Tyce placed his handheld on the table in front of them. "This comm is now encrypted, General Malar. I assure you our conversations are completely safe."

"Thank you. Please take a seat."

As they began to get settled, Max entered the room. He was very obviously surprised to see the *Loshad*'s crew. The last time they'd seen each other, Max had been in a medbed. "Hal, Vivi? You're back." He came to them and shook Hal's hand. Vivi gave Max a hug.

"Good to see you on your feet, Max." Hal nodded.

"Good to be on my feet." Max grinned.

"There is quite a lot to tell you, but perhaps I should get you all up to date," Ty began. "Before we joined you here, we were a salvage crew. We would go out past the border on permits to salvage Mudar technology. We got a tip from a friend about a downed Mudar ship in a mostly unexplored part of the border, so we went there and located it and what we found inside was...unexpected to say the least."

"Vivi found a silver sphere that we brought on board. We didn't know right away that there was anything to it, but there was," Hal said.

"How big was it?" Max asked.

"About this size." Hal held out his hands to demonstrate that it would fit in the palm of a hand but was slightly larger.

"I've seen those spheres before," Max said thoughtfully.

"Where?" Ty asked.

"In lab storage on Haleia-6," Max said. "I'm sorry, go on."

"Wait. The ACAS has Mudar spheres?" Vivi asked, stunned.

"Yes. They're only artifacts, really. ACAS used them to develop the nanites and interfaces for vats."

Ty exchanged looks with Hal and Vivi, trying to figure out what to say. Eira spoke before they could.

"Those objects are consciousness spheres," Eira said. "I was inside the one that Vivi and Hal found. My conveyance was destroyed, and I went into stasis when my ship crashed one hundred years ago. When they found a serviceable conveyance, my nanites downloaded me into the *Loshad*."

"Wait. This person on the comm is... a Mudar?" Max asked. "You have a Mudar on your ship right now?"

"Yes," Tyce said. "She downloaded herself into the computer as self-preservation. For a while we didn't know she was there, but after a time, it became apparent."

"Eira was on our ship when we came to save you," Hal said, turning to Max, "so you could say you owe your life to her. She made it possible for us to escape the ACAS that day."

"I regret the deception," Eira said.

Max glanced to Commodore Seren and General Malar, who was agape. "Did you know about this?" Terra asked Seren in a low tone.

"No. This is quite unbelievable."

"Bernon, are we in any danger from Eira?" Malar asked.

"Absolutely not." Ty went on. "Eira saved us many times as the ACAS tried to hunt us down and kill us for what we knew about her ship. When I was injured, she saved my crew by getting us to Al-Kimia. I know you may have reservations, General Malar, but Eira's people are not like we've been taught. They did not come for the destruction of the Coalition. They came to contact the Coalition," Ty said. "And the ACAS met them with hatred and fear."

Hal spoke up. "You know, it makes sense. The Coalition probably encouraged everyone's fear to consolidate their power. Humanity drawing together to fight a common enemy. Star systems doubtlessly begged to join up."

"So, you're saying that the spheres I saw in the storage were essentially Mudar...brains?" Max asked.

"Yes," Eira replied. "How many were there?"

"I...I'm not sure. No more than five. Most of them were cracked open...in pieces. There were one or two still intact at the time I was there." Max ran a hand through his hair. "Gods," he muttered.

Ty went on to explain Eira's struggle to exist in the memory of the *Loshad*, and their plan to contact the Mudar to help not only Ty but Eira.

Seren raised an eyebrow. "So. Did you find them? Were they able to help?"

"Yes. I can tell you more about meeting them later but suffice it to say, they didn't harm us or the *Loshad*. In fact, they fixed our drive."

Malar and Seren shared another incredulous look before Ty went on.

"There's more that particularly concerns you," Ty said. "On our way to the Mudar we found an ACAS cruiser. An Aquila class ghost ship, drifting out there for around a hundred years. We mapped its location, vector, and rate of drift. We should be able to go back and pick it up. Eira said it had been disabled by one of her people's viruses, which she can easily remove. Other than that, the ship only suffered minor damage," Ty said. "It could be put to good use against the ACAS."

"Did you board it? Any idea what happened to the crew?" Seren asked.

"Hal and Vivi boarded it. Hal?" Ty offered, knowing how important telling this story was for Hal.

He leaned forward. "When we went on board, we found that only part of the crew had abandoned ship. The second in command had been shot, execution style. Other than that, there were no nats on the ship." He lifted his gaze to take in Max, Seren, and Malar. "But the vats were still there."

"Still there?" Malar echoed, leaning forward, wide-eyed.

"They were murdered – locked into the sleeping quarters during programming and left behind...like equipment."

"How...how many?"

"All of them," Hal said, grappling with his emotions. "They were strapped into the sleeping harnesses and left to die."

Seren bowed his head.

"Gods," Malar whispered, sitting back with her arms crossed over her chest.

"They should be retrieved and laid to rest," Hal said, "and everyone should know what the ACAS did to them."

Vivi had called up their helmet feed on her handheld, forwarded it to the correct spot, and passed it to Seren and Malar.

They watched wordlessly, then pushed the handheld back to her.

"There's one more thing you need to see." Hal nodded to Vivi, who pulled up the XO's handheld vid. The effect on

Malar and Seren was obvious as they listened to the XO trying to save her ship's complement of vats.

"I'll need a copy of both of these to show to the First Minister," Malar said.

"Of course," Vivi replied.

"What happened next, Captain Bernon?"

Ty continued narrating their story, ending with Eira being returned to a body by her people and deciding to come back with them. "When her people refused to help us, she decided to return to fight the Coalition. I am sorry for not being initially forthright with you. We...we didn't want to bring her out until we were sure she would be protected." He glanced up, concerned as he met Malar and Seren's gazes. "If you'd rather we leave, we can do that, but I think you should talk to Eira face to face before you make that decision.

"I am willing to meet with you anytime, General," Eira said placidly from the comm.

Max, Seren and Malar looked at the handheld, as if reminded that it was there. "We should… ah… bring her in on this conversation," Malar said, standing. "Can we go now?"

Tyce and the rest of the crew stood up. "Of course. We do ask that Eira's existence stay secret as long as possible." He eyed the three of them as he took up his handheld.

"I think we can agree to that," Malar said. She was well aware of what the reaction to Eira would be if the news was widely known.

"My ship is in Hangar 15," Tyce replied as they followed him.

How will *this meeting go with the humans, Eira?* Runa asked.

The silver AI answered her over their private connection

that was always open between them. *It will go well. I believe the best of them.*

You are confident in your ability to discern their motives? Runa asked.

Yes. If Tyce trusts them then I trust them, Eira replied. *The risk is an acceptable one.*

I hope you are correct, Runa replied.

EIGHTEEN

When they reached the *Loshad's* small bridge, the crew entered first, and then Max, Malar and Seren. Once inside, the three stopped cold, agape at the diminutive, silver form in front of them. Max recovered the use of his voice first. "I'm M-Max Parsen. It's incredible to meet you, Eira," he sputtered.

"I know you, Max," she said, extending her hand to his. "I believe this is the customary human greeting, is it not?"

"Um...yeah," Max replied, shaking her hand tentatively.

"It is good that we should meet face to face at last."

Terra Malar was the next to step forward. "Eira, I am General Terra Malar. I am the leader of the Al-Kimian Defense Force."

"Please let me assure you, I am committed to helping the vats and Al-Kimia fight the Coalition. While the Mudar on my worldship have not yet decided to join the fight, I am committed to my friends. The technology of my people has been used to enslave vat soldiers, and this cannot be allowed. We must face this fight together. I know it may be difficult for you to trust me, but I am willing to do whatever it takes to earn it."

"Your return to us, without any guarantee of safety, says a lot," Seren said, taking her hand next. "How do you plan to help us?"

"I am a trained biologic specialist, and I have seen the way the Coalition has subverted the natural processes of beings like the vats who did not ask for such modifications. We must find a way to neutralize the threat of the vat kill device. We also must neutralize the virus that made the *Harbinger* non-functional and bring the ship back to Al-Kimia to lay the vats to rest."

"We have the same goals," he said, glancing to Seren and Malar.

General Malar spoke, "I would like to speak with Commodore Seren and Dr Parsen a moment."

"Of course," Eira said.

The two officers and Parsen stepped outside the bridge, and Ty could hear the low murmur of voices, but couldn't tell what was being said.

Eira faced Ty. "I have a theory. If we were to somehow rescue the surviving spheres from Haleia-6 and return them to the Mudar, we could possibly convince my people to assist the Al-Kimians. Rescuing me could be an anomaly, but if you were to bring two others to be restored, it might convince the council to assist the Al-Kimians, Betald and the rest of the Edge sooner rather than later," Eira said.

"How long does it normally take them to decide on something?" Ty asked.

"As I have told Hal, it took 80 years to decide to withdraw from the war with the Coalition," Eira said.

After a moment, Hal spoke thoughtfully. "Cap, she's right, you know. Al-Kimia, Noea and Betald are not going to be able to win this war alone."

Ty raised an eyebrow. "You know what this would mean. We'd have to go to the Inside Spiral, into Coalition space and into a lab facility on an ACAS base."

"Sounds like exactly the job for us," Hal grinned.

Ty was about to say how dangerous the idea was when Malar and Seren re-entered the room.

Malar spoke, shaking her head ruefully. "This is...an alliance I never thought to be making. There is much to consider."

"I understand your hesitation," Ty replied.

"However, we cannot turn down an offer from friends," Seren spoke. "As we see it, there are two objectives. Number one, Al-Kimia needs the *Harbinger*. This would be helpful not only for the ship itself, but for the confirmation of how the ACAS has treated vats."

"The story could sway other planets to our cause," Malar said, thoughtfully, "and we are greatly outnumbered. You say you can pinpoint the location of this ship?"

Ty nodded. "The *Harbinger* would be an asset for you, but you're going to need more ships than that." He glanced at Hal, to see if he had thought of the same thing.

"The Pirate Anklav has lots of ships," he said with a grin.

"Will they join our cause?" Malar said.

"Possibly. If they see some benefit to themselves," Seren mused. "They are already helping us ship weapons. I can send Patrin's team to Dela Prime to speak with them."

"We also need to find a way to neutralize the vat kill device," Max picked up. "The man who devised it, Dr Balen, is an evil son-of-a-bitch who will not be afraid to use it. I saw him test it against a..." Max's voice broke, struggling to get the words out. "Against a young vat. It was horrible. If we can foil Dr Balen's plans, I'm in, whatever the risk."

"I know Balen," Hal said in a low voice. "He ran the vat

facility on Chamn-Alpha when I was there. Calling him a son-of-a-bitch barely scratches the surface."

"There's another thing," Ty said, glancing up at them. "The spheres that Max mentioned."

Eira stepped forward, addressing herself to Malar. "General. If it were possible to rescue the intact spheres and return them to my people, they could be restored to a conveyance. I have asked the Mudar to assist the Opposition in resisting Coalition rule, but they hesitate, not knowing if they can trust in the humans' good will. This could go a long way toward convincing them to intervene for Al-Kimia."

"I'd go on a mission to retrieve them," Hal said. "If you leave them in the hands of the ACAS, they will just chop them up to develop some new weapon against the Opposition, vats and nats alike. None of us can afford that. And if there's a kill device protype on Haleia-6, we can steal that as well."

Malar eyed each of them for long moments, then she glanced at Seren. "Seren and I should speak with First Minister Adara. May I have your word that Eira will stay here, on the *Loshad*?"

"If that is what Captain Bernon wants of me, I will certainly follow his orders while you check with your superiors," Eira said. "I am part of his crew, after all."

"Please," Malar said, shifting her gaze to Ty. "I'm sorry, but I must insist."

"We'll all stay here to keep Eira safe."

"Very good. Thank you." Malar stepped forward and held out a hand. "I appreciate you for confiding in us. I hope to have some news for you soon."

Ty shook her hand. "The Coalition's left its mark on each one of us, so you can trust we believe in Al-Kimia's cause," Ty said, glancing at Hal, who agreed with a nod. "The Coalition has no friends here, General."

"I understand. Thank you. We'll be in touch soon."

THE RAPTOR'S bridge displays cast a light over each face hovering above them. Dai was navigating the little ship, excited at the challenge of running the blockade once again as they returned from Coren. "We're coming within range of ACAS sensors," she said, glancing up to see Patrin on weapons and Kat on the upper platform on comms. Lane manned the other data station on the right side of the bridge.

"Lane, pull up the distribution of ships in the blockade."

A holo appeared in the middle of the room, projected from a console. Al-Kimian space was mapped out, around which they could see the real-time movement of ACAS ships. Patrin joined her as Dai walked around it, then pointed at a certain area.

"What about there?" She pointed to an empty space, a path through that only had one ship nearby. "We might be quick enough to slip through."

"Yeah, that's a heavy cruiser. It won't be quick enough to catch the *Raptor*," Patrin said. "That might be exactly the place."

EIGHTEEN MINUTES LATER, the mood grew tense. Dai was watching the movement of the ships as she flew them closer. When it became clear she was making a run for the line, the ACAS cruiser reversed course.

Lane spoke from sensors. "ACAS ship is coming for us, Cap. Advancing on our position."

"Got it." Dai could feel the rush when it started, and she allowed herself a grim smile as she threw everything into the engines. Speed was going to be essential in breaking the line, and even with every bit of velocity they could muster, she still couldn't be sure they wouldn't take some hits.

"We're almost there, Dai," Patrin called.

As soon as they came within range, the cruiser fired across their bow.

"Typical blockader," Lane snorted. "They're sensing we'll be a quick prize."

"Screw that," Dai said, the rush thundering in her blood. She'd been a ship's mechanic her whole life, longing for, yet unable to fly the ships she worked on until she'd become a free vat. Now no one could keep her from flying. It was everything to her, and she liked it better than the rush. The ship began to shake while they continued to pass the heavy cruiser at a high rate of speed. "Take the shot when you have it, Patrin," Dai said as the cruiser scored a lucky hit that rocked them. Now the race was on.

"Yes, Ma'am," he replied. Dai could see he was enjoying this, and it made her experience a surge of confidence.

"Direct hit!" Lane called.

"That's okay," Dai murmured, trying to coax extra speed out of the *Raptor*. "Come on, baby. I know you've got a little more in you," she prayed to the gods of speed and dexterity, something that all pilots must have done since the dawn of space travel. Her voice was a soft litany that could barely be heard above the screaming engines. "Don't give up on me. Don't give up on me..."

But there was no need for her prayers – her bird was flying like an eagle, Dai realized as she dove away from the cruiser's guns.

Her good mood didn't last long; she was fast but not fast enough to escape damage, she realized as the ship rocked as it suffered a glancing blow from a rail cannon. "Fuck, looks like they went and pulled out the big guns, fellas!"

"We're being hailed," Kat called.

"Ignore the bastards," Dai bit her bottom lip as she mentally urged her ship to fly, fly, fly.

"Thirty seconds to Al-Kimian space," Lane said.

Dai pushed it, and the ship began to shudder and groan around them. They took one final hit to the rear shielding as they broke the line. Then it was all shouts and whooping as they realized they had made it.

The ACAS cruiser broke off their pursuit. Dai was the first to settle back in at the pilot's chair with a sigh of relief. "Setting a course for Al-Kimia. We made it, guys."

AFTER THEY'D LANDED Kat was packing her ready bag in one of the sleeping pods when Patrin found her.

"I'm getting my things together..." she said.

They had stayed behind to help Dai with the post flight checklist. Patrin knew that both he and Kat needed to eat something and try to ramp down. His blood was up—the rush was still humming in him, and he knew it would be a few hours before he could sleep. She had to be feeling the same way.

"Care for some company? I'm gonna be awake a while, yet."

She turned and smiled. "Maybe. We could share a couple of meal bars."

"Yeah. My meal bars or yours?" A couple of weeks ago, she'd been assigned to quarters in the same adjacent complex where Patrin and Seren stayed.

"Hmm..." She bit her bottom lip. "You decide."

Twenty minutes later, they reached his quarters. Eager and hungry for each other, they forwent the meal bars and moved into something that sated a deeper need. "Ah, gods..." Kat moaned as she leaned into him. He had pushed her up against the wall and his hands were keeping busy as he kissed her neck. "You sure about this?"

"Hells, yes," Patrin mumbled into the skin between her neck and shoulder where his teeth grazed. "Why?"

"My past record sucks."

"What if I like to take my chances?" His hands slid from the dangerous swell of her breasts to the hem of her shirt. He tugged it over her head and let his gaze caress the pale curves of her body. He hauled his own shirt over his head and growled when she ghosted her hands over his skin.

"You might be making a big mistake," she said, thinking of Jakob.

"Don't worry about your past. There's nothing but right now, Kat," he whispered as he pulled her in.

Finally, they reached the bedroom. He stopped by the bed as she tugged the tie from her hair, and it fell around her like a dark wave in a night sea. Her brown eyes flashed as her hands began to work at his belt. "Just don't say I didn't warn you," she said with a hungry smile.

THEY WAITED all day but heard nothing from Seren or Malar. Hal was impatient and edgy, so he'd retreated to the cargo bay to train. Moving his body helped the worry smooth out.

He hoped that Seren and Malar would be able to work it out where they could conduct a mission to Haleia-6. If Eira's people were being held in an ACAS facility, it was paramount they be rescued. There was no telling what evil ways the ACAS doctors could twist Mudar technology to keep their hold on the star systems they already had and prevent vats from ever being free.

Free. He paused a moment in his workout to get some water and glanced across the way where a group of four vats were unloading a cargo vessel. He was freer than they were, he realized. No matter if he had five extra years or ten, he would live longer than they would. While he was glad he'd undergone Eira's procedure, it was a lonely feeling to realize he didn't belong anywhere anymore. He was not a vat anymore, but he wasn't a nat either. He was between them both but belonging to neither.

He glanced back at the bag, and resumed a stance, working through combinations long embedded in his mind by ACAS training routines. Despite Eira's modifications, the routines were still there when he reached out for them and let his body slip into the preprogrammed moves, which left his mind free to think. He wondered if the Mudar would assist the Opposition if they brought back the surviving spheres from the ACAS base. Would they grant the other vats the same gift he'd been given by Eira? How many vats would give up the rush for longer life if given the chance?

He had no clue. The decision would have been difficult for him if not for Ty and Veevs. He'd wanted to keep the rush to protect them and had the opportunity come a year ago, he would've turned it down flat. But the way Ty, Beryl and Veevs cared about him and would miss him if he died...that was what had finally tipped the scales. Maybe vats that had a chance for a longer life would find a reason to live like he had – instead of throwing their lives away chasing the rush.

His timing had gotten off, he realized as his thoughts turned back to the heavy bag in front of him. He focused, trying to use some of Ty's meditations so he could get his head into training. It would be more important than ever that he be stronger and faster than an opponent since he wouldn't be able to rush. He would need every advantage in a fight.

He began to run through the routines again. The repetition helped him focus and was soothing in a way. *Double jab*

– *cross – left body shot – low kick*. He was dimly aware that he was zoning out again with the repeated patterns. He threw different combinations for a long time, letting his mind coast on autopilot, working on the sequences etched into his brain.

Unsure how long had passed, he moved around the bag and saw Vivi coming over.

"Hey," He paused to reach to the side for his towel and water bottle as the patterns in his mind faded. "What's up? Have we heard anything yet?"

"Not yet. You've been working out a while, so I wanted to check on you."

"I'm good." He took a drink. "Just punching the bag and thinking, you know."

"What about?"

"About the other vats. If they'd give up the rush for more time if they had the chance." He took a seat on the floor and began to remove his handwraps. She sat beside him.

"Are you sorry you went through with it?"

"Nah," he shrugged. "I'm trying to figure it all out." He paused a moment, unsure if he should share everything he was thinking. *Just tell her*, he thought. "I'm…I'm not sure where I fit anymore."

"What do you mean?"

"I'm not like them, anymore," he gestured across the way. "And I'm not a nat. I…I don't really fit in anywhere."

She thought a moment. "Does being different bother you?"

He let out a heavy sigh. "No…yes…I- I'm not sure. In the ACAS we spend so much time trying to be…like every other vat out there. There's a sense of…of belonging, you know." He shifted his gaze to her and saw her earnest expression. She understood him just like Ty. She *cared* about him. It did something to his heart that he was only starting to understand. "I'm not saying I regret anything. I've never been much for regrets. I just…it's an adjustment, I guess."

"Hal, I can't tell you I know what you're going through because that would be a lie," she said. "But I'm here for you when you need to talk. And if it helps, you should know that you fit with us. You belong on this crew with Ty, Eira, Beryl and me. I don't want you anywhere else but by my side."

He nodded slowly, sensing a weird tightness in his chest that he wasn't used to. He wanted to hug her but settled for taking her hand. "It helps, Veevs. There's nowhere else I'd rather be."

"Good because I wasn't planning on letting you go," she grinned, leaning against him.

"I love you, Vivi."

She drew back, surprised.

He went on. "You don't have to love me back. I mean, I'm probably going to muck it up anyway because I don't know how to do the things nats are supposed to do in a relationship, but I wanted you to know how I feel."

"Hal…I love you too."

Now, it was his turn to be surprised.

"I didn't tell you because I wanted to give you time to think about how you felt," she said shyly.

"When did you know?"

She shrugged. "After the first squads game we played, I knew I had feelings for you. Then when we were on Chamn-Alpha…that's when I was sure I loved you."

He pulled her to him with a gentle touch on her cheek and they kissed until there were catcalls from a few soldiers in the hangar. They broke apart laughing gently. The soldiers that had been kidding them moved on.

"Don't worry about mucking it up. Look at my previous relationship. I own the market on screw-ups," she said, standing up and taking his hand. "But this time, we're going to get it right together."

Ty got the word from command the next morning. They were going to be allowed to stay on base, provided that Eira remain on the *Loshad* for now. Seren and Max would explain the objectives and together with the *Loshad's* crew, they would come up with a plan for the Haleia-6 mission to be approved by Terra Malar and the First Minister. Since Eira was not allowed out, the best plan was for Seren and Max to join them on Ty's ship, at least to start out with.

The first meeting took place in the common area. Max had brought them all breakfast – dark Al-Kimian coffee and lightly sweetened flaky pastries drizzled with zeebee honey. They dug in. When everyone had something to eat, Seren sat back.

"So, we have three objectives, just as you laid them out the other day, Captain Bernon. We must find out more about the vat kill device and obtain one if possible, rescue any Mudar consciousness spheres that may still survive and get the Anklav involved in the movement. Terra Malar will handle the acquisition of the *Harbinger*." He looked to Eira. "If you will help develop a removal protocol for the virus, we would be extremely grateful. With the way things are going between Al-Kimia and the Coalition, it might be better to go retrieve it sooner, rather than later."

"I can program nanites to go in and restore the computers," Eira said. "Your people will only have to release the nanites at the computer port to start the process."

"Are there any other items that need repair?" Seren asked, making a note.

Vivi spoke up. "A full restart will most likely require more extensive work. You'll need large auxiliary power units until you can get the ship's drive restarted."

Hal chimed in. "You'll also need a few teams to repair minor hull damage that the ship would have suffered over the years, plus recovering the bodies of the vats will be...an undertaking in itself."

Seren was somber. "I will send a full crew."

"I can accompany them if you wish," Eira said.

"No. I do not think we can risk that," Seren spoke up.

"You can trust her. Eira has been with us for months now. She is in every way a part of my crew. She's had multiple chances to kill all of us, and yet she's helped us at every turn," Ty said with a fond smile for the Mudar. He glanced down at his leg, still braced. "Your doctors on Al-Kimia have told me that I would never walk without braces again, yet here I am almost walking on my own, thanks to Eira."

"What do you mean?"

"Eira used nanites...her nanites to rebuild the severed nerves in my back," Ty glanced to Eira's finely sculpted features. She regarded him with a beatific smile. "As time goes on, I may be able to leave this other brace behind. Perhaps that will explain how we can place our trust in her so freely."

"Gods..." Max marveled. "Is this for real?"

"Yes. Should we tell...all of it?" Ty asked, glancing to Hal and Eira. They agreed.

"If it will help you trust her," Hal spoke up, "you should know that she risked her life for me too. She used her neural nanites to block my rush response."

There was a beat in which no one spoke, then Max let out a breath. "Holy gods," he said, sitting back in his chair in shock. Seren glanced at Max, and Max drew the conclusions for him. "Seren, it means he won't die from adrenaline fatigue. How? D-did you deactivate his interface somehow?"

Eira shook her head. "I used my neural nanites to inactivate the node controlling his adrenaline."

"However, the procedure caused an inflammatory response in Hal's body, and Eira had to use so many nanites to fight it that she was no longer able to maintain her neural pattern in the *Loshad*. She began to decay," Beryl said.

"We barely got her back to her people in time to save her," Ty added.

"If we can convince my people to come assist the Edge, there may be a chance to refine the process I used with Hal and save many vats from an early death," Eira said. "Hal has asked me to do this, and I have promised to try."

Seren sat back, obviously stunned into silence.

"You can trust her," Hal said.

Max rubbed his face. "I haven't had nearly enough coffee for this," he said, getting up to go into the galley for a refill.

"It is not trust that is my concern. Now that we know all of this, we do not need to take a risk that Eira might fall into someone else's hands," Seren said. "If your people do not help us, Eira, you may be the only hope for the Edge's vats to avoid an early death."

"I understand," Eira said, bowing her head.

"In addition, because she is so important, we would like Eira to stay on Al-Kimia," Seren said.

Ty glanced to Eira, and she gave him a curt nod. "This is acceptable to me," she said.

"I will send you a list of needed supplies to retrieve the *Harbinger*, if you would permit me, Commodore," Vivi said, furiously typing with both thumbs on her device.

"Certainly," Seren moved to set his comm to receive it.

"This brings us to the next item on the agenda," Ty said. "The Haleia-6 facility. We know *what* we must do there – acquire any remaining Mudar spheres, as well as try to get a vat kill device – but we need some intel inside the facility so we can figure out *how*."

"It's an underground complex with four levels. I'll map what I remember and send it to you," Max said.

Hal was making notes on his own handheld. "If we go, we're going to have to have spotless ID's. Veevs, can you help with that?"

She shook her head. "That's ACAS encryption. I can crack a handheld or even most corporate stuff, but military's a whole other level of badass."

Hal glanced to Seren and Max.

"You'll need an identity that they can confirm in ACAS databases," Max said. "I was with Dr Balen and still had my ID double checked before they even let me go down."

"I was afraid of that," Hal said.

Seren leaned forward. "I will look into what the Al-Kimians can do for us in that area. In the meantime, keep thinking. We will want to send the *Harbinger* team and the Anklav team out as soon as possible."

"What about the delegation to the pirate Anklav?" Hal asked. "Patrin will handle that?"

"Yes. He and the crew of the *Raptor* would be best to send. I will talk with him as soon as possible," Seren stood.

"It's probably a 50/50 at best, but it's worth a shot," Hal said.

"I agree. We will begin planning and be ready to move soon."

"I'll walk you out," Ty offered.

When Seren and Max got to the cargo bay, Ty paused. "Look. I see the need to protect Eira. I certainly don't want the ACAS to have any opportunity to take her into custody. You'll protect her here?"

"Of course. I will find a place for her to be kept as safe as possible while you are gone."

"She could stay at my lab," Max said. "It's a secure facility and we can work together to try and find a way to replicate what she's done with Hal."

"That will be important work, Dr. Parsen." Seren turned to Ty. "We are indeed fortunate to have you on my side. I knew you were a good person when I met you."

"How?" Ty said. "I mean you have more than enough reason not to trust anyone, much less a nat."

"It was in how you treated Hal during our meeting aboard my ship," Seren said. "You care for him and the rest of your crew. It says everything about you, Tyce." He held out a hand and shook Ty's. "You can depend on me to keep Eira's secret. The fewer people that know, the better. If I do not see you before you lift off, please know that all my hopes go with you."

"Thank you," Ty nodded, watching Seren and Max go.

NINETEEN

Ty met Vivi in the galley late the next morning so they could strategize. "Hey, Max sent me a map of the Haleia-6 complex. I'll send it to you." He tapped on his handheld and forwarded the information to Vivi. "Where's Hal?"

"He told me he'll be working on one of the *Loshad's* Gpods," Vivi said, downloading the complex map into her handheld and her tecker node.

Ty threw a hologram up of the complex so they could study it together.

"It's underground," Vivi said thoughtfully.

"Yeah." It was bad news. "Limited ingress and egress. We're going to need a good cover story and the right fake ID's. If things go wrong, it's going to be tricky to get out of there."

Vivi bit her bottom lip. "I've been thinking about that. I might have...a way to get us into the ACAS databases. Remember when you took me aboard ship?"

Ty was slightly unsure what she was referring to, but he remembered how they'd stopped two guys from kidnapping her. "Yeah?"

"You know I was running away from a bad relationship at the time. My ex, Noah, was keeping secrets from me. What you don't know is I found out he was a member of Echo."

"Wait. You mean the hacking group, Echo?" Ty asked. Echo was one of the three main hacker entities in the galaxy. Where the Incogs hacked to steal identities and the Nils stole scrill, Echo was a bit more complicated. They claimed to be hacking for the good of the people. For example, Ty knew they claimed to steal from the Coalition's corporations to redistribute the wealth to the needy, but no one had ever been able to find proof that they actually gave the money away. They weren't known as being particularly dangerous, but not many people knew much about them at all.

"Yeah. I might be able to comm Noah and get him to put us in contact with Echo if he hasn't changed his second comm number. We could see if they could try to hack the database from a distance. If anyone could get in, it would be Echo."

"That may not be a good idea," Ty sat back, his arms crossed over his chest.

"What? Why not?"

"I don't want you to have to deal with that skeeze again." Ty shook his head.

"Tyce, that's sweet, but I won't even have to see him. I'll get him to contact Echo for us. Then we can take it from there. I'm willing to risk it for Eira's people who are trapped in that ACAS facility. And if they have a vat kill device…we can't afford not to do everything in our power to get there."

Ty frowned, but then he shrugged helplessly. They had to try. "Look, I'll check with Seren. If Al-Kimia can't get in, then we'll try it," he sighed. "I don't want to be overprotective, but you're not just crew to me…you're family. Do not contact or meet with this guy without Hal or me there. That's an order."

"I understand. Thanks, Ty," she said, giving him a quick side hug.

LATER THAT DAY Vivi was back in the common area, using her node connection with the computer to view Max's schematic from all angles. There were only three buildings on the surface: the vat barracks, the hangar, and a tiny circular building that contained the elevator that led down to the main part of the complex. Labs were on the first, second and third levels. Max had thought there was some sort of computer room near the secure storage for Mudar artifacts, but he couldn't be sure because they hadn't gone in there. With a few moves of her hand, she added a tentative sketch of where Max had said it was.

Ty's footsteps startled her from her work. "Oh!" she blinked as she saw him through the shimmering hologram. She tapped her node to deactivate her display.

"Where's Hal?" she asked. "I thought he was with you."

"He went to the rec hangar. I think he needed a break by himself for a while. I'm sure being cooped up for four months with all of us has been a strain," Ty said.

"Yeah, he's said the long hauls are the hardest for him," Vivi replied. She turned toward Ty as he sat beside her. "But...he's opened up a bit. He told me he's feeling...a little out of place."

"Because of Eira's procedure?" Ty asked.

"Yeah. He said he didn't regret doing it, but he doesn't know where he fits anymore. I reassured him that he fit with us."

Ty nodded thoughtfully. "Sounds like you said the right things."

"There's a little more. He said he loved me." She bit her lip nervously. "I told him how I felt too."

Ty grinned. "That's great," he said. "I'm happy for both of you."

"Yeah?" she said self-consciously.

"You've been the best thing that ever happened to him, Vivi."

"Second best. His friendship with you came first," she reminded him.

"I think you're overestimating my impact," he chuckled. "I came to find you because I heard back from Seren. Al-Kimia is not going to be able to break into the ACAS database. Apparently, they've been trying for months. So, even though I'm not wild about this whole Echo idea, you're up."

She pulled out her handheld. "I'll send him a message."

Noah, she wrote. *I need you to contact me. It's really important. Vivian.* She signed her full name – Noah had never called her by her nickname. That was for her friends. She'd decided last night that she'd keep him at a distance with a business-like demeanor if he did answer her.

After sending the message, she tucked her handheld away. "I'll fill Hal in on what we're planning when he gets back."

"Uh, yeah. I've been thinking about that." Ty rubbed the back of his neck. "You might want to leave out the fact that this guy is your ex."

"Why?"

"Hal's a little bit angry at Noah."

"Oh." It made sense. "We did talk about him before."

"Yeah. Hal told me he would be more than happy to pound Noah's face into a bloody mess. And I'm none too fond of this asshole either," he pointed out.

"Aww. That's sweet." She elbowed him gently. Then her handheld beeped.

"That was quick," Vivi said, surprised. She dug it out and saw an unfamiliar comm designation but answered it anyway.

Noah, her ex, was dark-haired, with dark eyes, a straight nose and chiseled jaw. They were model good looks, and it was obvious he knew it as she saw him smile, revealing his line of perfect white teeth.

"Vivian," he said, a smirk on his features. "I knew you'd come crawling back eventually..."

She took a deep breath. "Noah, I'm not coming back. I'm calling because I need a favor-"

It was obvious that her reply wasn't what he'd expected. "A...a favor? Are you fucking kidding me? After what you pulled?"

"I need to get in touch with your friends," she said.

"Is this a secure comm?"

"It's secure," she assured him.

"What makes you think that I'd do anything for you? You ruined a six-month op with your call to Bromcorp. Explain why you thought that was a fucking brilliant idea? The way I see it, you got what was coming to you."

Vivi sighed. "Look. We don't need to rehash all that. I've put it behind me, and you should too. I need to get in touch with your friends."

"What if I don't want to put it behind me?" he said.

Vivi sensed Ty stiffen beside her. She put out a hand to stop him from saying anything.

"Don't be an idiot. Are you going to do this or not?"

"What do you need to tell them?"

"I'll share that with them. Your friends will be very interested in what I have to say. It concerns certain governmental operations they may be interested in interrupting."

He raised an eyebrow at her. "And why would they want to believe a snitch like you?"

She tightened her grip on Ty's arm, hoping he'd understand what she was saying: *wait*. "You'd be surprised what I've been up to, Noah. And your friends will really be interested. What do they have to lose in contacting me? We both know they will be able to shield their location, so there's no risk there."

"Fine. I'll let them decide if you're worth their time," he said. Then he cut the call abruptly.

Vivi sighed and glanced to Ty. "What a blast," she sighed tiredly.

"Yeah. He sounded like a real piece of work," Ty said.

"He was different when I first met him," Vivi mused. "He could be really charismatic when he tried. He usually got what he wanted with it."

"He tried to blame you for his mistakes. What a piece of shit."

"Don't worry. I know who's to blame," she said confidently. "Ty, I'm not that same scared girl you guys rescued in that bar anymore."

"No, you're definitely not," he said. "I'm proud of you, Vivi. Asking you to work for me was one of my better ideas."

"Think so?"

"I know it," he replied.

TWENTY

Once they had returned from Coren and settled in, Patrin met Seren at his quarters the next afternoon.

"Take a seat." Seren took a chair in the living area and gestured to the other one. "I've been wanting to speak with you for a while now."

"Sir?"

"Very likely I won't make it to see the end of this conflict..."

"Sir, you can't know that-" Patrin interrupted.

Seren raised a hand. "Peace. This is something that has begun to weigh on my mind. It is most likely that you will be leading once I'm gone, and I want to make sure that you continue to help both nats and vats join our cause."

Patrin nodded, an uncharacteristic lump in his throat. He cared about Seren, more than he could put into words. The old man was the best friend he'd had since being released from service. Seren had given him direction and purpose at a time when he'd needed it badly and life without the old man was unimaginable.

"Always take care of ours," Seren repeated. "It's what

makes us different than the Coalition." As he spoke, he looked down at his own hands contemplatively. After a moment, he raised his gaze back to Patrin. "You should know that I have put you up for a captaincy."

"You...you have?" Patrin was surprised.

"The *Hesperus* will be yours when I am gone. It's a good ship and will serve you as well as it has served me. Her crew will be loyal to you, and I'm comfortable you will lead them like I would."

"Why does this feel like you are saying goodbye?" Patrin asked. Since joining the Al-Kimians, he and Seren had developed a close bond. Only since Seren's last bout with sickness had the elderly vat begun to focus on what would happen after he died. Patrin didn't know how to handle these conversations.

"I won't go on forever. When I am gone, there must be a smooth transition." His voice was calm and even, the opposite of Patrin's increasingly emotional tone.

"Sir, I'm not ready for this..." He'd been on Seren's crew ever since he'd been a station rat. Finding himself on Omicron, he'd chased the rush by fighting with anyone who challenged him at night and working during the day for the station, repairing micro-perforations in the station's hull, until Seren had shown up and given him a chance on the *Hesperus*. The thought of being without the old man made Patrin feel a sense of panic. "I've done my best, but command? I'm not sure I'm ready for that..."

"You're ready because I made you ready. As I've said, I won't go on forever and you need to prepare yourself. I don't intend on going anywhere anytime soon, though. We have a few vital operations in play."

Ok, this was a better subject to talk about. Patrin pulled himself together. "What kind of operations, sir?"

"Maybe the most important of the war. Number one: Tyce

Bernon and his crew have located an ACAS cruiser...specifically, a 100-year-old cruiser from the war. It's drifting in space past the border. I'm sending a crew to retrieve it."

Patrin was surprised about the ship. "How badly is it damaged?"

"It isn't. It was disabled by a Mudar virus. And..." he paused, struggling with his next words. His voice dropped. "The vats on board were all murdered by the ACAS. Locked in their sleeping quarters and placed in programming mode as life support failed. They are still there."

"What do you mean? How many..."

"All of them."

"They let them die?"

He nodded, then gave Patrin a minute to compose himself. "When we have the evidence, we will show the Spiral what the Coalition has done, but for now, we are focused on recovery."

Seren went on. "You should know about the other missions as well. Tyce Bernon and crew are planning to go to Haleia-6. There is a lab facility there that may contain the kill device the doctor told us about. They are going to get into the facility and bring a prototype back."

"That's...that's going to be difficult at best, and damn near impossible at worst."

"Yet, I believe they want to try, and the mission would be valuable. Your job is just as valuable."

"Are you sending me with them?"

"No. You'll be going on the *Raptor* to Dela Prime to contact the pirate Anklav. The Coalition will be winding up to attack the Edge. We need the Anklav to see that keeping the Coalition out of the Edge will benefit them as well as us. More ACAS in the Edge will hurt their business."

"They are not going to throw in with us," Patrin said. "Their leadership is too fractured." The Anklav had been led by a man named Tobias Guare 15 years ago. By all accounts, Guare had been a master at negotiation and had pulled together the disconnected crime and smuggling syndicates to function under the Anklav banner. He'd been murdered by an unknown assailant, and the alliance had fallen by the wayside, with each faction reverting to function on their own. It was said the different groups met to discuss issues a few times a year, but there was no clear leadership anymore.

"Maybe they won't. But there's a possibility. If they can be made to see that the Edge is in this together...perhaps they might join us."

"You should come with me," Patrin said suddenly. "You're so persuasive at getting people to work with us." During the early months of the movement, Seren had tirelessly worked at pulling vats and nats together and making the alliance with Al-Kimia. There was something almost supernatural about the way he did it.

"Not this time. I am needed here," Seren said. "This is your operation, Patrin. I know you will make me proud."

"Yes sir. I'll try my best," Patrin said, but he was not so sure.

VIVI HAD BEGUN to get worried about Hal because he hadn't returned yet, even after Max and Eira had met that afternoon. Ty wanted to talk over their part of the plans after dinner, and so, she'd come to find him. When she arrived at the rec hangar, she was greeted with all the noise and activity of a barracks full of vats and Al-Kimians – both men and women.

Was he still here or had he gone somewhere else? She headed for the entrance, where she was stopped by a solider.

"ID ma'am?" he asked.

Max had brought them base badges this morning. She turned the badge so that the soldier could see it – he'd obviously noticed her civilian clothes. The color of her badge marked her as a civilian in assistance to the Al-Kimian Defense Force and would get her access wherever she needed. There were a lot of civilian vessels that Seren had recruited as "friends" of Al-Kimia, and those people who were verified and working out of the base had a special blue ID.

"My name's Valjean."

"I'm Sergeant Brody."

"I'm looking for Hal Cullen. He's taller than me, blond hair-"

"Oh yes, ma'am. This way." The officer let her into the hangar. It was sort of a common area with a feed display, seating, several squads boards and weights/workout equipment. In the last corner was a ring.

It was louder in here, and she could hear the grunts and impacts of a fight going on. There was a group around the ring. Inside the ropes was a very familiar set of tattoos dressed in headgear, thin hand wraps and shin guards. Her stomach clenched as she remembered the last time she'd found Hal fighting for a crowd like this. She stepped forward quickly while Brody hurried to keep up.

Hal was fighting bare footed and bare chested, soaked with sweat. His opponent was a nat. As she watched a moment, Vivi realized Hal was sparring, not fighting for the whims of the crowd. She could hear the steady sound of his voice as he instructed his opponent, and it was obvious the young solider needed the tutorial. Despite knowing what was coming, he was unable to avoid the combinations Hal was throwing at him.

Hal used a left head hook, followed by a right low kick that caused the soldier to crumple to one knee. The solider held up a hand, and Hal backed off a moment, allowing the nat to get his bearings. They said something to each other, and Hal grinned and extended a hand to help the nat up. Then they began to go at it once more.

"He's a good fighter," Brody said. "I've been watching him train a few of the younger Al-Kimian soldiers today."

"He's pretty amazing," she said. "Hey. I notice you're not from Al-Kimia." His accent was a little different than the other Al-Kimians she'd met.

"No, ma'am, I'm not. I deserted the ACAS, not long before the blockade went up. I was stationed at Chamn-Alpha for a while, then transferred to Rinal Station."

"Why did you leave the ACAS?" Vivi asked.

"Well, one day, I was supposed to take a shuttle out to pick up a VIP from a cruiser, but I kept on going. I can't explain it, but I just...decided I couldn't be a part of that anymore."

"Are you glad you left?"

"Yeah. Best decision I made."

"Veevs?" Hal called from the ring, finally noticing her as he'd come to his corner to grab his water bottle. His sparring partner approached and gave Hal a pat on the back before he left. Sensing there was going to be a break, the crowd drifted away to other parts of the room. After saying goodbye to Brody, Vivi approached the side where Hal had taken a seat.

"Hey. You didn't answer your comm."

"Oh. Sorry. I took it off to spar. I needed to burn off some energy, and I guess I lost track of time. Everything okay?"

"Yeah. Ty wants to meet about the mission after dinner. He wanted to make sure you'd be there."

"Oh. Sure," he said, turning around to gather his gear. She climbed up onto the steps around the ring, to be face to face, and he turned back around with a conspiratorial grin. "Hey... wanna go a few rounds?"

She eyed the ring, interested...it was certainly better than sparring in the cargo hold.

"C'mon. You know you want to," he said.

She gave in easy. "Okay," she said, stepping through the ropes.

She took off her boots and strapped on the protective headgear, which was a little different than the one she normally wore aboard the *Loshad*. He pulled out a new pair of handwraps from his bag and tossed them to her. She wrapped her hands and wrists the way he'd shown her when they'd first started sparring. When he went to get a pair of shin guards, she took a second to glance around them.

Several people in the common area were now standing around in twos and threes, watching the ring. She stretched her legs and bounced on her toes a couple of times, before stretching the rest of her body. She knew that although Hal was a careful teacher and watched for errors or mistakes that could lead to injury, he wouldn't take it easy on her because people were watching.

"Ready?" he asked when she was suited up.

"Maybe?" she said, feeling a little nervous at the spectators.

Hal leaned in, grabbed her headgear and pulled her forehead to his. "Focus on me. Not them, Veevs. We're the only two in the room."

She nodded gratefully.

"Let's go." He gave her a tap on the side of the headgear as they broke and got ready. She put her guard up and saw him nod subtly, then he threw a jab/uppercut combination. She blocked both, and responded with a left push kick, right round kick combo.

As they kept moving about the ring, she realized he kept challenging her with more complicated moves as she fought to keep up. He kept her constantly on the outer edge of her skills, so that she'd have no time to think about the audience they'd attracted. She was tiring, and he noticed – he gave her a glancing blow to the headgear, something simple she could dodge, and she did. But when she ducked, her cross caught him hard on the jaw. He bounced back, shaking it off.

"Gods! Sorry, didn't mean to land it like that," she said, dropping her guard. He didn't reply but used the opportunity to leg sweep her and grapple her to the mat.

They were both breathing heavily, as he forced her into a head and arm choke, but then he let the hold go before she even had a chance to tap out. He stayed pinning her to the ground, however, and his pleasant weight and closeness made her body react with a flood of heat. "Don't ever drop your guard, Veevs," he said in a low voice meant only for her.

"Not fair. You didn't teach me that move yet," she said teasingly as she looked up into his blue eyes.

"I know I didn't," he said. "I might have taught you everything you know, but I haven't taught you everything I know." He leaned in and kissed her deeply. It was a heated, hungry kiss at first, that dissolved into both of them laughing at the catcalls of the regiment—reminding them of their audience.

Hal switched gears, bounded up, then pulled her to her feet, and they took a bow to claps and cheers. "You impressed them," Hal murmured in her ear as he helped her off with her headgear, and they got ready to go.

There were several whistles, cheers and pats on the back as they made their way to the door. Apparently, Hal had made a lot of friends who were now looking at Vivi with obvious respect. It felt good, she thought. Like after their mission to save Max. She'd felt like a real Edger--like she could handle any danger the universe would throw at her. The confidence was intoxicating, and she took a moment to luxuriate in it.

"That was...amazing," Vivi said. "I mean the crowd, the energy...you."

He caught her hand as they walked back to the *Loshad's*

hangar. "Yeah. Guess it's one of the reasons I used to like club fighting. Having an audience takes things to another level."

"Do you miss it?"

He shrugged. "I've got other priorities now. Like you," he said as he glanced sidelong at her.

"Yeah?" she squeezed his hand.

"Of course," he responded.

Kat settled herself down to wait on Patrin. He'd had some sort of meeting earlier, but he'd asked her to dinner at his place at 1800. About five minutes ago, he had sent her a message that he would be late and told her she should go on in. She remembered his hab unit code but didn't key it. Something about going in there without him felt wrong. It was as if she didn't trust herself in his place alone.

But waiting was boring. She was about to send him a message on his comm and see him later, when he came around the corner.

"Hi," he said. "I told you to go in."

"I know. You're late," she replied.

"I brought food," he held up two containers.

She playfully pretended she was reluctant to let it go. "You might be forgiven. It all depends…"

He handed her the boxes, then keyed the door. "Depends on what?"

"On what's inside," she said, peeking. "Oh yeah. Guess I have to forgive you now. You brought Keshen food?"

"One of the mess cooks is a nat from Keshen. He sets me up from time to time." Patrin took the food back from her as the door slid open.

"I can see now that there are going to be some benefits to hanging out with you," Kat smiled, following him in.

"What? The meal bars weren't enough of a benefit?" Patrin teased. He turned to get utensils, and when he turned back, she was right there.

"Oh, they were a benefit alright." She put an arm around him, fisted a hand in his hair and pulled him to her. They kissed until they had to break apart to breathe.

"Why do we always end up like this?" she panted as he nipped her neck with his teeth.

"Because you make me hungry," he growled, tossing the forks onto the counter and pressing her back against it. He yanked her tee up over her head and ran his fingers over the black bra she wore, then to her hips where he worked at the button of her pants, and she knew he was hers.

AFTERWARDS, they ate dinner sitting on the floor in the living area. The two of them shared bites from each food container as Patrin told stories of his time on Omicron before he'd met Seren. Kat found herself laughing at his jokes, as they finished the Keshen food and polished off the bottle of jet juice Patrin had brought out of the freezer.

"I'm going to miss you," Patrin said as he poured the last of the liquor into their cups. "I got another mission today."

"Where are you going?" she asked, sliding over to sit beside him.

"Can't say. Mission security," he answered.

"Aww, seriously? Can I go?" she asked, her pupils large in the dim lighting.

"Kat...the crew's set already. There's something different I need you to do."

She nodded slowly, sensing his seriousness. "Yeah?"

"I need you to keep an eye on Commodore Seren," Patrin said. "He works too hard, and he's..."

"Getting older," Kat finished.

"Yeah. You're being put on temporary assignment, assisting him. I'll be gone...for at least a week, maybe two."

She frowned. "I'll miss you."

"I know. Me too. But when I come back...we'll be able to see where all this goes with us." At her frown, he leaned down to catch her gaze. "I really want to see where this goes with you."

"Me too," she said softly, still frowning. There was thunder in the back of her mind. It hung in her thoughts, like an omen of things to come. It would start with his leaving, that much she was sure of. "When...when do you have to go?"

"Day after tomorrow."

"Good. That gives me time," she said distantly.

"Time for what?" he asked. She blinked at him a moment and realized she'd spoken her thought out loud. Her lips curved in a smile as she crawled into his lap and straddled him.

"Time to remind you why you need to hurry your ass and get back here," she said, kissing him. She managed to coax a grin onto her face, although it was the last thing she wanted to do.

TWENTY-ONE

THE NEXT MORNING, TY WOKE EARLY, DID HIS THERAPY exercises on his legs, and decided to try to go without bracing his weak leg. He'd been working hard to build up his strength, and with their impending mission, he knew that now was the time to test out his ability.

His muscles were tight, so he made his way down the hall slowly, trailing his fingers along the wall in case he stumbled. He limped into the galley, his right leg dragging, but he was altogether pleased with being able to get that far.

He found Eira in the common area. She was holding her hand over a silver ball, the size of a ball bearing.

"What are you doing?"

"These are nanites. I'm programming them to remove the Mudar virus from the *Harbinger*." She looked up at him. "Tyce, you are without your brace." Her silver optics examined him.

"Yeah. Thought I'd try it out. I need to start developing more strength in it..." For the first time, Ty began to wonder if he would be a liability during the mission to Haleia-6. He quickly dismissed the thought. He had to be there for his team, no matter what.

"You are doing well."

"Thanks to you," he said. "None of us would be where we are without you."

"I am able to say the same," she replied, smiling at him.

"How are you feeling about staying here with Max and the Al-Kimians?"

Eira turned more fully toward Ty at the galley table. "I do not understand. Is there an expected way I should feel?"

"No, I mean do you feel safe with them? I don't want to leave you here if you have any misgivings or worries." Splitting his crew wasn't his favorite option, and he didn't want to put Eira in any danger.

Her head tilted to the side in confusion. "Oh. I believe I understand now. You are being protective. Yes, Tyce. I am comfortable here. I will not be lonely," she reminded him. "Do not worry about me. Your mission has much more risk."

"Yeah, if it'll ever get off the ground." Vivi had not heard back from Echo, and Ty was still at a loss as to how they were going to get into the ACAS facility. Maybe they could go meet Patrin on Dela Prime to obtain fake identification if they didn't hear from Echo. He would throw that out to Hal and see what he thought.

Last night's idea session had gone on for quite a few hours after dinner. They'd filled Hal in as much as they dared about Echo without going into Vivi's ex as a connection. Hal agreed it was a good possibility. He had suggested that they might go into the facility as building maintenance, but Ty didn't like it. Two might slip in as maintenance, but that left them in a bad way if they were found out. It felt wrong for the mission.

Hal and Vivi entered the common area, making their way

to the coffee. "Up early for more strategizing, I see," Vivi teased.

"I never stop," Ty said.

Hal noticed right away that Ty wasn't wearing his brace. "Wow. No brace today." He remarked as he sat down with them at the galley table.

"Yeah, for a while, anyway."

"Five by five," Hal said. "Well, Veevs has solved our transportation issue."

"Yeah?" Ty glanced to her as she came over with a mug. Transportation had been another problem with the mission they'd batted around yesterday.

"Yeah. I talked to a guy named Brody in the rec hangar, and he said that he came here in a stolen ACAS shuttle."

"Is it still on the base?" Ty asked.

"I sent a message to Patrin, and he said he thought so. He should get back to me...oh, that's probably him." She reached in her pocket for her handheld and stared at it a moment before turning the screen and holding it up. "No, it's from Echo." The message was easy to read. *Borj Gaba, Harakat. Five days. Bring no more than two companions.*

"Now we know," Ty said. "I'll go find Seren. We may have to meet Echo, then plan from there based on what they say."

"We'll verify if that shuttle's still here, then I'll finish getting the *Loshad* prepped with the right Gpods in case we run into trouble," Hal said.

"Good. Let's all meet back here for the evening meal together. I think being together this last night will do us all good," Ty said. "I'll even cook."

"That's definitely a deal," Hal replied.

. . .

The following morning, a few hours before dawn, they transferred Eira to Max's lab. Hal had given her a hooded jacket, and Vivi had given her a pair of pants and shoes so that she could transfer from the *Loshad* to the base safely without drawing too much attention. With her hood over her head, Ty agreed she could pass as a human if she kept her head down and her hands in her pockets. The crew walked with Max through the complex until they reached one of the service lifts to get them to his lab.

The *Loshad's* crew followed her to the door. Max keyed a sequence, allowing Eira to watch. "This is the code to get in and out," he told her. "Come on in."

They entered. "You've got everything you need?" Ty asked, looking around.

"Affirmative," she answered.

"Come back this way," Max said. He led them into what had been a supply room. It had been converted to a room for Eira. There was a terminal, data pad and a bed.

"We...we didn't know about your requirements for rest," Max said, gesturing at the bed. "We can obtain anything you might need, just ask."

"This is fine," Eira said. "I do not sleep, but I have reflection periods where a room like this would be helpful."

"You are not a prisoner; you can get in and out of the lab and this room at any time with the code you saw earlier. Commodore Seren strongly requests that you *would* stay here, but if you have to leave, please let us know in advance so that we can ensure your safety."

"I understand," Eira replied.

"I'll give you all a few moments to say goodbye," Max stepped out.

"If you are the least bit uncomfortable with any of this, I'll pull you," Ty said, concern on his features.

Eira turned toward him. "There will be no need of that. Through this terminal, I can assume control of this entire complex in less than ten seconds if necessary."

"Maybe don't tell *them* that," Hal said with a grin.

"Very well," she agreed. "But there really is no need for worry."

Ty smiled, "You're right...I've simply gotten so used to you having my back that it won't feel right without you."

"I have a gift for your mission," Eira said, turning to Hal.

"Yeah?" Hal replied.

Eira held out a hand and reached in the pocket of her jacket to remove a silver ball-like object similar to the one she'd given for the crew going to retrieve the *Harbinger*. It was very small. "This is made of mytrite and allenium nanites. If you leave it behind in the lab, the nanites will replicate and inactivate all computers they come into contact with."

"Like a virus?" Hal asked.

"Yes, but smarter. The ACAS will not be able to counter it. I have tethered the nanites to you and your lifesigns, Hal. You merely have to touch them to a port and tell them when to activate their programming."

Hal held out a hand and she placed it in his palm. "Once you engage it, it cannot be recalled, so do it on your way out of the Haleia-6 base. This way, you will have the time to escape the planet."

"Thank you, Eira," Hal said.

"Could you do this on more of the ACAS's bases?" Ty asked.

"Not without more mytrite. I brought some extra mytrite nanites with me, but with this and the nanites I'm using for the *Harbinger*, I do not have enough."

"I get it," Hal said, looking down at the precious sliver ball in his hand. "Eira, I'll be very careful with this."

"We appreciate how dear of a sacrifice this is," Ty said. "Thank you."

"You are welcome, amatan."

"So, I guess this is goodbye," Hal said sadly.

Beryl shook her head. "Goodbyes are permanent. It's until we see you again," Beryl said, reaching out to hug Eira.

The Mudar remained very still, then tilted her head to the side.

"What?" Ty asked with a smile.

"I am attempting to understand your leave-taking customs. Like Beryl, I shall simply say we will see each other again."

"Yeah, I like that," Vivi said taking her hand and squeezing it before letting it go.

Hal stepped forward. "I'm going to miss you," he said, reaching out to hug her.

She hugged him back carefully. "I will miss you as well."

Finally, Eira turned to Ty. "Do be careful, Tyce. And please look after Runa for me. She has learned much, but she will need you to guide her."

"Of course," Ty promised.

PATRIN HAD SAID he would come to find her before the *Raptor* left at 0430, so Kat made her way to the hangar, her feelings uncertain.

She'd grown to really like Patrin in the past few months. Running operations with him and his crew had been exciting and had engendered a sense of camaraderie that filled a hole in her soul she didn't know she had. She *belonged* there with them. She *fit* in and it felt good. From time to time, thoughts of her mission...thoughts of the fleet admiral intruded, but not for long. What Patrin had told her about being free to choose her own path seemed to be coming true.

But after Patrin told her he was leaving on an extended mission, a thread of worry had begun unraveling in her mind. It was bad to be alone, and she was afraid of it. She wasn't exactly sure of what she would do once his steady presence was gone.

She'd left her quarters and made her way to the hangars, intending to board the *Raptor* and plead with Patrin for permission to go. The two guards stopped her at the ship's entrance, citing mission security when she asked to enter. Disappointed, she sat down on a shipping container nearby and sent Patrin a message that she was outside.

When he appeared at the cargo ramp, he saw her immediately. She could see his smile shine even in the dimness of the hangar in early morning.

"Hi," he said, reaching her and sliding his arms around her. "You came to see me off."

"Yeah," she said with a frown.

"What is it, huh?" he asked, leaning down to catch her gaze.

"Let me go with you," she said. "I...I don't want to be here alone," she bit her bottom lip as she waited for what he would say.

"I'm sorry. I can't. The people on this mission were picked by Seren himself. Almost everyone's been with us since the beginning."

"So, you don't trust me?" she dropped her head.

"No, Kat, it's not that." He tipped her face up to his. "It's not. This mission's just larger than the both of us. I promise, when I get back, I'll share with you everything about it." he kissed her. "I'm leaving you with the most important mission anyway. Take care of the old man for me, right?"

She nodded, her heart sinking as he enfolded her in his arms.

"I care about you. Don't think this is easy for me to leave," he added.

"I know," she murmured, burying her face against him.

After some moments, Patrin let her go, and she sat back to see Seren standing nearby.

"Saying goodbye is always difficult," Seren said, inclining his head.

"Yeah." Kat furiously blinked her tears away. Patrin put an arm around her.

"Can you spare Patrin a moment, Kat?"

"Um...yeah. Sure."

The old man took Patrin aside. "The *Loshad* leaves not long after you do."

"I talked to Ty yesterday. He's still putting together their plan, but if anyone can make it work, he will," Patrin replied.

A minute ago, Kat had been inconsolable at the thought of Patrin leaving, but now, she was straining to hear any of their conversation.

"Dai and the rest of the crew will need your leadership," Seren continued. "You have all my hopes going with you. We will do our best to hold things down here. Send a message via the new encoded channels when you know something."

"Yes, sir."

"Patrin, I never knew what it meant to nats to have children, but I think I might be starting to understand," Seren said. Kat glanced up to see Seren envelop Patrin in a hug.

She couldn't help but compare the situation to her relationship with the fleet admiral. He had never shown that kind of open affection toward her, and it made her chest hurt to see the deep care that Seren obviously had for his people. "I am proud of you," Seren added.

Kat teared up and for the second time, she couldn't have articulated what was causing her emotions. The cool detachment she'd had when she'd joined the Opposition had morphed into something completely different. Something was tearing her apart inside. She swiped under her eyes with her fingers and then focused on her boots as she waited for Patrin to re-approach.

"Hey, it'll only be a few weeks," he said, taking her hand.

She swallowed hard and looked up at him. "I know. I'm sorry. I realize I'm making it hard for you to go," she slid off the cargo container and wrapped her arms around him one last time.

"Whatever this is...it's going to be fine." He kissed the top of her head and held her close. "I know you've got things that are bothering you. If you need anything, talk to Seren. Talk to Max, even. They'll be here for you until I get back. I already asked them to watch out for you."

"You...did?" she asked, surprised. There were sounds from the *Raptor* starting up as it went through its pre-flight checklist.

"Of course." He took both her hands and squeezed them. "It's time for me to go."

"The sooner you go, the sooner you'll be back," she murmured, squeezing his hands and then letting them go.

"You bet." He walked backwards toward his ship until he was across the hangar. Then he turned and disappeared up the cargo ramp.

"He will be back before we know it, although he will be sorely missed." Seren had come to stand beside her as they watched the ship begin to lift.

"You're right," she said softly as her heart fell.

TWENTY-TWO

The *Loshad* left for their mission the same day. After four days, they found themselves arriving at Harakat, a grey planet shrouded in clouds. Ty guided them into the lanes of traffic leading to the planet's surface. "Hal, link us into the nav beacon for Borj Gaba."

"Linked. Turning nav over to them and going auto."

Ty sat back, eyeing the transports moving back and forth in front of them in the complicated maze of traffic in the skies around the capital city. "We'll be bunking on the ship," he said. "Runa, when we land, engage security protocol Obsidian Nova."

"Of course."

"Obsidian Nova?" Vivi asked.

"It's a security setting, Vivi. Are you expecting trouble?" Runa added.

"Not exactly," Ty replied.

"Harakat's just not the safest place," Beryl explained.

"It's best to keep ship security pretty high in case someone tries to jack the ship or sneak on board," Hal said.

"Is it very populated?" Vivi asked.

Just then, they broke through the clouds and saw tall buildings gleaming dully in the muted light of sunset. "Oh, that answers my question," she replied.

"Harakat has multiple levels—the sky level, mid-level, street levels, and multiple underground levels. The planet contains 235 separate offices for corporations; however, the ACAS presence is limited," Ty told her.

"Better for business," Hal smirked, glancing at Ty before turning back to the display in front of him.

"What do you mean?" Vivi asked. It was obvious both ex-soldiers knew the answer.

"Like Vesbra and Dela Prime, this planet has a thriving black-market economy. Having the Coalition around would spell trouble for the corporations here. They make money off the goods that the gangs and pirates sell, and in exchange, the corps keep ACAS off-world," Ty said.

"So, anything goes here."

"Yeah," Hal said. "That could be good or bad, depending on your point of view. One thing's for sure. No one's going anywhere alone while we're on this planet."

VIVI AND HAL were coming back through the spaceport with dinner when Hal paused, extending a hand to hold her back. He pulled them out of the walkway, putting their backs against a support column. While sweeping the crowd around them, he had obviously noticed something suspicious.

"What is it?" she said under her breath.

"It's..." he trailed off as he scanned, then he shook his head. "I thought I saw someone that we passed back by the street vendors." He was hyper-focused, the way he'd been when they'd rescued Max from Chamn-Alpha, and she was reminded that even though he didn't have the rush, he still had all the abilities that the ACAS had programmed him with. After a few moments, he relaxed, but only slightly. "Let's get back to the ship."

They entered the flow of traffic and turned left onto their concourse. As they made their way into the concourse proper, they noticed a little boy. He was about ten and dressed in an oversized, second-hand flight suit, just standing in the middle of the corridor. Hal's head was on a swivel, checking the area, but when the kid stood in their way he paused.

"Hi. This is for you, Miss Vivian." The boy stepped forward. He was holding out a comm—a cheap shredder that Vivi knew would be pretty much untraceable.

They approached carefully. "How do you know who I am?" Vivi asked.

Hal tensed beside her as he surveyed the crowd, hand hovering near his blaster.

"They showed me. I'm 'sposed to tell you they will call you, Miss Vivian." The kid pushed the shredder into her hands then took a few steps back.

"What's your name?" Vivi called.

The boy shook his head at her, turned and ran.

Several spaceport workers stood silently over by a support beam. There were three shady looking guys, maybe pirates, loitering over near a hulk of a vessel that looked like several other ships had been used to hold it together. Three or four prostitutes stood in the shadows nearby. Only the pirates were giving them a second glance, and Hal was glaring at them.

"See something interesting?" Hal called, bristling.

They retreated back into the shadows of their bay.

"I guess they know we're here," he said, glowering at the crowd which automatically gave him a wide berth. Hal took Vivi's hand, to keep her close. "Let's go."

. . .

By the time that Hal and Ty brought the food to the table, Vivi was already at work on the shredder comm. She'd told them she was going to make damned sure that the thing wasn't being used to watch or listen to them.

"You're good at that." Hal said, sitting back watching her work. She had disassembled the thing, searched it, and put it back together in about three minutes flat. He felt a lot more comfortable now that he was on the ship and his adrenaline spike was starting to fade.

She smiled at the praise. "Thanks." He watched her place it in the middle of the table. "We probably want to keep it out in case we get a message."

"So, I guess we simply wait until we hear something," Ty said as he took a seat.

"Yeah," Vivi said. "We're safe to talk around it now."

"How do you suppose they knew we were here?" Hal asked, reaching for one of the take-away containers.

Vivi shrugged. "I'm known to them. They could have been using spaceport surveillance."

Hal dug into the dish of chela, a stir-fried mixture of vegetables and spicy meat served with round flat bread called ogia. It was popular on Ty's homeworld of Celian, and it was one of everyone's favorites. "So, how many of these Echo guys do you know?" Hal asked as they passed around the containers of food.

Vivi's gaze darted to Ty and Beryl for a moment. "I only know one of them. From...back when I was in Uni."

"Beryl. I'm going to want you to stay on the ship during the meet," Ty said.

"Of course," she replied.

Hal noticed the change of subject and the look shared between the three of them. Something was up. "We should go armed. Maybe something smaller so we don't look overtly hostile, but we don't want to be unprepared. Vivi might know one of these guys, but...I don't know any of them." He glanced to Ty for verification.

"Yeah," Ty said. "I feel the same way."

Hal's gaze shifted between the two of them. "Good."

Vivi and Hal were cleaning up the galley after dinner when the shredder comm's annoying beeping interrupted them. "Shit." She pulled it out and her breath caught when she saw a set of coordinates and a timer. "Twenty minutes."

Hal was all business. "Okay. Runa, let Ty know we got the message to roll. Suit up, Veevs."

"Got it," she said, going back to her room.

She came out of her quarters with her blaster on her hip, and a black jacket covering it. Hal was already armed and waiting as well. "Runa. Please tell me the location of the coordinates I'm sending you."

"Vivi, the coordinates point to the twelfth underground level, less than a mile from your current position. I have sent the directions to everyone's personal comms."

Vivi switched comms, tucking the shredder into a pocket. "Runa, you're a sweetheart. Thank you."

"You are welcome."

Vivi saw Ty was exiting his own room, checking the charge level on his blaster. He was wearing his leg brace this time, she noticed. "C'mon, guys," Ty called. "Beryl's going to back us on comms. Let's go."

The lower levels of Harakat were different than the world above. The first few levels of the underground were relatively safe, patrolled by security hired by the shops and businesses there. The further down Hal, Vivi and Ty went, however, the seedier the areas became. Food smells drifted through the air as they passed hole-in-the-wall restaurants, street vendors and run down hab units. People watched them from the gloom of doorways as they wound their way deeper. Hal glared at them with open hostility and most of them backed off. A few kept looking but no one dared to follow them.

They found an unmarked door at the end of a passageway on one side of a restaurant. It matched the coordinates but was locked. They rapped, but nobody answered. Hal took a moment to examine the door, realized it opened inward and decided brute force was the best plan of action.

He threw his shoulder against it several times until it flew open, then pulled his blaspistol and flipped on the lighted scope. Making several signs to Ty, they both entered the room.

It was a ventilation station. Vivi stayed at the door, blaspistol in hand while the pair cleared the room. She didn't realize how tight her fingers were on the pistol grip until she heard each of them call out "clear," and she relaxed.

"I dunno, Veevs. Maybe the coordinates are off," Hal said, rejoining her at the door. "Let's scout around."

Vivi led them back out past a Sheni restaurant to another alley passage. The spicy smells of fried food drifted out of the open door and followed them. "Here," she said, looking at the alumicrete walls. "This is supposed to be it."

Hal came over and passed his hands over the wall. "There's nothing here."

Vivi turned around, glancing up at the three sides and the metal above them. Each was smooth with no seams. "Damn. We're running out of time."

"Maybe we're just supposed to wait for them?" Hal said.

Ty sighed heavily and turned around, looking back down

the hallway, scanning walls, ceiling, and floor. "It's below us," he said.

"Below?" Vivi came over. "Oh...," she murmured, seeing what Ty was pointing to. The outlines of a hatch were visible under closer examination.

"Is it a sewer tunnel?" Hal asked.

"No." Ty shook his head. "A service hatch...probably for an old transport system." Vivi watched him reach for the portal, working his fingers around it. As the shredder's obnoxiously loud timer sounded, the hatch popped open. He used his comm to shine a light down and saw a ladder. There was a damp, dank smell coming from the opening.

"Disconnect the shredder from the feeds." Hal murmured, in case it could be used to get a line on their location.

"Got it."

"I'll go first," Hal offered. He drew his blaster, then he slid down the ladder before Vivi or Ty could protest.

"You go next; I'll follow," Ty said.

Vivi went down the ladder, her feet tinking on the metal rungs. When she reached the bottom, she drew her blaster as well and looked for Hal, who was scanning the darkness in front of them. A depressed area with a monorail stretched into the darkness beside them. They could hear the soft whir of Ty's brace as he came down the ladder and closed the distance. A few silent signs between Hal and Ty and they were off.

They walked about four hundred meters in the dark. Ty stumbled once, and both Vivi and Hal turned back to help him, but he got up by himself, silently waving them off. Finally, they came to a blockage in the tunnel. A collapse of dirt and rock and other debris blocked off the monorail. The path to the service door in front of them was also strewn with debris but there was clearly a path through there. Hal signed, *Go on?* Ty nodded in response.

Vivi watched as Hal tried to key the service access door beside the pile of debris, but it was locked. He had tried to slide it open with no success and had just pointed his blaster at the keypad when it swished open.

The person on the other side was an older teenager, with red hair and extremely freckled skin. After looking Vivi over, he checked his comm. He lifted it and took a picture of the three of them, then sent a message, all the while completely unfazed by Hal pointing a blaspistol at him.

"We were asked to come," Vivi said.

"Yeah, that's right." The teen nodded after his comm binged and turned to walk back further into the dark. "Come on in."

"Aren't you going to ask for our blasters?" Hal asked, nonplussed.

"Nope. Guess we have to trust each other. Ours are bigger than yours anyway."

There was the click and whine as two automatic blaster rifles were powered up behind the teen. In the blue light of the battery packs, they could see that one of the gunmen was the freckled teen's twin. There was a girl as well, no older than sixteen, who was holding the other rifle.

"So, this is what you do when you want trust?" Ty asked. Slowly, he holstered his gun. Vivi followed suit and then Hal.

The teen sighed and rolled his eyes. "Fine. Guns down, crew." They complied. "C'mon. *He* wants to see you."

"Who?" Hal asked.

"The boss. That's who you came to see, right?"

The teen led them across the transport platform to another door that obviously used to lead to some sort of administrative area. He pressed his hand to a pad and the door slid open. Vivi saw a look exchanged between Ty and Hal and she realized they were taking note of everything, communicating in that silent way they had.

"Here you go, Beall," the boy said.

Beall was a man with short grey-hair, standing just inside the door. "Thanks kid. I'll take them in."

The teen looked at them and grinned. "Good luck, Oppos. You're gonna need it."

Beall led them down a hallway toward a battered metal door and gave a single knock. As he did so, Vivi noticed the tattoo on his forearm—double fives with a dagger. Apparently, Ty had too.

"ACAS?" Ty said, surprised. "Five-fives?"

"Yeah." The old man gave him a second look. "You?"

"Former ACAS. Fourteenth Strike Regiment," Ty replied.

"Iron Glaives, oohrah," Hal echoed automatically, at Ty's right shoulder.

"Both of us," Ty explained.

"Hmm," Beall mused thoughtfully. "I chewed up some space with the one-fours back in my day. Good to meet you." He started to say something else but was interrupted by the door sliding open.

"Bring them in, Beall."

The older man gestured, and they went in first. Beall followed, standing by the door. There was a room full of equipment and young people working on terminals. In the middle of it all was a shimmering holographic display, in front of a man in his late twenties or early thirties. He stared at them through the rapidly shifting numbers and colors, before closing it all with a swipe of his hand.

"You've been looking for Echo. What do you want with them?" He stepped forward, examining them all through a thick fall of chin length brown hair that he pushed back. Vivi noticed something strange immediately. The man's pupils were as dark as his hair, and it was almost impossible to see the color of his irises. It was as if he were rushing.

Was he a vat? Vivi checked the man's wrist, but it was bare.

"My name is Tyce Bernon. These are my friends Hal Cullen and Vivi Valjean, but I'm guessing you knew that already."

The hacker smiled. "I did, Captain Bernon. My name is Eli Sawyer." He gestured around him at the mass of computer equipment and teckers, including Beall in the movement. "We are Echo."

"We have come to ask for your help. Our information...is probably best given to whomever is in charge." Ty glanced around uncertainly.

"You can speak with me."

As Ty and Eli chatted, Vivi examined the set-up of the room. There were different stations, manned by teckers with nodes as well as kids with no such modifications. Mostly, they appeared to be monitoring things via surveillance cameras. Her eyes narrowed when she saw that one feed was trained on the *Loshad* in port. She had about neared the rear of the room when someone grabbed her arm from behind. Swinging around, she saw a familiar face.

"Vivian. I can't believe you had the gall to show your face here," the man sneered.

It was Noah.

Her heart hammered painfully in her chest and all of a sudden, it was *that* day again, and she could see the rage in his face, and the spittle flying from his lips as his fists slammed into her. Her ears were ringing, so even though his lips were moving, she found she couldn't hear anything.

"Wh-what?" she said, trying to back up and put a little distance between them.

"I said I finally get to see you make your excuses in person."

He dug his fingers into her arm where he held her and yanked her back toward him. "I sent two guys after you, but you gave them the slip on Jaleeth."

"You did what?" Vivi said incredulously. Then she shook her head. It didn't matter anymore. The meeting with Echo was all that mattered. "Noah—that's not why I'm here."

"Explain what made you think you could fuck me over like that and get away with it," he spat.

She tried to yank her arm out of his grasp. "Let me go—"

His fingers dug into her arm further. "You ruined months of work." He was growing angrier and angrier with each passing second. "How could you turn me in? You put me at risk. How could you be so fucking stupid!"

"Let go of me," she growled, stepping backwards and trying to jerk her arm away as he advanced toward her, now reaching for her other arm as well.

"No, you're gonna give me an explanation this time," he growled.

"Noah! You're hurting me—" They struggled a moment before she twisted out of his grasp. He was reaching for her again when she threw an elbow strike to his face. Blood began pouring from his nose.

"Bitch!" Noah said, pulling back his own fist.

Before Vivi could act or even take another breath, Noah was just gone.

HAL WAS LISTENING to Ty and Eli talk when he heard Vivi's voice take on a note he hadn't ever heard before. He knew she'd moved behind them, obviously taking a look at Echo's operation. At first, he'd actually turned to keep her in his vision, but when he saw she was only looking around, he'd brought his attention back to the Echo guy.

But then, he'd heard panic in Veev's voice. As his head whipped around, he saw a dark-haired man grab her arm with one hand and struggle to capture her other flailing arm. *What the fuck?* he thought. He heard the guy mention betrayal and call her Vivian...and then two and two came together in his mind and his body began moving. The look on Vivi's face said everything. He didn't have the power that the rush provided, but the adrenaline flood of uncontrollable anger provided a close approximation.

"You're hurting me—" Vivi cried as the man wrenched her arm.

She laid into his nose with a quick elbow strike after twisting away from him, and the man called her a bitch.

That was the last thing Hal was able to hear before the world narrowed to one target. When the man raised his fist to hit Vivi, it was practically over before it began.

When Ty heard Vivi's voice rise above the hum of the machines in the room, he glanced over his shoulder in time to see Hal plow into a man menacing her. His attack was brutal and swift, his momentum throwing the tecker against the nearest wall. Hal held his quarry in place with his muscled forearm while his fist, like a piston, slammed into the dark-haired man's face several times. The guy tried weakly to defend himself, but it did nothing. One of the nat's punches landed on Hal's cheekbone, but his fist might as well have been a fly lighting there for all the notice Hal took of it.

"Hey!" Ty reached Hal the same time as Beall. His friend might not be rushing, but Ty knew he could do a massive amount of damage even without it. Together, Ty and Beall hauled Hal back.

The vat growled wordlessly, trying to break free from the

grip of the two former ACAS officers. He was definitely struggling with a black threat level event, Ty realized. "Stand down, Hal!" he said, trying to get Hal to fix on him, instead of his opponent.

The hacker was injured, his face covered in blood as he sank into unconsciousness on the floor. Vivi's attention went from the man on the floor to Hal.

She reached him as he threw off Ty and Beall's hold. "Hal, please. I'm fine! Look at me!" She moved herself between Hal and Noah, and it worked to break his gaze.

Instead of going back again to resume the beating, Hal focused on Vivi. The only sound in the whole room was the harsh rasp of his breathing as he got himself under control.

"Him, right? It was him?" Hal asked when he could finally speak.

Vivi nodded. "He's the one who sent those guys on Jaleeth." She threw her arms around Hal and buried her face against his chest. Hal immediately folded her in his arms to comfort her, but over the top of her head, Ty watched him glare angrily at the fallen tecker. The altercation had been so fierce, even the twins from outside had heard it and come in. One knelt to check Noah over. He looked up at his brother and shook his head grimly.

Ty wiped sweat off his brow, glancing uncertainly to Beall, Eli and lastly the stricken faces of the teckers who had stayed to watch the beatdown. "Look, Sawyer. I'm sorry. That...that man's my tecker's ex. He beat her up before she left him, and Hal cares for Vivi. This guy, Noah... sent some thugs after Vivi when she left him. We stopped the guys from kidnapping her in a bar."

"Noah did that?" Sawyer asked.

"He just told me he did," Vivi said from the circle of Hal's arms.

"Ty and I beat the shit out of the guys he sent," Hal said.

Eli's gaze narrowed, and he glanced to Beall. "He's done." He called out, "Serafina?"

One of the teens, a pretty dark-haired girl with a tattoo of stars down one side of her face, came over. "Yes, boss?"

"303 his ass. Sever all connections with Noah Anders. Put out the word to all other cells to go to their blue safehouse." He made a circular motion with his hand, glancing around at all the teckers. "Pack us up. We're moving to location blue in three hours."

She began tapping on a handheld. It didn't take long. "Done, boss."

Eli turned to the twins. "Take this 303 to the medbay. Get his bleeding stopped and get him back on his feet. I don't want him bothering anyone else while our guests are here. I'll deal with him later."

"Ok...But boss, I don't think you gotta worry. He's not gonna be bothering anyone anytime soon." The twins hefted the still-unconscious Noah between them and carried him out the door.

Eli nodded, then scratched his chin thoughtfully. "I need a minute with Beall, please," he said to Ty.

The two of them left the room for a moment, which gave Ty had a chance to check on Vivi and Hal. "You two good?" He murmured low, glancing at the few teckers who hadn't scattered. They were all business, however, and had begun to pack up equipment.

"Yeah," Vivi said, stepping back. "S-sorry, Ty," she said. "He just came up and grabbed me."

Hal was still angry, glaring through the doorway the teens had taken Vivi's ex through.

"Hal?" Ty asked, placing a hand on the vat's bicep. He could feel Hal's muscles jumping from the adrenaline in his system, like they had when he'd gotten Hal out of his vac suit during the exploration of the *Harbinger*.

At the touch, Hal startled, and his head whipped to Ty. "What?"

Ty had expected to see the pupils of a rushing vat, but he saw with relief that Hal's eyes were normal. "You alright?"

"Yeah. Be better if I could take that guy out permanently." Ty noticed Hal's bloody left hand was still clenched in a fist. When he saw Ty looking at it, he wiped his knuckles on his pants and took a deep breath.

"You made your point," Ty said. "I don't imagine we'll see him again."

Beall and Sawyer returned to the room and called to Ty. "Why don't we talk somewhere a little more private while my people work?" Eli asked. "If you'll follow me."

They were led to another area in the underground complex. It obviously used to be an office of some sort, with a table and chairs.

Sawyer gestured to the table. "Please have a seat. Ms. Valjean, I'm sorry that happened. I assure you that I did not know of Mr. Ander's past behavior toward you. I do not sanction kidnapping...even of those that disrupt my operations," he said with a slight smile.

She blushed as she took a seat, "I'm glad you didn't hold that against me."

"I figured it was worth listening to your story, Miss Valjean," Sawyer replied.

Ty glanced up as Beall handed Hal the med kit for his skinned knuckles, then leaned in to talk to Sawyer. The former ACAS officer spoke softly, but Ty managed to catch some of the words.

"You've been going for three days...you're gonna need to rest soon," Beall said, laying a hand on the hacker's shoulder.

"I'll be fine a little longer," Sawyer said, turning to the three at the table and taking a seat. "So, what do you want with us? The message you sent Noah led me to believe you may have friends in the Al-Kimian quadrant of the galaxy?"

Ty shrugged. "It's possible."

"Nice little war that's shaping up to be. Good for the corporations. War's always good for the inner spiral's economy, while the Edgers pay the price," he said. "Is what we hear true? Are the Edge's released vats heading to Al-Kimia?"

"Yeah, they are," Hal said.

"Interesting." Sawyer glanced to Beall, then back to Ty. "So, what can Echo do for you?"

"We need spotless credentials in the ACAS personnel database," Ty said.

"ACAS database?" Eli whistled. "That's a tough one."

"So you can't?" Ty asked.

"I didn't say I can't. I simply said it would be tough." Sawyer sat back and crossed his arms over his chest. "I'd have to know what you're going to do with them," he asked.

"Aren't you a hacker? Why would you care?"

"Maybe I'm curious." He eyed Ty. "Maybe I don't work only for scrill."

Ty glanced to Hal and Vivi, who both nodded. "There are two reasons for the trip. The ACAS has developed a weapon against free vats, using their implant against them somehow. You press a button and the vats within range die instantly. We don't know exactly how it works, but if we can steal a device, maybe we can make vats immune to this weapon. If we don't get them, every free vat in the Edge is a potential target, whether they've joined Al-Kimia or not."

He went on, leaning forward. "My crew and I salvage tech past the border. We recently found out that the ACAS also has access to some Mudar artifacts that could have been used to make the kill device. Who knows what they'll dream up next? Our second objective is to steal the artifacts so they can't be used for nefarious purposes."

Sawyer didn't say anything, but he shared a glance with Beall.

"A kill switch for vats?" Beall muttered. "Godsdamned rat bastards." The old man was angry.

"How do we know you're not going to sell this type of tech on the black market to the highest bidder?" Eli said. As he spoke, Ty noticed him look down at his hands, which were trembling. When he saw Ty notice, he moved them under the table and shifted his body in his chair.

It was Vivi's turn to speak up. "Mr Sawyer. Our crew is not only a crew. We're family. And we're well-aware of what unscrupulous governments can do." She glanced to Hal, then squeezed his uninjured hand. "Our plan is to put this technology far beyond the reach of the ACAS or anyone else who wishes to exploit it."

"We'll look into it." Eli swiped at his forehead with one hand. He'd grown pale and sweaty while Vivi spoke. It was then Ty recognized the signs of someone coming off of Amp without a neutralizer shot. Some nats used the drug to stay alert for multiple days, and although doing that was against the law, it wasn't really enforced. Maybe the hacker was using it to stay alert. Amp wasn't extremely addictive, but he was aware that some nats became compulsive users. Was this hacker an addict?

Hal interrupted his thoughts. "Look. You have to help us. If we go in there with any ID less than perfect, we're dead. We've got the scrilla to pay."

"We'll look into it," Eli said again. An expression of pain crossed his features and he almost folded in half. "Um...I'm gonna have to go..." He spoke through gritted teeth.

"Eli?" Beall asked, watching the tecker get to his feet.

"I'll get back to you," Eli muttered. He took a step towards the door and stumbled, falling into the wall and sinking to the floor. He curled into a ball with a groan.

"I'll get the neutralizer," Beall said.

The older man exited the room, leaving Sawyer with them. "What is it?" Vivi asked as another round of spasms shook the hacker.

"Muscle cramps," Hal said, helping Sawyer sit with his back to the wall. The man was heaving with pain. "It's amp, right?" Having been through the spasms, he knew what they were like.

Ty gave Hal a nod. "How long has it been since your last dose?" Ty asked Sawyer.

"Two days," Eli groaned out through clenched teeth. "Almost three."

Ty and Hal shared a look. With vats, amp could last an entire day or maybe a bit more if the individual was on a rush, at which time you either got the neutralizer or another dose to extend the effects. It made sense that a slower metabolism like a nat's would cause the effects to last longer.

Beall returned with a medjet. He lifted the hacker's sleeve and pressed it to a bicep and Ty had time to notice several other bruises from previous injections there. Eli seemed like a pretty regular user. "It's the neutralizer," Beall said. "He's been up a couple days and needs to sleep. Mind helping me get him to a bed? Two hours' sleep, and he'll be back up and at it."

"No problem," Hal and Ty lifted Sawyer up and carried him a room a few doors away where there was a bed. By the time they laid him out, he was unconscious.

"How long has he been using?"

"A while. To stay sharp while running ops." The old man shook his head, obviously frustrated. "Look, we've got a lot going on with this move. Give us a chance to look into it, and we'll get back to you."

"How long?" Vivi asked.

"Tomorrow," Beall said. "If it means anything to you, I think it's a good op, but Eli has the final say. I'll get someone to walk you back out. We'll be in touch."

It was the best he could ask for. "Thank you," Ty replied, offering his hand, which Beall shook.

TWENTY-THREE

WHILE KAT SLEPT, SHE DREAMED. SHE WAS SIXTEEN AGAIN and the admiral had her on Invern for training. It was just the two of them, under the tall coniferous trees flanked by a steep cliff and the ocean down below. Green needles covered the ground, but she could no longer smell their scent like she could when they'd first arrived. There were only the odors of dirt, sweat and blood.

"Again, Katerine." The admiral raised his bare fists and waited for her to put up her guard. They had been sparring for over two hours, and she was exhausted. Her cheek was cut and her mouth was full of blood where he'd busted her lip against her teeth. The knuckles of both of her hands were scraped and oozing. But the admiral was indefatigable. She spat blood and lifted her fists again. It didn't occur to her to cry – it would be pointless. There was only the hot rasp of air in her lungs, the unyielding stone of the admiral's fists and the metallic taste of blood.

They fought, and she actually hit him with an uppercut

twice before he struck her so hard in the side of the head she fell to the ground.

She laid there trembling. The world was a blur of greens and browns. She felt like throwing up but clenched her teeth against it with a groan.

"Get up," he ordered.

Her legs twitched under her, but she couldn't. The strike had landed near her interface, and the world was spinning.

His boot toe nudged her. "It's an interface hit, Katerine. Fight through it and get up." Next, he would kick her if she wasn't able to start moving again. She tried again, but her feet just scratched at the dirt weakly.

"Are you defective? Do you need reprogramming, girl?" he asked, his voice deceptively gentle as he knelt beside her and took the ponytail of her dark black hair between his fingers, running his thumb over the strands. Then she sensed the lightest brush of fingertips on her neck. He spent so long watching her that fear began to squirm in her guts. "Perhaps you are not as strong as I thought," He mused, letting go dismissively and standing up.

She squeezed her eyes shut and summoned energy from somewhere outside herself to force her legs to *move*. She got to her knees and the nausea threatened again. He watched her struggle with it, then walked past her to their camp.

"Good. Get to your feet, Nyma."

The nickname he'd given her along with the praise caused something to bloom inside of her, and she used the burst of endorphins to crawl to the nearest tree and pull herself to her feet. When she turned, lifting her fists again, he was approaching her with a bottle of water, which he held out. She took it with a shaking hand.

He drank from his own bottle, watching her appraisingly.

"I'm worried about you, Katerine. You haven't fulfilled your programming. Do I need to motivate you differently?"

She lowered the water bottle and spoke in a pale voice. "No sir." Despite her trembling, she stood stock still, looking to the side so that she wouldn't appear impudent by eyeing him. "I will follow your every order."

He drew near again, and Kat knew he was studying each micro-expression on her face, sensing for any weakness. "Then tell me what your mission is, Nyma." He put one finger under her chin to lift her gaze to his own. His other hand trailed down her cheek in an almost tender gesture before it closed around her throat. As she struggled to breathe, she broke into pieces.

"I am supposed to... to gather information."

"And?" he asked, raising an eyebrow and tightening his grip.

"And report to you!" she rasped.

"Then it is time to fulfill your programming. Do it, Nyma, or I will end you."

She awoke with the admiral's voice in her ears. Her heart throbbed as she sat up in bed, the dream melting around her. Expecting to see him and the forest around her, she found nothing except the darkened bedroom of her new hab unit. The silence was terrifying.

It's time, Nyma, his voice rumbled through the dark corridors of her mind like thunder. It was a dream, she realized. She knew what they were because of her trips to train with the fleet admiral. During the days that they were separate from the others in the vat facility, Kat hadn't been receiving her nightly programming, and she'd begun to dream. She had woken terrified at first, until the admiral had realized what was happening and explained it.

She wasn't asleep now, but she still heard his voice in her mind. *Time to call in.*

"No, no, no, no," she whispered.

Time to call in.

She got out of bed and began to pace. "I can't do this," she pleaded, swiping at the tears that streaked her face.

Time to call in.

She reached the far wall, then put her back against it and slid to the floor. Tears obscured her vision, and she buried her face against her knees and sobbed, but the voice was relentless.

Time to call in.

"Call in?" she whispered, but she already knew what he meant. She wrapped her arms around herself at the sudden chill in the room. Blankness threatened the edges of her mind. She didn't want to do it. In fact, she'd been trying to put it off for weeks now, distracting herself by spending time with Patrin.

But without him around, her thinking had begun to shift. It was exactly what she had been afraid of. Like what had happened at the spaceport when Jakob had died. The coldness took over and she was able to look at the situation with some vision and distance now.

The facts were clear. She had to call in and tell the Admiral everything; the set-up of Al-Kimian command, the mission that Patrin had gone on, the coming and going of patrols and the civilian ships working for Al-Kimia in the Edge. There were also whispers of a mission to the Inside Spiral. She had plenty to tell him; he would be pleased. If she had gathered enough information, perhaps he would let her deal with the traitors and return to the ACAS. The cold part of her hoped that would be the case. The longer she stayed in contact with people like Seren, the more she was slipping.

And there it was again, that other voice in her mind crying in horror at the thought of rolling on her friends. The tension pulled her so taut she was afraid she would break. She pounded a fist against her head in frustration as the conflicting emotions threatened to pull her apart.

"Shut up. Shut up," she hissed in a whisper, tears making hot paths down her cheeks. She stood up and made her way to the bed. She wound herself into a ball and cried until the traitorous voice in her head died away and she fell asleep again.

"THE COMMAND POST has lost contact with the *Terrapin*, sir." Kat entered the small ready room off headquarters and reported to Seren. "They were returning from a supply run. Sensors have detected ship debris in the area—it's thought to be lost, no survivors."

Seren looked up sharply. He'd known the crew of the *Terrapin*—the ship's captain was an old man named Jacobs who had helped turn civilian ships into gunships during the mounting tensions between the ACAS and Al-Kimia. Along with Al-Kimia's regular fleet, it was this informal fleet that would be called on to defend Al-Kimia when the ACAS decided to come for them. "I see."

"Did you...know them?" she asked.

"Yes, Kat." He bowed his head sadly, sitting back with his arms crossed over his chest and his eyes closed a moment. "I knew them."

"I'm sorry," Kat said, softly.

"Thank you, young one," Seren said.

Quietly, Kat turned back to her desk in the corner where she'd been monitoring the newsfeeds on her datapad.

After long moments, Seren tried to get back to his work as well. Even though people had died, the fight had to go on. But after he'd read and reread the same paragraph five times on his display, he sighed heavily and sat back. As much as Terra Malar appreciated his insights, he wasn't going to be able to focus on his work without a break first, he thought sadly as he glanced to Patrin's protégé. She'd been a great help the past few days. The ACAS had taken out three blockade runners, including the *Terrapin*, in the last two days, and command had been working around the clock to get messages out to the rest of their "civilian fleet" to lay low. He was feeling more and more as if war wasn't far off.

"Kat. Let's take a break for now." He locked his terminal, then scrubbed his face a moment.

"Yes, sir," Katerine said, turning toward him.

"When's the last time you've eaten?" he asked.

"Ration bar this morning, sir. What about you?"

"Can't remember." Seren stood, arching his sore back. "Ah, vats weren't meant for this kind of work," he complained. Both of them knew that his arthritic joints were from his advanced age, but neither remarked on it. "Let's walk down to the chow hall. The change of scenery will do us both good."

"Yes, sir," she stood and waited on him.

"You have been a great help to me, Kat."

"I am learning a lot from you, sir. It truly is amazing to see how vats and the Al-Kimians are working together."

They left headquarters and began to walk across the quad to the mess hall. It was a fine summer day, sunlight dappling the walking paths when it shone down through the leaves.

"Do you believe that...the Al-Kimians will keep their word to vats if they were to win in the war?" Kat asked.

"Yes," Seren replied.

Kat glanced at him uncertainly.

"You don't agree," Seren observed.

"It's hard to imagine nats...being so accepting."

"What were your CO's like in the ACAS?" Seren asked.

"Brutal, like all of them," she answered, thinking of Quillon's training sessions. "They saw us as a tool. Nothing more.

We were replaceable to them. We tried so hard to please them, but they never appreciated it."

Seren seemed to understand. "They are not all that way. Some of my CO's...were people like Terra Malar. People who valued vats and treated us as they themselves wanted to be treated."

"It's hard to believe that there are such people," she said softly, looking around at the vats and nats eating their noon meal together.

"Yet there are," Seren said, with a small gesture. "They are right here in front of you."

She looked up at him and was suddenly afraid he might be right. "Maybe they are," she said softly. "Maybe I've been wrong all this time."

"We've all been wrong sometimes," he replied, picking up a tray and going through the serving line. "It doesn't matter, as long as you come to set your feet on the right path."

She didn't know what to believe anymore, but she nodded as she was expected to do.

Kat woke with a blinding headache the day after she'd had lunch with Seren. The only headache comparable was the one she'd had when she'd first came to Jaleeth after the extended programming she'd undergone. She managed to comm Seren about her absence from duty and then she tried to sleep it off. By the afternoon, the pain was unbearable, and she made her way toward the medcenter lift. Her vision was blurring, and she could barely see to press the floor number.

She had stepped out of the lift when the world greyed out and she sank to the floor. The last thing she heard was a startled medic calling her. "Ma'am? Ma'am!"

• • •

She woke up in a medbed. As soon as she groaned and moved, she felt a hand on her arm. "Kat." The voice was familiar, and she peered up at Max Parsen's concerned face.

She licked dry lips, terror flooding her veins. "I...Where am I?"

"We're in the medbay. They found you collapsed on the floor, crying that you were in pain. Where does it hurt?"

"On my left side. By the interface. It's better now." Her voice was a paper whisper as she watched the traitor warily.

Parsen brought up a medscanner. "Everything is normal with your implant. Let me try some medication for you."

Don't worry, he can't read your mind, she thought. "I had these headaches on Jaleeth," she rasped. "I was taking Mopen for them."

"That's a pretty standard migraine medication. Let's try it first, then. I'll be right back."

Kat nodded, her eyelids drifting closed until she heard a voice.

Nyma. Don't you have a mission to complete?

She dared a glance to see the Admiral's gaze weighing and measuring her. He was standing across the room, by the window, watching her with folded arms.

Time to call in.

She didn't question how he was here—she now understood that he was, and he would know if she faltered.

"I know what I have to do," she whispered, as the voices in her mind died back and the headache finally began to abate. By the time Max gave her the shot, she no longer felt anything at all.

TWENTY-FOUR

They'd returned from the trip to Echo's hideout about an hour ago, and Hal was pounding the bag in the cargo bay while Vivi and Ty made dinner. Vivi was spooning some cheese into the noodle dish Ty was showing her how to make, and she slipped it into the microwave warmer.

"So, let's take a seat a minute." Ty gestured to the table in the galley.

Vivi wiped her hands and followed Ty over. "What's up?" she asked.

"I wanted to make sure you're okay after all that today." He hadn't wanted to ask her earlier in front of Hal; it was obvious the vat was still worked up from the confrontation with Vivi's ex.

She rubbed her arm where Ty noticed she had finger shaped bruising. "I'm fine. Noah got worse than I did."

"Yeah. He got what he deserved. You got a good hit on him too, before Hal waded in. I gotta admit, seeing Hal give that guy what he had coming was pretty damned satisfying." Ty smiled at her.

"Yeah," she said.

"Vivi...I wanted to talk about Hal. I've known him for over seven years, and I've never seen him as steady as he's been since you came into his life."

"Yeah?"

Ty nodded. "Before you, Hal always struggled with day-to-day life. He was released from service before I finished my tour, but I promised him I'd look him up when I got out." Ty looked down at his hands. "I guess I was just so used to watching out for him, I didn't know what to do without him. When I tracked him down, he was living on Omicron in a run-down hab unit. No handheld, no food in his apartment to speak of. I found out he was fighting in the vat fights there for extra scrill." He paused a moment trying to think of how to explain it. "The fight promoters juice vats up on drugs and get them as hyped as possible before turning them loose on each other. You've seen some of it that time in the vat club. It's a bad situation. Lots of vats end up hooked on drugs like null and jack from their time in the ring."

"He stopped one time to give some scrill to a null addict. When I asked about it, he told me that if not for you he would have ended up like that."

Ty couldn't help remembering finding Hal blissed out on null in a back alley on Jaleeth not long after they'd purchased the *Loshad*. It had only happened once that he knew of, but even now it made him nauseated. "Yeah...he makes some bad choices sometimes. Hal's always had trouble staying focused when he gets bored. But he's been a different person since he became focused on you.

"I saw it when we had to pull him off Noah. He wouldn't listen to me, but he calmed down when you talked to him. The whole reason I'm even having this conversation with you is that you need to know when you say something to him, there's a good chance that he's going to take it like a military order from a commander. It's how he's programmed."

"You're saying this from experience."

"Yeah, it's...a responsibility. Sometimes it's a heavy one. Hal's devoted himself to protecting you like a commanding officer or part of his squad and will most likely do anything you ask him. It's a holdover from his programming, I think. I know you wouldn't intentionally misuse it, but you must be careful not to because it can happen without you even realizing. Your opinion will mean a lot to him, so you have to be careful where you use it."

She bit her lip and nodded. "I'll be careful, Ty."

"I know you will," he said. "That's all. I just...when I saw you calm him down today...I knew we needed to have this talk." They both stood and Ty came around to her, wrapping her in a bear hug. "Thanks for being there for him, Vivi."

"I always will," she promised.

AFTER DINNER, Hal was on his bed, flipping through the data for Haleia-6 for the twentieth time when he looked up to see Vivi in the doorway. She was ready for bed, dressed in sleep shorts, shirt and bare feet, looking as beautiful as the first night she'd shown up in his room. He tossed the handheld to the side and sat up when he noticed the worried crinkle of her forehead. "What's wrong?" he asked, sliding to his side of the bed for her to crawl up.

She took a few slow steps forward, something obviously on her mind. She'd been quiet at dinner all night. "You aren't upset with me?" she asked.

Alarmed, he scanned her face. "What? No, Veevs. What gave you that idea?"

"I didn't tell you about Noah being my Echo contact. I

started to, and then we got the message…and I didn't get the chance."

He sighed in relief. "Oh, that. No." She was still looking at him worriedly. "Veevs, I'm not upset. I promise." Still, she said nothing, so he gestured. "Will you come here?"

She crawled up on his bunk and situated herself facing him. "I was afraid it would upset you…and I didn't think he would actually be there because I told him it was over and… then he was just *there*…and…" she finally stopped speaking when she ran out of words.

"Vivi. I'm *not* mad. Ty told you not to tell me, right?" She nodded, reluctantly. "I wouldn't have told me about him either," he shrugged. "If I'd known he was going to be there ahead of time, I probably would have shot him on sight. Then Echo would have been pissed at us, then people would have pointed guns at us, we would have pointed guns at them – it would have been a godsdamned mess. At least we're all still alive." She laughed softly, so he went on. "Look Veevs, I love you. I'd never be mad with you. You did what you thought you had to do."

Suddenly her eyes were full of emotion, shining like green glass. She struggled to say something, but instead threw herself into his arms. He wrapped her in an embrace, surprised.

"So, I guess this means you're staying with me tonight, right?" he asked.

"After that? Try and make me leave, Hal Cullen."

He kissed her in response and was still kissing her with the promise of more to come, but the chime on the door interrupted them. "Yeah?" Hal called.

"It's me," Ty said from outside.

. . .

EARLIER, Ty had returned to his room after dinner and sat on the bed, beginning the complicated series of latches and straps that would release his leg from the one brace he'd been wearing. After he tossed the brace to the side, he rubbed the sore spots on his knee and upper thigh where the straps held him in.

He tackled physical therapy every morning either by himself or with Beryl or Hal, but it was clear to him that he was not as far along as he'd hoped to be. It only took about 30 minutes of walking without the brace to tire him out, but he was trying to think positively. They needed him on this mission; he couldn't disappoint them.

After finishing some stretches, he took a seat and began working his way out of his boots, now going over possible cover stories for the op. They would be going into the heart of the ACAS—to Cardela Base on Haleia-6, which was sure to be heavily guarded, staffed with soldiers and scientists. How were they going to make it in? He knew that Vivi thought the Echo would round them up some great credentials, but who knew how those ID's would hold up under scrutiny? Brass was sure to take a deep look into any new faces on base, right?

He tossed his boots to the side, laid back on his bed and thought. They needed a good way in.

A reason to be there, that not many people would question. An excuse.

Maintenance? He discarded the idea right away, just as he had the first time it came up. Their team would have too many for that and the story would be too easy to check.

A surprise inspection would get them in, but there were sure to be questions. Base personnel would report it to superiors and the ruse would be discovered. He'd have a small team, but too big not to be noticed.

Nothing was coming to him. In frustration, he brought a hand up and kneaded his forehead, his mind chewing at the problem. What branch of the ACAS could move pretty much wherever they wanted with little question?

The answer hit him like a Celian beacon light.

"That might work..." he muttered to himself. He forced himself to go over the idea once more to make sure there weren't any holes. By the time he sat up, the plan was fully formed in his mind.

"Ty? Your heartrate suddenly increased by twenty-one beats per minute. Is everything alright?" Runa asked.

"Yes. I got an idea."

"What is your idea?"

"I know how we're going to get into the facility on Haleia-6. Comm Hal for me. No, never mind. I'll go there myself." He got to his feet, and despite the tiredness in his complaining muscles, he made his way down the hall to Hal's room, ringing the doorchime.

"Yeah?" Hal asked.

"It's me," he said. "You weren't asleep yet were you?"

"No." The door slid open to reveal Hal and Vivi.

"I...didn't mean to interrupt, but I figured out how we can get into the vat facility."

"Come in. I've been thinking about it, too," Hal said, scratching his head. "And I couldn't come up with anything besides going low key and hoping our new friend could develop some ID that would hold up. What's your plan?"

"Arcteck," Ty said triumphantly.

"Damn!" Hal grinned. "That would work." He grabbed his chair from the table surface and brought it over for Ty so he could sit.

"Thanks, Hal," he said gratefully.

"What's Arcteck?" Vivi said, looking from one to the other.

"A special operations branch that salvages Mudar tech. It's semi-autonomous...their chain of command goes through the

Ministry of Archeological Technology and that branch is under the doyen's control. But they work with the ACAS—they use ACAS ships and vats to search and recover the tech to reverse engineer it, but the ACAS is not always kept up to speed on what Arcteck is doing. We were called in to support a team past the border once. Remember, Hal?" Ty said.

"Yeah, those guys were a bunch of dicks," Hal smirked.

"I remember. We had to do whatever they wanted. We ended up hauling them from the border all the way back to Chamn-Alpha. It would not be beyond the realm of possibility that an Arcteck team would be bringing back some Mudar artifacts to Cardela Base's lab on Haleia-6."

"What about the pieces of Eira's original sphere? It's still in the smuggler's hatch," Hal said.

"Oh, that's perfect," Vivi said.

"It will definitely help verify our backstory," Ty said. "If Sawyer decides to help us, we'll see if we can get him to set up Arcteck identities."

"We're still gonna have Lane rendezvous with us, right?" Vivi asked. "Bringing the shuttle?"

"Yeah. We'll have to get an ID for her as well," Ty nodded. "As soon as we tell her what's up, she'll bring the right uniforms." Malar and Seren had told him to let him know what they'd need for the disguise, and they'd send it. "All we need are basic fatigues and hats with the Arcteck badge."

"This should be easy," Vivi said.

"Yeah, but Haleia's Inside Spiral, Veevs," Hal said. "Don't underestimate them." He glanced over to Ty. "I do think Arcteck's gonna work, though."

"Well, that's all I had – I just wanted to run it by you," Ty said as he stood up. "I'll leave you guys alone."

"You can get back to your room?" Hal asked, nodding toward Ty's braceless leg.

"Yep. All good. I'll see you two in the morning," Ty said, getting gingerly to his feet and placing a stabilizing hand on the door frame as he left. He didn't miss Hal and Vivi's concerned glances and they echoed his own worries about participating in the mission. He wasn't sure if he should just go on with it, call things off, or send them alone, which he really didn't want to do. He knew he had a day or two to decide, but that didn't make it any easier.

HAL AND VIVI were sparring in the cargo bay when Beall and Sawyer returned the next morning.

"Good morning," Sawyer called from the bottom of the ramp.

Hal paused in his sparring and Vivi took the opportunity to smack him gently on the jaw. "You got distracted," she teased.

"Oh, that's how it's gonna be, huh?" Hal lowered his head, grabbed her around the waist and tackled her to the mat while her laughter pealed around them. Finally, the two of them got to their feet.

"Sorry, someone needed to be taught a lesson," Hal teased, taking a swipe at Vivi. "What can we do for you, Sawyer?" He noticed that the hacker was not under the influence of amp today.

"Call me Eli. May we come aboard?" he asked.

"Of course," Vivi said, grabbing her towel and water bottle.

When they were on board, Hal closed the ramp and locked it.

"Take them to the galley, Veevs," Hal said. "I'll get Ty."

A FEW MOMENTS LATER, Hal and Ty met them in the common area.

"Good to see you," Ty said as he shook their hands.

"We came as soon as we had news," Beall said.

Eli and Beall accepted mugs of coffee from Vivi. "I accessed the ACAS database," Eli said. "I can put in whatever personnel records in that you want, all I need to know is who and what rank you want to have."

Ty pulled out his handheld and tapping on it to bring up a file. "Here's the relevant information and cover ID's." Eli tapped on his handheld to accept the file. "We want to be set up as an Arcteck unit. We'll need a captain, Vivi as a lieutenant. Hal and another female colleague of ours will be vats under nat command."

"I can handle that," Eli said, making a note of it. "Look. Beall and I are game to come along. Screwing the ACAS would be the best heist ever. If you have any problems getting into locked areas, I can open the locks, and Beall's been on Cardela Base before. He actually knows the place. And maybe I could find the research and specs for the item. Makes more sense to steal what we can and erase the rest."

Hal glanced to Ty, eyebrow raised.

"Look," Eli said. "We're no friends of the ACAS."

No one said anything, and finally Beall spoke. "Think we could talk in private for a moment, Captain?"

"Yeah, let's take a walk."

They made their way to the cargo bay. Ty limped over to a crate and took a seat.

"Injured in the field?" Beall asked.

"After," Ty replied. "It's a long story."

Beal didn't ask. "I got out of the ACAS years ago...I didn't re-up because of Mags, my girlfriend who had gotten out a year before me." He pulled his handheld and showed Ty a picture of a beautiful, dark-skinned woman with high cheekbones and short cropped hair.

Ty nodded slowly, giving Beall time to unwind his story.

"Mags was a vat. We were happy during the time we had." He gestured toward the front of the ship where the galley was. "Like the two of them. Then nature took its course. Fucking adrenaline fatigue." His jaw clenched and Ty could see the tears standing in the old man's eyes as he tucked the handheld away.

"Damn, I'm sorry," Ty said, looking down. The old man's pain was evident, and Ty gave him a minute to collect himself while his thoughts turned to Hal and Vivi, who most likely had been lucky enough to escape that fate for a few years yet at least. Time would tell.

"It was a slow decline. She held on for a year before she... died from a stroke." Ty could see the pain on Beall's face. "So, what I'm saying is that you can trust us. I have a vested interest in fucking over the ACAS. And Eli's gonna do this for me. Let us help you."

Ty held out a hand. Beall took it. "We'd be glad to have you, Beall."

"I've trained the kid since he was about sixteen. He won't be a liability on the mission."

Ty let out a sigh and scrubbed his face tiredly with one hand. "Yeah. But I'm afraid I might."

"Your leg?"

"Yeah." Ty sighed again. "I got injured about six months ago in a fight with an ACAS vat assassin."

"You must have really pissed them off," Beall said, with obvious respect.

"Yeah. Recovery's not coming along as fast as I want or need it to. Problem is that someone with my kind of disability would be mustered out of the ACAS, but my leg's not strong enough yet to do a lot of steady walking without the brace."

"Oh?"

"Yeah." He thought a second. "Beall, could you lead this mission with Hal? If there's anyone I can probably trust this to, it's you and my team. You know the base; you know the protocols." Ty was surprised; he hadn't known he was going to ask it until he did, but here was Beall...a former ACAS with a vat girlfriend who had died. He had a good reason to go. He'd been an officer like Ty. Both facts weighed heavily in the plus column for him. As much as he wanted to deny it, Ty knew the truth: he wasn't ready.

"You sure this is what you want?" Beall asked.

"Yeah. I can't risk the mission by going. But Beall... you should know, Vivi and Hal are more than just crew. They're my family."

Beall held his gaze. "I understand. I feel the same way about that kid in there."

"Good, then. Let's head back and tell them."

"So...I think it's best if I let Beall lead the mission," Ty finished up.

Hal nodded slowly, glancing to Vivi. Last night before they'd fallen asleep, they'd talked about their concerns that Ty was pushing himself too hard to be ready. Neither one of them had known how to bring it up to Ty, but now Hal realized that Ty had been evaluating his own progress the entire time.

"Ty. You sure about this?" Hal asked.

"Yeah. Very sure." Ty glanced to Eli. "Beall can go in as captain. You and Vivi should be the same rank, Eli," Ty said. "Think you can arrange that?"

"I can put in the records. I don't do the fake badges personally, but I know a guy who does, and he owes me. They'll be flawless. With the records I'll set up in the database, they'll see everything's legit when they do the surface check."

Ty explained the Arcteck division to Eli. The hacker listened with rapt attention and typed notes on a handheld.

"The Arcteck ruse sounds like it would work. The thing I can't figure out is how we're gonna get in? If we plan to land this big J-Class in there, we're gonna need a good cover story," the hacker said.

"We have a stolen ACAS shuttle, ready to rendezvous at our word. I need to get in touch with our people, and they'll update the uniforms to what they need to be as well," Ty said.

"Damn. Good deal. Let's get some 3D's of everyone for the ID's, and I can get that rolling."

"Black shirts," Ty said, glancing to Vivi and Hal.

"I'll put the background in later," Eli said. "Can I get a scan of your tattoo, Hal? For the file," he added.

Hal stepped forward and let Eli scan his wrist with his handheld. Then Vivi and Hal went to find the requisite black shirts.

"IF IT'S LONG ENOUGH, ACAS females wear their hair pulled back," Hal said.

Slowly over the weeks, Vivi had brought more and more of her things into Hal's room, and they were getting ready together. She ran her brush through her hair, then pulled it back in a tie. It was barely long enough. She turned toward him once she was finished. "What about makeup?"

He took a look at her. "You're fine. Female nat officers might wear it, but it's a bit reserved."

"What about vat females?" she was curious.

He shook his head. "They don't have time for nat stuff like that. You're gonna have to remember that dealing with vats is different if you're playing the part of an ACAS nat."

"What do you mean?"

"It's just different. You can't treat us like...friends or even people," Hal said. She could tell that it was hard for him to describe it. "It's like we're...a means to an end. Not important on a personal level. A tool like a powerhammer. You can't show you have feelings or care for us." He was at a loss for how to describe it another way.

She scanned his face and could tell he was trying hard to explain, so she nodded.

"Check with Beryl or Ty - maybe they can give you a better insight from a nat's point of view," Hal shrugged, heading for the hatch. She nervously tucked a loose strand of hair behind her ear and followed him.

RUNA WAS able to pull a still of Lane from the *Loshad*'s security cams footage during the Chamn-Alpha op. Eli said he'd be able to manipulate it into an ID scan and by lunchtime, the hacker was on his way to work his magic. They would be ready to leave in two days.

That left Ty to get in touch with Al-Kimia through the underground network and send a message as to what they would need, and where and when Lane would meet them with the transport. Other than that one necessary transmission, they were running comm silent for the rest of the op.

With his access to the ACAS computers, Eli would also get them the landing codes they would need for the base. Ty had finished his message to Lane and turned to a newsfeed on his monitor when Vivi found him on the bridge.

Sensing she needed to talk, he muted the vidfeed. "Everything alright?"

"Yeah. I...um...wanted to ask you something," It took a moment to gather herself. "Hal said I need to work on how to deal with vats as an ACAS solider. You know, in order to play my part well. Can you...I mean, would you mind giving me an idea?"

"Sure. Um...try and imagine that you're a natural-born, ACAS soldier. You become an officer and are assigned vats. To you, the vats are like...a piece of equipment. They do a job, serve their purpose. If they fail, the ACAS will send you ten more just like them. You probably don't even see the vats you work with as people with wants or desires. They are...merely mechanisms to fulfill your will at best. At worst, they're violent animals that have to be controlled."

Vivi frowned. "You heard someone say that...?"

"Yeah," Ty nodded, face tight. "That's how nats in the ACAS are taught to see it. Vats won't look you in the eye, or talk back, or say anything to disapprove of you and your orders, but if you're thinking like an ACAS, you still don't trust them. Be ready for that. Officers will notice immediately if you treat your vats differently."

"Vats won't even look you in the eye?"

"Not in a situation with a superior officer. The vat would be showing that he thinks he's an equal with a nat. Or that he or she is challenging a nat. That's a pretty severe punishment."

"He wasn't comfortable talking about it. Now I understand why. You didn't ever think of them that way, did you?"

He shrugged. "No. I never bought into the ACAS's bullshit. Every vat I ever commanded did their job as well or better than any natural born. I treated them with the same respect they gave me. But I got a lot of flak for it. It's the main reason I never made a rank above captain."

"You made your vats feel valued."

Ty shrugged. "I tried."

"No, you did more than try. Hal told me about you, and he said that. He's aware of how you valued his opinions and ideas."

"Yeah?" Ty shrugged. "I...I simply tried to treat him like the person he is."

"Tyce, I am reluctant to interrupt you, but there is a report on the newsfeed," Runa said.

Their focus was drawn to the monitor as Runa unmuted it. "—I repeat, there are reports of the ACAS massing ships around Betald. In the past weeks, the planet has expressed sympathies with Al-Kimia's stance against ACAS expansion. Now we go to Roger Triuna on Haleia Prime for his remarks."

The serious older man who appeared on screen was the Head of the Coalition Senate. "Good afternoon. Everyone is aware of the increasing tensions between the Coalition and Al-Kimia. First Minister Amias Adara has shown that he is unwilling to discuss ways for the Coalition and Al-Kimia to resolve their differences—instead he is stirring anti-Coalition sentiment throughout the planets of the Edge. This hostility has subverted the good people of Betald and made them pass laws to restrict Coalition commerce. Also, Coalition citizens living and working on Betald have been unfairly targeted by pro-Al-Kimian gangs. This is why we are moving in to support President Terzin's administration with the strength of the Coalition. Free vats, another target of the Al-Kimian gangs, have been rescued and housed temporarily on Omicron Station. We will keep Edge space free of Al-Kimian pirates and safe for Coalition citizens everywhere, especially our valued vat veterans. Thank you."

"I'm surprised he could say that with a straight face," Vivi said in disgust.

"Remain riveted, denizens, we'll be back in six with more on this and other stories," the announcer said.

Ty stabbed the button to shut off the noise. "Things are heating up. They'll move to Noea next. Solidify their presence on both planets, quell any uprisings, then move in on Al-Kimia and anyone else brave enough to stand up against them."

"Why are they moving vats to Omicron? What about the virus?" Vivi began to remember how they'd heard something about a vat virus, but they'd heard no more about it beyond the initial reports. She searched Ty's face uneasily.

"I think the virus talk was to come up with a feasible cover to empty Omicron. As for keeping the vats there... at the best, they're trying to keep them from joining Al-Kimia. At the worst...they could be preparing to use the vat kill switch," Ty said, suddenly nauseous. Would the ACAS go that far to keep vats from joining Al-Kimia? He knew they would.

"Oh gods," Vivi whispered. "It keeps getting worse."

"It'll get worse before it gets better," Ty said. "Now at least we know what's at stake on this mission," he said grimly.

Vivi nodded, her mouth set in a grim line. "We'll get it done."

"I know you will," Ty said.

TWENTY-FIVE

Fleet Admiral Quillon sighed as he waited for Dr. Balen, the head of the vat program to meet him on the *Vetra*. His disdain for Balen had been decided long ago; they'd had a few heated exchanges over the comm until finally he'd ordered the scientist to a face-to-face at Rinal station, where the *Vetra* was currently docked. The man was manipulative and was more self-interested than loyal to the ACAS and as such, the admiral despised him. Quillon had ordered him here to prove a point. He was no vat to be manipulated by this scientist.

"Good afternoon, Fleet Admiral," Balen said. He moved to take a seat in the one chair in front of the desk.

"You can stand. You won't be here long," Quillon said, leaning back in his chair to assess the man. "The doyen has requested an update on your progress on the kill device."

"The device works well-" Balen began.

Quillon cut him off – he didn't want to hear a lot of bi-horn shit. He already knew the problems with the kill device, but the point of this was to confront Balen on it and maybe get the man off his ass so progress could be made. "Have you been able to refine it and make it more reliable? Are the problems with the range solved yet?" Quillon imbued his words with impatience. As he saw it, this scientist was far too comfortable in his job being the head of the vat program for almost twenty-eight years. He never would have kept a man in a position that long—it always gave a subordinate a sense that they were invulnerable to being replaced, which caused most to get lazy. "Will it distinguish between released vats and vats still in service?"

"Not yet, Fleet Admiral. We are moving our work to the more secure Haleia-6 facility as you requested, and that's put us behind schedule-"

"The doyen won't care to hear your excuses," Quillon said, cutting him off.

Balen was getting flustered. "With all due respect, we've made a great deal of progress, considering the delays we've run into. The range increases the power usage exponentially—that's the difficulty we are running into-"

"You better solve the problems with your device. The doyen wants results, and he's not as patient as I am." Quillon smirked as he enjoyed the effect his words had on the scientist.

The admiral was not surprised to see Balen back down. "Yes sir, we will do our utmost. We have already set up an opportunity to test the revised device on Omicron once it is ready-"

"I am well aware of that, Balen. You need to go supervise your people on Haleia-6 personally. The doyen wants results in the next few weeks, or he will have to see if there are others who might have new ideas."

"Of course, Fleet Admiral Quillon," Balen said coldly. Chastened, he turned and left the room like a whipped dog.

Quillon smirked as he watched Balen go.

TWENTY-SIX

PATRIN WAS REVIEWING THE PIRATE ANKLAV INTEL ON HIS handheld when he glanced up and saw Orin standing in the open doorway of the sleeping pod on the *Raptor*. They'd landed on Dela Prime earlier in the day and Patrin had said they'd get started as soon as the sun went down. That way they wouldn't have to spend more time than they had to on this gods-forsaken rock.

Hi boss, Orin signed. *You wanted to see me?*

Yeah. Patrin gestured to the bed opposite where he sat. *I haven't heard from our weapon contacts in the Anklav, so tonight, we're going to go to the Palisade and get the lay of the land. Maybe we can just happen across someone.*

Orin nodded. *So, you need me to have your back.*

Yeah, Patrin said. *And then when we know more, we'll bring Dai with us. I think for the first time out, you and I can handle ourselves alright.*

Orin agreed.

. . .

THE PALISADES WAS a gigantic complex with a large vat patronage. There were the typical sex workers, glittering gambling casinos, ruthless vat fights and a tide of alcohol high enough to wash the whole place out to sea. It sat like a flashing jewel atop a cliff overlooking the dripping hues of sunset as Patrin and Orin stepped off the transport.

They made their way into the breezeway of the market, passing retail shops and going toward the rowdier sections of the complex. *Here*, Patrin signed, turning to go into a shady-looking bar attached to a large but tattered-looking casino.

Loud music and neon light spilled out into the street. When they entered, they saw the first room was a sort of dance floor and bar, but further in there were other, quieter areas where deals might be done.

Patrin entered the quieter area, taking a seat at the bar alongside Orin. Several nats at the nearby tables gave the big man a second look, then returned to their drinking.

A man sitting next to Patrin glanced at him as he raised his glass of amber liquor; Patrin saw the vat tattoo on his wrist.

"What's good here?" he asked as he saw the bartender heading over.

The grey-haired vat shrugged. "I like the Haleian whiskey or the jet fuel...depends on what kind of mood you're in. If you're trying to get fucked up and don't mind searing off your tongue, take the jet fuel. If not, definitely the whiskey."

"Thanks," Patrin said, ordering the whiskey for himself and Orin. He summarized the conversation with the stranger for Orin.

"What's up with him?" the vat asked.

"He's deaf. He's my ship's mechanic."

"Mm," the vat gave Patrin a nod. "He a nat?"

Patrin realized that the vat hadn't seen Orin's tattoo. "No.

He's one of us, brother." He paused a moment. "I'm looking for someone in the Anklav."

Patrin did not check the crowd directly, but he saw several people glance up in his peripheral vision at the comment.

"Looking for work? Or someone particular?" the vat asked tilting his glass to the side and watching the amber liquor move in the dull light.

"Looking to talk."

"The way I hear it, if you want them, they'll find you," the old vat laughed, polishing off his drink and swinging himself off the stool with difficulty. "If you're worth finding, that is. Where you staying?"

"The city spaceport."

"Alright. Have a good evening, my friend."

"What's your name?" Patrin asked.

"Rafe."

"Just Rafe?"

"Yeah," the old man said. "See you around, newcomer." He made his way off through the crowd.

Think he's going to be any help? Orin signed.

Who knows? Patrin shrugged.

They spent the rest of the evening drinking cautiously...or at least cautiously for vats. Patrin kept thinking of Seren's face as he'd set the mission before him. Disappointing the old man was unthinkable, especially so near the end of Seren's days. At the thought of the old man, there was a peculiar tightness in his chest that he didn't understand. He tried to feel around all the edges of whatever it was bothering him, but he was afraid to delve deeper. Instead, he ordered another double and downed it.

What's up? Orin asked.

Just like normal, Orin could sense his moods by the expressions across his face. He had an uncanny ability to read people,

Patrin remembered. Focus on the mission, he told himself. There was no way he could allow them to fail.

Just don't want to disappoint Seren, Patrin signed.

I know what you mean, Orin said.

It was getting late, but the bar didn't close, it just switched shifts in the early morning. About three, the crowd began to thin out. Patrin signed to Orin it was time to leave and slipped off his chair. He stumbled a little and realized that last drink had hit a little too hard.

You good? Orin signed.

Yeah. I think it's time to get back, he replied.

We can try again.

Patrin looked up at the big man's face, the scar from his interface to his cheek, still thinking of Seren and the rest of them, rapidly growing old. How many years did Orin have before his expiration date? How many years before he himself would find his strength and health ebbing?

He sighed heavily and echoed Orin's signs. *Yes, we can try again, my friend.*

THEY HEARD nothing from the Anklav the next day and Patrin's mood grew darker. He tried to distract himself helping Orin and Dai repair some light damage they had taken on their way out of Al-Kimian space. Before leaving, they would need to purchase a scudplate to replace one of the rear shields, so Dai was looking into where they could find the piece. For the rest of the day, they sat around at the ship, doing too little and getting bored.

He and Dai played squads that afternoon, but when the sun set on Dela Prime, he decided to head out on his own. He moved from club to bar, trying different parts of the city that he and Orin hadn't investigated yet. As the night wore on with no sign of the Anklav, he began drinking more heavily.

He couldn't exactly remember how long he'd been in the dark, dank bar he found himself in, but it matched his mood perfectly. There were a couple of mountainous bundles of muscles guarding the front door; it was a good idea – with drunken vats it was best to have capable bouncers on hand. While drinking, Patrin noticed three quarrelsome vats get ejected from the place.

When the excitement was over, he turned back to the alcohol. The mission was starting to weigh on his mind. He was becoming sure that Seren's trust in him had been misplaced. What would happen to Al-Kimia if he failed to secure the Anklav's help? His gun-running contacts had not replied to his requests for a meeting and poking around in the Palisades was not netting him any returns on his effort.

"Another," he ordered, watching as the bartender approached and poured another jolt of jet juice in his glass. He was getting shitfaced at a rapid rate. The thought of Kat brushed his mind, and he drew a fingertip through the moisture on the bar. He now wished he'd brought her along. She meant so much to him, in a way he couldn't explain.

They had something that he'd never had with any of the other women who had shared his bed, and he found he missed her. There was something strangely sad about her, and her worried look when he'd left had troubled him, but not completing the mission was unthinkable. He scrubbed a hand over his face. The sooner he could get this done and get back to Al-Kimia, the better.

Taking another look around the bar, he caught a brown-haired man greeting another with a furtive hand gesture. He didn't know what it meant. If not for his knowledge of ACAS hand sign and Haleian Sign Language, he probably would've missed it altogether. The man sat with the newcomer and they ordered a round of drinks while they talked. Not long after, the man and his friend shook hands and left. Patrin threw a few scrills on the bar, then followed them out and saw that they had gone their separate ways. He followed the brown-haired man toward the spaceport. When he turned the corner to a concourse, he saw that the man had vanished. Had his shadowing been that obvious? Cursing silently, Patrin headed back to his own ship.

He tried to be quiet as he headed into the *Raptor's* galley, but Leila was there when he entered. She scrutinized him, sensing something was wrong. "You okay, Patrin?" she asked him.

He glanced at her and slid into a seat next to the table. Pillowing his head on his arm he shook his head. "I'm drunk and stupid," he sighed.

She placed a gentle hand on his shoulder. "You might be drunk, but you're not stupid. Would you rather have some coffee or water?"

"Water."

"Good choice." She brought him a cup of water, placing it at his elbow. She sat across from him. "Patrin, I know the whole world seems like it's on your shoulders alone, but it's not. We're all in this together, and it's going to be okay," she said.

"I'm supposed to be the one reassuring you."

"Yeah, you might be in charge, but I'm the den mother of this ship," she smiled, tilting her head at him. "Reassuring you comes with the job."

"Thanks," Patrin said, smiling faintly at her. "We've been pretty unsuccessful so far. How can you be so calm?"

She laid a hand on his arm. "Because I know you. You'll get this job done. Get some sleep and tomorrow, things will look better."

. . .

Later the next day, Patrin found himself with Dai and Orin, heading into the local junkyard/chop-shop to pick up the replacement part. It took them an hour to find a scudplate that would bolt onto the *Raptor*; they paid in scrill and then headed back toward the spaceport, through a more industrial area adjacent to the Palisades.

Orin had hefted the scudplate on his shoulder, and he followed Dai and Patrin to the west entrance of the spaceport. They began to wander their way back toward their ship's berth, but before they arrived, Orin signed to get Patrin's attention.

Over there, he said, leaning the scudplate against a nearby wall.

Patrin glanced over, seeing the same brown-haired man from the other night being hassled by three others in an empty bay. The harassers had thrown their victim up against the wall. He gave Orin and Dai a nod.

They silently approached what looked like a robbery in progress.

"Scrill now, nat!"

"Three on one? Now that's just not fair," Patrin said loudly.

Two of the vats turned, and Patrin saw that they were rushing like a vat on amp. "Get the fuck out of here if you know what's good for you," one of them snarled.

"This isn't a fight you're going to win," Patrin said.

"They're vats." The bigger one said.

"So are we," his companion said, advancing slowly, spoiling for a fight. "Let's fight this out vat to vat," he said, putting up his fists.

Patrin grinned as he raised his own hands. Getting in a fight was fine by him – he needed to blow off some steam anyway. "Sounds about right to me."

The first blow was a punch meant for his interface. Patrin dodged it but took a body blow to the ribs. He was able to return with a punch that split the skin over his opponent's eye. Orin and his adversary were slugging it out, and he was similarly successful, using his size and weight for advantage. As their two rivals stepped back, they eyed Patrin and Orin warily, wiping blood from their faces.

"Had enough?" Patrin asked.

"Not nearly," the vat in front of him said, and they went at it again. Patrin took a blow to the eye but got in a jab that connected with his opponent's interface, sending the vat to the ground twitching. He stepped back, glancing to Orin's foe, who had a broken nose and was snuffling blood.

"You're done here," Patrin said. "Get the fuck outa here."

The vat regarded him appraisingly, weighing his options in the middle of his rush.

"I can end this real quick if he's not done, boss," Dai said. She'd leveled her blaster at Orin's opponent. Patrin knew her eyes were black with the same rush he felt rolling through his veins. There was that quality of synchronicity with his team, and Patrin knew he wouldn't lose this time. He smirked. "You've been bested. Don't make us kill you."

The vat growled. "Fuck it. Berman, let's go."

The vat named Berman let the captive nat go, and the two of them came to their unconscious friend.

"Good idea," Patrin said. "Get him outa here."

"Preferably to a medcenter before he bleeds out," Dai said with a smirk.

When they'd hauled the unconscious vat off, the brown-haired man stepped forward, nursing a busted lip. "Don't know what made you help me, but I owe you," he held out a hand.

"I like helping the underdog," Patrin grinned, shaking his

hand. "Why don't you come aboard my ship and let us patch you up?"

"Okay. That sounds good," he said, limping out of the empty bay and following them.

"What's your name?"

"Fallon. Yours?"

"I'm Patrin," he said, offering his real name. If this was the same man he had seen last night and did have some connection to the Anklav, he would need to go by his real name.

"I appreciate the help, Patrin."

When they reached the *Raptor*, Patrin helped his new friend up the ramp and into the main area of the ship.

"Have a seat," Patrin said, gesturing to a chair.

Leila was standing in front of the feedscreen in the galley, chewing on a fingernail. She obviously hadn't noticed their guest. "Guys," she said, gaze riveted on the screen.

Patrin turned to watch, but the story was at the end. He just caught the chyron scrolling past: "Vats in Protective Custody on Omicron."

"What did it say?" Dai asked.

"They're moving released vats to Omicron for holding," Leila said. "Rounding them up on Edge worlds like Betald."

The *Raptor's* crew shared uneasy glances. Their mission was even more important than ever. Patrin brought them back by gesturing to his guest. "Leila. Could you help out our friend here? He got on the wrong side of some thugs."

Leila turned to see Fallon. "Oh! Of course. I'm sorry I didn't see you there."

"It's fine," Fallon said.

"Let me get my medkit."

That's bad, Orin signed, gesturing to the feedscreen.

Patrin nodded, then turned back to Fallon.

"The big guy," Fallon gestured, "and you. Did you two serve together?"

Patrin shook his head. "We met later," he said, knowing Orin would read his lips.

Leila returned and began working on Fallon's lip, cleaning the blood away, disinfecting and then sealing the cut. "Did they hit you in the head?" she asked, scanning near his blackening eye.

"Just in the eye. I'm sure I'm fine."

"I'll be the judge of that," Leila said, giving him a smile. The scanner beeped. "Ok, yeah, You're fine. What's your name?"

"Fallon. I'm in...cargo," he said, glancing at Patrin. "Anklav cargo."

Patrin's eyes went wide.

"Look. I heard from a few that you've been asking around. Are you looking for someone to ship something for you?"

Patrin came to sit across from him. "Could we have a few minutes?" he asked as Leila finished up.

"Boss?" Dai said.

"I'll be fine. Go make sure Orin's patched up. I'll call if I need you."

Dai, Leila and Orin went to one of the sleeping pods, leaving Patrin with his guest.

"So," Fallon said. "I was trying to figure out which berth was yours when our three friends became interested in what I was doing skulking around. One good turn deserves another. What can I do for you?"

"I have a...need for more than shipping cargo," Patrin said.

"Guns for the Oppos?"

Patrin shook his head. "I'm gonna be plain because that's what I'm good at. I want to speak to the Anklav heads. As many of them as I can."

"At one time?" Fallon asked. He shook his head. "That's impossible."

"Why?"

"They haven't met like that in years. Why do you want to talk to them?"

"Al-Kimia needs help. We all know the ACAS is coming for them," Patrin said.

"I know it sounds harsh, but that's their problem. We run our business and the Coalition leaves us alone. That's the deal."

"Do you really think you're going to remain untouched here? Once the ACAS comes for Jaleeth like they came for Omicron, you're next on their list. And when the Edge worlds are under the Coalition's heel, you're going to look very, very good to them with the amount of money that flows in and out."

Fallon sighed heavily. "What is it you want? Other weapons?"

"Not exactly. The Anklav has a lot of ships."

Realization dawned on Fallon's features. "The Anklav is not going to give its ships to Al-Kimia."

Patrin shook his head. "No, that's not it. We want you to join us. Support us. Betald's effectively fallen, Noea's not far behind."

Fallon ran a hand through his hair. "That's a tall order."

"I know," Patrin said. "Look, the Anklav has helped Al-Kimia out so far. We've shipped our blasters through you, but it's not enough. Set it up so I can appeal to them."

"They're not gonna all come to one place…The Anklav's not organized anymore. Different factions do what they want."

"That's okay. Put out the word so I can talk to as many of them as you can get all at once, via the feeds or in person or whatever," Patrin said.

Fallon sighed heavily, then retrieved his handheld from a

pocket. He made an audio call. "It's Fallon. I need you to get a message out for me."

"I can try," the voice on the other end said.

"Let everyone know I want to request a meeting of the captains. I have a proposition that might be of interest to them," Fallon said.

"A meeting of the captains?"

"That's what I said."

"Give me a couple of days to get it out on the network. End of the week, maybe?"

"Yeah. Thanks." He disengaged the call, setting his handheld up to receive. "Let me get your comm designation. I'll call you when everything's set up."

Patrin sent his designation, and Fallon fixed him with an appraising stare. "Look, if it makes you feel better, I don't believe you're fucking with us. I checked you out after I figured you were looking for someone in the Anklav, and I know the shipping arm has been helping Al-Kimia. But you should know this. If I'm wrong and you're setting us up, you're going to regret it."

"I'm not," he answered. "The only mission I have is to keep the ACAS from taking the Edge."

"Okay, then." Fallon slowly got to his feet.

"Look, I can send one of my crew with you in case those guys are still skulking around."

The Anklav member shook his head. "I'll be fine. I'll contact you end of the week."

"Sounds good," Patrin said.

TWENTY-SEVEN

ELI GOT THE IDs AND LANE WAS BRINGING THE uniforms that Al-Kimia had provided along with the shuttle. They had invited Beall and Eli to stay on the *Loshad* while they waited for all the pieces of their disguise to come together. This allowed everyone to get to know each other a bit better. At first Eli was busy supervising the movements of his cells to their new locations, but by the time they left on their way to Tranesh, the small uninhabited forest moon where they were to switch from the *Loshad* to the ACAS transport, they were feeling more comfortable with each other. Ty had become even more certain of his decision to let Beall and Hal go on the mission. As much as he wanted to go with them, he would take the *Loshad* back to Al-Kimia to wait for their return.

They landed about the same time as Lane, and they had all spent the evening mission prepping. Ty took Lane to the side and got her up to speed about Eira, the spheres and the dual reasons for their trip: not only to get the kill device, but the Mudar spheres as well. Last night, he'd also had a private

THE RUSH'S ECHO

conversation with Hal on the bridge, who assured him he was comfortable with Beall on the mission.

They were up early the next morning, gearing up for the mission. Once done changing, Eli and Lane had said goodbye to Ty and boarded the transport where they sat talking together. Then, Hal and Vivi appeared.

Ty was waiting for them on the ramp. Vivi was wearing the fatigue uniform of Arcteck and a black cap bearing the Arcteck insignia of a trowel and data chip. She'd tugged it down over her hair and was wearing a backpack. Hal looked as he always had in uniform—black tee, black cargoes with a fatigue jacket that had the same insignia on his collar, to show that he was one of Arcteck's vats. Whoever had made these uniforms on Al-Kimia had known what they were doing, Ty thought. Everything was right down to the smallest detail, but it still did little to make him feel better about staying behind.

"You both look perfect," Ty said. He'd scrutinized the ID's when Eli had brought them and declared them good. He'd even compared them to his old one and swore that he couldn't tell the difference.

"Thanks. It's weird to be back in uniform," Hal said, adjusting his fatigue jacket.

"Yeah." Ty realized the two of him were waiting for his blessing. He opened his mouth to speak, but words failed him, and he ended up glancing down at his leg, strapped into the brace. Admonishing himself, he returned his gaze to Hal and Vivi, making himself say what they needed to hear. "You're ready for this. Both of you." He hugged Vivi first, holding her close for a moment and hating himself for worrying that it might be the last time he saw her. "Take care of yourself out there, Vivi."

"I will," she said.

Ty turned to Hal. When his friend had heard that the

Coalition was holding released vats in protective custody on Omicron, he'd taken it hard. He was chomping at the bit to do something...anything to strike a blow against the ACAS. Ty supposed Hal was ready for this, but it didn't make it any easier. He had to inspire confidence.

"I told you it's time for you to take the lead on things, and I meant it. You brought everyone back from the mission to get Max and you'll bring everyone out fine this time," Ty said.

Before he could decide whether to shake Hal's hand or give him a one-armed hug, the vat stepped forward and uncharacteristically clapped him in a full bear hug. "No worries, Ty."

"So...just making sure. You and Beall are clear on everything?" He asked again, looking toward the cargo bay where Beall was. He felt more secure knowing they'd have another veteran with them, which meant Hal would have someone to back him up and keep him steady. With Beall's past experiences...Ty knew he understood vats in a way that most ACAS officers didn't.

Hal had, of course, picked up on Ty's glance to the cargo bay. "Yeah. He's five-by-five," Hal said. "Don't worry."

Ty gave him a nod and glanced at Vivi again, appraising her disguise. "Let me see your soldier face," Ty said.

Vivi took a wide stance, and narrowed her eyes at him, settling a hand on the blaspistol at her hip. Then she laughed softly, completely breaking the spell. "We love you," she said simply, giving him one last hug.

With those words, Ty was almost overcome. "Yeah. I feel the same way. Take care you two."

"We will, Cap. Don't worry," Hal said, stepping down the ramp with Vivi.

Beall came out, his gaze following Hal and Vivi over to the transport.

"Beall. There's something you've gotta know," Ty said, speaking low.

"Go."

"It's a long story, but Hal doesn't have the ability to rush anymore," Ty said. "He's completely capable of whatever you need him to do. He's fast, strong and smart – he can think on his feet, but he won't have the edge from the rush. It's not something we mention to everyone, but I thought you probably needed to know."

"Was he wounded in the field?" Beall asked.

"No, not exactly," Ty glanced back at the shuttle. "It's a long story…something that we probably should go into another time. I thought you should know before the mission."

"Thank you, Ty." Beall held out a hand. Ty shook it. "I'll do everything I can to be successful."

"I trust you will," Ty said.

TWENTY-EIGHT

"Lights to sleep cycle," Seren called before heading into his bedroom. It had been a long day, going over contingency plans for the Al-Kimian Defense Force's reaction to the fall of Betald.

He took off his belt and made his way to the closet to hang it up. Shrugging out of his fatigue jacket, he heard a soft, but clearly audible thump behind him. He was able to snatch his viblade from its sheath on his belt without much movement and slip it under his shirt in his waistband next to his skin. Then, he waited in silence as his intruder spoke.

"Hands where I can see them."

His heart fell as he turned slowly, hands up. "Now it makes perfect sense. I should have expected you would be the one to come for me."

Kat stood in front of him, her hair pulled back in a severe tail, in true ACAS style. She wore black clothes and gloves, her knees and elbows marked with dust from the vents above. Her eyes showed she'd been crying, but there were no tears now.

Her face was set in stone. "It's time for you to die, traitor," she said.

Seren chuckled sadly at the irony of her words. "It's past time for that, Kat. We both know I've been living on borrowed time. But you're struggling with this – I can see it in your face. You should ask yourself why you're doing it if you hate it so."

Her face twisted for a second, and her mask of righteous anger slipped. She reached for her temple with her free hand, as if she was having the mother of all headaches. "I...I'm not s-sure..."

Seren took a step forward. "Let me help you," he said, hands open.

She focused back on him and snarled, "I don't need to ask myself anything. I follow orders. 'I am the fist of the ACAS.'"

"Then why have you not shot me yet?"

"Shut the fuck up," she said coldly, one hand going to her head in obvious pain again.

While she was distracted, Seren reached for the viblade in his waistband and stepped forward. He was able to strike a glancing blow on her shoulder as she twisted out of the way. At the same time, she pulled the trigger, the bolt hitting him on the right side. Her blaspistol went flying as he slammed into her, and his weight toppled them both to the floor. They wrestled, and he pushed her back with a monumental effort. She rolled with it and once she was up on her feet, she was holding her own viblade.

He had gotten to his feet as well. Her vibrating blade slashed him across the forearm that he put up to block her. Wary now of letting him pin her, she stepped back.

"Don't do this, little one," Seren said, breathing heavily and switching the blade to his uninjured side.

"I am the fist of the ACAS! In war, I am strength! I bring the justice of the Coalition to its enemies! Victory...is... mine!"

she hissed through clenched teeth, each word sounding like it brought with it a burning pain.

Seren prepared himself for her strike, but she was young and fast, and his arthritic joints slowed him down. In a powerful strike, she plunged the knife deep between his ribs. The vibrating blade scraped bone as she drew back. He lunged out at the same time and managed a deep cut on her bicep as she dodged to avoid his blade. She backed away as he went down, but there was no need. He was hurt badly. She watched him struggle. Wheezing heavily, Seren kicked his feet in his own blood, trying to put space between them.

After he had retreated enough to put his back against the wall, he tried to get to his feet, but couldn't. The wound in his side was a red-hot agony, and breathing was becoming difficult. The blood he was coughing up was a bad omen, and his strength was ebbing.

Kat took a few steps toward him, then dropped her viblade. Her breath was harsh in the sudden silence of the room. She clutched her head and fell to her knees near him, sobbing. It was obvious to Seren that she was being torn apart inside. The ACAS must have programmed her to kill him when the chance offered itself, and now the programming was tearing her apart. "Gods...I...I didn't want to do this!" she sobbed.

"Kat, it's okay." His voice was a rough whisper, but she heard him.

"What?" she asked, suddenly staring at him in horror.

"It's not your f-fault," Seren said hoarsely. "I don't b-blame you..."

His breathing was getting slower and slower; he could feel his life spilling out with every pull of air. She shook her head at his words, tears spilling down her face.

"They...did this. N-not you, young one," Seren said.

"He's...in my head. I hear him all...the ti-time," she sobbed.

It was a mammoth effort for him to reach out and brush her hand. She latched on like a drowning person. "Kat..." he said, his eyes drifting closed for a moment as he took a desperate breath. "Listen to me. It's not your f-fault." At her sob, he renewed his focus on her. "Under-understand?"

"I'm s-sorry," she was crying freely now, tears cutting paths in the blood splatter on her face. "I'm so s-sorry." She squeezed his hand.

"I...I know," he whispered, holding her gaze until his very last moment.

WHEN HIS HAND'S touch grew slack, she knew he was gone. Kat crumbled. "Seren," she cried.

But he didn't answer. His kind expression had lost its focus, and he stared past her into nothingness.

She sat on her knees for a long time, wrapping her arms around herself and sobbing helplessly. When she was utterly exhausted, she lifted her head and looked around the room, everywhere – anywhere – but at Seren's dead body.

Her viblade was nearby; she grabbed it and stuck it in her belt. By the time she got to her feet, her face was empty. Her mind began to distance itself and coolly access the situation as the tears and blood dried on her face. Cleaning up and getting away were the objectives now. She stepped over the body to get to her blaspistol, holstering it. It was then she saw the blood running down her arm and dripping from her fingers. Pressing a hand against the cut in her bicep that she hadn't felt, she realized she needed to do something. Darting into the bathroom, she found a towel and pressed it to the wound with her shaking hand, catching sight of her face in the mirror.

Her eyes were black holes in a pale, dead face.

Her blood ran cold when she saw Quillon watching from behind her, his face visible in the mirror.

Nyma, you have done well, the Admiral praised. *Clean up the evidence and go.*

Feeling the automatic burst of endorphins at his approval, she nodded. If he was pleased, she would be happy. "Sir, yes sir," she whispered.

Taking the towel into the bedroom, she stepped past the traitor to stand in the middle of the room. She knelt to rub the towel over the smears on the floor, then realized that there was nothing she'd be able to do – the traitor's blood was mixed with her own and there was too much of both. Standing, she turned around in a full 360, her gaze brushing over the floors and walls. So much blood. This was sloppy. They would know. There was no way she could escape being identified.

She had expected to shoot Seren and flee up the vent, leaving no trace, but her hesitation, fraying nerves and his fierce defense had made that impossible. "I...I can't cover this up," she whispered, turning around in a circle again. "I can't." She let out a panicked moan.

There was no answer from the Admiral, but he didn't have to speak. She knew. She would have to run. Seren's schedule for the next day meant it would be a while before he was discovered. Wiping the blood from her chrono, she saw that she had six, maybe seven hours before the treasonist's body would be discovered.

With a leap up, she grasped the edges of the vent's hole and pulled herself up into the ductwork once more. Reaching down, she snagged the hinged opening and pulled it shut behind her. Trailing blood, in the midst of one of the strongest rushes of her life, she made her way back to her quarters.

. . .

THE RUSH'S ECHO

Ten minutes later, she was sobbing again, huddled on the floor of the shower as the hot spray beat the tears out of her. She was awash in a sea of grief as flashes of what she'd done replayed in her mind. She'd murdered Seren, one of the few people who ever treated her like someone who mattered. This had been her one chance for...something new. Freedom. And it was utterly lost.

The storm of grief spent itself as she watched the pink water swirling down the drain. When she came back to herself, the water was clear, and the swells of emotion had faded into numbness. Her emotionality was coming and going like a bad comm signal, but she couldn't let it get in the way of her escape. It had been the same when she'd lost Jakob, but this time it was worse.

The next thing she was conscious of was standing in the bathroom, using wound glue on her still bleeding shoulder, then her arm. Her bathroom was covered in blood, but she no longer cared. Once her bleeding had stopped, she wiped her arm down with a towel and let it drop to the floor.

She dressed mechanically, then tugged her still-wet black hair into a tail. Then, she grabbed her ready-bag and began to add to it. Next, she found herself chewing on a ration bar from the kitchen with no memory of leaving the bedroom. It tasted like paste, but her metabolism would need the calories to recover from the massive rush she was on. A wave of nausea made her think she was going to throw up, but she gritted her teeth until it passed, and she could think again. It was time to find a blockade runner and stow away. By the time they found the traitor's body, she planned to be long gone.

Two days later, Kat clenched the shredder comm in one hand and her blaster in the other in the wan light of the cube's crysplas feedscreen. Her hands were clean, yet she still felt the stains of Seren's blood on her skin. She dropped the shredder and the blaster and rubbed her palms compulsively on the black cargos she wore. Would her hands ever be clean again?

The ship she'd stowed away on had left Drena base, headed to Sora. She had hidden in the cargo bay until it arrived at its destination at midday, which had made her escape easier. After disappearing into the ebb and flow of Sora's foot traffic, she bought a shredder comm and rented a cube.

Her two choices stood out starkly. Comm the fleet admiral or use the blaster to blow her brains out in this cheap cube of a room? She stopped compulsively rubbing her hands to pick up the weapon and run her fingertips over the dark metal. It was what she deserved. Patrin had trusted her. Seren had treated her with fairness, and she'd repaid all of that by killing him. She hit the charging lever and listened to the whine as the blaster powered itself. Could she do it? Abruptly, she pressed the business end to her head, right by her interface. She trembled on the knife edge of action. It would be over so quick she wouldn't feel it. Looking up, she saw Quillon watching her from the reflection in the feedscreen and she began to tremble and let the gun fall.

On autopilot, she began to dial a number on her comm, unconscious of what her fingers were doing. She stared down at the screen, feeling the ache of her physical wounds and the black hole that threatened as she tried to forget Seren's last words. *They did this, not you.*

She wasn't sure who the traitors were anymore.

The fleet admiral's face appeared on the screen of the shredder, and she immediately looked away.

"Katerine."

"S-sir." Her stomach knotted itself at the sound of his voice.

"At ease, Nyma. What happened?"

"I...I...killed the vat leader, but I was injured and had to flee," she said simply. The comm was shaking, so she reached to steady it with her other hand. "Evidence...was left behind. It got...m-messy."

"Just one. No others?" Quillon eyed her intently. "I am disappointed."

She cringed at his words as if wounded. "Th-things...did not go as planned, Sir," she said. "I can explain—"

He cut her off. "Send your coordinates. You will be retrieved. We will discuss your failure when face to face again."

"Sir-" He did not wait to hear her words but signed off before she had finished speaking. She had to type in the coordinates twice because her hands were still trembling so badly. Then she walked unsteadily into the bathroom and threw up the ration bar she'd eaten earlier. She rinsed her mouth, washed her hands again for the tenth time since she'd been in the room and went back to the bed. There was a message waiting for her that said expect pickup in the Sora spaceport in 12 hours.

It had never occurred to her to run away. The admiral was like a gravity well. If she ran, he would pull her back in. There was no escape.

TWENTY-NINE

Patrin entered Fallon's ship bay, feeling the slight prickle in his senses as he tried to take everything in at once. He was following Fallon, flanked by a vat named Sutherland.

They'd made their way across the spaceport to some of the nicer bays, where a sleek black freighter sat. As they'd stepped in, he noticed that there were two atop her. He could barely see the people, but the barrels of their blasrifles were easily apparent from his angle. They were being careful of him, it was obvious.

"I'm not here to cause any trouble," Patrin said.

"Trust but verify, my friend," Fallon replied with a soft chuckle.

Two familiar looking men stepped outside the craft. "It was a set up!" Patrin said, recognizing them from the fight a few days before.

"All part of the verification," Fallon grinned.

They stepped inside to see a few crew in the cargo bay and to hear a high-pitched yell and giggle as a little boy burst through the tall crew.

Fallon knelt and caught the child in his arms, swinging him up. "Hey, you little Owlet."

"Hi," the boy said back, looking at Patrin shyly, then hiding his face against Fallon's shoulder.

Patrin watched the two of them for a moment. The boy had brown hair, and wide eyes like Fallon, obviously his offspring. He was confused as to why they would have the child on the ship. Not having much experience with children, Patrin wasn't good with ages. He could only tell that the child was smaller than he, himself, had been when he'd started in vat training school. The boy was holding something in one arm. Taking another look, he saw it was a small representation of an animal, part of one ear missing. A feline, it seemed, by the pointed ear, tail and whiskers.

He considered that perhaps the child was being trained to take Fallon's place, but then dismissed it. The nats had schools for their younger ones, he knew. Their children were not trained or accelerated like vats, but allowed to grow and learn naturally, instead of being supplemented. He wondered why the nats would choose such an inefficient way to educate their children, but he knew there was probably a reason. Being a vat, he just didn't understand it.

"Time for a nap, kiddo," Fallon said. "Patrin, this is my kid Ollie."

"Hi, Ollie," Patrin said.

The child's tiny feline representation fell from his fist as he wrapped his arms around his father's neck. Patrin knelt down and retrieved the item. As he glanced up, he saw Sutherland step forward.

"He's been wide open all day," he said to Fallon. "Would you like me to take him, sir?"

"I'll carry him to his room. You can put him down for his nap. Come on, Patrin."

Patrin followed Fallon and the vat down the hallway to Ollie's quarters. "You can have him if you take care of him," Ollie said, over his dad's shoulder.

Patrin was confused for a moment, then realized the child was trying to give him the cat. "Oh...I don't...um..."

"He doesn't have time for pets, buddy," Fallon said, "but that's a nice thing to do. Time to sleep a while." The pirate keyed the door and handed off the boy to Sutherland. "See you when you wake up, Ollie."

They made their way to the bridge where a tecker was working on the ship computers. "Sorry, but I'll need the bridge a moment," Fallon said.

"Sure, Cap," the female tecker replied, tapping off her node and heading off the bridge.

Fallon made his way to a table and began to bring up a holographic display.

Patrin took in the bridge, unsure of what to do. He held the cat in his hands, turning it over as he did. He remembered now; nats called these toys—they were given to nat children. He wondered what they did with these besides carry them around. Vats didn't have such things, so it was a mystery. Gently he set the cat down on a nearby console.

"We'll do the meeting in here," Fallon said.

"Sure. I put Ollie's cat over here."

"No problem. Kid leaves his toys everywhere anyway," Fallon said.

"You let a vat care for your offspring," Patrin noted.

"Sutherland's been with me a long time. I trust him, and Ollie loves him," Fallon noted. "My kid's mom died, and I needed help. The rest of the crew helps too."

Patrin nodded thoughtfully. It was like a vat batch, he supposed – each person devoted to the good of the whole group.

"Ok, I'm getting ready to start the conclave. You ready?"

"Yeah," Patrin said, feeling a bit uncertain. He'd spent the last two days planning on what he would say, but every time he thought he had an angle on it, he changed his mind. Now, however, he knew that everything rested on his ability to speak to the members of the Anklav. With the right words, the idea would spread, like a secret at first, then like a revolution, just as Seren had always said.

Fallon brought up a screen with many faces on it. He greeted a few of the early arrivals, and then they waited a few more minutes while more and more people joined the conclave. Some screens showed faces, others were anonymously dark.

Finally, Fallon spoke. "Hello. As a lot of you know, I'm Fallon Guare."

Patrin was floored. *Guare? Was this the son of Tobias Guare – the last Anklav leader?*

"I want you all to know that I would not have called this meeting unless it was about some issue crucial to all our survival. My father taught me that the Anklav was family, and we protect family. There are enough of you that remember him, I see, by your attendance here today. I thank you for that.

"I have found the man who is about to speak to you to be truthful. I have talked with him at length, and he brings up much to think about. His name is Patrin Kerlani, and I will let him speak to you now."

Guare glanced to Patrin, then turned the screen and its camera so that he could be seen.

"Al-Kimia asks your assistance," Patrin began. "As you know, the ACAS is extending itself into the Edge, strengthening its hold on the Edge worlds. They have taken Betald and Omicron station and are now holding released vats with no cause. They call it protective custody, but we all know why they are doing this. Because vats have sided with Al-Kimia in a bid for the Edge to remain free.

"The ACAS has turned a blind eye to the Anklav, but who do you think they will come for, once the planets of the Edge have fallen? Anklav business is lucrative, and once the ACAS has settled the problem posed by the Opposition, they and the corps they represent will not hesitate to turn their eye to you. Freedom for Dela Prime and the Anklav has never been in the corps best interest, and once we are conquered, you will be a small matter for the doyen to settle. They keep us divided by saying you are protected, but when the threat of the Edge is conquered, you will be the only thing between them and total domination. You will stand alone, and you will fall.

"It doesn't have to be this way, though. Many of the civilians of the Edge have entered into voluntary service with us. Their ships support those protecting Al-Kimian space. But ACAS ships are massing, and our fleet is not going to be enough. My message is simple: we need all the inhabitants of the Edge to band together against the threat against us. Every vat, every nat, every being that calls these planets their home must rally at this moment. Our destiny is at stake."

He glanced at Fallon, who was looking at him thoughtfully. After a moment, the pirate took the screen back. "I will not tell you what you should think, conclave. I would only urge you to look at the facts and share them with others in our organization. Each ship...each crew will have to make its own decision. My crew has yet to decide, but I see much sense in this man's words and will urge my crew to join. Those who are resolute should join me. Those who are not, may do as they will, of course. When you are ready, call the conclave together again. Thank you."

With a press of a key, the screen went dark. "You make a

good argument, Patrin. I cannot speak for my crew, but I will share your words with them."

"Thank you," he glanced over and saw that Sutherland was standing in the open doorway that led back to the main hall.

"Is Al-Kimia truly offering sanctuary to released vats as we hear?" Sutherland asked, studying Patrin.

"Yes. They are offering a place to belong," Patrin said. "It's not a ploy to gain more soldiers. They treat vats as equals. In fact, General Terra Malar's closest advisor is a vat – my captain. It is no lie."

Sutherland nodded thoughtfully. "I will speak to the vats on our ship, Fallon."

"I know they will hear you," Fallon said. "Now we must wait, Patrin. The word will get out and spread. I don't know how it will go, but you gave it a good shot." He stood up and Patrin did the same. He held out a hand and Patrin shook it. "I will be in touch."

THIRTY

The Locust CD-8 which had brought him to Haleia-6 touched down in the hangar and Dr. Riley Balen stood, stretching his legs after the long flight. His face was still burning with rage from being called on the carpet by Quillon. The fleet admiral had been only a boy when Balen had started his work with the ACAS, and he didn't appreciate being treated like a subordinate. Every vat Quillon had on his staff had been created in facilities designed and run by Balen and those like him. That bastard knew nothing.

He would talk to the doyen about the man, but he knew he had to wait until he could deliver a working kill device. Then Doyen Meyer might be inclined to listen. Until then, Quillon undoubtedly had the upper hand.

He stepped to the transport's hatch as it slid open, revealing a captain and subordinate.

"Sir – we were told by command to meet you and escort you to the lab."

"No need," he said dismissively as he swept past them and toward the lift building. "I know exactly where I'm going."

When Balen stepped across to the lift, he came face to face with another pair of guards. The vat that stood directly in front of him averted his eyes and stepped to the side, deferring exactly like he'd been programmed to. Balen smirked as he entered the lift and headed down to his new research lab on level three.

"How far now?" Hal asked as he peered at the piloting displays. They'd just began the approach to Haleia-6 and the base there.

"Less than an hour. I hope those landing codes Eli got us were legit, or it's gonna be a real short mission," Lane said, glancing up at him.

"He's got issues, but being a good hacker isn't one of his problems," Hal said, slipping into the co-pilot's seat. "Here." Hal handed her two sprays of Amp and the neutralizer. "Just in case we get in the shit. There's more in the supplies we brought."

"Thanks," she said, tucking them into a front pocket of her fatigue jacket.

"Lane, there's something you need to know."

She gave him a sidelong glance, about to crack a joke, but she saw he was serious and turned more fully to him. "What is it, Cullen?"

"I don't have the ability to rush anymore." He waited a second, to see her reaction. "Our friend Eira...figured out a way to stop adrenaline fatigue, but I had to give up the rush."

"Holy shit. You're fucking serious?"

"Yeah. Vats have repurposed Mudar nanites, so she was able to use her own nanites to stop mine."

"Is she gonna be able to do that for more of us?" Lane asked.

"That's what we're hoping. If we can recover these spheres, the Mudar might be willing to help us do that."

"Fuck me," she whistled, looking at him closely. "This op is more important than I realized."

"Yeah, it's gotta be successful. We could help a lot of vats. The other thing I wanted to mention was, if we get in any trouble in there, you make sure to get Vivi out if you can."

"You think something bad's gonna happen?" Lane asked.

"No, but where we're going…it's dangerous. Beall gets it, but Veevs and Eli don't. They don't get it like we do."

"Yeah. She's a nat, but she's a nat I like. I'll keep my eye on her." There was a long pause, then she spoke in a lower voice. "Kinda weird to be going back in, right?"

"Yep, I gotta say going back on an ACAS base wasn't on the top of my list of things I wanted to do before my expiration date," Hal said grimly.

"Me either. Think those routines'll come back to us?" Lane said.

"Yeah. Easy like flatcakes."

Hal sat with her until they were growing close to Haleia-6, then he stood. "I'll let everyone know we're close." They'd discussed the plan earlier, and Vivi had shown both Eli and Beall the sphere they would be using as an artifact to make their story seem legit.

Even though he couldn't rush anymore, he felt the typical pre-op excitement, tempered with his worry about the nats in his care. He found himself acutely aware that he didn't have the edge he needed. He would have to be extra careful, using his increased ability to focus to make up for the loss of power and speed that the rush would give him. He hadn't wanted to jinx anything by telling Lane about his concerns, but it would pay to be extra wary.

"Hey. We land in about 45 minutes," he said as he passed Vivi, Beall and Eli, heading to the back of the shuttle to check everyone's weapons. The familiar process eased his mind a little, and he was running through the steps when Vivi came up beside him.

"Got any last tips?" she said.

"Let Beall take the lead. He knows ACAS codes and procedures. If you get called on something, let them know quick that you're a tecker, not a soldier. You can lay on the attitude too. Arctecks think they're the doyen's gift to the Spiral." He eyed her weapon. "Fully charged, right?"

"Yep." She touched her belt near the back where another two powerpacks were. "Got backups too, like you taught me."

Hal could see she was getting scared behind her façade of confidence. Something about the tightness in her jaw and the stiff way she held herself communicated her inner thoughts. He placed a hand on each shoulder and slowly rubbed the stress out. "Just stay natural, as if this was another day's work, right?"

"Yeah."

"And think about what a great story this is gonna make for Ty. He'll want to know every detail."

She smiled, then turned to hug him. He returned the embrace. "I love you, Veevs," he said against her ear.

"Love you back," she murmured.

LANE GAVE the landing codes Eli had stolen, and then navigated their transport to the lab facility at Cardela Base. Beall saw them set down inside the hangar, where it appeared they were the only ship. As Lane landed, Beall looked at each of them in turn. "Ready?" he asked.

"Yeah," Hal replied.

Eli grabbed the ACAS pack that contained Eira's sphere and Hal swung a blasrifle onto his back. Vivi and Beall joined them. Hal gave Lane her blasrifle as she came down from the pilot's chair.

"Sir," Hal said, addressing Beall but diverting his gaze over the former ACAS's shoulder in the customary manner. "Lead the way."

Lane took up the rear, behind Beall and Vivi as they exited the transport to find two ACAS officers waiting for them. The soldiers saluted Beall's rank of colonel. He returned the salute and the older of the two soldiers spoke.

"I would like to apologize for the small welcoming committee. We weren't expecting another transport today, sir."

"Of course, Lieutenant," Beall replied. He waved a hand, warming naturally to the role. "We have some valuable cargo to take down to the lab."

"We get advance notices for everyone that goes down to the lab. This is most unusual. If I could check your identification, please."

Beall handed over his ID, and the other soldier checked Vivi and Eli's ID's. No one questioned the two silent vats, standing with hands clasped behind their backs and eyes averted from the nats around them.

"Colonel Loeb." The officer read the name on Beall's ID. "I'm sorry, but I really should call this in."

Beall let his irritation show plainly. "These teckers haven't slept in two days—all we need to do is drop this off, then get them some rest. I hardly think you need to hold us up longer than need be, but by all means, be sure. And I'll be sure to report our treatment to the base commander."

The younger officer whispered to the older one, who shrugged. "Sorry Colonel. I'm sure we can avoid holding you up longer than needed. Please allow us to escort you to the lifts."

There was a mechanical sound behind them, and Beall glanced back as their cargo ship's platform was rotated and slowly lowered into the holding bay below. He tried not to let it bother him, but he didn't like the idea of his getaway vehicle being hemmed in.

They were led out of the hangar and across the yard to a lift building. When the soldier keyed the door open, they were able to see the small building had a pair of lifts in it, with one man standing on guard. The man, a vat, snapped to attention and saluted all the officers there.

"Private Chall, these three and their vats are cleared for the complex. I already checked their ID's."

The man gave a curt nod. "Sir, yes sir," he said, coming around the desk to unlock one of the lifts.

"Have a good visit, Colonel Loeb," the older nat said as they left, leaving the guard alone with them.

He stood at attention beside the lift door. "Is there anything else I can do for you, sir?" he asked, standing stiffly and avoiding their gazes. Beall barely looked at him.

"No," Beall said curtly, seeing that the lift slid open. "Let's go."

They entered the lift and the doors slid closed. Beall keyed the lowest level, which was three. "There's a different lift down to level four," he said. "I'll remember more about where it is when we get to level three."

Vibration told them the car was moving. Beall kept watching the lighted display and saw when the car's progress slowed. The heat of earlier gave way to coolness as they sank further and further below the planet's surface.

"Lab level three," Beall said.

The doors slid open, revealing a white tiled hallway in front of them. An overweight grey-haired doctor stepped into the doorway from the side and startled. He was surprised to see them.

"Good afternoon," Beall said stepping out. He read the man's ID badge with a quick glance: Dr Nantrell, a biotecker with an orange level security clearance.

The scientist didn't salute. "We weren't aware of shipments arriving today."

"Arcteck doesn't announce their shipments, as you should know, tecker."

"I am a doctor here!" the flustered man retorted.

"Oh, my mistake. I supposed a doctor would already know how we operate," Beall said, smirking.

"Well!" The doctor said, offended. "I just wasn't aware that Arcteck uses...many vats. Isn't their job best done by a natural-born?"

"We take what we're given. They're good enough," Beall said, grudgingly, glancing at the two vats. Hal stepped up, as if to ask the colonel what to do. Beall nodded.

Mindful of the security cameras, Hal continued moving forward, drew his sidearm in one quick motion, and jammed it against the doctor's side, all out of view. "Choose your next action very carefully," Hal said in a low voice.

"What...what is this?" The doctor said in a hoarse whisper.

"This is you, showing us around the place," Hal said, not blinking. "That's all. You're going to take us to the secure lab storage, or I'm going to leave your guts on this floor. And the wall, and probably me," he shrugged. "Won't be the first time I've been covered in blood, and it sure as hell won't be the last."

"I..." the doctor's gaze shifted to Beall.

"I'd trust him," Beall said. Hal jammed the gun against the

doctor's side more firmly, and he nodded quickly, obviously afraid.

"We know the storage is on the fourth level. How do we get there?" Beall asked.

"We have to go d- down that h- hallway," the doctor pointed.

"Good," Hal said. "Don't make me shoot you." He holstered his blaspistol but stayed close to the doctor as they made their way down the hallway. Beall met Hal's eyes over the doctor's head and gave a nod.

Hal held his breath as they passed the first few windows, which looked in upon the labs. Two of the labs had frosted plasglass windows, but he could see into the last three. There were scientists in there, but most of them paid them no notice. In the last lab, there was a vat in fatigues, unconscious or dead, strapped to an exam table. Hal didn't want to think about what was going on there. He caught Vivi's glance as she saw the same thing. He shook his head, trying to forget the disturbing scene. There was nothing he or any of them could do for the vat. It only tightened his resolve to make this op work. They took a right at the end of the hallway.

There was a service lift on their right, but there was no button, just a pad. "Biometrics," Eli said softly.

"Yes." The doctor put his hand on the pad and the elevator opened for his touch.

"Go on," Hal said, following the doctor in. The doors slid closed, and everyone breathed a sigh of relief to be away from the cameras they knew were everywhere. "Beall, check him for a comm," Hal said.

"Got it." Beall found it and tucked it in his own pocket. "How many guards below?" he asked.

"None," the doctor said.

Lane pulled her blasrifle from her back and jammed it into his side. "Care to answer that one again?"

"Ok...ok...two guards."

"Cover him," Hal said to Beall, moving to the front of the doors with Lane. "We go out first."

"Be careful," Vivi said as Hal pressed the button to send the lift down.

He met her worried expression. "I will. Stay in the lift until we call for you."

Hal swung his blasrifle into his hands. "I'll go left. You take right," he said to Lane.

The lift opened and the two vats exited. Hal immediately saw two hostiles at the desk to the left. They hadn't been expecting him, so he got the jump on the vat standing guard. The man drew a blaspistol, but Hal pumped two bolts into him before he got the chance to use it. Unfortunately, that gave the nat time to draw and aim. He and Hal fired simultaneously. The nat caught it in the throat. Hal took a shot in the shoulder as Lane finished the nat off from behind him. "Shit," Hal said, feeling the burning agony of a blaster wound. Normally, the pain wouldn't be a problem with the effect of a rush to dull it, but now, Hal felt it all.

"Clear," Lane called, coming to him. "You okay, Cullen?"

"Yeah." He grimaced and switched to his blaspistol, carrying the rifle across his back. The pistol would be easier to handle with one hand.

Vivi, Beall, Eli and the doctor came out of the lift. "We're gonna need to hurry," Hal said, grimacing. There was no need to hide the bodies because of the blood spatter on the wall.

"You're wounded," Vivi said.

"I'm good," Hal said. "We need to go."

Lane had grabbed Dr. Nantrell and shoved him toward the door. "Open it, nat."

The doctor pressed his palm against the lock.

Hal and Lane went first, and Beall, Vivi and Eli followed with the doctor as they entered the room. It was almost a warehouse, filled floor to ceiling with rows upon rows of shelves. Upon the metal shelves were tons of artifacts. Hal recognized hexagonal shaped panels like the panels on Eira's people's worldship. There were also many Mudar weapons: hand weapons as well as ship weapons. Parts of ships and hunks of allenium were sitting on shelves, collecting dust.

"The allenium alone here is worth millions," Vivi murmured to Eli.

"Yeah. With just the tech you could buy your own planet," Eli responded. There was a door in front of them as they came to the end of the first row. "Where does that go?"

"Answer him," Beall said, grabbing the man by the collar and shoving him.

"The towers for the whole facility," the doctor said grudgingly.

"Open it," Eli ordered.

The doctor placed his hand on the scanner and the panel turned green. Eli darted inside. "Make it quick," Beall said.

"You got it, old man," Eli replied.

"Where's the big stuff?" Hal asked the doctor. "The Mudar spheres?"

"S-spheres?" Nantrell said, pretending not to know.

Hal took Nantrell by the coat and slammed him up against the wall near the doorframe. His wound was starting to slow him down and his irritation was showing. "Let's try this again," he said through gritted teeth.

"That way," the doctor pointed. "End of the rows and turn left."

They moved quickly through the row and came upon a room, sealed off from the larger lab storage by a thick plasglass door. It was a cube-shaped space with walls, ceiling, and floor made of thick plasglass. On the built-in shelves they could see two shining spheres, the exact same size as Eira's. Two others were cracked in half like Eira's sphere.

"Oh, my gods. There they are," Vivi breathed.

Hal shoved the doctor to the door. "Unlock it."

"Look. You can't carry these out of here. Nanites can be dangerous!" the doctor said.

"I promise you, you're in more danger from me," Hal threatened.

The doctor looked from Vivi, to Beall and then to Hal. He paled when the vat's blaster jammed into his back. "Do we need this guy alive?" Hal said impatiently, glancing to Beall. "I could cut off his hand just as easy." With his free hand, he pulled his viblade, thumbing the switch. The hum was like the drone of a great angry bee.

The doctor quickly placed his hand against the panel. It turned red, then green and the door popped open with a hiss.

"Get the spheres," Hal said. "Take them all, even the broken ones."

Vivi gathered them up, placing them in her backpack, and came out.

"Where do they keep the vat kill device?" Hal asked.

"W-what? I...I don't know what you're talking about."

Hal put the barrel of the blaster to the scientist's head. "You better figure it out real quick. The vat kill device. Where. Is. It?"

"I'm only a biologist. Something like that would be classified... at a higher level than me. Check my ID." He held it out. "I don't know anything."

Hal eyed the ID and Dr Nantrell, then he shoved the man toward the door. "Get in," he said.

"W-what?"

"Get in." Hal shoved the doctor to the floor of the little room. He pushed the door closed and shot the doorpad, causing the metal and plasglass lock to melt. Then he pulled on it. The doc wouldn't be able to open it without help.

"Let's get Eli and get the hells out of here," Beall said.

"Yeah," Hal replied.

MAKING their way back to the door of the computer lab, Beall and Vivi ducked inside to retrieve the tecker.

When Hal remembered Eira's gift, he turned to Lane. "Stay here."

He entered the room. It was dim, but Hal could see the computer towers that stretched up to the high ceiling. This was the perfect place for Eira's nanites to start their work. He reached in his pocket and found the tiny ball, warm under his fingers. At his touch, a soft susurration of this living part of Eira began; Hal could hear it now because his hand was in contact with it.

"It's time to run your programming," he said, unsure of exactly where to put it. He held it up, intending to place it inside one of the ports when the ball became liquid and melded with the metallic casing around the system.

"Damn," he swore, watching as the indicator lights on the tower began to shut off.

He turned toward Eli and saw he was still working on the system through his node.

"Eli...Veevs. Time to go," Hal said, the stress evident in his voice.

"He's still searching for schematics on the kill device," Vivi said.

"If he takes much longer, we're gonna get to see what it does first-hand," Hal deadpanned, glancing at the security cameras. "Eli! Let's go."

"I didn't find it yet."

"It might not matter," Hal said, glancing to Vivi. "Eira's gift."

"You used it?" Vivi asked.

"Yeah," Hal nodded, then grabbed Eli's shoulder and pushed him forward. "We need to move, double time." Outside, they found Lane and ushered everyone into the lift from the fourth to the third level. Apparently, once on the secure floor, you could easily take the lift back up with no bioscanner needed.

When the lift reached its destination, they exited and headed back toward the original elevator.

"There's a corridor on two that will get us to the ship, but we have to make it there," Vivi called.

Once they reached the lift, Lane stood beside Hal at the door, ushering everyone in. "Stay against either side," she said. "If they're onto us, we might get shot at when the doors open."

Just as they arranged themselves, the elevator stopped on the second level, but the doors stayed closed.

"Shit," Hal cursed, glancing to Lane before he moved to pull the doors apart. When he did, there was an instant shot of blaster fire from outside. He crouched and began to return fire through the narrow opening he'd made in the door. Lane fired high, facing the opposite direction.

Not expecting any trouble at this facility, the ACAS hadn't laid it out to deal with threats from the inside. Hal and Lane took out the three ACAS that were waiting for them, and then

Hal pried the doors completely open. Three hallways radiated out from the central area.

"Which way, Veevs?" Hal asked, turning to keep all the tunnels in sight.

He saw that Vivi was focused on the dead nat lying on the floor near her. The man's lifeless green eyes were staring at the ceiling as a rivulet of blood traced a vertical line down his cheek.

"Veevs, focus. Which hallway?" Hal asked. He approached her and laid a hand on her bicep, trying to keep her attention.

She focused on him and steadied. "The m- middle one." She pointed to the center tunnel. "It's supposed to lead to the hangar elevator."

"Thanks," Hal said. There was the sound of the other lift coming back down. "Lane, you take point, and I'll bring up the rear. Beall, Eli, and Veevs guard those spheres. Go!"

For a moment, Hal thought Vivi wasn't going to follow his instructions, but she looked at him, saw he meant it, and gave a curt nod. He felt a burst of pride, seeing he'd taught her well. Hal followed them into the hallway, as he heard the lift doors opening. The reinforcements were running silently—he heard no orders or commands, but knew they were out there, stalking him, and those he was supposed to protect.

He backed through the hallways, past darkened labs, trying to stay out of sight as he felt them approach with his heightened senses. With a grimace of pain from the wound in his shoulder, he holstered his blaster and swung his blasrifle back into his hands.

After the third hallway turn, the point man came around the corner, and Hal shot him in the face before backing quickly around a curve in the passage. He had intended to put on a burst of speed and follow the rest of his group, but a blaster bolt hit him in the hip as he ducked back.

It was a searing pain, but Hal kept up the suppression fire until he was able to slip back beyond their range, right leg dragging. Quickly he keyed his comm. "Double time it, Lane! When you reach the ship, get the fuck out of here, no matter what. They're right behind us and coming fast."

"Affirmative!" she replied.

Please, he thought. *Get them out, Lane.*

Two more soldiers appeared, and Hal held the line, but missed both of them as they backpedaled. "Fuck," he swore, his hand brushing his blood-stained side. The shot had gone right through the standard ACAS vest he wore, striking him underneath the cuirass, at his right hipbone. Mobility was going to be a big problem.

He could hear more troops coming, so he sprayed the wall with a flurry of shots, to give himself a second to think. He might not be rushing, but his programming was telling him to stop this pursuit and protect his unit. Not saving Vivi and the rest was unthinkable.

He was at the top of a T-shaped passage. Looking to the right, he saw a sign that pointed the way to the lifts that led to the landing platform. This was where he had to make a stand. He couldn't let this squad of ACAS get past him.

His hand slipped behind him and grabbed an Armacorp Titan plasma grenade from his ammo belt.

"Where are you, Hal?" Vivi's panicked voice came across the comm.

"Veevs, finish the mission. Get the hell out of here."

"What?! No!" Her startled voice came across the comm.

Hal squeezed his eyes shut for a moment, fixed her face in his mind, then spoke. "I love you Vivi, more than anything. Now do what I ask and go."

When he looked again, he saw the curve of an ACAS helmet peek around the corner. He could barely hear Vivi's voice, yelling into the comm – there was no time to listen. He had to focus now. He sprayed the wall with blaster bolts, then moved down to the left-hand turn. He squeezed the grenade in his hand. The decision was surprisingly easy. Most likely, he wouldn't survive with the explosion that close.

It would be enough to collapse the tunnel and kill him as well, but he was dead either way. The only thing that mattered was Veevs and the mission. He turned, thumbed the button and tossed the grenade, aiming for twenty meters. Then he limped back behind the corner of the wall and waited for the blast.

THIRTY-ONE

When Hal's last transmission came through, they had entered the lift to the ship bay. Vivi stopped and turned back, yelling Hal's name into the comm. Beall grabbed her arm and an explosion shook the complex around them as they stood in the lift door.

There was no answer but the static whine of her open comm.

"Hal! Are you there? Are you hurt?" She looked at Beall and Lane desperately. "We have to go back."

"I can't let you do that!" Lane said, stepping in front of her.

"We can't leave him! I won't leave him!" she cried, struggling with Beall's grip on her.

"Vivi," Beall's quiet voice commanded respect. "I'll go back to get him. All of you keep going." He made eye contact with Lane. "Wait as long as you can, then go."

"Yes, sir."

"Careful, Beall," Eli said.

"I will be, kid," Beall murmured, before he vanished back down the hallway.

A knot in her stomach threatened to turn into a black hole, but Vivi followed orders. What had happened to Hal? Had they thrown grenades at him? Was he still alive? The thought of him being dead was impossible to contemplate.

"Hey." Lane shook her out of her thoughts, her hand on Vivi's shoulder. "Come on. We've got to keep moving. I need you with me." She yanked Vivi into the lift and pressed the button to send it up to the sunken flight deck where the ships were stored.

Vivi drew her blaster with a shaking hand and tried to pull herself together. Beall would find Hal. He had to. Her heart was pounding in her chest like a hammer.

"Just breathe, Vivi," Eli told her. She wiped the sweat from her face with her free hand and struggled to control her emotions. "All you have to do is focus on right now. Stay low and put one foot in front of the other."

"Right," she whispered thankfully. Then the door slid open.

As they stepped cautiously out of the lift, they saw platforms in front of them that would rotate up to the surface, which was about fifty feet away. Each one was either empty or filled with a ship.

There were several transports very much like the one they'd flown in on, in fact, one was cued up and ready in front of them. "It's a CD8. A 'Locust,'" Lane murmured. She checked the perimeter, then silently signaled forward.

"Can you fly it?" Eli hissed.

"Yeah."

They ran across the open space one at a time, each covering the others. Lane went first, then Eli, but when Vivi took the same path, a blaster bolt caught her in the arm. She returned fire immediately, but it was Lane that shot the ACAS soldier off his perch in the ceiling of the hangar. He fell like a dead bird, hitting the platform with a weighty thud.

Eli came back for Vivi. They entered the ship, and Lane covered the door while Eli searched for the medkit. Vivi paced back and forth, watching Eli glance into what seemed like a cargo bay before he snatched at something on the wall and came back with a bag that had a red star: a medkit.

"Get down," Eli said, pulling her low. "Sit and let me take a look."

She sat but her focus was on the corridor across the way. "Why aren't they coming?" she whispered, as Eli examined the blaster wound to her arm.

"I'm not sure." He began to clean her wound with some gauze and placed a coag/antibac pad over the burn-damaged flesh before wrapping it.

"He's got to be okay," she whispered.

"Need you two over here," Lane hissed from the door.

Vivi and Eli both came over with weapons, crouching as well and looking out. One of the lifts opened, revealing three ACAS vats. One appeared to look a lot like Lane, with her long dark hair pulled up into a ponytail. Lane took aim, but she hesitated, so Vivi took the shot. The woman fell like a tree. Lane switched her target and killed the blond man with a shot to the chest. Then Vivi stood up, pushed past Lane and began firing at the third man so furiously that he ducked back inside the elevator while returning fire. She wanted to kill him. No, she wanted to kill every last ACAS in this facility. As she lifted her blaspistol, and stepped further out, Lane grabbed her around the waist and try to pull her back.

"Godsdamn it!" Lane growled in frustration. "Get your ass down before-"

Lane's words were turned into a grunt as a person slammed into them from above. Vivi went sprawling. Whether the person had been in the transport above them or on the platform, she wasn't sure.

The ACAS soldier had a hold of Lane's gun arm and was trying to wrench the blaspistol from it. Vivi was stunned, but soon gathered herself and leaped on the man, wrapping her arm around his throat in a headlock to get him off Lane. Hal had taught her this move in their training. The ACAS disengaged with Lane and staggered back, slinging Vivi back and forth as she held on. She was applying the chokehold as firmly as she could, but the man just wouldn't go down. As she tried to adjust her hold, her opponent's teeth found purchase in her forearm. She yelled in pain, but at the same moment, Lane had recovered enough to find her viblade and sink it into the ACAS's stomach. "Die, motherfucker," she spat as her blade slid up through the soldier's chest.

He sagged almost immediately and both he and Vivi tumbled to the floor. Lane helped Vivi up, as she kept her gaze trained on the elevator doors. They were closed now.

"You good?" Vivi asked.

"Fuck yeah," Lane replied, slinging blood off her hand. "Let's get under cover," she warned, and they all backed into the Locust waiting for Beall and Hal or the next group of hostiles.

When the elevator opened again, it was Beall. Lane stepped outside their craft to meet him. He shook his head at the question on her face. "This place is crawling with troops searching for us. We have to go now, or we won't make it," Beall said.

Vivi watched Beall enter the transport alone, and he could read the devastation on her face. "Oh no," she said softly, shaking her head and backing away from him.

"I'm sorry," he said in a quiet voice as the shuttle's exit sealed behind him. Lane headed for the cockpit.

"What happened?" Vivi asked in a trembling voice. "What did you see?"

"That blast was from a plasma grenade. The tunnel must've collapsed on him. There's no way, Vivi. He couldn't have made it..."

"Oh my gods," she whispered as she dropped into a seat, wrapping her arms around herself. Her face crumpled, and when he sat beside her, she fell into him, sobbing.

Beall did the best he could, holding Vivi as Lane slipped into the cockpit and linked into the ship lift. He could hear her reciting the preflight checklist to herself as the lift took them to the surface.

"I'm so sorry, kid," he soothed Vivi as she cried. Eli was watching with pity. "Her arm?" Beall asked.

"She took a hit," Eli said. "I bandaged her the best I could. I haven't had a chance to look at the other wound." There was a lurching as the ship took off, bursting out of the hangar.

"Go help Lane with the guns, and I'll stay with Vivi."

Once he got the pain medication out of the medkit, Beall dosed her, and she began to calm down. The tears never stopped, but the violent sobbing slowed. He held her tight through the storm of grief and the respite as the ship lumbered into the atmosphere. "That's right. Let it go, kid. I got you," he whispered.

IN THE FRONT of the ship, Lane had pulled herself together enough to give Eli a quick down and dirty overview of firing the transport's weapons as they lifted off. There would certainly be hostiles on the way.

"We've got to give the nav computer time to compute a

course, so we have to hold our own for at least a minute. Ever shot at anyone from a ship before?"

"Just a few times," Eli said, flipping on the heads-up display.

"Then do a good job, and we might actually make it out of here." They flew up through the exosphere and were waiting on a course when she noticed the contacts on Eli's targeting screen. "Right on schedule. They've launched fighters from the base."

The blips were two hard-burning Stormhunter-class Interceptors that were presently at extreme range but were closing fast. Almost as soon as she saw them appear, two smaller dots blinked on the screen. The Stormhunter pilots had fired missiles. Not close enough yet for a target lock; they were simply hoping to get lucky. Obviously, the ACAS hadn't expected them to get off planet. Lane knew the fighters would be burning at full thrust to catch them before they got far enough from Haleia-6 to go to FTL. If they caught up, the shuttle would be a sitting duck for the advanced fighters following them. "Fire some shots to keep them on their toes." Lane instructed Eli while she pushed the transport's engines as far as she dared.

Eli began firing rapidly, not getting any locks, but throwing out as many shots as he could to try and slow the two menacing ships.

"Damn those missiles are coming fast!" he swore. A tone sounded; the defense computer was telling them a missile had locked on and was tracking them.

"Those godsdamned motherfuckers," Lane muttered to herself.

"What do we do?" Eli sounded panicked. She didn't feel so good herself as she pushed their speed so much that they could hear the ship groaning in response.

"Locusts have a cargo bay," she said. "Think there's anything in there?"

"Two multi-terrain vehicles," Eli said. "I found them when—"

"That's perfect," she cut him off and moved her hand to the switch to open the doors.

"Missile's closing the distance, Lane," Eli said, alarmed as the tone became louder the longer it went on. Now the shipboard computer had added a verbal "proximity alert" warning.

A heartbeat later, the nav computer beeped, and Lane grinned. This would work, and if it worked well, the ACAS might think they got the transport after all. She stabbed the button for the cargo bay, then slammed the Bixby drive into operation. There was a brilliant light behind them for a split second before they hit the FTL, and the stars disappeared in front of them.

"Holy shit," Eli breathed, relieved they'd escaped. "What did you do?"

"Old smuggler's trick – the jettisoned cargo acted as a decoy for the missile. Its guidance systems honed-in on the closest target," Lane said, smiling as she glanced to her copilot. "We made it."

"Yeah, but not all of us," Eli said sadly, looking back at Vivi. Lane glanced toward the rear and could see the nat cradled in Beall's arms. Her eyes were closed – Beall had probably dosed her with pain meds for the shoulder wound. Eli's next question jostled her out of her thoughts. "Hal and Vivi...they were in love, weren't they?"

"Yeah," Lane said, slumping back in her seat as the news hit her anew. "Gods," she scrubbed at her face. She really liked Hal and couldn't even begin to come to terms with the loss that Vivi, and the rest of the *Loshad*'s crew would be facing. It would be like losing Orin. She shook it out of her mind. "Fuck this shit. I gotta get us back home. That's first. Time for the rest of it later," she whispered, blinking tears away to focus on the displays in front of her.

"Are you oka-"

"Give me a few minutes," Lane said in a desperate voice. "Go check on Vivi or something."

Thank the Gods, Eli figured it out. He laid a hand on Lane's arm as he got up, then left her to herself.

It wasn't until she was alone, with the ship on autopilot and nothing else to do, that Lane allowed herself to cry.

IT WAS DARK. Vivi got to her feet unsteadily, stepping over Eli and Beall on her way to the bathroom. Her head was fuzzy and light, as if the ship's gravity had gone wonky somehow. She found the bathroom in the back of the ship and caught sight of her face in the mirror. Her eyes were glassy and shadowed, and her face was pale, with two hectic spots of color on her cheeks. She was hot and shaky, as if she had a fever. There was blood on her clothes. Staring into the silver metal of the sink, she began to put the pieces of the last hours together. There had been a mission. They had found the spheres, Hal had delivered Eira's nanites, and they'd escaped in a transport.

So why did it seem there was some horrible secret about to come crashing down on her? She brought her hand up to rub her forehead and realized her arm was throbbing. There were two sets of bandages on her arm. She'd been shot and the ACAS guy had bitten her when she'd tried to choke him out. Beall had gotten her cleaned up and under the blood they'd found the deep punctures in the shape of two half-moons on her arm.

Where was Hal? she wondered. The question was like a dark wave threatening; the answer was a stone to the skull. She grabbed the sink to hold herself up, but eventually, she slid down between it and the wall, tears slipping down her face.

She remembered now; they'd left Hal behind. The explosion. He was dead.

She buried her face against her knees and sobbed – the loss threatened to suck her in like a black hole and never let her go. Hoping for oblivion, she gave herself to it and allowed the dark ocean of grief to swallow her.

She was so deep in her sadness that she didn't notice when Beall found her.

BEALL HAD THOUGHT his heart couldn't break anymore, but he'd been wrong. He lifted Vivi up into his arms and carried her out of the tiny room back to the pallet they'd made her on the aisle. He tried to lay her down and make her comfortable, but she clung to him like a child, so he ended up pulling a blanket over her and sitting with her leaning against him.

He called Eli softly, waking him. "Eli, she's burning up."

Eli got to his feet, going for the nearby medkit.

"This will work for pain and fever," Eli said, reading the medjet before administering it.

"Vivi. Please drink some water," Beall urged, as Eli held out a bottle.

She sniffled against him and let out a hiccupping sob. When he tried the second time, she held the bottle in both hands and took a long swallow before handing it back.

"That's good. Sleep for now." When she finally fell back asleep, Beall laid her on the pallet again and re-covered her with two of the thin blankets he'd found in one of the under-seat bins. Then he went to find Lane. "How much longer?" They'd already been flying four days. He knew it would be a few more before they reached home.

"Four more days," Lane said. She'd used another race of amp when they had stopped to give the Bixby drive a rest, and Beall knew that as the best pilot, she'd keep going until they made it home. She was chewing on a protein bar in the way that said she wasn't hungry, but she knew she'd need the energy.

"Vivi's developed a fever. I'm concerned."

Lane's mouth tightened into a thin line, and she returned to the controls. "I'll try to wring as much as I can out of the engine."

"Thank you. I know you'll do your best," Beall said. He made his way back to watch over his charge. Vivi reminded him of himself, back when he'd lost Mags.

The first head of Echo—a former corporate tecker named E. B. Colbert—had recruited Mags and Beall to oversee security risks. They'd met E. B. on a trip to Coren—drawing his attention in a novel way. E. B. had been going to the recreation planet on a "vacation" when their transport had gotten hijacked by some of the pirate Anklav. Together Mags and Beall had defeated the would-be hijackers, and after saving everyone on the ship, E. B. had found them at their resort and offered them a job at his "tech company," which had been the cover for Echo. Mags, who'd always had a mind and love for technology jumped at the chance, and Beall joined her.

He'd not regretted the decision. The job had a taste of danger, which satisfied Mags's vat desire for excitement, and it was a way for them to both to be together most of the time. The two of them had completely understood the short amount of time allotted to a vat, and so didn't like to be apart much.

And they hadn't. Mags had lived to thirty-five, and then she'd died from a massive stroke. She'd been just starting to get the pains of early arthritis – the beginnings of a slow decline. When she died it was still a shock, however, but eventually, he'd come around to realize she'd died exactly as she would have wanted – before a final decline could make her completely helpless. If not for E. B.'s steady presence, Beall knew he probably wouldn't have made it through losing her.

Thinking of Mags and thinking of himself, he watched over the sleeping young woman, checking her temperature from time to time. Hours later, when she stirred, Beall was there to keep her steady.

She sat up, looking at him with her eyes luminous in the dim light. "Beall," she said, her voice raspy from so many tears. She wasn't crying now though; she had that blasted look of someone who'd seen too much and didn't have a reaction left anymore. It was a sort of battle fatigue—he'd seen it before in his natural born soldiers.

He handed her the bottle of water. "Drink some more for me, kid."

She allowed him to press the water bottle into her hands, then she lifted it to her lips and drank greedily.

"Slowly," he warned her. He checked her temperature again and saw that it was less than it had been. Her fever was holding steady at 101, providing they kept up with the medication. "How's your pain?"

"What?" she said, lowering the bottle.

"Your arm. You were hurt."

She looked at it like it wasn't her own. "It's...it's really sore, I guess."

"Let me see." He pulled on a pair of gloves and unwound the gauze from the two wounds on her arm. When he removed the coagulant pads, he saw that the wounds still appeared red and angry, with streaks and pus coming from the bite mark. It took a few minutes to clean everything with antibac, like he'd done several times so far, but he had a sinking feeling that the medicine wasn't going to slow down whatever this was. She grimaced as the fluid bubbled in the puncture wounds of the bite before he wiped it gently away. "I know it hurts," he told her while he rebandaged. He found the antibac medjet in the medkit and dosed her again, along with something for pain. The antibac might at least hold the infection at bay until they could get her back to Al-Kimia.

"Think you can eat something?"

She swallowed hard. "M-maybe?"

He found a ration bar out of their pack and opened it for her. After chewing a bite mechanically, she swallowed hard. Immediately she grimaced. "No more," she said, handing it back to Beall and reaching for the blanket.

"Just a few more days," Beall said to her as he pulled the blanket up around her shivering body. "You gotta hang in there, Vivi."

"It doesn't matter anymore..." she whispered dully. She laid down, staring into the dim interior of the ship while tears ran down to soak the carpet under her head. Knowing there was little he could say to make this any easier for her, Beall took his own fatigue jacket and covered her with it.

BERYL WAS STRUGGLING to get to sleep. The first four days on the *Loshad* without Hal and Vivi had been tough. The ship's soul was gone as they made their way back to Al-Kimia.

Ty spent a lot of time by himself, either practicing walking, or compulsively monitoring the feeds to see if the mission had been compromised. Beryl had made them dinner a few hours ago, but he had barely eaten before retiring to his room, and she couldn't help but be concerned.

She'd almost drifted off when Runa's electronic chime sounded. "Beryl. Please wake up. I believe Ty needs you."

"What's going on?" Beryl asked as she reached for her robe.

"He is in the common area, showing signs of elevated heart rate and blood pressure. He is distressed and will not answer me."

She grabbed a medbag, just to be sure, and flew out the door.

When she got to the common area, she heard the drone of the feed on the crysplas display and realized that the Bixby drive was disengaged for the power down cycle.

Broken glass littered the floor and the sharp smell of Celian whiskey permeated the room. One of the table's benches was upended and in the corner of the room was Ty. His arms were crossed on knees that had been brought up to his chest. He'd buried his face against them. Blood spotted his sleep pants under the brace he wore and dripped off the fingers of one hand. She could see the shuddering of his shoulders. He was crying silently.

Oh gods, she thought. *What now?* She said a silent prayer to Iren, the god of hope on her home planet, then she swallowed hard. "Ty?" She knelt beside him after making sure there was no glass in this area. "Tyce, talk to me."

His face was twisted in an emotional pain so profound she could feel her own heart ripping in response. "There," he said hoarsely, pointing to the feed.

Beryl had been so focused on Ty that she certainly hadn't paid attention to the feed. But now she saw the awful banner. It read: "Attack on Haleia-6 Foiled by ACAS!" The serious-faced anchor was reporting, but Beryl could hardly hear it over the pounding of her own heart. "Raise the volume, Runa."

The announcer's smug voice went on at a level where Beryl could hear it. "-a target in the Spiral. This time, it was a military installation on Haleia-6. And this time, it was foiled by the brave actions of the ACAS. According to initial reports, ACAS fighters pursued the terrorists and blew them out of the skies above the planet. The authorities have verified the presence of ship wreckage in Haleia-6's orbit. No clues were left behind as to the identity of the terrorists."

The other anchor spoke. "It seems the Opposition terrorists found a different reception than the last time, Angelian."

"We were ready for them," Angelian replied. "We'll have more on this story as it develops...In other news..."

Beryl turned back to Ty, fighting the tears that threatened. "You don't know that they're... dead. The ACAS lied before," she whispered weakly, reaching out to grab Ty's shoulder. "Listen to me. We still don't know anything."

Ty wiped at his face and drug his hands through his disheveled hair. "There was wreckage, Beryl."

"I don't give a godsdamn what they said. They're not dead," Beryl swore, reaching out to hug him. He'd obviously been drinking, seen the report and lost his mind, wrecking the galley and slicing himself open in the process. With a confidence she didn't feel she went on, "They're not dead. Do you hear me, Ty?"

He scared her by not answering, so she held him tighter. When she got him calmed down, she would seal the wounds to his hand, clean up and make them both some coffee. Then they would talk, but for now, she just couldn't bear to let him go.

THIRTY-TWO

Ty parked the *Loshad* just inside the main hangar at Drena Base. It had been a rough few days and an even rougher landing; he'd flown through the darkest clouds and heaviest thunderstorms he had ever seen, but they'd made it to the hangar safe.

But he felt wrong. Actually, he felt like shit. The *Loshad* was too quiet without Hal and Vivi. Having Beryl around had been a great help, but he hadn't really wanted to talk since his outburst a few days earlier.

He turned to Beryl as they landed. "I'll be back later. I need to check in with Seren and Malar and update them on the mission."

She met his eyes and nodded. "Then you need to rest."

"Yes, Tyce," Runa agreed.

"Um...thank you, both of you. I know you've been trying to help by talking to me the past few days to keep my mind off worrying...and it's appreciated," Ty said, giving Beryl a meaningful smile. "I'll hook the *Loshad* up to utilities, then I'll go. I should be back before too long."

He had exited the ship and was securing it, when a group of security officers made up of vats and nats approached. "Sir." The vat wearing the highest rank spoke respectfully. "General Malar requests you report to her office."

"No problem. Has something gone wrong? Is this about my people's mission?" he asked tersely, muscles stiffening as he prepared himself for the worst.

"No. It's Commodore Seren."

Ty wondered if the vat's condition had taken a downturn. "Is Seren alright?"

"He's dead," the vat said, clenching his jaw. "Murdered a week ago."

Ty struggled for words. "W-who killed him?"

"Someone we thought was one of our own. Please come with me. General Malar will fill you in."

AN EXHAUSTED TY returned to the *Loshad* after his meeting with Malar. The information about Seren's murder was gruesome. Apparently, his assistant Katerine Neval had knifed him to death in his quarters. She'd escaped, probably on a blockade runner, and was now well beyond Al-Kimia's reach. It was a horrible end for someone who had been such a good person.

He had gone straight for his last bottle of whiskey in the galley when Runa spoke. "What is wrong, Tyce?"

Beryl had apparently been up waiting on him because she entered the galley not long after.

"Jacent Seren was murdered after we left Al-Kimia." He spun the cap off the bottle and brought two cups to the galley table.

"Oh my gods," Beryl whispered.

"Who did this?" Runa asked.

"A vat named Kat Neval." Ty sat and poured himself a cup.

He took a drink, then poured Beryl a glass. His second swallow didn't burn on its way down as much as its predecessor had. "He didn't deserve a death like that," Ty lamented.

"I am sorry," Runa said.

"Why did she do it?" Beryl asked.

"Only the Gods know," Ty breathed, settling his head in his hands a moment.

"You are sad," Runa said.

"Yeah." Ty scrubbed a hand over his face. It was unthinkable and it had shaken him badly. It was proof that the worst could happen, and he couldn't help but think of Hal and Vivi, Lane, Eli and Beall. His stomach burned and he felt like throwing up. He bit it back and drained his glass.

"Runa," Beryl asked, "do you...do you understand what sadness is?"

"My feed search tells me it is an emotion of regret. A wishing that things had been different."

Ty bowed his head. "Yeah. I should be with them, you know. With Hal and Vivi...wherever they are," he swallowed hard and managed to look up at Beryl. She took his hand, and they stayed that way for long moments.

"Look, I gotta...I gotta get some rest." He hadn't slept well since the night of the broadcast about the mission failure on Haleia-6. Very carefully, he got up and made his way back to his quarters, trying not to let the combination of alcohol and his leg send him sprawling. The alcohol had warmed him pretty good, and he was starting to think he might be able to sleep a while.

"Tyce. Should I be concerned?" Runa asked.

"Why...um...why would you be?"

"Because you haven't slept very much lately. You have only averaged 4.2 hours of sleep a night and you are unsteady on your feet."

"I'll be fine," he said, flopping on the bunk. He was too tired to even undress.

"Please try to rest. I will turn the lighting down to night cycle level and lower the temperature 2 degrees for optimal sleeping. If you wish, I will also silence your comm unless it is information about Hal and Vivi's mission."

"Thank you." Ty yawned and rolled over. "I...I appreciate it."

"Of course. Sleep well, my friend."

HAL BECAME conscious in a fog of agony. His eyes were gritty and painful and there was the taste of blood in his mouth.

He found himself in a familiar room, strapped down to an exam table set in the vertical position. Everything was familiar; it was ACAS issue. This was the worst possible outcome. He hadn't died as he'd planned; he'd been taken prisoner instead.

Hal glanced down his body and saw that he was dressed in the loose white sleep pants and tank you got if you had to stay in an ACAS medbay a few days due to injury or programming. Someone had obviously cleaned him up, bandaged him and strapped him down to be studied like a bug. He was weak, possibly from blood loss or lack of nourishment. The last time he'd eaten was a couple of ration bars before the mission, and he wasn't sure how long ago that had been.

There was an ACAS officer watching him intently, along with two scientists in the room who were both facing away from the interrogation table. "It's awake," the officer sneered, eyeing Hal with disdain.

The older scientist with a familiar voice spoke from behind Hal. "Good. Find out who this one is."

The younger scientist came over and scanned Hal's wrist. He tried to make it difficult for them, but with the officer holding his arm, the doctor got a good scan, then read the display on the datapad. Then the man frowned and did some tapping on the screen. "Somebody's changed the records. There are two records for this service number. One of them is surface information, probably in case they scanned him when he came into the facility. The other record is more complete and only comes up when you search released vats."

"Who is it?" the older scientist asked.

"Halvor Cullen. Last rank held: sergeant. Gestation date, 2434. Scored 148 on the Petersen scale. Mmm," the doctor hummed as he scanned the pad. "Wasn't bred for it but earned elite status in training."

The older doctor turned, and Hal saw with horror it was Dr Riley Balen. He'd been the head of the Chamn-Alpha facility when Hal had been a rook. At his name, Balen examined him more closely.

"I might forget a face, but I never forget a name," the doctor said. "Why did you come here, Cullen?"

It took everything Hal had not to look away from the man that had terrified every rook in his batch. All the young vats had lived in fear of attracting Balen's attention, good or bad. Hal still remembered the flogging he'd taken at the man's order. He couldn't have been more than two or three years out of the exowomb when the doctor had found him fighting another vat who had been terrorizing the newest batch of rooks. It had not been the first time he'd been cited for such a transgression.

After checking his record, Balen hadn't even allowed him to explain. He'd ordered the nearest officer to take Hal into custody and set the punishment detail at 10 lashes. Afterwards Hal had done everything he could to stay clear of the man. Now, Balen was older with more grey hair, but other than that he hadn't changed; seeing him still sent a shiver through Hal. Despite that, he met the doctor's gaze head on, not answering as the younger doctor went on reading information about him off the datapad like he wasn't even there.

"Ok...here we go. The military record shows some issues. High rush index. Aggression. Fighting with vats and nat officers. It says here this vat was flogged when he was still a rook..." the young doctor shook his head. "He should have been adjusted before leaving the rook program."

"There were very few rooks flogged at Chamn-Alpha..." Balen mused, taking the pad from his subordinate. Hal watched him smile as he suddenly remembered. "Ah, yes. I remember now. Cullen. I'm not surprised that you have ended up consorting with the Opposition. Did they send you to steal the Mudar spheres?" He asked as he approached Hal with a medjet in his hand.

Hal growled and yanked at the straps holding him down.

"Knock it off. You're not going anywhere you jar-bred bastard," the ACAS officer said.

"Fuck you, nat," Hal growled. Then the ACAS stepped forward and hit him so hard he was dazed for a moment. This was a bad situation. Balen would pry information out of him with drugs, or programming or both. He had to keep that from happening. The ACAS watching him had a short fuse. Maybe he could use that to his advantage. He glared and spat at the officer leaning over him.

The nat made a fist again and went for Hal's face. The blow split his lip and he tasted blood. He laughed to taunt the man, even as the blood dripped down his chin to mar the white tank he wore. "That's...the best...the best you got, huh?"

"Fuck you, traitor."

"Let me out of these straps, and we'll see who's the best."

The nat hit him again, an interface strike so hard his vision greyed out. When he came back to awareness, he saw that the young doctor was holding the ACAS officer back from killing him.

"Enough of that. There are some that pain does not work on. That's why we have these." Balen held up a medjet. "They're all the same. We'll calm him down, like an angry dog," the older doctor said, pressing the injector against Hal's arm hard enough to bruise.

Hal's heartbeat ramped up as he wondered what they'd juiced him with. In his mind, he tried to go over all the programming drugs they could have given him. There was Drowse—the one that induced a heavy sleep right for deep programming. Aura was another one—a vat who got that would hallucinate until they didn't know what was real and what was not. When the hallucinations stopped, usually they would believe anything the ACAS told them. Then there was Mean Blue. The Blue made you feel good at first, but its downside was that steady doses would alter your personality. Vats who got too much of the Blue had no conscience left and were capable of brutality bordering on atrocity. It was often used to toughen up vats who were too soft. If too much was given and the vat became uncontrollable, however, they were euthanized or sent off to serve as assassins for the ACAS.

He was sure he knew more programming drugs, but as the medjet took effect, the worry and pain left his body. He struggled to think through the haze.

"Shit," Hal mumbled, his head tipping forward as if he couldn't keep it up anymore. He drifted in a pain free cloud for long moments.

"That's better. It'll be easier this way." Balen pushed Hal's head back against the headrest and held it there. "Do you feel like talking to us now?"

"No," Hal said. "What- what did you give me?"

"What were you here for?" Balen asked.

"To fuck you over." Hal licked the blood from his lip. "Get revenge for all those vats on that derelict ship."

"What derelict?" The doctor leaned in, fascinated.

Balen's interest shook Hal; he was hemorrhaging information and clenched his teeth against it.

"Why aren't you rushing by now?" Balen murmured, reaching to his pocket to bring forth a small light. He shined it into Hal's eye, checking his pupil responses. "You know what we're going to do to you—you should be humming with adrenaline by now."

Hal glared at him but couldn't remember why he was supposed to keep quiet.

"Tell me what your primary function is, vat."

"Protect the unit's nats first, then the vats," Hal replied before he even realized he was speaking. A programmed burst of endorphins hit his blood when he completed the recitation.

"Good. Recite the Vat's Creed..."

Hal growled in frustration and gritted his teeth against it. He squeezed his eyes shut, fighting the compulsion drummed into him since his days as a rook. A doctor asking him a question was trigger enough for the impulse.

"Follow my orders, soldier."

Hal slammed his head back against the interrogation table in an effort to distract himself from the war taking place in his mind. They were trying to weaken his resolve, to put him into programming mode and erase him. "Fuck off," he spat.

The doctor leaned in. "Look at me solider."

Hal did.

"Recite the Vat's Creed, now!"

As if something outside him took over, Hal began to speak through clenched teeth, every muscle rigid. "I am the fist of the ACAS. In war, I am strength..." He paused, his chest heaving with effort. "I bring the justice of the Coalition to its enemies..."

Like during a task echo, Hal's sense of self began slipping away. The compulsion to follow orders was just too strong. "Victory is mine. I will gladly fight to the death..." he hesitated.

"Finish it," Balen said.

"I do not surrender to exhaustion or fear. I am inexorable...I am steadfast and tenacious in the face of adversity. I am the ACAS." Hal finished, unable to fight it anymore.

"Good," the doctor praised, looking him over clinically. Hal's head tipped forward and his eyes closed. He was drifting, only dimly aware of his mind blanking out as he waited for the next order. It was good to wait to be told what to do, wasn't it? Words and phrases floated to the top of his mind in a soothing current of reinforcement he hadn't felt since being in the ACAS. Following orders was the action of a good soldier. He should want to be a good solider. It was his job to make sure that the orders of the ACAS were carried out.

Hal became dimly aware of Balen talking. "Scan him. I want to know why he's not rushing. Maybe a node has malfunctioned?"

Hal could sense people moving around him and snatches of conversation. "Ah! A device...Maybe a foreign implant in his head?"

"What the hell? Let me see."

With extreme effort, Hal began to focus more on the voices around him.

"That location lines up with the node that controls adrenaline. It's only slightly bigger than the node."

"Have the godsdamned Al-Kimians begun making adjustments to our vats?"

"But why? What benefit could stopping adrenaline have..."

There was a comm beeping somewhere. Then murmurs. Hal drifted again. The programming would start soon, then he would know what to do to make them happy. But at that thought he frowned. There was some kind of danger in doing what they wanted, but he no longer remembered what it was.

"This is going to have to wait. They are requesting us upstairs. The order is to put this one out for a while. Can't have him escaping." There was a sting on his neck as they injected him with something else. "Bring the scans of his node," Balen said.

Hal caught a glimpse of the doctor peering at him intently. Then the table was tipped completely horizontal and the lights went out. The medication in his blood smothered his consciousness, and he knew no more.

On the inside, Quillon was apoplectic with rage. The fool he was talking to had allowed enemy agents to infiltrate one of the most important ACAS facilities in the Inner Spiral and then get away scot free. His stoic expression betrayed nothing however as he waited for Colonel Hansen, the commandant of Cardela Base, to make another excuse.

"M-my best fighters claim they shot the enemy down as they came out of Haleia-6's orbit," he sputtered.

In a level voice Quillon said, "No, they are gone with whatever data they stole from your computers."

"B...But Admiral...."

"But nothing. You will relinquish command of base to your second and send the vat prisoner to my flagship. Then you may consider yourself under arrest for gross dereliction of duty."

"I...I don't understand..."

"What's not to understand? Your career is over, and unless you are very lucky so is your life." Quillon stabbed the comms button, turning the shocked colonel off.

THIRTY-THREE

Hal woke up slowly, feverish and nauseous, his head aching from the drugs they'd been using to keep him unconscious. There was a metallic taste in his mouth, and he was painfully aware of the blaster wound in his side. He had no idea how long he'd been out, but now that he was coming to, he didn't want anyone to know he was awake. At least until he figured out what was going on.

"So, where's this fucker going again?" he heard a voice ask. The bed he was on was being wheeled up a ramp.

"The *Vetra*, Quillon's ship."

There was a low whistle. "This guy's screwed, then."

Hal felt sick. He had heard of Macallister Quillon before. Quillon was the only nat to go through the complete cycle of vat training. He supposedly understood vats better than any man in the fleet. Cruel, heartless and sadistic, he kept his vats in line by fear and brutal intimidation. Hal had heard that Quillon had flogged two of his vats to death, and probably more.

Footsteps, then another new voice. "So, why are we not

getting our shot at this guy again? He broke into our facility, so we at least deserve the chance to crack him, and I mean literally." The man checked that the bindings were secure; Hal could feel the metal tightening on his wrists.

A voice replied, "Quillon wants to deal with this vat personally. He has a tecker who writes programs for him. If they can't break this vat down, they'll reprogram his interface until he tells them everything they want to know."

"Or they could do a complete wipe." The younger scientist from before spoke.

"Well, either way he won't like what's coming to him. Works for me. If he wakes up, at least we won't have to listen to him down here," the ACAS officer spoke.

"Listen to me. We have him strapped down, but you're not gonna let him wake up. He gets a shot of this every four hours until you arrive at the *Vetra*. He was a little high-strung." The doctor said. "You'll need to dose him up once you get started good."

Hal listened to them move off into the other areas of the craft. This was likely a CD8-GPC, the typical ACAS cargo hauler. A schematic of the CD8's layout floated to the surface of his mind as implanted information sometimes did.

When he no longer heard anyone, he opened his eyes and took stock in his situation, confirming where he was. He could sense movement, which he assumed was liftoff. He was strapped down to the gurney he was on, and his wrists were shackled to the bed. He twisted against the straps and there was no give in them at all.

With a rising sense of panic, he used his gaze to search around the cargo hold of the CD8. There were some jump seats in one corner and some cargo containers in the other. Would there be any way to escape? He knew his chances would plummet to zero once he reached the *Vetra*. He struggled against the straps again with no success.

"Ah, so it *is* time for another dose," a voice said from behind him.

Hal looked up and saw it was the same ACAS that had been present earlier at his exam. The officer had come up behind him and was now eyeing Hal with a mixture of disgust and fascination. "Just in case you're wondering, they're sending you to Quillon to be cut up so they can look at that thing in your head. Who did that? The Al-Kimians? Are they controlling you?"

"I'm not telling you shit, nat," Hal growled in a low voice.

"Have it your way," the officer said. He produced a medjet and jammed it against Hal's neck. There was a hissing sound and the sting of the injection, and within a minute, he lost consciousness.

THIRTY-FOUR

Tyce was waiting when the stolen ACAS shuttle carrying Vivi and the rest of the team landed. He'd suffered through four days of anxious waiting before the call from Malar. Four days of too much coffee, too many hours of watching the newsfeeds and too little sleep had caught up with him. He'd been dozing in the common area on the *Loshad* when Malar had called him and Beryl to the landing area. Eira, who had joined them the same evening they'd arrived, had stayed behind on the *Loshad*. There were two squads of "Shadowstalkers" – vats and Al Kimians – waiting to meet the ACAS shuttle, in case it was some sort of trap – but it wasn't. When the ship landed, Eli Sawyer was first off. Behind him, Beall and Lane were supporting an injured Vivi between them.

Her bandaged arm hung loosely around Lane's shoulder. And she looked wrong. She was too pale, with feverish spots of color in each cheek. Ty picked up his step to get to her, with Beryl keeping pace.

"She's hurt," Beryl said with concern as they drew close.

"Hey. Don't stand there and gawk!" Lane yelled to the vats

and nats watching. "I need medical over here, you useless fucking rooks!"

Ty made it to Vivi first. When she saw him, she disengaged from Lane and Beall and hugged him tightly. "I was so worried about you and Hal," he spoke into Vivi's hair as he hugged her back.

Then he realized she was crying, and his heart knotted in fear. He let her go enough to see her face, twisted in grief. "Ty, Hal's gone," she managed.

"Gone..."

She nodded, and Ty fumbled for what to say. "Y-you mean he was taken prisoner?"

"No. He...there was a tunnel...an explosion..." She shook her head and sobbed, clinging to him. He replied by wrapping his arms around her and holding her tightly.

"He...he didn't make it," Beall said softly, laying a hand on Ty's shoulder. "The tunnel collapsed on him."

"I'm sorry, Ty. I'm so sorry." Vivi wept against him as he held her up. If not for his brace locking him upright, they would have fallen to the ground together.

The world spun. He didn't know how long they stood there, arms around each other, before he heard someone speak. "Sir... sir... she needs medical attention." Someone was trying to disentangle Vivi from his arms, but he only held her tighter, afraid if he let her go she would disappear like Hal.

It was Beryl who eased Ty into releasing her. "Ty, you need to let go. She's wounded, and we need to let the medics examine her."

As Ty released his grip, he realized she *was* burning up with fever. The nearby medics guided her to a gurney and began to do a quick evaluation. Another medic was taking a look at Lane. Beryl stepped over to speak to them while a blur of medical personnel and soldiers moved around them. Ty turned to Beall, shell-shocked. "You're sure? About Hal?"

"Yeah. He was covering our six. There was an explosion; it had to have been a plasma grenade. I went back for him, but the tunnel was completely collapsed. Gods, I'm sorry, Ty."

Ty nodded numbly. The medics were moving Vivi's gurney toward the medcenter.

"C'mon. We need to stay with her," Beryl said as she came over, ushering them both along.

When Vivi woke, Ty and Beryl were right beside her. She blinked slowly, trying to remember where she was and why she felt so weak as Ty took her hand. "Hi," she whispered.

"How are you feeling?" he asked her gently.

"Tired." Her eyes welled with tears, but she didn't know why. Then it hit her all at once. The op. The explosion. Hal. She let Ty's hand go and covered her face as it all flooded back. "Oh gods…it's…it's my f-fault…"

"Oh, Vivi, no," Beryl murmured, laying a hand on her shoulder.

Ty folded her in a gentle hug as best as he could from the side of the bed. "It's not your fault," he said in a hoarse voice. "It's not."

For long moments, they stayed in each other's arms. When Vivi had cried herself out, she leaned back, wiping her face. Ty and Beryl both were struggling with their emotions as well.

"Uh…think you can eat something?" Ty asked.

"Maybe," Vivi answered. "You're not looking great either. When's the last time you had a meal?"

"Too long," Beryl said disapprovingly.

"How about we just stay focused on you right now?" Ty said, raising an eyebrow.

"I think we're going have to all watch out for each other from now on," Vivi said softly, blinking through more tears.

"Yeah. I...I think Hal would want that," he murmured, as they both noticed Beall standing at the curtain of the medbay.

"I'll go get something for all of you," the older man said, turning back into the medcenter.

"I'll come with you." Beryl followed him out.

"Thanks," Ty called. "Vivi, the docs said you got a nasty infection from a bite, but you're going to be fine."

"There was an ACAS guy on Lane. I put him in a chokehold, but he bit me. Lane killed him with a viblade." She swallowed hard, feeling nauseous. "Ty, we completed the mission, but they came for us on the...on the w-way out..."

Ty took her hand. "That part can wait. Rest." He reached out and smoothed her hair off her forehead. "You're what we need to focus on now."

Just then, Lane appeared at the curtain. She had on a hospital bracelet and was dressed in some clean sleep clothes. She looked tired. "They told me I could some see you for a minute, then I'm back to bed to crash. I needed to know you'd be alright first."

"Yeah. I'm good." Vivi's voice cracked on the last sentence, and she wiped at her eyes again.

Lane came over to her and stood. The dark-haired woman shifted from foot to foot uncertainly, then quickly reached down and squeezed Vivi's hand and knelt by the bed. "You listen to me. You did what you had to do, exactly like he did. There was nothing any of us could have done differently."

Vivi got herself back under control quickly. "Please don't worry about me. Go rest. We can talk when you're up and around again." She knew that Lane had flown them back the entire way and needed to crash after the multi-day rush she'd been on.

"You get some rest too," Lane murmured.

"I'm gonna try."

When Lane was gone, Beall and Beryl showed up with a nurse who brought them two bowls of soup and a loaf of soft bread. By the time they finished eating, Vivi was wiped out and ready to sleep. "Her fever's down, but we need to keep her overnight. She needs to continue the IV antibiotics," the medic said, after checking in on her. "If her numbers look good, we may discharge her tomorrow by late afternoon. If not, another night with us. We'll be back in a few hours to check vitals again. Until then, get some rest, Ms Valjean."

"Okay," Ty nodded. "I'll stay with her tonight."

"You don't have to..." Vivi began.

"Yeah, I do," Ty said. As he spoke, Vivi realized Ty needed to do this to give him something to do, to keep his mind off Hal. Tears threatened again, and she clenched her teeth against them.

"I'll go update Eira on Vivi's progress," Beryl said. "She was very anxious when I spoke to her earlier." Beryl leaned down and kissed Vivi on the top of the head. "You're in good hands here. I'll be back," she promised, glancing to Ty. "Call me if you need a break."

Ty kicked out the footrest on the chair beside the bed. "I'll be fine right here."

"Okay then," she said, placing a hand on Vivi's shoulder. "I'll see you in the morning or even sooner."

Vivi watched her go. "Thank you for staying with me," she whispered to Ty, closing her eyes. Ty squeezed her hand once before she fell asleep.

VIVI ENDED up spending two days in the medcenter, but on the morning of the second day, the doctors told them she was going to be released after dinner. They'd given her enough antibac to kill even the worst creeping itch in the brothels of Dela Prime, as well as fluids to combat her dehydration, so Ty was confident she was out of danger.

The same morning, Ty had gotten a message from Terra Malar requesting a meeting. Beryl offered to stay with Vivi while Ty went. She was probably the only person on the base besides Eira that Ty would have trusted with Vivi at this point. He knew he was being too protective but couldn't help it.

They were all reeling from the loss of Hal. Neither Ty nor Vivi could bear to return to the *Loshad* right now, so he'd decided to ask Malar if she'd help the crew out with quarters for a few nights. Having something to do helped him keep from focusing on Hal's absence. He'd been holding his feelings at bay since his breakdown at the shuttle, and it was starting to fray his nerves. Going back to the *Loshad* would be unbearable.

He wanted to put in a good word for Eli and Beall as well, who had decided to join the Opposition to the ACAS. After what they'd seen in the facility, both had a desire to help Al-Kimia fight back. From what Beall had told Ty, they had already been debriefed by the brass, but no decisions about them joining the movement had been made. After what had happened with Kat and Seren, he could see how the Al-Kimians wanted to be extra careful of outsiders.

The vats and nats guarding Malar's passageway went ahead and ushered him through as soon as he stopped to explain that he'd been called there. It was obvious they knew who he was, and he was wearing his base ID.

As he entered Malar's office, he glanced around. The room was carpeted with the rich patterned rugs common to Al-Kimia, and there were decorative glass lamps that cast warm light in pools throughout the room. The general was in the corner of the room, examining holographic real-time representations of Al-Kimia, Noea and Betald. The blue blips denoted the Opposition ships. Ty saw the huge buildup of red blips around Betald, Al-Kimia's oldest ally.

"I saw the news reports. So Betald's fallen?" he asked, causing her to look up at him through bleary eyes.

"With a whisper," she frowned. "Apparently, they didn't put up much of a fight. ACAS'll go for Noea next and that fight won't be as easy." She stood up, smoothing her slightly wrinkled uniform. "I heard what happened to Cullen. Gods, I'm sorry, Bernon. How's Valjean?"

Ty ran a hand nervously through his hair. "She's doing as well as can be expected, I guess. I...I wasn't sure who to ask about accommodations. Vivi needs some time before we go back on the *Loshad*." Her nod told him she understood. "Are there any quarters available that we could have on a temporary basis? A week or two, tops?"

"Of course. I will have my yeoman set you up." She used her handheld to send a quick message to her subordinate. "You'll need an escort for Eira to be brought there, correct?"

"Yes, if possible." Moving Eira around the base took special effort. Even dressed in human clothing, she required guards to clear the way for her and keep her from getting seen.

"I'll arrange an escort for her. Take a seat and speak with me for a moment," she said, gesturing to a pair of chairs over by a glass lamp with an amber shade. It cast a warm soothing glow like firelight. Once seated she went on. "Our sources report a mass evacuation of Haleia-6's residential areas. The Coalition has kept it off the newsfeeds so far, but something is going on there. Any ideas?"

"Eira gave Hal a computer virus to deploy. She said it would disrupt the ACAS systems. Could that be it?"

"I don't know. They are evacuating the planet with the same protocols that would be used in the case of a bio-attack."

Terra steepled her fingers and rested her chin on them. "I will let you know if we hear anything else in this area." She thought a moment, then continued. "Captain Bernon, Jacent Seren always advised me in the matters concerning vats, and he appointed Patrin to take over when it was time. With Patrin having been gone, and Seren's death, I must admit, I'm struggling."

"Yes, ma'am. I heard about the investigation into Seren's death. Not that you need my approval, but I thought it was a smart move to appoint a vat to oversee the investigation." She had appointed head of security Lieutenant Jenkins, a well-known vat on base. It showed Malar's ability to delegate to the right people—Tyce could tell she was a capable leader able to see moves ahead.

"Well, I'm leery of making a mistake that might cost us some of our most valuable soldiers and friends. I want to ask you if you'd assist me in being a temporary liaison between the vat officers and Al-Kimian leadership. Both nat and vats will listen to you..."

Ty shook his head. "Wait, ma'am. They don't even know me."

"Captain Tyce Bernon, while you are very modest in person, your reputation precedes you. There are some vats here that still remember you from the ACAS 14th where you were known as a fair commander to vats and nats alike."

Tyce shrugged. "I did what any decent person would do and commanded my soldiers the best I could."

"You understand vats and you have experience getting nats and vats to work together. I have a need for someone like that by my side."

Ty scrubbed a hand over his face and the scruff of a few days' beard. With everything going on, he hadn't shaved in a while. Hell, he'd barely eaten in the past two days. "General,

I'm not in any shape to do that right now. Things are kind of rough," he said, his head dropping. He was exhausted. Doing what the general wanted felt like a mammoth task that he wasn't up to.

"I need you to take this commission, Tyce Bernon," Malar said, not letting up.

Ty shook his head. "I've put my crew at your disposal and run missions...but I can't do it this time, Ma'am. But there is someone who can – Hieronymus Beall. He has experience in the field with vats, and he understands them. Eli Sawyer and Beall...they're going to be powerful allies in the fight against the Coalition. Eli got us in there, and Beall helped bring..." he swallowed hard, "most of my team back safely. They're eager to help."

Malar nodded slowly, leaning back in her chair. "So, you think that we should include them in our ranks?"

"Yes, Ma'am. Eli is a talented tecker with an established network that could probably do a great deal to disrupt ACAS operations. And Beall's a previous ACAS officer who knows how they operate. You can trust them both."

"How do you know this?"

"It's not my story to tell, ma'am, but after the service, Beall was in love with a vat. He lost her to adrenaline fatigue. He hates the ACAS... probably as much as I do."

She contemplated it a moment. "We will certainly consider it," she said. "And now, I know you need to go. Your crew needs you. Take as much time as you need with the quarters, and please let me know if you need anything."

"Thank you, Ma'am."

THIRTY-FIVE

"I want you to reinforce all of Katerine's programming. Her time with the Opposition has undone some of our hard work," Quillon said, standing at the window in his quarters. He could see the surface of Rinal below and traffic coming to and from the station to the ship and the ship to the station. There was the gentle thrum of the *Vetra's* engines, keeping them in orbit.

He'd sent a transport for Kat and had her brought back to the ship. She'd arrived several hours ago and had been receiving a checkout in medical.

"Have you spoken with her yet?" his tecker asked.

"No."

"Fleet Admiral, I have a suggestion, if I may."

Quillon turned and focused on his personal tecker, Wyatt Romal. The man was not part of the ACAS – he was a consultant for the military, developing new routines for the subliminal vat training for the past fifteen years. Routines he'd written were a part of every vat in the fleet. If Balen couldn't come up with anything on the vat device, he would see what Romal could do. The sheer joy of being allowed to solve a problem that had stumped others would be likely to wipe out any moral hesitations his tecker might have. Somehow, though, Quillon didn't think morals would be a problem for Romal.

"What is your suggestion?"

"Perhaps we should start over with another vat. Katerine's had a great deal of programming. When we had her psych done before this last time, I told you that she was a little shaky."

"And you told me you could fix that," Quillon said in a low voice.

"And I did. I shored her up, the best I could. But you must understand, sir. What we're doing here is so experimental that there's no way...no way to know the effect it will have-"

Quillon spoke through gritted teeth. He was losing patience. "This vat is mine. Another will not suffice. You have a week to come up with something."

"It's not time I need. She's getting close to the usual release time. Perhaps we could release her and...."

"I will *never* release her from service. She is *mine*," Quillon said in a low voice. "Do you understand me?"

Not wanting to challenge the admiral any further, Wyatt glanced down at his datapad and made a note, pursing his lips. "Yes, sir."

"Then go. You have a lot to do."

Romal left without another word. Quillon weighed the situation in his mind. It wasn't like Katerine to be careless in her work. She had always executed orders with an intense focus on detail and accuracy. He would have her reprogrammed completely if this was something that Wyatt couldn't fix.

And if she couldn't be fixed, he would kill her himself, but he would never let her go.

. . .

When Katerine had arrived on the *Vetra*, the commanding officer escorted her to medical to be checked out. Once she was there, she had received a check and rewrap of her wounds, the obligatory antibac medjet and an examination of her interface. A medic assistant brought her a clean fatigue uniform, and Kat was pulling the shirt over her head when she heard the medic approach her.

"The fleet admiral would like to see you in his quarters, Neval," the medic said almost apologetically. Kat wondered if he knew her story but dismissed the idea. It was obvious that he was only following his orders.

"Yes, sir."

She stood and walked out the door on unsteady legs. In the hallway, her knees tried to give out under her as she wondered what she was in for. Willing herself to walk, she began to head to his office. There would be no avoidance because he would never allow it. She would have to face his disapproval head on and take...whatever the punishment was.

She knocked as her stomach tied itself into knots. The wait felt like 5 hours, but in reality, it was no more than two or three minutes. He always made her wait – it was a test, she knew, and she had always passed it before. She couldn't afford to fail it now.

"Enter," he called.

She opened the door and walked the path to his desk and remained standing at attention.

He stared at her from his seat and said nothing for two full minutes. A bead of sweat rolled down her face as she stood straight-backed and unmoving.

"Sergeant Neval."

"Sir, yes sir," she said, her voice as steady as she could make it.

"Describe to me the circumstances of your return." She

could see from her peripheral vision that he had sat back in his chair and steepled his fingers in front of him, watching her intently. He did not release her from attention, so she stood straight, her gaze averted and her body unmoving.

"Yes sir. As...as I had told you, I had begun running missions with the Al-Kimian military. Weapons running, picking up supplies, that sort of thing. Then Patrin Kerlani, the second in command, left to go on an extended mission, and he asked me to assist Commodore Seren while he was gone. That was when...I knew it was time to strike against the leader. I broke into his room, but he fought back with a viblade and injured me. I shot him with a blaster and finished him off with my own blade."

"But you left evidence." Quillon leaned forward, intently.

"Yes, sir. Unfortunately." Her mouth was dry with fear.

Quillon stood up, and walked slowly around his desk, examining her. "You are not usually so sloppy, Katerine."

She shuddered at his negative words and saw how his interest intensified. Seeing him enjoy this made her feel sick to her stomach. A tear slipped down her cheek.

He reached out and touched a strand of her ponytail. "Poor Nyma, your programming *is* slipping, like I thought, isn't it?"

His soft voice took her by surprise. She trembled as she responded in a fearful whisper. "I...I don't know. My head... hurts a lot of the time. Nothing makes sense..."

"I will make you better, Nyma. After some reprogramming, things will be clear to you, and you will be mine again."

At the very word *reprogramming*, her stomach dropped, as she remembered her last programming session and how blank and cold she'd been after it. She began to panic, and her chest tightened. "Reprogramming, sir? Why? I've done everything you asked me to," she pleaded, her voice desperate as she searched his face for any quality of mercy. Just as quickly, she dropped her gaze, realizing the enormity of her mistake by the rage in his eyes. Quillon was not Seren. Her panic had caused her to slip.

Quillon's manner immediately changed. "What did you ask me?" Quillon's voice was low and deadly. When she didn't answer he reached out and grabbed her by her hair, turning her face toward him. Years of experience and programming kicked in, and she did not dare look at him.

"I'm sorry s- sir."

"That's not what I asked. What did you ask me, Sergeant Neval?"

"Sir. I asked the fl...fleet admiral to ex- explain his a- a-actions." Her trembling became an all-out shudder as she struggled to keep her head up and her eyes steady.

"You know the penalty for insubordination."

"Yes sir," her voice was a soft whisper. "Punishment detail." She'd witnessed many punishment details but had never been the victim of one. They were horrible. Quillon used a multi-headed bi-horn leather whip to flog compliance into his vats on a regular basis. Last year, he'd beaten a vat to death for consistently fighting with his fellow soldiers on the ship. The ACAS had said nothing about the loss, but simply sent Quillon a replacement.

"We will take care of your infraction now. Ready yourself and face the wall."

She swallowed hard. Usually, punishment detail was a public event, used to remind them all of the penalty for failure, but apparently this was different. *Maybe he doesn't want any witnesses if he kills me*, she thought.

She turned to the wall and pulled her shirt out from where it was tucked in. Her hands were shaking with fear as she pulled it over her head, then slid her bra off. Her top bared, she braced herself tightly against the wall with both of her hands pressing against the surface and squared with her shoulders in front of her. It never occurred to her to think of modesty—she'd seen this process often enough, and she knew what would play out. Vats were treated the same, males and females.

Before he stepped backwards to have enough room to swing the whip, he laid a hand on the unmarked flesh of her back, right between her shoulder blades. She shuddered violently at the almost intimate touch, bowing her head.

The first strike was liquid fire laid across her back. "Vats crave rules as well as correction when they break them," Quillon said. "Isn't that right, Nyma?"

She knew what the answer was. "Sir, yes sir," she said through clenched teeth as she struggled against crying out.

He waited a full minute to hit her again, as if he were testing whether she would remain still or not. Frequently, vats subjected to punishment detail had to be restrained, and those were the ones who bore the worst of the Admiral's wrath. As she wondered if she would survive this, the second blow split her skin; hot blood welled to the surface and spilled down her back.

"Your job as a vat is to fulfill the will of your natural born commanding officer," he said as he hit her again, opening more rents in her skin. "You have no will of your own, correct?"

She was clenching her teeth so hard her jaw ached, and she was only able to let out a moan.

"Answer me!" The sharp edges of the bi-horn leather bit into her skin again as he hit her with all his might.

"Yes, Admiral!" she sobbed.

He began to hit her again and again, crossing the stripes from earlier. She shoved her fist against her mouth, stifling her screams.

When it was over, she heard him approach, and she began to tremble. The fear was a bone-deep terror of him that she'd never understood. Gently, he reached out and brushed the only unmarred area of her shoulder. "You did well, Nyma," he breathed. "This means you can be retaught."

"Gods...please..." Kat sobbed, sliding down the wall to her knees, curling into herself. She wasn't sure if she was begging for mercy or asking for Quillon's guidance.

"I chose you. I made you what you are. You will be mine, Kat. You will follow my orders, or I will end you," he dropped the whip beside her and turned abruptly toward the door. Outside, he spoke to his stone-faced lieutenant. "Take my vat back to medical and clean up the godsdamned mess."

THIRTY-SIX

It was well after one AM when Tyce entered the *Loshad*. He keyed in the code to unlock the ramp, then unsteadily stepped onto the quiet ship, bottle of alcohol in hand. It was his first time back since Vivi had returned with the news about Hal, and he had made sure he was good and numb before he even tried it. They had gotten Vivi settled in their new quarters and she'd fallen asleep for the night. Her pain meds meant she would most likely sleep through, but he'd still told Beryl and Eira to stay with her tonight. This was something he had to do alone.

Vivi would need him to be strong when she finally had to come back to the ship, so he knew it would be best to deal with his grief now. Maybe it would help him to hold it together for her when she finally had to face Hal's empty room.

He let his hand trail along the wall as he walked down the hall, remembering the day he and Hal had bought the *Loshad* from a used ship dealer on Dalamar. Before they'd gone to see it, he'd found himself standing on the shoreline of a light blue-green sea with Hal, who had been struck speechless.

"What's wrong, Hal?" Ty had glanced at the vat. They'd come around the corner of a street to see the ocean spread out in front of them.

Hal had shaken his head. "It's...it's so big," he managed.

"Yeah." Ty nodded, carefully watching Hal as he began to understand. "You never got stationed anywhere to see the ocean before, huh?"

"We flew over one once, but I never got to see it like this." Hal shook his head, glancing at Ty as if asking for leave to cross the street to the water. Ty knew from his experience that the permission-seeking was a holdover from Hal's conditioning at the hands of the ACAS, so he gently reminded Hal that he could do what he liked. "You don't have to ask me. Go ahead. I'm right behind you."

They crossed the street to the sand dunes beyond, Hal leading the way.

When they were at the shoreline, he stood silently, watching the waves rolling in to gently brush the sand. After a long time of watching, he asked, "Do they always do that?"

"Do...do what?" Ty looked up and down the beach, unsure of what Hal was referring to.

"Crash against the shore like that."

"The waves? Oh, yeah," Ty said with surprise. "They do." It occurred to him that even though Hal was a skilled fighter with an incredible ability for strategy, he was in many ways so inexperienced as to be almost childlike. When Hal had been his sergeant, there had not been time for noticing these types of details. There had been a divide between them, the separation that always existed between commander and the commanded, nat and vat, but now Ty realized that he alone would be responsible for tearing down that wall. Hal most likely wouldn't know how. Ty would have to be the one to teach him how to relate on a different level.

"I'm really glad you came to Omicron, Ty," Hal said, his eyes fixed on the horizon where the light blue sea met the sky.

"I told you I would," Ty said, remembering the conversation they'd had on the day Hal had been released from service. He'd promised the vat he'd meet him on Omicron in a few months after he, himself, was discharged. "You didn't believe me, huh?"

"I didn't know," Hal said, finally glancing at him. "I mean, I'm just a vat, and a pain in the ass one at that. I thought you might change your mind about us working together."

"Hey, one thing I don't do is change my mind about my friends or my family," Ty clapped him on the back. "You're not my sergeant anymore, Hal. You're more than that now."

Hal had blinked in confusion a second. "But I am your sergeant. I mean I always have been. What else can I be?"

Ty squeezed his shoulder. "Family, Hal. You look out for me, and I'll look out for you." At Hal's confused expression, he went on. "Don't worry about it. We'll figure it out as we go."

"But vats don't have family."

"You do now. What do you say we go find something to eat in this city, then figure out where we've gotta go tomorrow to take a look at this ship?"

"Yeah," he nodded, tearing himself away from the rolling waves. "What's the ship's name?"

"The *Loshad*."

Ty stood in front of Hal's door, staring at it as the memory faded around him. For a moment, he'd felt that Hal was there with him – the memory had been that strong. He took another large pull from the bottle and didn't feel it burn anymore as it went down. Raising an eyebrow, he looked at the plain bottle filled with clear fluid. It was something the vats on base cooked up, which meant it packed a punch. He'd be hung over as fuck tomorrow, but this would be done, and he could try and find a sliver of peace to hold onto. "Godsdamn it," he whispered, looking up at the door's silver exterior and seeing a blurry image of himself reflected in its surface.

He keyed it and it slid open, revealing Hal's room during the night cycle. "Lights up half," Ty said in a rough voice.

"Good evening, Tyce," Runa began.

"I'm sorry, but I don't...don't have the heart to talk right now, Runa," Ty said, entering the room.

"Of course," she replied gently.

He stood there a moment, taking in Hal's quarters. The vat had begun keeping it neater in here since Vivi, Ty realized with a pain in his heart. Another gulp of vat hooch deadened that emotion. "Hold it together..." he muttered.

There were clothes on the floor, as if Hal had been in a hurry suiting up for the mission on Haleia-6. Ty set his bottle on the nearby table after taking another slug. Then, almost reverently, he picked up the clothes, folding them gently and carefully before placing them in a neat pile beside his bottle.

He turned and noticed Hal's unmade bed, so he made it, replacing the blanket and the two pillows. Hal didn't have many personal possessions, so in the space of ten minutes, he had the room and attached head neat again. He'd thought about packing some of Hal's things away into his trunk, but he couldn't bear to do it. Vivi might need that kind of closure as the days and weeks went on. When the time was right, maybe they'd both be strong enough to do it together.

Runa spoke gently, with emotion. "Tyce, I'm sorry, but what has happened? Where is Hal?"

They hadn't told her yet, he realized. He tried to keep his voice even. "He's gone, Runa." Ty took up the bottle again and went to sit on the floor near the bed. "He..." Ty swallowed hard. When he spoke again, his voice broke. "He... died."

"I am so sorry," she replied.

"Yeah." He allowed the tears to fall unchecked as he hung his head, feeling the ocean of his grief fully, for the first time. The hole Hal's absence had made would never be filled, he realized bitterly as he drank more to deaden the pain.

When the door slid open, half an hour later, he didn't even look up.

Vivi and Beryl had found Ty in Hal's room, his head buried in his arms against his knees. She'd come as soon as she and Beryl been woken by Runa's worried comm. Even though she was sleepy and a little groggy, Ty needed her, and she was out of the bed in a moment, ignoring Beryl's protests and the pain in her heart at the thought of going back an empty *Loshad*. A *Loshad* without Hal.

When they'd found Ty in Hal's room, she'd shared a sad look with Beryl, who had wrapped an arm around her and gave her a hug before they both went to Ty.

Ty was not okay. His overwhelming grief was apparent in his broken posture.

Summoning up a strength that she didn't know she had, she came over and knelt beside him, wrapping her uninjured arm around him and pulling him into her. "Ty," she said.

"Vivi – no," He mumbled. She only held on to him tighter. Beryl knelt on his other side and put a hand on his shoulder.

"It's alright," Vivi soothed. He leaned into her, giving into his emotions, and she held him as if afraid the sobs would shake him apart.

Finally, the tide of grief subsided enough that he pulled away and wiped at his face – making an attempt to pull himself together. Vivi and Beryl needed a minute to compose themselves as well. She took his bottle, drank deep and coughed hard.

"Damn," Vivi exclaimed. "What the hell is this stuff?"

"Vats on base distill it," Ty said. "It's the strongest jet juice I ever had."

"It has to be," she took another long swallow and handed the bottle to Beryl, who downed a mouthful.

"Gods. I think my tongue is numb now," Beryl said, trying to lighten the mood.

Ty laughed weakly as he met their watery eyes. "You're supposed to be resting, Vivi."

"Well, if my captain wasn't wandering around in the middle of the night, I would be," she looked around the room and took a shaky breath. "Ty. We need some time before... before all this."

"You can't do this alone," Beryl said gently. "None of us can."

He let them help him to his feet. They leaned on each other as they went for the door, and Beryl lowered the lights as they left. "It'll be here when we're ready. When we're all ready," the medic said softly.

THE NEXT MORNING, Ty left his room to find Beryl and Eira at the table in the kitchen area. They both glanced up, concern in their eyes.

"Hey," he said self-consciously, smoothing down his hair and running a hand over the scruff on his chin.

"How are you?" Beryl asked.

"Hung over," he complained, crossing to the coffeemaker. He poured a cup and took a sip. "Vivi still asleep?"

"Yes, Tyce," Eira replied.

"She's had bad dreams again," Beryl spoke.

Ty came and took a seat between them. "I...I'm sorry. I should have been up with you watching over her."

She waved her hand dismissively. "It's fine. Eira took over when I fell asleep, and you needed the rest."

"Grief does unpredictable things to humans," Eira said, placing a hand on Ty's arm. "You needed some rest."

He stared down into his cup for long moments as Beryl gave him a one-armed hug.

Their caring loosened up the words inside of him. "I miss him, you know. I spent so damned long watching out for him... that I don't know what to do with myself anymore," Ty murmured, almost too low to be heard.

"I know," Beryl said quietly. "We're gonna find a way past all this, Tyce."

He shook his head slowly. "I'm trying, Beryl. I keep thinking if I can hold Vivi together, that'll keep me together."

It had been an unspoken plan between them that they would trade off keeping an eye on Vivi over the next few days, and they had not left her alone for any length of time, unless she was sleeping.

"Just put one foot in front of the other for now," Beryl said softly.

After a few moments, Ty glanced up and saw Vivi standing in the doorway. She was dressed in sleep clothes, her bandaged arm in a sling. They'd said she could go without it in a couple of days, but for now, they wanted to keep her arm and shoulder stationary. "Nobody woke me up," she said. She ran her free hand through her tangle of blond curls, then scrubbed her face sleepily. "What time is it?"

"0800," Ty said.

She walked to the coffee machine, poured a cup and came back to the table with them. After she took a sip, she rested her head on her hand and peered at him. "You doing okay?"

"Yeah," Ty said. "I...I appreciate you and Beryl coming for me. How...how did you know?"

"Runa commed us," Vivi said.

"Oh."

"Hey, I'm going to take a shower. When I get out, I'll make breakfast for everyone," Beryl said.

"I am supposed to meet Max," Eira said. "My escort is..." there was a ring from the doornote, "here, I see."

"We'll see you later," Ty said.

Once Eira had left, Ty and Vivi turned to each other. "How are *you* feeling?" Ty asked.

"The same," she shrugged and looked up at him with the first light he'd seen in her in days. "I want you to know that when I'm healed up, I'm going to join the Al-Kimian Defense Force officially."

It rendered him quite speechless for a moment. Ty turned his cup in his hands, thinking before he spoke. "Vivi. You need to give yourself some time. It's not a good idea to do this right now."

She raised an eyebrow. "Why not?"

"It's for the wrong reasons."

"What's wrong about wanting to fight back against the Coalition? Isn't that what you're doing? Isn't that what we've been doing all this time?"

Ty sighed heavily. "No. It's not what I'm doing, and I'm not letting you tear ass out of here trying to get revenge for Hal."

Her green eyes were bright with frustration. She clenched the fist of her good arm and pounded it on the table. "You should be right there with me," she said, exasperated.

"Don't think doing it hasn't crossed my mind," Ty said vehemently and a little too loudly. He sighed and placed a hand over Vivi's clenched fist. "Revenge causes people to make mistakes. Don't think that a large part of me doesn't want to go out there because it does. I want to fly back to Haleia-6 right now. Losing Hal –" His voice caught.

"Ty," she whispered, her own voice hitching at the struggle on his face.

"But I can't afford to make those kinds of mistakes. Beryl needs me, and you need me. And I need you here until you get your feet back under you again and your head in the right place. That's an order."

She frowned, frustrated. "You can't protect me forever."

"That doesn't mean I can't try." He sighed tiredly and went on. "Vivi, Hal meant everything to me. He was my best friend. My brother." His voice caught on those words, and he didn't speak again until he was sure his voice wouldn't shake. "All I can do for him now is watch over you. He would want me to protect you from making a big mistake."

Her head was down, and she was looking away from him. "I'm sorry. I just m- miss h- him, T- Ty," she stammered. "I... don't know what to do without him."

When she sniffled and wiped at her eyes, Ty put an arm around her. She leaned into him for comfort. "I know," he said.

They sat together for a long time, until Vivi lifted her head. The newsfeed had caught her eye, "Look, Haleia-6. Something's...something's happening there," she pointed up at the feed, reaching to unmute it.

The thin, pointed face of the newsfeed reporter looked concerned as Vivi unmuted her mid-sentence. "-lockdown taking place on Cardela Base on Haleia-6. Colonel Mauery, the new base commander, has not made a comment on the lockdown, but as you can see from our vidfeed, soldiers have established a perimeter around the base and are not allowing anyone in or out. We are attempting to get a statement from the colonel and will report further on this feed when we have it. In other news..."

"Malar told me," Ty said. "They're evacuating who they can. Eira's virus must be working."

Vivi frowned. "I hope it brings the godsdamned place to its knees," she said.

"Yeah," Ty agreed. They'd paid a great price for this victory. He hoped it would be worth the cost.

"I'm sorry, sir. You still can't leave the complex yet." The vat in front of him and his partner were blocking the lift to the surface. "We're waiting to hear from command."

With a disgusted grunt, Balen turned and headed back to the lab. He was livid. As soon as he'd arrived upstairs, upper brass made him aware that they were transferring Halvor Cullen to Quillon. The idea that the ACAS didn't trust him to interrogate Cullen was outright insulting. He hadn't had much time to stew about it, however because not long after the transport carrying Cullen lifted off, every device in the complex had shut down. Lifts, computers, comms, the feeds, everything. The only thing that worked in the whole place were the emergency lights and the lifts, which were now being powered by an APU on the surface. Twenty-four hours later and the entire base was still locked down. Balen and his staff had not been able to access any of their research in this time. Thinking it was a power problem, they'd commandeered one of the alternative power units to use on their computers, but it had not worked.

Balen frowned as he reached the lab. Athers, his tecker, was examining the computer system where their research was stored, and it didn't look good. The tecker glanced up with defeat in his eyes.

"Any luck?" Balen asked, already resigned to the answer.

Athers shook his head and picked up a handlight. He pointed it at the inside of the computer. Bejeweled spiderwebs had been spun across the memory board. There were silver crystals like mica hanging on the spiderwebs. "Look at this. If you'll pardon my cursing, sir, it's fucked beyond all I've ever seen. It's like someone or something crushed the memory crystals...and this stuff...it's made of metal. We can't scan it because the equipment's down,"

"What about the scanners sent down from the surface?" Balen said.

"They became inoperative as soon as they brought them to the lab."

"What do you think it is?"

"Some sort of nanite attack...by the Opposition, maybe?" Athers shook his head. "The device is the same." He gestured to the countertop where the three prototypes of the vat kill device lay. They were all disassembled and there was a scattering of tarnished metal particles. "The same webbing was inside, but when I touched it, it crumbled to dust. The memory crystals were much the same. All our research is gone."

Balen sat down heavily on a nearby lab stool. If what Quillon had said was true, the doyen was going to be extremely unhappy.

This was very, very bad.

THIRTY-SEVEN

Kat walked down the hallway much as the condemned headed toward their execution. She'd spent three days healing up in the infirmary after taking the fleet admiral's punishment. Even now, her back was still a twisted mass of healing scars, but she was numb to the physical pain.

Nothing, she told herself. *You feel nothing.*

The truth of it was that she was close to breaking. She was jumpy and irritable, her dreams troubled with memories of blood and murder. She'd murdered Seren, a man who had treated her as an equal and a friend, and every time she thought of him, she had to fight back tears. If she was caught crying, she could be shut down permanently.

She entered Specialist Walker's lab to find a man in grey pants and dark shirt with a lab coat thrown on over it – Wyatt Romal, the fleet admiral's personal tecker. Throughout the years he'd appeared from time to time during her training; he would question her about her emotions and actions, then administer programming sessions. Nausea swept over her as she forced herself to enter the room she'd been summoned to.

"Sergeant Neval. You'll be here a while. Please make yourself comfortable." He gestured toward the head, and she entered, the bluish lights shining in the metallic bathroom.

She went in, took one look at her pale face, then threw up everything she'd eaten that morning. Trying to keep her thoughts blank, she rinsed her mouth and exited the bathroom.

"Everything okay?" Romal was standing by the bed, holding his datapad.

"Yes, sir," she said, approaching him warily.

He gestured to the bed and brought over a tray of medjets and a chair for himself. "Please sit."

She did, folding her hands in front of her and letting out a shaky breath.

"How are you feeling, Katerine?"

"Fine," she lied. The tecker said nothing and the longer the silence unwound between them, the harder it was to keep a clamp on her emotions. Eventually, a tear slipped down her cheek. She wiped it away with a trembling hand.

The tecker watched her carefully and waited.

"Sir. I'm sorry," she kept her gaze averted as she spoke to him. "I'm not...not myself."

"Relax. You can speak freely in front of me. I'm going to make everything a lot better for you, Kat." The tecker examined her coolly. "You had a very hard time while you were with the Al-Kimians, didn't you? Did you find your sense of right and wrong slipping?"

"S-sir?"

"Did you feel compassion for the Al-Kimians?" he clarified.

She squeezed her eyes shut and more tears streamed out as she nodded.

"That's a good thing to know, Kat. You were brave to confide in me. Why don't you lie back, and I'll tell you what we're going to do to fix this. First, stay calm."

"Sir. I...I want to be a good soldier. I'm just...so confused..." she rambled as she laid back on the bunk.

"Stop. No need for excuses. You will be a good soldier. Say it."

"I will be a good soldier," she repeated it while he dosed her up. The flood of heat let her know it was a relaxant, probably drowse.

"That's good," he murmured gently as she began to sink into the chemical sea slamming her brain. The cold metal of a compnode attached over her interface. "You're going to feel a slight sting on your right hand," he said. "Then you're going to get very sleepy. I want you to go with it."

"Will the admiral stop hating me after this?" she asked, as the routines in her brain began loosening their hold. She imagined her mind, unlocked and open for whatever Romal was about to do to her, and she was worried, despite the drugs in her system. If it made the admiral happy, though, she would do it.

"Yes, Kat. You will be his perfect Nyma once more and there won't be anything else to worry about." She watched as Romal taped down the IV to her hand and then started the flow on the line. A dark blue substance began dripping at a rapid rate into her vein.

An incredible sense of peace and calm flowed into her. The pain from her back, the fear that her mental state would be revealed to the Admiral, the panic of becoming a failure to him faded out. "The Blue..." she whispered as she watched the drops fall into the drip chamber. He'd done this to her at least twice before.

"Yes," Romal said. "Blue Rendal will help repair you. It will make all these emotions you're having just fade away, Kat. Then you will know how to be a good soldier again. Go to sleep. When you wake up, this will be an entirely different world..."

. . .

THE VAT WAS SO eager to obey his directive that she never heard his last few words. Romal brushed his hand over her head, then lifted first one eyelid, then another. She was drifting deep. After a few minutes, she was in the heavy sleep of intense programming, so he connected to her interface. There was no sound as the new routines began flooding her mind and taking residence in her neurons.

"Sleep, Kat," he urged her as he watched her vitals fall into target limits, "and learn well."

THREE DAYS LATER, Kat entered the fleet admiral's office at his order and stood at attention by the door. Quillon ignored her for long moments, continuing to key information in at his terminal. Finally, he got up and crossed the room to her. The entire time he'd been watching her, she'd never so much as twitched.

"At ease," he said to her, weighing her every move. His gaze roved over her uniform, looking for anything out of the ordinary. Every piece of metal shone like a star, and her hair was pulled back in a severe tail, no strand escaping the tie. Her eyes were fixed on the wall across from him as she flawlessly slid into the 'at ease' posture: feet shoulder-width apart and arms clutched behind her back. "Romal said you have completed your programming sessions with him."

"Sir, yes sir."

"Good. You are reassigned to my direct command." It was the first time she'd been assigned to him personally. Before there had been a need to keep her training secret, but now there was no need of that. Word had traveled of the vat they called "Quillon's dagger" who had struck a blow against Al-Kimia by killing their vat leader. His purpose in keeping her close was not to honor her, however. He wanted to keep an eye on her in case she showed signs of cracking again.

The pleasure of proving herself to him and fulfilling his command showed plainly on her face. "Yes, sir."

"Romal said you will need another day's rest. You can begin your duties tomorrow. I have a vat prisoner arriving in the morning at 0800. You will escort him to the brig. He is a special one and must arrive safely."

"Yes, sir," she replied.

Kat and two vats were waiting on the shuttle from Haleia-6 when it landed. The ramp began to lower, and she used it to meet the nat officer in the cargo bay of the CD8. She averted her gaze respectfully as she began to speak.

"Good morning, sir. I am Sergeant Neval. I have been sent to take control of the prisoner."

"I'm due to turn Cullen over to Quillon himself," the nat officer shook his head. "Not to you."

"I will comm the fleet admiral for you, then," Kat spoke as a perfect vat, pulling her handheld from her pocket. "He may not be pleased at the interruption, sir, but I'm sure you can make your reasons clear to him."

She could see that the nat was weighing her questionable tone with annoying Quillon. Wisdom apparently won out, thank the gods. "That probably won't be necessary, but I'll have to see him stowed."

She gave a curt nod. "Whatever you wish, sir."

Kat followed the sergeant into the cargo bay and saw Cullen lying bound on a gurney. He was not what she'd expected.

The blond man was familiar, maybe someone she'd seen on Al-Kimia, but certainly not someone she'd interacted with. She examined him closely. He'd obviously put up a fight somewhere; his face was bruised and cut, along with his left arm. Cullen was dressed in the typical sickbay loose pants and tank with bare feet. "He's sedated, sir?"

"Yep." He handed her a nearby medbag. "He's due for the next dose at 0900."

"Time enough to get him locked down. Take off his wrist cuffs for us. My men have their own binders."

The nat moved to the wrist cuffs and unlocked them.

OVER THE LAST HALF HOUR, Hal had come slowly awake. Upon feeling the throbbing of a large ACAS ship's engines, he'd realized with a sinking heart that the transport had reached its destination while he'd been unconscious.

When he heard footsteps, he pretended to be unconscious. There was the ACAS officer who had helped interrogate him on Haleia-6 and a new voice, talking about him. The female told them to unlock him, and he knew this was his only chance to do something. It was a desperate move, but it was all he had.

He gathered himself, trying to ignore the pain in his injured hip as he got ready. One of his hands was unlocked, then the other.

He made his move.

KAT WAS CHECKING Cullen's record on her handheld while they set about moving him. She looked up in alarm when the vat, who was supposed to be unconscious, kicked the nat officer in the face. The officer fell back, stunned. Then, with most of his weight on his hands, the vat twisted his body off the gurney and went straight for Vaughn, the nearest vat. They went head-to-head, blow for blow in the narrow space between the gurney and bulkhead before Vaughn dropped. Katerine stuffed her handheld in her pocket and backed up to make Cullen come to her.

Once his opponents were incapacitated, Cullen and Kat were left face to face. With her adrenaline pumping and a rush in her veins, Kat readied herself for his attack. She expected a possible side kick, but then she realized Cullen was hurt. He was favoring his right side, placing most of his weight on the left. "You're gonna have to kill me," the blond vat rasped as he stepped forward and turned to protect his injured side.

Without looking, Kat motioned behind her to Janson to lower his weapon. "Killing you is not in the plan...yet," she replied with a grim smile. "I don't mind putting your ass on the floor, though."

"Try it." Injured as he was, she was well-aware the traitor vat was still dangerous. She was conservative, blocking his punches with compact moves, until one caught her under the eye. She growled and shook it off as she stepped back and regrouped. It was time to go all in. Cullen was tiring, so she advanced again, catching him with a body blow and an elbow strike to the interface that sent him sprawling. He laid there, shuddering, as she glanced to Janson still behind her. "Cuff this godsdamned motherfucker," she yelled, still angry. She kicked Cullen in the ribs, to make the point. Something about kicking him when he was down made her stomach turn, however. Trying to shake off the feeling, she stepped back.

Janson moved forward and rolled the twitching vat onto his stomach. He roughly cuffed Cullen's wrists behind his back and then went to check his comrade who was coming to. She checked the ACAS natural born lieutenant, whom she saw was named Nixen.

"Lieutenant Nixen," she said, helping him to a sitting position. She could see the darkening shadow of a bruise on his jaw. "We subdued Cullen, sir."

"Shit. Sedative must have worn off. His metabolic rate must be higher than the docs estimated," Nixen said, getting to his feet.

"Yes, sir," Kat said. She glanced to Janson who nodded as he and Vaughn pulled the vat up between them. Cullen was no longer struggling, still dazed from the hard, focused strike to his implant. Well, she *had* learned from the best. She spoke over her shoulder to the nat sergeant. "Follow me, sir. I'll show you where the fleet admiral wants him stowed."

THE BRIG WAS LOCATED in the bowels of the *Vetra*; Kat could sense the thrumming of the command cruiser's engines in the floor as she led them to the brig. Surprisingly, Cullen didn't put up a fight as her subordinates chained his feet to a cleat in the floor. There was only enough slack in the ankle chains to take a few steps, but he didn't stand; he remained in a heap where they'd dumped him.

She stayed behind as her vats went to show the nat lieutenant where the medbay was. When Cullen came back to himself, she was looking over his records. He groaned and pushed himself to an upright position, sitting with his back against the far wall.

Her eyes studied him. He was exhausted and in pain. "Why did you join the Al-Kimians? I see here that you were an elite, Cullen. You earned a Nova Star."

He glared at her a moment before answering. "Doesn't mean shit," he said, spitting blood. She'd obviously busted his lip against his teeth. "It's lies. Vats mean nothing to the ACAS."

"Vats are here because of the ACAS," she said automatically. "You owe them not only your life, but your loyalty." She continued skimming through his information on her device, hoping that he'd say something else. Something she could take back to Quillon. If she could retrieve some useful information, it would reflect well on her. But Cullen didn't speak. He just eyed her.

She decided to go right to the heart. "Why did your team steal the Mudar spheres? Were you all vats? Did Al-Kimia put you up to this?" She paused. "What did they promise you to disobey your government?" He turned his head away bitterly, saying nothing. "Why have all devices on Haleia-6 gone dark?"

There was no reply.

She glanced back down at his record a few more moments, looking for anything she could use to get him to talk to her.

"You know what Quillon's going to do to this vat, little one."

The familiar voice from behind her froze her blood. It became impossible to breathe, and she turned her head slowly toward the plasglass door, her pulse throbbing with fear. Seren was standing there, face and clothing splattered with blood. His expression was grave.

Her brain refused to believe what she was seeing. She dropped her handheld as she backed into the nearby wall. The plastic bounced once before skittering toward Cullen's bare feet, but she couldn't focus on it. Her eyes were glued to the apparition in front of her. "You c- can't be here."

"Who are you talking to?" Cullen whispered.

"Seren," she breathed, unable to tear her gaze away.

"Seren? You know Jacent Seren?" Cullen asked in a low voice.

"Yes." She let out a shaky breath as the apparition disappeared between one blink and the next.

She turned back towards Hal. "You didn't see him?"

"See? Who? Seren?" he asked in a soft tone. "How do you know Seren? Hey. Look at me. What's your name?" Cullen asked, sliding her handheld back toward her with his foot.

"Kat," she replied as she turned, knelt and took it back, all the while watching him suspiciously.

"I'm gonna be honest with you. I'll never answer your questions, and I'm not afraid of death, Kat. You might as well have them kill me now," he said.

"I...c- can't. I'm sorry," she whispered.

"Please."

"No." She stood quickly, making her way toward the door. "Guard!" she yelled, pounding the flat of her hand on the door twice.

"Kat..." he called.

She didn't look back. It didn't take long before the guard came to the door and let her out. She spoke quickly and assertively. "This is Quillon's next special project. He's already tried to escape once. Make sure he stays put or it'll be your ass."

"Yes, Ma'am," the guard saluted.

She fled from Cullen's imploring stare.

HAL SPENT the night chained to the cold floor. There wasn't enough play in the chain to get to the flat panel sticking out from the wall that passed for a bed, and with the thin pad he saw on it, he figured it couldn't be much more comfortable than the metal floor anyway.

Earlier, he'd been checked out by a medic and given injections. Two guards had stood behind the medic the entire time, blaspistols trained on Hal, so he hadn't tried anything. The medic had told him his hip wound was infected. He also noted a couple of broken ribs, and numerous bruises. Hal had been able to tell the medic was angry about the lack of treatment he'd received, but the man didn't dare voice his disapproval, his fear of Quillon keeping him silent.

An hour ago, they'd tossed in a bottle of water and a couple of meal bars on the medic's order. Hal had eaten quickly, realizing he was starving. Then he'd curled into himself, favoring his wounded side, and tried to sleep. For a while he managed to keep his mind off Vivi and Ty. But eventually, he found himself wondering if they were alright. He assumed Vivi had made it out with Beall, Eli and Lane, or they would be using her against him. The thought was the only positive thing he had to hold onto. He didn't have the rush and wouldn't be able to make it out of here, but Veevs had made it out and was beyond the reach of the ACAS. That meant he could face what was going to happen.

He'd thought at first that this Kat might help him, but it was clear she wouldn't. He knew all too well where he was headed. They would jack him up on programming drugs and pry everything out of him, bit by bit, and there would be nothing he could do. Maybe the officer on Haleia-6 had been right, and they would cut his brain into bits to get at Eira's nanites. Surely that was their plan once they'd gotten as much information as possible.

He pulled his bound arms into his chest and closed his eyes firmly against the thoughts swirling in his head. There wasn't much he could do but try to make it as hard for the ACAS as possible.

KAT RETURNED to her private quarters. The fleet admiral had gotten her rooms on the same level as his own, justifying it that he needed her close for her new duties.

Living alone aboard the *Vetra* wasn't as strange as those first few days on Jaleeth Station, but it was close. She keyed the code to her quarters and the door slid open, revealing the tiny living area and bedroom beyond. She was only required to report for programming twice a week now, so most of her nights would be spent here.

She allowed the door to slide closed behind her, then double locked it and headed into the sleeping area. It was only then that she was able to let her grip on her emotions go as she laid on the bed and curled into a ball. "Lights off," she murmured. Somehow, she felt safer in the dark. She needed to be alone, to think, but her mind ran in circles like a wild animal in a cage and nothing was clear.

The lights dimmed and the display panels in the wall lit softly, showing a star field background. The liquid crystal panel was programmed with 300 different views, giving the appearance of a wall-sized window overlooking some fantastic backdrop. It had automatically started up the first night she'd had these quarters. Some vistas were from real places – like the pink sand beaches of Tesia where the water rolled into the shore all night. Other backdrops were entirely fantastic artworks brought to life. The star field was one of her favorites, and she'd fallen asleep to its silvery glow the past two nights.

She rubbed her aching head as her mind turned to what had happened in the cell with Cullen. What she'd seen couldn't have been real. Seren was dead by her hand. Once again, she had the sensation of *slippage* – the feeling that she didn't know what side she was on. She closed her eyes and rubbed her temple, near her interface scar. She had to keep control of herself. If Quillon found out she was slipping, he would kill her.

THIRTY-EIGHT

When the *Raptor* landed at Drena Base, Patrin, followed by Orin, exited the ship to see two people waiting near the hangar for them. "Something's up," Patrin signed to Orin. The feeling didn't abate when they reached the two soldiers waiting for them.

"Terra Malar needs to see you immediately. She is waiting on the *Hesperus*."

"Why is she on Seren's ship?" Patrin asked.

The nat solider didn't answer the question but gestured ahead of him. "Sir, she's waiting."

Patrin frowned at Orin, then headed toward the *Hesperus*. His mind was moving from worry to worry. Had the crew gone out on mission and things turned out badly? Or had something happened to Seren? No. That couldn't be true, he told himself. Kat would have come to meet him if that had been the case.

When he entered the ramp, he saw that some of the crew were lining the cargo bay. Terra Malar stood near the entrance to the ship's hallway. "Please give us a moment, friends," she said to the vats and nats around her.

They all left, except for Lane who came to Orin. The big man wrapped his arms around her and pressed his face against the top of her head.

Patrin was alarmed. "General. What is going on?"

She approached. "I have news which is hard to give."

Patrin could sense handsigns flashing between Lane and Orin, but his eyes were on Malar. "Just tell me. What happened?" This was not what he had expected. He had thought he would deliver his news about the Anklav and then debrief with Seren.

"Jacent Seren is dead, my friend," she said, placing a hand on his arm.

"Dead?" Patrin said.

"He was murdered."

"What?" Patrin shook his head, backing away. "No. This can't be true."

She stepped forward, her hands open. "There was an assassin among us, Patrin. None of us knew. There was no way anyone could have known."

"Who?" His fists were clenched, and his voice deepened with anger. "Who did it?"

"Patrin," Lane stepped forward. "It..."

His voice went hard. "Who was it?"

"It was Kat," Lane said.

Patrin shook his head. "No. There must be a mistake. She wouldn't..."

"Patrin. She did." Lane grabbed his shoulder firmly. "She did it."

He turned away from them, reeling from the news. He could sense their stares, boring into his back, but he couldn't bring himself to let them see the war of emotion on his face. Seren was dead by Kat's hand – the news was like a gravity well pulling him in, and then he wasn't in control anymore.

. . .

Lane was startled by Patrin's scream of grief and the sudden pounding of his fist against the metal wall of the cargo bay. Orin was there before he could hurt himself any further, pulling Patrin into a protective embrace. As kind as the General was, Lane knew this was a private moment that wasn't meant for nat eyes.

"Give us some time with him," Lane whispered, her own vision glassy with tears. "Can we find you in your offices?"

"Yes, of course. Thank you, Lane."

"Yes, ma'am," she whispered. When the General left, she joined Orin and Patrin.

It was said vats could not cry. Like the rest of the shit that nats said about them, it wasn't true. Seren had cared for each of them since he'd collected them from the detritus of the Edge and made them into a family and losing him was like missing some vital part of their anatomy; the old man had meant everything to them. She brushed at the tears on her cheeks and laid a hand on Patrin's shoulder. "Patrin, it's not your fault. There's no way we could have known."

As Patrin turned to her, Orin gestured, struggling with obvious emotion on his face. *How did it happen?* the big man signed.

She signed as she spoke. "She stabbed him. The old man fought back fiercely and did not go down easy."

"She escaped?" Patrin asked. The question came out more like a statement.

Lane nodded. "They believe she hopped a blockade runner."

"Godsdamn it." Patrin turned away a moment, scrubbing the tears off his face.

"It happened while we were on mission," Lane said. "I

didn't find out until three days after I returned. I was out of commission."

"Were you injured?" Patrin asked, turning to her with concern.

"No. I had to rest up from a multi-day rush," she said. "We were successful, but we lost Cullen."

It was another blow. "I'm sorry."

She bowed her head. "He saved the mission by staying behind."

"Did they...did they have some sort of service for Seren?"

She shook her head. "They were waiting for you. I'm sure Malar will speak with you about it when you're ready."

"Give me a bit to pull myself together...then we'll see Malar." He reached out to them and pulled them in to an embrace. "You're both...like batch-mates to me. I want you by my side to make these decisions."

We're here for you, Orin signed.

"Of course, boss," Lane replied.

"Good. Let's go...break the news to Dai and Leila. It...It'll be better if they hear it from friends."

THIRTY-NINE

The morning after Cullen arrived, Kat was requested to report to the brig. She found Quillon standing quietly in front of Cullen's cell, watching him.

"Sir," she said softly from behind him.

She was more stable this morning. When she'd awoken, she had convinced herself she'd imagined Seren last night. Was it a guilty conscience that had made her see him? Perhaps, but this wasn't the time to be thinking about it.

Quillon was focused on the traitor and barely glanced back at her. "I heard there was an escape attempt when you brought Cullen in."

"Yes sir," she replied.

"Why was I not told?"

"Sir, it was not a problem. I put him down directly."

Quillon raised an eyebrow at her. "What is your opinion of Cullen?"

"Sir, he's a member of the Opposition, clearly."

"And your evidence?" Quillon asked.

She replied flawlessly. "I mentioned Seren's name. He reacted as if he'd known the man."

Quillon gave a slight nod. "Have him taken into the programming suite. Romal is setting up the room now. We will examine this Al-Kimian implant and interrogate him about Haleia-6. If he doesn't respond well…I will try other methods."

"Sir, yes sir," she said, stepping up to the cell door as Quillon left down the hallway. She was now able to look into the cell to see Cullen sitting on the floor in the back. He was awake and watching her warily as he took the last swallow from a nearby water bottle.

She keyed her comm. "This is Sergeant Neval. Send three soldiers to the brig to transfer a prisoner." She wouldn't allow there to be any problems this time.

They acknowledged her, and she cut transmission. After a moment, she stepped to the panel, then keyed it open.

KAT ENTERED and tossed him a meal bar. "Here," she said. "Eat quickly because we're moving soon."

"Your meal service sucks," Hal smirked.

"Yeah," she said, arms crossed over her chest as she watched him.

He tore the wrapper off with his teeth since his hands were still bound together. He was starving as his body was trying to accelerate to heal the damage he'd suffered. His hip was starting to hurt again, and Hal realized the medication the doctor had given him was most likely wearing off.

"So. That him?" He nodded toward the cell's entrance. "Your CO? Quillon?"

"Yes," she said simply.

He took a thoughtful bite and watched her as he chewed.

The bar tasted like wet paper and sat in his stomach like a rock. "Ever have any friends?" he asked. "I mean real ones."

A look of something passed over her face, "No." There was a long pause. "Maybe," she whispered. "Maybe once."

He watched her a moment, then nodded. "Then you understand what I'm gonna have to do." He chewed another mouthful and swallowed hard. "I know they'll make me talk," he gestured to the door where the soldiers that had come to get him were waiting, "but I've gotta try."

Kat's face slipped, and for a second Hal saw the same vulnerable, frightened person he'd seen the night before. There was a moment of connection between them, but then she looked away and it was gone. She fled to the door. "Bring him," she ordered the soldiers.

Hal got himself ready.

HE'D BEEN UNSUCCESSFUL AGAIN, he thought as he woke on an interrogation table. The three soldiers had been prepared, but he'd still attacked them as soon as they had brought him out of his cell. They'd slapped him with a sedative as he fought, weakened by fever, pain and hunger. Now with his wrists and ankles secured, he was helpless. He tried pulling against the straps but only managed to roll his head toward the speaking voice. It was as if his arms and legs were no longer attached to his body.

"He's coming around," the guard said.

"I need one more scan of the J72 node location. Hold his head to keep him still." The man speaking was slight of frame, with unnatural white hair cut short enough to be spiky. He was dressed in a lab coat, so he had to be a biotecker or a doctor.

Another man leaned over the table and Hal felt hands on either side of his skull while something cold was rolled across his forehead. There was a noise and a soft beep, then his head was let go. Hal drifted again as the voices floated through the mist in his mind.

"That's perfect. You can leave us alone, now."

"Very well sir," the other voice replied.

There was the snick of the door closing as someone entered or left. Hal looked up to see the fleet admiral from earlier in the day. The man was examining him intently.

"Romal. What have you found?"

"Something very interesting. Let me show you." Hal closed his eyes again and concentrated on the doctor's voice as he began to describe the results of his scans to Quillon. "Cullen's J72 node...the adrenaline node...has been modified."

"How?"

"There's an unidentified metal encircling the node. Scans can't get through it. I'm assuming the original node is still there, but we won't know unless we excise it, but I do have a theory. The metallic substance could be there to prevent the rush response or to prevent adrenaline fatigue. It is similar to some of the nanites found in Mudar brains."

"Fascinating. Perhaps it is a reward for joining up. Sergeant Neval, were you offered such a thing during your time with the Al-Kimians?"

"No sir," Kat replied.

"Did you hear of anyone having such a thing done?"

"No sir."

"Is he awake enough to answer questions?" The fleet admiral asked the doctor.

"Possibly. He's still a bit sedated, which means he may be more compliant."

"Unlikely. This one's a fighter. I have a feeling he will prove quite a challenge. Sit him up," the fleet admiral said. The interrogation table adjusted so that he was no longer laying on his back but upright. The Admiral regarded him coldly. It took effort not to fall into the old routines as he shifted his gaze to meet Quillon's head-on. "So. You're the one who led the assault on Haleia-6's lab. Very enterprising."

Hal mentally struggled for a moment, then remembered what he wanted to say. "Fuck off. You're not getting shit from me."

Kat stepped forward and punched him in the midsection, leaving him gasping. *Well, that was unexpected,* he thought. "You will address the fleet admiral with respect, traitor," she said.

When Hal got his voice back, he rasped out, "Sorry. I mean to say, 'Fuck off, *sir.*'"

She hit him again and again, until the Admiral held up a hand. "Enough."

Hal had a chance to breathe again as she stepped back. "I've had enough ACAS lies," Hal rasped. "So you can go ahead and shut me down, you nat bastard. You're not getting shit."

He steadied himself for a response as anger shadowed Quillon's face. The admiral's hand clenched into a fist for a moment before relaxing again.

"Ah. I see." Quillon shook his head. "You think to bait me into killing you. It's much too early for that, Halvor Cullen. I have questions that I require answers to. Send him to the bay," he said to Kat. "This is going to require a more direct approach."

"Yes, sir," she replied.

"How long have the Al-Kimians been using Mudar technology on vats?" Quillon asked. He didn't expect a response yet, but one had to start somewhere.

The traitor vat had been stripped to the waist and locked into the wrist shackles that hung between two supports in the isolated storage bay. The disobedient bastard swayed on his feet, still groggy from Romal's concoction. Quillon had little worry; the pain would make the vat more alert soon.

He stepped forward, letting the whip tails fall from his left hand as he got ready. Cullen had not responded to Romal's cocktail of drugs, so Quillon was ready to break him. He glanced back at Kat, who stood nearby, face composed and stone-like. This would be instructive at reminding her of her duty as well as reminding her of what these traitors deserved, so he'd required her to be present.

"I will not ask again," Quillon said, giving Cullen one last chance to answer.

"Fuck you, nat," Cullen slurred. His knees buckled under him a moment, then he forced himself to stand.

That was when Quillon hit him. The whip made a satisfying noise against the flesh of the vat's back. Cullen didn't scream, but the buckling in his knees said everything.

"Why did your team come for the spheres? What weapon did you deploy on Haleia-6's computers?"

No answer. Quillon lashed him again with all his might, drawing blood. Cullen groaned, lost his balance a moment and hung in the shackles. Slowly, the vat got his feet back under him.

"Nothing to say?" Quillon asked.

"Why don't you... let me out of these shackles...and we can settle this vat to nat?" Cullen said, gasping against the pain. "If you win, I'll tell you... everything you wanna know."

"It's a pity about your regimental tattoo. It won't be recognizable when I'm done. But perhaps it's not such a pity. Your lack of loyalty is obvious," Quillon replied with more blows that opened up another set of long gashes across the vat's back.

After fifteen lashes, Quillon paused, glancing over his shoulder. Kat's gaze was downcast, as if she couldn't bear to look.

"Katerine!" he growled. Her dark eyes snapped up at her full name. Frowning, he returned to the vat in front of him. He could not and would not show mercy. Cullen was still standing, but barely, and his feet were slipping on the bloody decking. "Let's start again," Quillon said. "How long has Al-Kimia been using Mudar technology to modify vats?"

There was a long pause. "Fuck off," Cullen rasped through the pain, hanging in the shackles, barely upright.

"I see more instruction is needed. Very well," Quillon said, raising the whip again. This time, Cullen did scream.

KAT OVERSAW CULLEN'S trip to the medbay after Quillon was done with him. She'd had to watch him flogged until he was unconscious. Then two medical paras had come and loaded the vat face down on the stretcher. He wasn't lucid or in any condition to escape, so she'd only lightly strapped him down.

You know what happens next, little one.

She glanced around at the voice. "What did you say?" she asked.

You know what happens next, little one. It was a familiar voice, right near her ear. Seren.

One of the paras glanced back at her nervously. "Sergeant?"

"Never mind," she said, picking up her pace and ignoring the goosebumps that rose on her arms. She tried to focus on what she was doing as she watched the stretcher rolled into place in a bay of the medical floor. "Another one of the Admiral's?" the attending medic asked, not seeing Kat in the corner of the bay.

"Sir-" the para gestured slightly toward Kat and the medic paled. It was obvious the paras had recognized her as the fleet admiral's vat.

"Yes, well." The medic cleared his throat nervously and began to examine Cullen. The paras departed and Kat approached.

"Medic, the fleet admiral requests that you treat him and get him ready to spend time in extended programming," Kat said.

"I understand, sergeant," the medic replied. "We can cushion these wounds, but it won't be comfortable for him to lay on his back that long."

"The fleet admiral is not interested in this vat's comfort," Kat said. "Just keep him alive."

"Yes, sergeant," the medic said.

AFTER HER SHIFT with the admiral the next day, Kat made her way to the brig to check on Cullen after his programming session. She found him lying on his side on the pallet, gaze focused across the cell at something she couldn't see. She noticed there was a tray filled with ration bars and a bottle of water on the floor near the door that didn't appear to be disturbed.

"Has he eaten anything?"

"No, sergeant. The medics put him on the bunk, and I don't think he's moved."

"I'm going in," she said. "I have to make sure he eats, or the fleet admiral will be displeased. I'll knock on the door when I'm done."

"Yes, sergeant," the guard replied.

She stepped inside and the door slid shut behind her. She

reached down and grabbed a couple of ration bars and bottle of water.

"Cullen," she said, coming over to him. She saw that his hands were still shackled together, but he was no longer chained to the ring in the floor.

His mouth was moving as he whispered something without sound. He had the dulled look of a vat on drowse.

"I have food," she told him.

He stopped whispering and noticed her for the first time.

She set the ration bars on the pallet and helped him sit up, being careful of the bandages on his back. Tearing the wrapper off the end of a meal bar, she handed it to him. He stared at it.

"Please, you should eat something," she gently urged. The programming they had him on was obviously disorienting him.

He began chewing the meal bar without enthusiasm, bite by slow robotic bite. "Are you in a lot of pain?" she asked, worried about the wounds the fleet admiral had inflicted. Her concern didn't make sense – she shouldn't care about the traitor, but she hadn't been able to get him off her mind the entire day.

He ate another bite but didn't reply. Obviously, he was still numb. Then she remembered that drowse would do that. When it wore off, she knew he would be in agony from firsthand experience. The vat glanced around him, then back at her. "W- where are we?" he asked.

"You're on the *Vetra*," she told him. "Cullen, you need to tell the fleet admiral what he wants to know. It makes no difference now. The ACAS is going to move on Noea and Al-Kimia. The Opposition can't hope to win."

"Did I get hurt in battle?" he asked.

She shook her head.

"Did I get transferred? Did Captain Bernon transfer me?" He raised hands to his head and rubbed. "Wait. That's not right. He sent me on a mission, but after that I can't...I mean I don't know. Did the mission fail, Ma'am?" He trusted her, and it made her heart seize up because it had happened so little in her life. He was obviously confused and thought he was back in the ACAS again.

"No," she whispered. "Quillon had you brought here, not Captain Bernon. You're not in the ACAS anymore," she said in the softest voice she could. Maybe surveillance wouldn't pick it up. "You transitioned out of service." Maybe her words would be enough to reorient him.

"None of this makes sense," he rubbed his forehead, near his interface scar.

It had to be the drowse. She didn't want to think it might be due to what they did to his brain in programming. "Have some water," she opened the bottle and gave it to him.

He lifted it to his mouth and drank, slow at first, then greedily. Finally, he lowered it. "Why? Why are you helping me?" He searched her face as if looking for what he'd lost. He held the bottle out and she took it back.

"I'm trying to convince you to see reason. Do what he asks. Or they're going to reprogram you and get what they want anyway." She capped the bottle and set it at her feet.

He narrowed his eyes, and she saw some realization dawn on his face. "I can't do that."

"You have to." She watched as he laid back down carefully. "Cullen-"

"I can't help you," he murmured. "Leave me alone. I want to sleep." He buried his face against his arm, ignoring her.

"Cullen."

When he didn't acknowledge her, she didn't know what else to do, so she went for the door. Then she knocked and waited for the guard to let her out.

. . .

HAL'S MIND was moving slow. As he laid on the bunk, watching the lights go from bright to dimness that signaled the beginning of the sleep cycle, he found familiar lines in the seatide of voices in his mind. *I am the fist of the ACAS. In war, I am strength...* At first, he clung to the words. They were familiar, soothing even. The echoes in his mind repeated the creed endless times.

The creed. Learning it was one of his earliest memories. It had been echoing in his mind on the day he'd been born at the facility. He remembered how the amniotic warmth had drained away from him as they released him from the exowomb he'd grown in and how cold the air had been and how he'd found himself shivering so violently he couldn't speak as a nurse wrapped him in a blanket. He'd wondered back then if he would ever hear the voices he remembered from his long sleep again.

But he'd heard them again that very night and every night thereafter, pouring into his mind over and over during sleep. He'd asked Dr. Leah, the psychologist at the vat facility, what the voices were saying, but she'd told him to relax and let them happen.

He wanted to find purpose in those inner voices now, but something was holding him back. He focused on that thing, that specific voice, instead of the creed. When the voice came again, its caring shone on him like a sun.

Halvor, I know... I know that you have this, this drive inside of you to seek out trouble. And that you can't quiet down that voice in your head because of what the ACAS did – to you and all the other vats.

What had the ACAS done to him? Programming. That's what this fog in his brain was. They were confusing his mind and clouding his thoughts. He opened his eyes and fixed his gaze on a scratch on the wall in front of him. He needed his thoughts to turn outward, not inside where the maddening routines were. There were no answers inside, only numbing circles of repetitive thought. He needed to concentrate. The ACAS wanted him blindly loyal, but that wasn't right. Loyalty couldn't be demanded; it was given to someone like his captain. Ty. Ty and Beryl and Vivi and Eira. He remembered them now.

He'd forgotten them!

He scrubbed his face. Vivi's features came back to him in sharp clarity, and he remembered she was safe. He'd stayed behind so that they could escape Haleia-6. That was fine; he was at peace giving his life for hers. It was the only thing he had to give, and it meant something. That was all he'd ever wanted if he had to die. To die for something worthwhile.

I forgot you, he thought. *They made me forget you for a while, but I remember now. I won't forget you again,* he swore, clenching his eyes shut and trying to ignore the pain in his heart, which far outweighed the pain in his body.

"I HEARD your conversation with Cullen last night," Quillon said. "You were convincing with him."

Kat nodded from where she stood in front of his desk. "I did the best I could, sir," she said, her skin prickling with fear. So, Quillon had watched the surveillance of her. Did he know she was feeling sympathy for the Opposition vat? If he knew, she was certain he would kill her.

"Escort him to programming. I have a call with the doyen. When they're done with Cullen, take him to the bay. *I'm* not finished with him yet."

"Do you think he will break?"

"Eventually. Alive or dead, we'll get answers from Cullen."

"Sir, yes sir," Kat replied. She turned smartly on her heel and left the room.

He'd obviously had slept badly. When she entered his quarters, he glared at Kat and her escort, while they disengaged the door.

"We're here to take you to programming," she said. "Step outside."

He got to his feet, slowly and painfully. Something in his posture told her to be ready, so she palmed a medjet from the pocket of her fatigues as he shuffled toward them.

One of her overzealous guards grabbed him by the arm and yanked him out into the hallway. Cullen reacted almost immediately, using his cuffed hands to hit the larger of the two guards. The metal of the binders caught the guard across the face and blood flew.

Cullen turned to plow into the other vat, throwing him back against the wall. Kat noticed the regular brig guards were coming down the hallway, guns drawn.

"Guns down," she called, at the same moment stepping forward to slam the medjet into Cullen's bicep.

It had absolutely no effect. He kept grappling with the guard, who was beginning to lose the battle. Cullen had head-butted him, and it had disoriented the both of them.

She hit Cullen with the medjet twice more and watched as the sedative finally took effect. He slid to his knees and went over onto his side in a heap. He focused on Kat, until his eyes rolled back, and he fell fully unconscious.

"What the fuck was he trying to do?" one of the nat guards said as they came up. "Trying to get himself killed?"

"Yes," she said softly, stepping back so her men could

collect Cullen once they were done wiping off blood and cursing.

"And you're going to watch it happen," Seren's voice said from right beside her. "I thought better of you, young one."

She kept her gaze on Cullen but could sense Seren's tall form beside her. It was impossible to bring herself to look at him. If she saw his blood splattered face, she'd scream until they took her away along with Cullen.

Their trip to programming was mostly silent, with Kat trying to keep her composure. Seren's unseen presence haunted her the entire way there.

The two guards dumped Cullen on the bed and then headed for the *Vetra's* medbay to get their own wounds attended to.

With shaking hands, she freed Cullen from the bloody binders, then strapped him down to the medbed. Walker and Romal were talking in the office so she had a moment alone. Just as she got him secure, Cullen woke up.

She drew back with a quick intake of breath, catching the woozy glare from the vat as he tried, weakly, to get loose. His breath was coming fast. It reminded her of the very first time Quillon had taken her on a survival training and had caught a rabbit in a snare. When they'd come upon the poor beast, it had been breathing rapidly and quick, like Cullen was now. She had almost seen the animal's heart thudding in its chest. Quillon made her hold the poor beast down as he took a knife and spilled its blood over her hands. It had been the first time she'd looked death in the eye. And now, she was about to watch the same thing happen again.

Cullen was speaking softly. As she listened, she heard him whispering something over and over. With focus, she realized they were names. "Vivi, Ty, Beryl, Eira," he whispered, eyes not seeing her. "Vivi, Ty, Beryl, Eira."

Names. Names of fellow Opposition members? Her heart caught, and she knew that these were more than comrades...he was terrified and murmuring their names like the prayers she'd heard nats saying right before a combat.

Romal interrupted her thoughts when came from the supply area with an IV kit. She frowned when she saw the bag of Mean Blue in his hands. He hung it above the bed.

Noticing her focused stare, he frowned back. "That's it, Kat. He'll be here until 1800. You're dismissed."

A crazy idea seized her. She could kill Romal...with her bare hands or with her blaspistol. And she could stop him from what he was about to do. Then she could kill Walker, the other tecker, and she and Cullen could escape. Her hands itched, and she could barely breathe.

"Did you hear me, Sergeant?" he said, tilting his head at her as if intrigued by her hesitation.

She stepped back as if she'd been slapped, now terrified by her violent thoughts. "Sir, yes sir," she said, a little too loudly as she turned and fled the room.

SHE ARRIVED BACK at her quarters ten minutes later. When she opened the hatch, she stepped inside and called "Lights up 75%."

The lights brightened as she turned and saw her entire apartment was covered in blood. She recoiled so fast that her back slammed against the hatch.

Seren was lying on the floor, in much the same position that he'd been when she'd killed him. His gaze was fixed and dead, and she crept forward. "Gods," she sobbed. "What is happening?"

He wasn't dead. "Kat..." His voice was the barest whisper. When she heard it, she took four unwilling steps forward.

"Come closer, little one," he whispered.

She knelt beside him, as she'd done that day. "Not again," she sobbed, tears streaming down her face.

He reached for her hand, and terrified, she took it. It was warm. "They've taken so much from you, haven't they?"

"There's nothing left," she sobbed, her head dropping.

"Kat, you're wrong."

She looked up, at him again. "What do you mean?"

"Ask yourself why you are crying," he whispered. "You still have your heart. Use it."

"I...I can't."

"Yes, you can. You know what is right." Seren moved to sit fully up, and when she met his eyes, they were full of amber fire. "It's time to take back what you've lost," he placed a hand on her shoulder. "Strike back at them. Show them the full measure of the warrior they've created."

She had thought there was only one road left to follow, but now she trembled on the edge of seeing another way. "On my own terms..." she whispered.

"Yes, little one," Seren agreed in reply.

FORTY

SPECIALIST WALKER FROWNED AS HE CHECKED IN ON THE brain activity in Romal's most recent subject. The vat wasn't progressing as they'd hoped, and before leaving, Romal had applied a comp node and increased the blue Rendal drip. It did seem to be having a slow effect. The subject's Beta and Gamma brain waves were climbing into the acceptable level, so he had to be learning something.

Being in the room alone with this prisoner, however, was worrisome, if not downright frightening. Word was that this vat had led a mission into the heart of the Inner Spiral – he'd killed at least 10 ACAS and survived a plasma grenade blast. After setting him up, Romal had gone to find a late dinner, which left Walker counting the minutes until he got back. He could just see this new vat waking up, breaking his bonds and ripping Walker's head clean off; a muscled vat who had fought his guards despite a triple dose of drowse running through his veins was probably capable of anything.

When he finally glanced up, he saw the shape of someone standing in one of the pools of shadow – the lights were automatically set to night cycle for vats in programming, so it was too dark to see who it was.

"There's no specialized programming tonight," he said as he stood up.

"I'm not here for programming," the familiar voice said, stepping into a pool of blue-green light.

It was Katerine Neval with her service blaspistol pointed at him. For a moment his brain was frozen; it was as if he couldn't process what was going on. He saw her enlarged pupils, though, and realized immediately she was a vat who meant business.

"Neval, w-what is this?"

"Stand up and put your godsdamned hands behind you." She kept the gun on him as he complied. "Turn around."

"I...I don't understand. D-don't do this."

She shoved him against the wall and snapped a pair of binders on his wrists. Then there was a blinding pain, and nothing.

KATERINE TURNED from dragging Walker to the head and made her way toward the inert form on the bed. She had disconnected the IV, and removed the comp node from Cullen's temple, when she realized that he was so deeply sedated he wouldn't be able to wake up. Also, routines were still flooding his brain if he was in programming. The loss of the comp node had only turned down the volume.

She turned around, looking for the computer to stop the programming. Like most vats, she was aware a computer controlled the simulations and routines. She didn't know how it all worked, but she'd seen enough biotechers with their datapads. She strode to Walker's desk and picked up his datapad.

Waves were displayed on the screen along with other data

she didn't understand. She'd seen them monitor with this program enough. Over the years she'd spent a lot of time in special programming. This was the one.

After slamming the datapad against the edge of the desk once, twice, and then over and over until it broke into two pieces, she slung them against the wall. They shattered.

Strands had come loose from her ponytail, and she took a second to slick the sweat-damp hair back again. With her rush, her body temperature was climbing. Now, she had to wake Cullen up. She tried shaking him and then she slapped him, but it didn't work. Frowning, she looked around the room. Time was ticking. It was said that the admiral had a second sense, and she didn't want to wait around long enough for it to kick in.

"I don't know if this is gonna work, Cullen, but if I don't try it, this is gonna be a real short escape," she muttered pulling out the amp medjets that had come from her ready bag. She'd stuck three of them in her pocket before leaving, knowing that she might need the amp herself to get Cullen out of here. She snapped off the top and pressed it against his neck for a quicker effect.

"Come on!" she said, her body thrumming with the need to get going. He started to stir but it was slow. Too slow. She immediately dosed him again with the second vial of amp.

It was fifteen seconds before he woke and focused on her. She was about to hit him with the third medjet when he caught her wrist in his hand. "W-where am I?" he asked.

"Still on the *Vetra*. I'm breaking you out of here," Kat said. "Are you fit to move?"

"What..." he gestured around. "Where would we go?"

She leaned down and took his face in both hands. "Listen to me, Halvor Cullen. They are going to kill you if you don't get off your ass and get the fuck out of here. I'm your ticket. This is your one chance. If you want to see your friends again...Bernon and whoever else you care about, this is your godsdamned ride. Do you hear me, rook?"

"Yes, ma'am," his voice was faint.

She let him go, and he tried to push to his feet and stand. He promptly lost his balance and sat back down hard on the bed.

"You need this last one," Kat said. "You've gotta be able to walk and maybe fight if they find us out."

Hal groaned at the injection and when he glanced up at Kat, she was surprised to see his rushing pupils. "I thought they said you couldn't rush..." she murmured.

"I can't," he placed his warm face against the cold metal of the bunk frame. "I don't know. Just – just I need a second."

She heard the door swish open. They both stayed motionless. "Walker?" Romal entered and the door swished closed behind them.

Kat drew her blaspistol, staying turned so that her body hid the weapon in her hand. "Sir," she said softly. "I have a message from the admiral. I entered and found Cullen unattended."

"He shouldn't be awake," Romal said, a crease on his forehead. He stepped forward and Kat drew her weapon on him.

"Stay absolutely still," Kat whispered. "Throw your handheld and your wristcomm on the deck."

He complied. "Look, Kat. This is not like you."

"No. It's very much like me. You never bothered to find out who I was. Your only objective was to mold me into what you wanted. You made me a murderer."

Romal shook his head. "Focus on me and listen, Kat. I...I think you're suffering an egodystonic episode. I can help you-"

"Help me?" She laughed sarcastically. "Fuck you, nat. You've done all you're gonna do to me." There was the sudden whine of the blaspistol as it signaled it was primed to go. "All these years, you kept taking and taking who I was...and putting in what *you* wanted instead."

She glanced at Cullen and saw a deep understanding in his eyes.

Romal stepped forward. "I've cared for you all this time, Kat. I wrote your programming. I know you. I know your thoughts."

She spoke through her gritted teeth, "You don't know anything about me," she said, and squeezed the trigger.

It was a head shot. One moment, Romal was reaching out to her, slowly getting closer and closer – the next minute she fired. A hole burned through his forehead and into his brain, searing it from the inside. His body fell with a thud.

"Holy shit," Hal said. "You killed him."

She let out a shaky breath and turned her gaze on Hal, the blaspistol in her hand. She could see he was surprised by her actions. *Well, a lot more are going to be surprised before I'm done today,* she thought with dark intent. For the first time in her life, she felt strong and free.

"Hey, it's fine by me, Ma'am." Hal held up both hands.

"Fuck him," she muttered, shoving her weapon back in her holster. "We've got to go." She reached down for Romal's arms and dragged him into the head. He left a smear on the floor. When she came out, she was holding Walker's comm in one hand and her blaspistol in the other. She blasted the lockpad when the door slid shut.

Hal stood up again, wavering. He wasn't going to be able to pass as an ACAS soldier, she realized. He was too drugged.

"Look. You're gonna have to keep the binders on for now. You're too woozy. They're going to think I'm moving you, at least until we get to the lower levels. Maybe by then you'll be more steady. There's a supply room down there, and we can dress you like a pilot. Then we're gonna have to make a run for it."

"Where are we going again?" he asked, looking around as if seeing the room for the first time.

"To the flight hangar. I'm going to put you on a transport out of here."

He squinted his eyes and rubbed at his forehead. "Sorry. I can't...I can't seem to remember. Things keep shifting in my head."

"It's the programming. Give me your hands," she said as she took his wrists and bound them behind him. When she was done, she came around to the front. "Cullen, listen to me. Keep your head down, do what I say and don't talk to anyone. I'm keeping the key in my hand. If I need you to help me, I'll press the button and the cuffs will fall off. Hear me? Then you fight like hell."

"Everyone else is the enemy?"

"Yeah. Now you're getting it. Come on." She took him by the arm. "Eyes on the ground. Follow orders."

"Yes, ma'am," he replied, as they moved out into the hallway. He did it so quickly that she wondered if he was really following her orders instead of just acting the part. Either way, she guessed it didn't matter. The further away he got from here, the better he'd be.

She led him through the brightly lit halls, trying to keep him moving. Cullen was following her instructions, but his balance was off. She kept him upright without looking too obvious about it as they stepped into the lift.

After she pressed a deck number, the doors slid closed. Thank gods they had the lift all to themselves. She saw Seren standing beside her in the shiny surface of the door, but when she glanced in his direction, he was gone. She swallowed hard and turned back to Hal, who was leaning back against the rear of the lift watching her.

"Why are you helping me?" he asked.

"I...I don't want them to do to you what they...did to me." She bit her bottom lip. "Those names you were saying earlier... You have someone? Back on Al-Kimia?"

"Vivi."

"You get back to her safely, Cullen. That's the only thing that matters to me. Hear me?"

"Yes, ma'am," Hal said as the doors slid open.

She pushed him out, her hand on his arm. "Sir," she saluted the nat officer on the other side who was waiting for the lift.

"Sergeant. Taking him back to the brig?"

"The admiral's private bay. The fleet admiral has special plans for this one," she shoved Cullen in front of her. "Hear that traitor?" she sneered. Cullen didn't reply.

"Well, then. Carry on sergeant."

They continued down the hallway. "Left," Kat said when they came to an intersecting corridor. They made two more turns and stopped in front of a door. It was labeled "supply/armory."

She keyed the lockpad.

"In," she ushered him, glancing around.

The supply room was dark. "Lights up 50%," she said. When the door closed, she released him from the cuffs.

The lights came up showing racks and racks of weapons. She walked past the blasrifles and searched around. "I've got to find a distraction for getting you out of here." After a moment, her eyes landed on a box of Titan plasma grenades. "Hells, yeah," she muttered to herself, stooping to gather three of them. She attached them to her belt and pulled her fatigue jacket over them.

When she glanced back at Hal, she saw he was leaning

heavily on a group of storage crates. He was still in sleep pants and barefooted. "Back here. Let's see if we can get you in something less conspicuous."

After searching around, she found a set of fatigues and boots for him, and when he assured her he was alright, she gave him a moment to change while examining the rest of the storage containers in the front area. She had just opened a box of CP-5 blaspistols when she heard the swish of the door to the supply open.

It was a nat officer with a vat subordinate. Saluting as she was supposed to with a nat officer, she hoped to gods this was not a search for Cullen and that he would hear them and stay put in the back of the supply area.

The officer returned the salute. He glanced over at the private behind him. "Go. I'm sure what you're looking for is back there."

The nondescript vat made his way into the back storage area where there were bins to the ceiling, stocked with all manner of equipment.

The officer turned back to Kat. "You're one of the vats in command, correct?" he asked, measuring her with his gaze. "I've seen you somewhere before," he took a step forward, into her physical space.

She took a step back to put space between them and then glanced down into the box like she'd been looking for something inside. "Yes, sir. I serve in command," she said, hoping he'd leave.

"Yeah, I thought so," he put a hand on her arm, and the back of his hand brushed her breast. She knew immediately what kind of nat he was. "I'm not surprised I noticed you. You're pretty godsdamned hot, you know." He'd probably forced half the vat females on board to sleep with him. Many vat females were easy marks for nats like this. It was either go along or fight back. Those who fought risked being reprimanded and reprogrammed. They were supposed to be able to report these kinds of predatory actions to superior officers, but the CO's rarely did anything about it. It had happened to her once and she'd fought back, despite the risks. When she'd been brought before the admiral for striking a superior officer, she'd told him what happened. And she'd never seen the nat who did it again.

This one must not realize who she worked for. When his fingers closed around her other arm, she knew she was going to have to kill him. The idea didn't scare her anymore. There was only the mission of getting Cullen out of here.

"Sir..." she pulled away, her hand going for her blaspistol. He didn't know what hit him when she brought the gun up and put one through his chest. He slumped against her and fell to the floor and she grimaced at the hot blood seeping through her shirt as she stepped back.

She glanced to the nearby doorway to the larger area of storage and saw Cullen standing there. "They were the enemy right?" Hal asked, still hazy with the drugs coursing through his bloodstream. He had the private's blaspistol in his hand.

"Yeah. Did you kill the other one?"

"Yeah."

She came over and checked him out. His pupils were still enlarged; he was rushing like she was, so he was probably feeling no pain. She could see the dark patches on his back and hip that meant some of his healing wounds had probably reopened during the fight.

Getting a fatigue jacket, she came back, holding it out for him. "Here." He moved to slide the jacket on and zip it over his bloody shirt. It would also hide the marks on his wrists from the binders. He'd already put on the fatigue pants, and she helped him with the boots. After rummaging around a moment, she found a jacket to hide the blood on her own shirt and checked her reflection in the shiny surface of a nearby metal crate.

"Ever flown a transport before?" she asked, wiping at the spots of blood on her cheek.

"Yeah."

"Good. We're going to find a ride."

THE ADMIRAL'S bay was on the same level as the flight deck. When Hal and Kat turned the corner, nearing the bay, they saw a man step out, carrying a small duffel bag.

It was Dr Riley Balen along with a subordinate. He was busy looking at his handheld, probably a schematic of the ship so he could find his way about. He didn't see them at first, so Hal had a chance to realize what was about to happen. Even with his mind moving slow, he knew this would be bad if Balen had a chance to out them.

The Doctor saw him just as they got close enough. "Cullen?" he said, shocked.

Kat's reflexes were faster. She had her blaspistol in her hand first. "Into that bay or I'll spray your brains on the wall."

Balen and the scientist with him backed into the nearby bay. It was the same bay where Hal had been flogged; the bloodstains were still on the floor.

"What's going on here?" Balen asked, an authoritative note in his voice. She leveled her gun at the other scientist while Hal focused on Balen.

"Who's your commanding officer?" Balen's eyes went from Kat to rest on Hal. "Who do you answer to here?" He fiddled with his handheld, trying to call someone up.

Hal slapped the device out of his hand and grabbed Balen's shirt with one fist. "I don't answer to anyone," he said in a low voice. The weight of everything he'd been through at Balen's hands came back in strobes of memory. He threw the doctor against a column and was dimly aware of Kat struggling with her opponent.

"What did the Al-Kimians do to you?" Balen whispered.

Hal threw one arm across Balen's neck, pinning him down. "This isn't what they did to me. It's what you did to me," he said. "You turned me into what I am. A killing machine for the ACAS. How do you like what you created?"

"What?" Balen rasped.

"What gave you the right to do what you did to all of us?" Hal growled, pressing harder against Balen's throat and thinking about all the vats done to death in the vat facilities and on the field. The scientist's face was turning red, and he was struggling. "Answer me!"

It was obvious Balen was angry. "We created you to serve a need. You're nothing more than a tool to be useful," he coughed. "We made you what you are to serve the ACAS."

The anger was like a thunderclap. Hal growled and punched Balen in the face. Something in his mind made him halt, though. The old man's split lip bled freely as he coughed and sputtered, stumbling back and falling to the floor. Hal wasn't sure how his blaspistol got to his hand, but there it was, and he was pointing it at Balen. The rush thrummed through him.

"Stand down, rook," Balen coughed out.

The compulsion to follow orders was triggered again, and he tightened his grip on the blaspistol. No. He would not let this scientist dig into his brain. He tried to focus his mind on the all the vats who had died. Who were they? He could only see rows and rows of boots. Bunks with dead bodies. He wasn't sure where he'd seen them, but he knew they'd been vats killed by the ACAS. His finger tightened on the trigger.

"You don't want to kill me. You want to follow orders. Put

the weapon down." Balen's voice became stronger as he caught his breath.

Hal's hand on the blaspistol began to shake. Was it his programming making him falter? Why couldn't he pull the trigger? He gritted his teeth and growled as he tried to fire again.

"What is your primary function, rook?" Balen said, something dark and hungry in his eyes. Hal suddenly realized that Balen enjoyed this. The power he had over them was at the heart of everything. "Recite it."

Against his will, Hal's hand dropped and his mouth began to form the words of the answer: *protect the unit's nats...* but he was able to clench his teeth against it, winning the war muscle by muscle.

"Recite."

"No," he said, bringing up his blaspistol again, to take the fatal shot. At the same time, a bolt caught Balen in the throat and he fell back, lifeless.

Kat had shot him. "Fucker," she spat.

Hal felt like he'd woken from a bad dream. She came over and put two more in Balen's chest. "Just to be sure," she said through gritted teeth. "You're gonna be okay?"

It was disorienting seeing Balen lying at his feet, and all he could do was gape.

"Hal?" She reached up with one hand and turned his face toward hers. "You with me?"

"Yeah." Hal glanced over and saw the other scientist lying face down on the floor. Again, nothing was making sense. The world tilted, and he wasn't sure what to do.

"That one's dead too," she took his arm. "We gotta get you out of here," she said, pulling him along. They exited and, after checking around for witnesses, she shot the doorpanel to keep the door closed.

. . .

THE REST of the way to the flight deck was uneventful. They passed several vats and techs, but Hal was walking better now and no one took notice of them. They reached the large hangar and stood looking out. The halo of brightness he usually experienced when rushing was extremely brilliant this time. His body was thrumming with the strongest rush he'd ever felt.

Which was wrong. He wasn't supposed to be able to rush, but he couldn't remember why. His thoughts had grown tangled and confused. He tried to focus as Neval chose a transport on the far right. "There," she said.

They reached it with no problems. Everyone had a job to do, and they were hurrying to get it done, paying little attention to the two of them. "Stay here," Kat said. "I'm going to go retrieve the ship's codes."

"Yes, ma'am," Hal replied, waiting by the transport.

Staying focused on what was going on was a struggle. He was uneasy, and the deck was a hub of activity he couldn't make sense of. The last time he could remember being in a flight hangar, he'd been under Ty's command, and he looked around, suddenly thinking that Ty would be here somehow.

But he wasn't. Time was all mixed up in his mind again. It had been such a long time since he'd seen Tyce. Had Cap transferred him to this fleet admiral? As soon as he thought that, he knew it wasn't true.

He remembered a time, right after he'd been made Ty's comm sergeant. They'd been coordinating an attack on an Anklav base when the comm unit had gone dead. When Ty asked him for the extra power pack, he'd found he didn't have one.

They'd reached another unit and borrowed their comm, so everything turned out alright, but Hal had believed he'd blown his chance. When they'd gotten back, he'd reported to Ty's quarters, expecting a transfer. He'd even packed his gear, but

Ty had set him straight. He had promised not to ever transfer Hal unless Hal himself asked to be transferred. It had been the first time a nat had promised him anything. So, Ty wasn't the reason he was here. Ty didn't break his promises. He knew that as well as he knew how to break down a blasrifle.

Then why had they sent him for special programming? Why was Balen here? His mind was jumbled. If he could only remember, he thought, as he rubbed his aching head. He could remember not being in the ACAS, but then here he was, on an ACAS ship in fatigues. What was going on?

Even with the rush, amp and the drowse warring in his bloodstream, he could still feel the throb of the wounds in his side and his back. He leaned against the ship carefully, the coolness of the metal seeping through the back of his jacket. It eased the pain a little.

"What are you doing here?"

Hal stiffened to attention at the tone and saw the nat out of his peripheral vision. The man was an officer, but not a very high ranking one. He automatically saluted anyway. "My CO told me to wait here, sir," Hal said, eyes downcast so the officer wouldn't see he was rushing.

"I'm readying this shuttle for transport to Rinal station. You'll have to pick somewhere else to wait." The officer turned dismissively and began to key the entrance to the shuttle. When he took a step in, Hal dove for him, sending them both to the ground. They grappled, exchanging punches. It took a moment before Hal realized the officer had pulled his blaster. His opponent shot Hal once in the upper shoulder, as the vat landed a massive punch.

The officer's face exploded in blood as Hal broke his nose. He didn't scream; he was only able to let out a gurgle. Hal used his forearm to put pressure on the officer's windpipe as his other hand grappled for the ACAS's blaster. They struggled a moment, and the blaster went skittering under some seats. Then the officer's struggles got slower and slower until they stopped altogether.

When the man was dead, Hal rolled off him and got to his feet, hissing in pain and placing a hand over his new wound. He searched around for the medkit then glanced up to see Neval in the doorway.

"Fuck," she cursed, stepping forward and closing the door quickly.

"He was going to take the shuttle," Hal said, leaning against one of the seats, catching his breath.

She guided him to sit down. "Wait here." In a minute she was back with the medkit. She applied a pressure bandage and a shot of coagulant to stop the bleeding. She eyed the Meliox medjet and glanced up at him. "You have so many chemicals in your bloodstream, I'm afraid to dose you in case you fall asleep again. Can you handle the pain right now?"

"Yeah," he said as she helped him to his feet. He allowed her to guide him to the cockpit of the shuttle, past ten rows of seats. "The rush is helping dull the pain a bit."

"Are you gonna be good to guide this back to Al-Kimia?" she asked.

"I'll do the best I can, if you need me to, ma'am," Hal said, wincing as he settled down into the pilot's chair. His head was pounding with the rush trying to keep his body going and the need to crash.

"Good," she replied. She pulled the comm off her wrist and handed it to him. "This is a private frequency. Don't leave until I get to command and message you with a clearance."

"Wait...you're not coming?" He was stunned. "I thought we were escaping together."

"No. I...can't go back, Cullen. But you can." Then Kat did something strange. She turned to her left and shook her head.

"He won't make it out unless I get to command," she murmured, swiping tears from her eyes. "It's an acceptable sacrifice after all I've done."

What was going on? Hal felt horrible as he watched her begin to crumble in front of him. "Hey, are you alright? Who...who are you talking to?"

At his worried look, she appeared to pull herself together. "Do you know Patrin Kerlani?"

"Yeah."

"Tell him that I'm sorry for how it turned out. I did care for him if it means anything to him."

"I don't understand. Why can't you go back to Al-Kimia?"

"It's...it's safer this way."

"They'll let you come back."

"You don't understand. They won't. After all the programming, I can't trust myself. The admiral chose me as a rook and had me specially trained and programmed. I gave him everything," she said through clenched teeth. "I tried to be...everything he wanted me to be. And he still flogged me. I'm nothing to him," she said with hatred.

"Kat," Hal murmured.

"Now he's in my head." She wiped tears from her face with the palms of her hands, then rubbed miserably at her interface scar. "I keep...flipping from me to something...colder. Like I'm not who I want to be. I don't have control of it. I can't let him make me switch sides again."

"You can't stay here. Quillon will kill you for helping me escape."

"It doesn't matter, Cullen. My time's short already. If the admiral gets me first, at least I'll be free. I deserve death." She took a few steps backwards. "But maybe...by saving you, I save myself. By finally doing that one right thing." Her voice shook.

"Kat," he pleaded.

"You're going to get out of here for them. Your crew. Keep them in front of you, Hal." She began to leave.

"Wait," he called, dragging himself to his feet. A wave of dizziness overcame him, and he held on to the pilot's seat to steady himself.

She turned toward him once more. "It's too late for me, but not for you. At least let my death mean something. You'll give Patrin the message for me, right?"

Hal was at a loss. "I...I will."

"Good. Wait until you get my signal, then find your way home, Hal Cullen," she said, and left.

FORTY-ONE

Kat kept a careful pace as she went down the hallway. She didn't want to run, but every moment was another chance that either she or Cullen would be discovered. The adrenaline rushing through her system was like an acceleracer slamming into her brain.

"Steady young one," she heard Seren's voice to her left, wrapping around her like a warm blanket and giving her courage.

"I have to hurry," she murmured to herself, stepping up her pace. "I can't lose my nerve."

"You are the solider they made you into. You are strong," Seren murmured into her ear. She could sense the weight of his hand on her shoulder. "You will not fail."

She whispered as she reached the lift. "I will not fail." Stepping inside, she examined their reflections in the shining metal of the door that slid closed in front of her. She wiped under her eyes and smoothed back her hair so that no strand was out of place. "I can't fail," she whispered.

. . .

Hal was working his way through the flight checklist on the heads-up display, waiting on Kat's call when an arm fastened around his throat. He'd thought he'd killed the ACAS officer, but evidently, he had not.

Neither one of them spoke – the struggle was too great for that. Black spots threatened his vision as he scrambled for his blaster and the nat struck him repeatedly in the head with his free hand. Before he could get it loose, the nat pulled him from the seat and they tumbled to the floor.

Kat made it to the bridge without drawing attention. When the door swished closed behind her, she keyed the lock, then turned. There was a sparse crew; the *Vetra* was in orbit around Rinal, so there was no need for everyone to be present.

She'd hoped the fleet admiral would be on the bridge. He kept a close eye on the crew and customarily checked the bridge crew at this time. But he wasn't there, she realized with a frown.

"It makes no difference," Seren said. She turned to see him standing beside her. "Do what you have to. Take back what you have lost."

She shot the lock panel to the bridge and turned to the surprised faces of nats and vats.

The XO stood, her face darkened with anger. "What is the meaning of this, Sergeant Neval?"

Kat advanced, "Hands up," she said, her blaster raised.

Some of the bridge crew complied. One vat was reaching for his blaster. She shot him and he fell.

"Stand down, Neval!" The XO said, thinking her order would have some effect on Kat. The rest of them were aware that she was the admiral's pet vat, and they hesitated to shoot her, not wanting to be the recipient of the admiral's displeasure.

She frowned. "Sorry, Ma'am, I can't do that."

"We'll see what the fleet admiral has to say-"

Kat shot the XO. The woman crumpled.

There was movement out of the corner of her eye, and Kat pivoted to the comms officer who had raised a blaspistol in his hands. She caught him with a shot to the throat. He fell thrashing.

There was a searing impact to her back as she was shot by the last vat at engineering. She'd missed him or he'd flanked her somehow while she was occupied with the XO. She whirled, firing rapidly as she did so until he wasn't a threat anymore.

The pain caused her to drop to her knees. Holding her weapon with one hand, she lifted the other to her face and wiped the sweat with a shaking palm.

"They will be coming Kat. You do not have long," Seren spoke from behind her.

"Right," she replied. She pulled herself to her feet by using the nearest chair, then collapsed into it. She sent the fleet admiral's clearance code through. It would get Cullen out as quickly as possible. "It's time," she commed Hal as she sat in the XO's chair.

There was no answer. "Do you hear me, Cullen? You need to leave now," she was going to wait until he'd cleared the bay before she blew the place. It would cause the most confusion and hopefully Cullen could slip away during the chaos.

There was still no answer. "Cullen, you better move your ass!" she growled, plucking the grenades from her belt and setting them on the console in front of her. She knew the shot in her back had nicked something important; as she moved, the hot, wet stickiness of blood soaked through her shirt. The world greyed out around her for a time.

A pounding behind her on the bridge door brought her back from the fuzzy darkness. She turned her head that way, realizing it would be a minute before they made it through the hatch. It was meant to hold out against intruders trying to take the bridge and they'd need a heavy-duty plasma cutter to get through it.

"Damnit, Cullen. Answer!" she called in frustration, her voice weak.

"Yes, ma'am," Cullen's voice came back breathlessly.

"What happened?" Kat asked.

"That officer wasn't dead before, but he is now," Cullen said.

"You need to go. Now. I don't have much longer up here," Kat said, tapping at the panel in front of her. "You're cleared to take off." she said finally, sinking back against the chair.

"Kat?" he called.

"I'm here," she said, pushing herself forward enough to take two of the grenades, one in each hand. The thumping was getting insistent at the hatch, and she could hear some grinding noise, as if they'd found that plasma cutter they needed.

"What are you about to do?" Cullen asked.

She smiled tightly. "You'll see it. Once you're away...push the engines hard. Get the fuck out of here. Back to your friends."

The short range comm was beginning to lose signal. "Kat?" he called again.

"Tell Patrin how sorry I am," she murmured again, her eyes filling with tears. The noises from the hatch were louder now. "I'm done, Cullen. Now it's your turn. Make them pay for what they did. Make them pay for what they did to all of us," she said, her anger rising again as she shut off the comms.

The bridge door slid open. Fear brought her to her feet.

"Katerine!" Quillon's voice made her turn. She held both grenades in her hand tightly.

She turned to see Quillon behind her, blaspistol drawn.

"Where is Cullen?" he asked.

"Safe. Away from you," she replied.

"What is it you think you're about to do?" Quillon asked carefully, lowering the gun. She could sense a carefully controlled rage under his words. It made her skin prickle.

"Why did you choose me?" she asked, watching him warily. "Why did you do this to me?"

She could see the flash in his eyes, but he was too crafty to let his anger loose. With her hands on two plasma grenades, he had to be careful. "You pleased me because you were fierce, Nyma. I thought that you could be made into something worthwhile. Perhaps I was wrong."

"Worthwhile?" Her stomach turned. "I did everything you asked of me! Everything, but it was *never* enough. You kept taking more and more of me... until there was nothing left." Her tears spilled over, and she depressed the buttons on the grenades and held them. Letting them go would cause the grenades to explode: a dead man's switch. "I didn't breathe without thinking to please you."

"Katerine, disarm the grenades." He knew with a swipe of her thumb on the side of the grenade she could kill the switch.

"Did you ever care about me at all?" she asked, letting her emotions show clearly on her face in front of him. It was a freedom she'd never had before, and it was like fire in her heart. "Or was I only a tool for you?" She was starting to feel tired too; the blood loss was catching up with her and her rush was fading. It wouldn't be long, she realized.

"You are mine," he said, stepping forward. "Everything I have done, I have done to make you faster and stronger – so you can be of use to me. I gave you your will, your strength, your very thoughts. Whatever you are, you owe me."

She stared at him as his words sank in. He was right in a way. Everything she was going through...all the pain...the guilt...it was his fault. Her murder of Seren...those actions had not been her own, they had been Quillon's, programmed into her by his tecker Romal.

"Yes, little one. You understand it all now," Seren's voice said from behind her, his hand on her shoulder. "You know your path."

"You made me everything you wanted. Are you satisfied, Admiral?" she asked, gesturing to the dead around them.

"Nyma. Disarm the grenades. We can find a way to help you." Quillon took another step forward. It was obvious he was more confident that he was in control, now. He took another step.

"You mean you will have me shut down. No. I'm going out on my own terms," Kat said wearily.

When Quillon dove for her, she let the grenades drop from her hands. They fell, Quillon slammed into her and there was a bright flash, then nothing.

HAL HAD CLEARED the ship's launch bay when a flash of light lit up the cabin. He turned to glimpse a brilliance out of the starboard side viewport. "Shit," he breathed, watching the explosion travel outwards from what he assumed had been the *Vetra's* bridge; the ejected material was moving at a rapid rate. Neval had been in there, he was sure.

"Kat!" he called on the comm. "Are you there?"

Static was the only reply as bits of the bridge pelted the transport.

. . .

"Situation report." Lieutenant Commander Schaff of the *Vetra* barked as he entered the secondary bridge. Nats and vats were bustling around, and when he entered, the activity increased.

"Sir, I've got reports from security that there's been an explosive decompression on the bridge. That's all I know at this moment, but I have ship's engineers and security on the way. We've locked down the bays as well," an engineer said.

"Do you have security data from the bridge?" Schaff asked.

A nat tecker tapped away at a terminal, then turned to them. "Sir...I- I think you should see this." He backed away so that Schaff could get a look at the display.

Schaff watched as Quillon's vat entered the bridge, shot the lock pad, then proceeded to murder the bridge crew. His face was carefully composed but inside he was shocked. What had happened? He saw her line up three round objects that looked like plasma grenades and then he could see her mouth moving. *Who was she talking to?* Schaff wondered.

He commed specialized programming but there was no answer, so he tried the brig as he watched the footage of Neval reaching for the grenades.

"Do you have the prisoner? Where is Cullen?" he asked them, watching Quillon enter the bridge and talk to Neval. He could see the Admiral edging toward her as she held out two of the grenades.

"Sergeant Neval took him to programming."

The display he was watching went white as the bridge imploded.

Schaff closed his eyes a moment. So, she had blown herself up and taken Quillon and the bridge with her. One of the vats was watching the screen out of her peripheral vision and he saw her swallow hard at the explosion.

"Send security to programming and find out what's happening there," Schaff said, rubbing his forehead. This was going to be a long night.

FORTY-TWO

"There's no way this is not a trap," Spenser remarked as he pulled on a webmesh chest protector and then moved to grab his helmet. "An ACAS transport drops out of FTL into Al-Kimian space and shuts down? Why?"

"I dunno." Tobias, his fellow soldier, glanced up as he flipped the switch and heard the comforting whine of his blas-rifle powering up. "Not responding to hails; that's what Saraph in communications said."

"She that hot as hell comm officer?"

"That's her. She keeps me informed." Tobias winked.

"I bet she does."

They both chuckled, then Tobias became serious. "Look, first thing I see moving on that transport is getting a bolt between the eyes," he swore.

"Oohrah," Spenser replied. "Let's go. Kline's already at the docking rings."

. . .

When the three vats breached the ACAS transport that had dropped out of FTL, Tobias didn't know what to expect. It was dark inside, with only the center row lit up with blue-green light, as if it were the transport's night cycle.

Tobias, Spenser and a female vat named Kline flipped down their night vision goggles and silently made their way down the center aisle, weapons at the ready. Tobias stopped and gestured ahead where the dim light from the cockpit illuminated the still body of an ACAS soldier. From the pool of blood and fixed look on his face, it was evident that he was dead. A peek at the wrist and Kline signed *nat*.

A flurry of handsign began. Tobias and Spenser moved forward and peered around the corner of the cockpit, while Kline covered their rear. There was no one in the pilot or copilot's seat, however they found a body slumped on the floor nearby. There was a dark pool of blood underneath the torso.

"What the fuck? Why would two ACAS kill each other?" Kline whispered, as she glanced over her shoulder at them.

"This one's not dead yet," Tobias responded. "Call a medic, Kline."

Ty was in command, meeting with Beall and Malar. He had a lot of experience against resistance fighters on Bel-Prime and other planets, so the General had thought he might have some insights into what they could do on Noea to slow the ACAS's advance. They had just gone over the Al-Kimian Defense Force order of battle when the General stepped outside to take a call. She stepped back in, while still on the comm.

"Yes, please. Someone's on the way."

Beall stood up. "Ma'am?"

She held up a hand as she signed off, then spoke quickly. "One of the outer patrols reported an ACAS shuttle dropping out of FTL. It wasn't responding to hails, so we boarded it. There were two men onboard, but only one was still alive. We have reason to believe it's Halvor Cullen. Ty, he's not in good shape. One of our shuttles is ferrying him to the surface now."

"Where will they land?"

"Hangar 13. They're ten minutes out. I've put Dr. Parsen and a medical team on standby in the medcenter. Go on, both of you."

Ty and Beall began a brisk walk toward the Hangar.

"Are you calling Vivi?" Beall asked.

"Yeah. She needs to know." He activated his handheld. "Vivi?"

"Ty, what's wrong?"

"Is Beryl there with you?"

"Yes."

"I need the two of you to meet me at Hangar 13. I don't know how to tell you this, but it seems Hal...he's come back to us. They said he's in bad shape. You need to be there."

There was a stunned silence, then Vivi's voice came in a whisper. "Gods, Ty. We're on our way."

THEY STEPPED FORWARD as the ramp opened from the transport. Ty could see people inside, then he saw the gleam of a metallic antigrav gurney guided forward by some medics.

"Ty," Vivi came up at his side. He wrapped his arm around her as the medics brought Hal off the ship.

His face was bruised, his lip was cut and he was covered in dried blood. "Oh gods," Vivi murmured. She angled closer to the stretcher and placed a hand on his hair. "Hal. I'm here. We're all here."

He gave no sign that he heard her.

"We're taking him down to level four," the medic said to

them as they glided Hal toward the cargo lift. There wasn't room for the rest of them inside, so they had to wait for the elevator's return.

"Ty..." Vivi said. "Is he going to make it?"

He swallowed hard. "I don't know."

"He's a fighter. He's going to make it," Beryl said, putting an arm around Vivi.

Finally, after what felt like ages, the lift opened again to take them down.

Vivi chewed her bottom lip as she looked out the window at the steady rain. The storm had begun not long after they'd wheeled Hal into surgery, and it was still going strong now, hours later. On Al-Kimia, late spring was the rainy season, when storms swept the temperate zones to encourage growth in the forested areas of the planet. What rain nature didn't provide; weather drones supplemented.

She needed the soothing patter of the raindrops to keep her calm. Max and Eira were consulting on Hal's treatment, and Eli had been called away to review the cargo ship's systems so they could get logs and camera footage. Beryl was in the operating room, so she and Ty had been left to a silent, anxious watch.

Vivi had slept for a little while, finding rest while leaning against Ty's shoulder. Now, however, Ty had been called away to speak to General Malar, so she was alone. Staring out the rain-streaked pane, she saw a figure in blue scrubs appear in the plasglass's reflection.

She turned and saw it was Max. She took a few hesitant steps toward him.

"Is it good or bad?" she asked.

"Hal's situation is a bit complex. Sit down with me, Vivi," Max said.

Feeling like she was about to throw up, Vivi came to sit beside Max. She took his hand. "Tell me, Max. I can't take much more waiting."

"Hal came back to us in bad shape. He's been shot in the shoulder, and there's a half-healed wound in his lower hip that's infected. Cuts, bruises, a head injury and..." he hesitated.

"What?"

"He was severely flogged."

"Oh my gods, Max," she whispered, thinking of comments Hal had made about vats being flogged in the ACAS. It was a brutal, inhuman treatment far beyond anything she could imagine. When she glanced up, she saw Ty at the door. From the look on his face, she could tell he'd heard the news.

"He's coming out of surgery pretty weak right now," Max said as Ty came over. "As you probably know, vats heal faster because of their rapid metabolism. They usually eat more at those times to manage their need for increased energy, or we put them on IV nutrient if they're unable to eat. Hal's had neither, and his body's been running at a high metabolic rate. We're going to take steps to help his body recover, but it could take a while before he's fully healed. It will be days before he's even conscious enough to talk to us."

"But is he out of danger?" Vivi asked.

"I think so, if everything goes well."

Vivi bowed her head, saying a silent prayer.

"Can we sit with him?" Ty asked.

"Yes. I put the two of you and Beryl down as family members, so you can come and go as you please. Follow me."

. . .

HER PATIENT WAS SLEEPING the dead sleep of a vat recovering from an intense multi-day rush and multiple severe wounds when Nurse Perlan came back to check on him. They'd had Cullen in an intensive care room for the first few days, but now his vitals had been stable enough so that he could be brought into a regular room. The damage from the blaster bolts and the three broken ribs would heal over time, just like his back, and the raging infection was being dealt with, so barring anything unforeseen, the vat was out of danger.

He'd been attended constantly by the members of his crew. Their medic was keeping an eye on Cullen's treatment and the captain of their ship had finally coaxed the young woman downstairs to get her first real meal in several days. While they were gone, she was going to change Cullen's IV line and the bag of intravenous nutrition keeping him alive.

She was reaching down for the new bag of fluids when Cullen woke. In one smooth motion, he sat up and grabbed her by the arm.

"WHERE IS THIS?" Hal demanded. His voice was raspy with disuse, and he was horribly thirsty, but he had to focus on the woman in front of him. Was he still on the *Vetra*? Or had Quillon moved him somewhere else?

"What?" she asked, startled.

"Where are we?" Hal shook her. "Who are you?"

She stumbled over her words, "My name's Perlan. I'm your nurse. We're... we're on Al-Kimia." He stared at her, uncomprehendingly. "Look, you've been very ill."

Hal shook his head. "Liar!" he cried. He let her go and pulled the IV out of his forearm. He began ripping at sensors attached to his chest and inner elbows while trying to swing his legs off the bed.

"Please stay calm." When he reached for her again and missed, she held out both hands and backed away, pressing a button on the wall as she passed it. "We need assistance in 142!"

Hal had just tried to stand when someone else dressed as a medic came through the door.

"Cullen. It's alright. You're back home among friends," the man said gently.

Hal stood upright for a moment, but stumbled back, bracing himself against the wall. "That's a lie," he growled.

"No, it's true. Try to calm down. No one is going to hurt you." He held out empty hands, then gestured to the nurse. "Come back this way."

She edged toward the medic. Once she reached him, she stepped into the hallway, and disappeared.

Hal's eyes were wild as he looked around, expecting some new torture from Quillon. He wanted to believe he had escaped, but he couldn't remember anything but the endless questioning, interspersed with hot, searing pain. "If this is Al-Kimia, where's Ty? He would be here."

"He's on the way, Cullen. Hang tight."

Hal's legs were trembling, and he found himself sinking down to the floor. He was too weak to fight anymore. Closing his eyes, he curled up against the wall to protect his injured side, knowing it was all he could do. He struggled to remember what had happened. There had been a mission. Something had gone wrong, and he was in the hands of the enemy, who was trying to force him to do something. The memories were blurry, and his mind was moving slow.

A familiar touch on his shoulder startled him. "Hal."

His entire body stiffened as he looked up, not knowing who or what he was about to face. But it was Ty. There was a long beat where they took each other in before Hal could speak. "T-Ty?"

He nodded. "We're here."

"Both of us," another familiar voice said behind him. Hal turned to see Vivi had knelt on his other side.

"Veevs?" he whispered, tears blurring his vision.

"It's me." She embraced him gently, but he swept her up in a hug so tight her breath caught.

"I love you," Hal murmured against her.

"I love you, too," she replied, smoothing his hair with a gentle hand. "You're going to be okay."

After long moments, Ty spoke. "We need to get you back in bed."

Hal's eyes searched the room, still grappling with everything overwhelming his senses. The volume of everything had been turned up. His skin hurt, his body ached, and the lights were all too bright.

"This...is real? Not a sim?"

"It's real." Vivi assured him again, allowing him to lean on her as they lifted him to his feet. Together she and Ty got Hal back onto the bed and resting comfortably again.

It was three more days before Hal was well enough to stay awake for more than a few minutes. Ty and Vivi were taking turns sleeping so that someone was always awake when Hal was. Shortly after 0200 on the third day, Hal sat straight up in bed. Ty saw him looking around as if trying to orient himself. "Hey, it's me. You're safe," he said, leaning forward in his chair.

Hal blinked at him in the blue glow of the night cycle lights. "Ty...Where are we?"

"You're on Al-Kimia in the medcenter," Ty said. It was the

third or fourth time he'd asked that question. Max had said that Hal might be disoriented. "Do you need me to get a doctor?"

"I...No." He shook his head. "I'm fine," he murmured, grimacing at the pain in his back as he laid down and turned toward Ty. "I keep thinking I'm back there. Bad dreams."

"Want to talk about it?" Ty said, pulling his chair closer. He glanced across at Vivi, who was lying on the small makeshift bed near the window and saw she was still sleeping.

"Yeah."

"How...how did you escape, Hal? We thought you were dead in that explosion."

"A woman named Kat saved me...but she died, Ty."

"Who saved you?"

"A vat named Kat Neval."

Ty's was stunned. "Kat Neval saved you? Tell me what happened."

"I was prisoner on the *Vetra*. She helped me steal a shuttle, but she stayed behind. To make sure I got out."

"The *Vetra*." Ty knew what that probably meant. When they had Hal in custody on Haleia-6, they had moved him to vat-breaker Quillon. Ty grimaced, remembering the man's record from his time in the service. "You were... ah...questioned by Quillon?"

"Yeah," Hal said. The shadows under his eyes told Ty all he needed to know.

"Gods, Hal."

"I tried not to tell them anything. But the programming... I'm not sure."

Ty went pale as he came to another horrible realization. "They programmed you?"

"Yeah. I was confused, and I kept thinking you'd be on the ship. Neval came, and I'm not sure. She was there most of the time before, during the questioning by Quillon and taking me to programming, but... she wasn't well, Ty. I think they programmed her in some way that she wasn't right anymore. Like she was falling apart...breaking down.

"We got to the flight deck, and she said she wouldn't come with me. I...begged her to get out of there with me. But she said to tell Patrin she was sorry. Sorry about everything. I get the feeling that there was something between them. Is he here? I'm having trouble remembering."

"Yeah," Ty said. "We'll ask him to come by when you're up for it." He was cold all over, his mind replaying what he'd been told about Neval's attack on Seren. That she was a mole, sent to get close to the leadership and kill them. Neval had shown no signs of working for the other side, and Malar said it could have been possible that she'd been programmed to do it and hadn't even known until she'd done the deed. Had they done the same to Hal? It was unthinkable...but possible.

"I'm gonna have to tell him, Ty. I promised her."

"There's something you should know..." Ty murmured, sitting back heavily, as if he'd been punched in the chest.

"What?"

"Kat...ah...she killed Seren. I found out when I got back here. He was discovered in his quarters knifed to death. The blood trail led back to her."

Hal's eyes went wide. "She...killed him?"

"Yeah, I'm afraid so."

Hal's face fell. "If it means anything, she was so sad. She told me she'd done things...things that meant she couldn't trust herself around anyone. I didn't understand then, but now..." After a long moment, he spoke softly, "I didn't think I'd see you or Vivi again."

Ty's eyes quickly filled with emotion that he tried to blink away. "Yeah, we didn't think we'd see you again either, buddy. Vivi took it pretty hard."

"She was pissed at me, wasn't she?"

"No, Hal. She wasn't pissed at you. She wanted to join the Al-Kimian Defense Force and give the Coalition hell. I talked her into waiting a little while." Hal gave the first small smile that Ty had seen so far. It was great, but he looked exhausted. "Why don't you try to get some more sleep now? How's your pain level?"

"It's okay." Hal was tiring, and Ty knew the look from their years on the battlefield and in medcenters. Hal's system was pushing him to sleep again, in order to heal itself more efficiently. He drifted off a moment, then woke again. "Oh. When we were on our way out, Kat gave me three doses of amp, and I was rushing."

"You were?" Ty asked.

"Yeah, didn't think I was going to make it out. I was gonna lay down and give up, but then the rush happened." Hal closed his eyes again. "Maybe they did something to me to counteract what Eira did, I don't know. I was in and out a lot."

Ty was sick at heart. "Don't worry," he murmured. "Just sleep a while. We'll be here when you wake up," he said, sitting back in his chair as Hal drifted off. Ty didn't think he'd be able to sleep, so he let Vivi continue to rest past the time he was supposed to wake her. She needed it, and he had a lot to think about.

FORTY-THREE

The next morning, Max brought Vivi and Ty the breakfast pastries that they were all growing so fond of and then checked Hal's wounds. During the examination, Ty and Vivi had stepped out to the nearby patient consultation room to eat and take advantage of the thermal carafe of rich Al-Kimian coffee that Max had brought them.

Vivi sighed with happiness as she opened the carafe and inhaled the scent. "Remind me to hug Max."

"Yeah," Ty smiled tiredly.

She poured a cup and gave it to Tyce. "You need to make sure you wake me up to spell you."

"You needed the rest." Ty took a sip and sighed. "He was up for a while last night."

"Did he say anything about what happened to him?" She sat back, wrapping her arms around herself. It was always cold in the facility, and Vivi had taken to wearing Hal's jacket when they'd thought he wasn't coming back. The larger jacket made her look even smaller as she regarded Ty, and he hesitated, almost afraid to burden her with everything Hal had shared.

She went on. "Look. Don't try to protect me. You need to tell me so that we both know what we're dealing with. It's obvious they did more to him than...what we can see," she swallowed hard.

She was right, so he shared the story of Hal's escape. When he was done, she sat back thoughtfully, wiping her eyes. "So, the vat that killed Seren just helped Hal leave? It seems too easy."

When she echoed his fears, he knew they were valid. "Yeah. He said he was programmed. If they did the same thing to him that they did to her, he could be a bomb, waiting to go off."

"I don't think he would hurt us," she whispered.

"As long as he knows us, he wouldn't," Ty said. "Hal says this vat that killed Seren and helped him escape was mentally off. *Breaking down* – those were the words Hal used. That they'd done something to her in programming that was causing her to fall apart."

"Gods."

Ty leaned back himself, crossing his arms over his chest. "I've been thinking about it all night. We need to determine if Hal's a danger to others or even himself. He seems steady, especially for what he's been through, but this Kat did too."

"So, you think he could be...could be programmed to kill someone on Al-Kimia in command?" Vivi said, lowering her voice to a whisper.

"It's a possibility that we have to consider. Or he could be here to gather intel and report back. Or maybe he wasn't programmed long enough. He told me Kat Neval interrupted a programming session and set him free. From what I understand it requires repetition to program someone. That's why Hal has those task echoes. They're the echo of the repetitions he had to go through to learn something."

"I suppose General Malar needs to be told," she said as she chewed her bottom lip.

"I think so. I want to talk to Max and see if he can find out what they did, but I wanted to run it by you first. And then of course, Hal. I'm not for making him do anything he's unwilling to do. He's been through enough. I don't want to, but we can take him and the *Loshad* and set up on one of those border planets and wait this godsforsaken war out." He sat back a moment, then let out a sigh as he tried to figure out how to tell her the rest of it.

"What is it?" she asked.

"Kat gave Hal amp to get him up and moving when she got him out of there. He said she gave him three doses and he rushed." Her eyes widened, and he continued. "Look. It might be that he was too under the influence to remember what was going on. I'm not sure. We won't know until Eira can confirm that her nanites are still functional. I called her, and she will come see him tonight. There's nothing we can change right now. I thought you ought to know in case he mentions it."

She nodded. "We're going to have to confide in Max."

"Yeah. Maybe there's some way we can find out what happened in those programming sessions. Then we'll know what step to take next."

EIRA CAME THAT NIGHT. Her escort waited outside as she stood at Hal's bedside. "Amatan. I am so happy to see you awake," she said, laying a hand on his arm.

"It's good to see you, Eira," Hal said.

"Can you tell me what happened to you while you were in ACAS custody?"

He went through the short version he had told Ty the night before. There was no need to make them worry by telling them all the details, he thought, especially when he noticed Vivi's worried expression.

"I am supposed to communicate with the nanites to make sure they are still in place. This will not hurt you," she said softly.

"Go ahead," he agreed.

She placed her hand on his forehead. There was a susurration that Hal could hear; it came from somewhere inside of him and continued for several moments. It was comparable to the whispering he'd heard in the *Loshad* so long ago before they knew Eira had come aboard their ship. Then the noise died away.

"Your mytrite nanites are indeed intact and functioning perfectly," Eira said.

"Then how did I rush?"

"Your nanites allowed you to rush due to the damage to your system. You were in danger of dying."

"So, you're saying that it wasn't something the ACAS did to him?" Ty asked.

"No. It seems my nanites applied my instructions in a novel way," she said, almost appearing proud.

"What do you mean?" Hal asked.

"I told them to protect your life, meaning to stop you from rushing. They extended the parameters to protecting you at all costs. When they thought you would die, they did the only thing they could and allowed Hal's system to slip into rush mode."

"I wouldn't have made it out without it," Hal said.

Vivi took Hal's hand. "Thank you, Eira."

"You are welcome, of course, amatan."

. . .

HAL KNEW something was on everyone's mind the day he was supposed to be released from the hospital. Ty was in and out of the room, and Veevs was too quiet as she helped him get dressed. Now, he was sitting on the hospital bed, waiting to go, Vivi beside him.

Did this have something to do with the conversation he'd had with Patrin yesterday? Ty had let Patrin know that Hal needed to see him. He and Ty had given Kat's message to Patrin, and the vat's emotional reaction had been difficult to see. Ty had seemed sure it would give Patrin some closure. Hal hoped he was right.

When he looked up, he saw Max had come in.

"So, what's the word? Is everything go for me to leave?" Hal asked.

"It is," Max said, glancing to Ty. "Is this a good time?"

Ty nodded.

"What's up?" Hal said. "What's wrong? Just come out with it."

"It's no secret," Ty said. "I wanted Max to be here for this conversation, Hal. I told him about everything that happened to you on the *Vetra*. And there's some things we might need to be concerned about."

Max came over and pulled up the stool that the doctors used when they came in to check on him. "I know you met Kat Neval, and she helped you escape the *Vetra*. You know what she did to Seren. And we missed it. She had obviously been programmed to slip in, gain our trust and then murder some of the upper leadership. She only succeeded in killing Seren, however, before she went on the run.

"Maybe she didn't even know what she was here to do. She fit in seamlessly with us and ran operations with the *Raptor's* crew. They didn't suspect anything. When she came to us, we tried to question her, but she couldn't tolerate the truth drugs.

Based on her behavior and some voiceprint questioning, she was allowed to stay."

Max went on. "Can you describe the programming sessions *you* underwent on the *Vetra*?"

Hal shook his head. "It's all a jumble. I mean I know I went. Two times, maybe?" He glanced at Ty. "You're thinking I was programmed like her and sent back."

"It's a possibility, however slim," Ty said.

"They're developing new programming methods all the time," Max interjected. "During my last year at the facility, they were trying new techniques, changing what they normally do with vats. We think some sort of new programming is how they are going to be able to try and keep vats in service more than 7 years. Maybe they used this with Kat.

"But there is a way we can check for any malicious programming. After Kat...did what she did, I've been working on teaching several other doctors questioning techniques so that we can be sure of the vats who come to us. What I would do is give you certain truth drugs and question you to see what programming is there and if you have any hidden objectives... but only if you agree to it."

Hal didn't reply immediately, so Ty jumped in. "It's unlikely they were able to implant suggestions like that in two or three programming sessions anyway, Max says, but we've spoken with the General and after what happened with Seren...she's got to be sure. But if you're not ready..."

Hal shook his head. "No, I can do it."

"Are you sure?" Vivi asked.

"Yeah, I gotta know. When can we do it, Max?"

Max thought a few moments. "How about tomorrow? But if you wake up then and you don't feel up to it, you can just let me know and we can delay a few days. You need to take it easy on yourself for at least three more weeks while your body repairs the damage that was done and you regain some strength."

"I want to do it tomorrow," Hal said.

Max glanced to Ty, who nodded. "When I come, I'll bring what I need to the *Loshad's* medbay. I know you'll be more comfortable there."

"I'll be ready," Hal said.

FORTY-FOUR

MAX AND TERRA MALAR CAME THE NEXT AFTERNOON. The *Loshad's* ship assistant opened the ramp for them. Malar had asked one of her guards to wait outside and the other trailed behind them silently as they entered. "Welcome back, Dr. Parsen and General Malar," Runa said. "You will find the crew in the medbay. Exit the cargo bay, turn right, then make a left at the end of the hallway."

"Thank you," Max said, glancing at the General.

"Lead the way," she gestured.

The medbay hatch was open and Hal was sitting on the bed. Beryl had pulled out a pack of medsensors that Max had said they'd need. "You're sure you're up for this? We can wait a couple of days if you need to," Max said, noticing the dark circles under his eyes.

"No. I'm ready," Hal insisted.

"General," Ty stepped forward, hand out.

"Bernon," she nodded, taking his hand.

"Thanks for having me patched up again," Hal said.

"Of course. We are so glad you've come back safe. What we

have to do today is regrettable after what you've been through, Cullen. If there was any other way..." she said.

"It's fine. I've been through worse," Hal remarked. "What really matters to me now is knowing the people around me are safe."

"Hal..." Vivi began.

He shook his head. "I'm okay with it, Veevs. I trust Max."

"I'll take the greatest care," Max said, placing the medpouch he'd brought with him on the counter by the bed. Inside were the combination of medications to slip Hal into a mental state where they would be able to access his programming. "I learned to do this during my residency at Chamn-Alpha before I specialized in genetics. Let me explain everything I'm going to do." Max said, taking the medsensors and applying them to Hal's inner elbow, collarbone and neck. "I'm going to give you something called Bupariol to get you very relaxed. It's like drowse, but you won't fall asleep. Then there's Xendicam. It's one of the stronger truth drugs that will help us access your programming levels. I'll ask you some questions about what happened on Haleia-6, give you some keywords to check that your programming is intact and then you'll sleep a while." He turned to Ty, Vivi and Malar. "I'm so sorry, but I'll need the medbay as distraction free as possible." It was a small medbay and they all barely fit in it as it was.

"C'mon, Vivi. Beryl can let us know if there's any trouble," Ty said. "Would you like to join us, General Malar?"

"Of course."

Malar, her escort and Ty exited the medbay and stood waiting in the hall.

Vivi hung back. "Are you sure you're good with all this?"

He gave her a tired smile. "Yeah, it'll be fine. Sleeping for a while sounds nice. Go with Ty." He pulled her close for a hug, then she left and the medbay door slid closed.

"Thanks for doing this, Max," Hal said, glancing nervously at the medjets needed for the procedure.

Beryl noticed the change in his demeanor and put her hand on Hal's shoulder.

"I'll be right here," she promised. "Runa, lower the lights fifty percent."

"Are you comfortable with the procedure I described?" Max asked.

"Yeah."

"Good. Lie back, Hal, and we'll start when you're ready."

"I'm ready now." Hal said, getting settled. "Let's get this done."

It was an hour and a half later before Max and Beryl joined them in the common area. Ty had broken out a bottle of Celian whiskey to ease the waiting and Vivi looked up from the amber liquid in her plasglass cup to see Max coming over. "Got an extra one of those?" Max asked tiredly.

"Make it two," Beryl said.

"You bet." Ty poured the two of them a generous measure and pushed the extra cups their way.

Beryl took a drink and then settled into a seat across the table from Vivi. "He's sleeping right now. He'll probably need to nap on and off for the rest of the day," she said.

"What did you find out, Dr. Parsen?" Malar asked.

"Hal wasn't programmed enough times for anything to stick. Under questioning, he told me that he had been through only two programming sessions when Kat Neval freed him. When I checked his programming using keywords, there's nothing new there. His original objectives and routines are still intact."

Vivi bowed her head and said a prayer. "Thank gods."

"They were focused on Hal's implant. They seemed to think Al-Kimia modified him so that he didn't rush."

Ty glanced at Malar, but she didn't seem surprised, so he guessed that someone had probably filled her in on Eira's modifications to Hal.

Max drained his glass. "But two things make me pretty certain that Kat Neval wasn't just playing a role of letting Hal go."

Ty leaned forward. "What do you mean?"

"First, she shot Fleet Admiral Quillon's personal tecker right in front of Hal. This was the man who programmed her since she was a rook. Secondly...she gave Hal the means to escape in the confusion by blowing up the bridge of the *Vetra*."

"She...what?" Malar asked.

"Apparently, when Hal exited the *Vetra* in the transport, she blew up the bridge. Hal couldn't raise her on comms after that. He's convinced she died."

"He saw the bridge explode?" Ty asked, refilling Max's glass. "There's been no news about an accident or explosion on an ACAS ship."

"He said he saw it. He would've died on that ship, if not for Kat," Max said. "Seems like she tried to make up for what she'd done to Seren. The way he described her, she seemed tortured...almost falling apart. It was becoming harder and harder for her to behave normally. I think we can be very sure that Hal has not been programmed like Kat."

"How awful for her," Vivi whispered, sitting back with her arms around herself.

"Yeah. It seems she did kill Seren at Quillon's order."

"Then she is not to blame," Malar said thoughtfully. "I must return to command, Bernon. You do not know how relieved I am at this outcome. I will pray that his recovery is soon and complete."

"You and me both, General," Ty said. "I can show you out."

"No need," she said. "I can find my way. I will call to check on you in a few days. Take this time to rest and rally around Cullen."

"Thank you, General."

HAL WOKE SITTING on the floor of his quarters on the *Loshad* while the nightmare did its best to convince him that he was back on the *Vetra*. It had all returned in the dream: the endless questions, the searing impact of the fleet admiral's lashes against his back and the heavy scent of sweat and blood in the air. He sat there for long moments, his emotions heaving and the vat's creed thundering in his head. His stomach lurched and he got to his feet, went to the head and threw up.

When he'd pulled himself together enough to enter the bedroom again, he saw with relief that he hadn't disturbed Vivi. He could just see her form in the watery lights of the *Loshad's* night cycle, stretched on her side with one arm under her pillow and the other one tucked into her chest. A glance at the chrono told him it was late, 0230.

He knew he wouldn't be back to sleep for some time, and he was reluctant to wake her up by tossing and turning, which would surely happen if he laid back down. Burdening her or Ty with his churning thoughts didn't seem like the right option either. He'd not been more specific about what happened to him since that night in the medcenter with Ty and he didn't intend to be. Some things were best forgotten. Leaving his quarters, he made for the galley. He grabbed the whiskey and didn't bother with a glass, and after a long, steady drink, he headed to the bridge.

The *Loshad's* lights were low, which suited Hal fine. He sank down at his station and ran newsfeeds through his display.

It was more for a background murmur than anything else; the ship was too quiet and lonely at night. Eira was with Max, working on a redistribution of medical supplies needed for vat members of the Al-Kimian Defense Force.

"Hal. You are typically asleep at this time. Is there something wrong?"

"I'm fine, Runa," he lied. "Just need some time to think, and I didn't want to wake anyone."

"Very well. Please let me know if you would like to talk."

Hal nodded, turning the bottle up and taking another long drink as he sat back and tried not to think about the *Vetra*, but that was impossible. It was like walking through it with Max had brought back every excruciating detail.

He knew he should wake up Ty or Veevs, but there was nothing they could really do. He'd feel guilty for bothering them and they'd obviously been through enough. Thinking he was dead, coming to grips with that and then having him come back had taken its toll on them. From what he'd been told, Vivi had been injured in the escape and had had a difficult time, yet they'd stayed by his side every moment so far. He knew they would continue to do so, but they wouldn't understand. The programming, the sensation of being erased, the fear that he would betray them...the fucking helplessness of it all were things impossible to communicate to them. Somehow, he knew he'd have to come to grips with it on his own.

What he wanted was payback. How many vats had Quillon destroyed in his time as an ACAS officer? Hal knew the man had been determined to break him or kill him trying. And what he'd done to Hal had been nothing compared to what he did to Kat Neval. He'd clearly driven her mad. Hal wondered what he would have been like without Ty's leadership in the ACAS. If he'd been under one like Quillon...he'd probably have been dead long ago.

If they'd had a day or two more to work on him, Hal was sure that was exactly where he'd be... or he'd be a mole, like Kat had been. The thought made him sick again, and he took another drink to push that back. He was getting drunk, a bit drunker than he'd been in a while. For good measure, he chugged another mouthful. It would make thinking about this shit easier, he hoped. He could still see Quillon's cold dark stare in his mind. "I hope you killed the motherfucker," he whispered to Kat in the dark.

Glancing at the feedscreen, he saw hovertanks and vat troops. Still holding the bottle, he sat up and called to Runa.

"Runa, turn up the volume 30%."

She did and he listened as the sound of a feedcaster came on. "...on Betald, where anti-Coalition sentiment is being curtailed. This vid feed is live from Betald's capitol. Resistance to the Coalition has been rising after the signing of the accord, and with Betald's help, the ACAS has deployed enough troops to suppress the last of the terrorists threatening daily life on Betald. Free vats who had settled on the planet are being evacuated to Omicron for their own safety."

There was vid of MH-12 Hammerstrike hovertanks patrolling the streets and ACAS vat units fighting with insurgents.

"And once again, here's the footage from earlier today when President Terzin has signed legislation to join Betald to the Coalition of Allied Systems in hopes of quelling the uprising on his planet. This is a historic event, and we can only hope that other Edge planets decide to follow suit for the good of all."

Hal watched as President Terzin, surrounded by ACAS officers, signed his name to the legislation. The man did not make a speech, but simply stood there uncomfortably as other members of his government clapped politely. They had obviously been forced to capitulate to the pressure of the Coalition.

"Noea and Al-Kimia will be next," Hal murmured ominously.

"It is the prediction on 91% of the newsfeeds," Runa replied.

The feed went on, showing vats being shuffled off an ACAS transport onto a crowded Omicron station. If the Opposition failed, would they round him up one day like that?

"Runa, turn the feed off," Hal said, sick at heart. He could see it all in his mind, as if it were playing out on the darkened screen in front of him. It was like a squads game but on a galaxy-wide scale. Betald, Noea, then Al-Kimia. The ACAS expected to weaken Al-Kimia's allies, then go for the heart of the movement. Once it was done, no other Edge planets would dare think of coming to Al-Kimia's rescue.

If they had any hope at all, it would be in rallying the Edge. He had to do something. The last time he'd asked General Malar and Seren about it, they'd put him off. *But now...fuck waiting*, he thought.

"Runa, can you bring up the *Harbinger* vid that Vivi and I were working on?"

"Certainly, Hal."

She showed it on his screen, and he watched it, sitting back in the chair.

Vivi had shot the vid in the cargo bay, with the lights lowered so that details of the *Loshad* couldn't be discerned and his face was partially shadowed. "I have a message for the inhabitants of the Edge. Information you need to see has fallen into my hands about how the ACAS treats its vat soldiers. This footage may not be pleasant to watch, but you need to know the truth."

The feed from their exploration of the *Harbinger* was

shown, without sound. The hatch to the barracks slid open, revealing the bodies of the vat soldiers. It was easy to see the faces of the dead vats as Vivi had slowed down Hal's helmet feed. There was a voice over to explain. "This is the *Harbinger*, an ACAS ship lost during the Mudar War. It was found by some salvagers, who discovered the escape pods jettisoned. All the nats had abandoned ship, but the vats were left aboard, to die in their sleeping harnesses."

Hal confirmed again that the feed did not identify either Hal or Vivi as the "salvagers" who had discovered the ship.

"The salvagers of this ship found even more. Here is Natalie Johnson, the XO of the *Harbinger*." The vid showed a picture of her smiling face, one of the pictures from her handheld. "This feed was found on her personal device. It was recorded a hundred years ago." Here, the vid switched to Natalie Johnson speaking: "The *Harbinger* sighted and pursued a lone Mudar ship. Captain Sterat decided to attack, but the ship fought back. Then our weapons and engines went inexplicably offline, which allowed the enemy ship to escape. Sterat sent the vats to programming and told us to prepare for evac. They're planning on leaving the vats here," her face showed how distraught she was. "I would like to state for the record that I am opposed to this action. The vats are ACAS soldiers. They cannot be left behind like...equipment." She stood up, reaching for something beyond the scope of the camera, then they could see her seating a blaster at her hip. "I am going to try to convince the captain to change his mind. May the gods help him see reason." She reached out and the feed paused, then morphed into Natalie Johnson's frozen corpse with the blaster hole in her head.

Hal's voice was ominous. "She was not successful."

The feed came back to Hal's shadowed face. "The ACAS believes vats are something to be discarded when no longer needed. How do you think they'll treat the inhabitants of the Edge planets? Do you think you will be valued more than the ACAS's loyal vats? The same vats they're rounding up and holding without due process on Omicron, for shadowy reasons that remain undisclosed?

"I'm asking all Edgers, nats and vats, to offer help however you can to keep the Coalition from extending their stranglehold. It's time for us to rally and fight back against them in whatever way we can before it's too late, or the fate of these vats will be the fate of all."

The screen went black. Hal remained staring at it for some time as he finished off the bottle, then set it next to his chair. "Runa?"

"Yes Hal."

"Veevs stripped out all the identifying information from this vid right? What did she...call it? The meta...something."

"Metadata? Yes, Hal. The last time she worked on this, she said it was ready to distribute. There were three different feed sites she had been researching to use."

Hal sat back for a moment, thinking. Then he said, "Send it out to all three."

"Would you like me to further cloak the origin of the transmission?" Runa asked. "There is a program called 'circuitous' that Vivi used with the Echo communications to make them more secure."

"Yeah," Hal agreed. "Do everything you can, then send it out."

"Very well. The vid is posted," Runa said. "There is no way it can be traced back here."

Part relief and part satisfaction washed over him. He couldn't get his hands on Quillon, but this was the next best thing. Striking back made him feel like less of a victim.

"Thanks, Runa," he grabbed the empty bottle and got to his feet. "I think I'm gonna head back to bed."

He wavered a little getting to the hatch, then made his way to the galley. Leaving the bottle on the counter, he continued down the hall, keeping his hand on the wall for balance. He had to key the hatch to his room twice to open it, then he entered and tried his best to lay down without waking Vivi.

Before long, he was asleep.

Ty HAD SET the coffee machine to brew when he received a comm from General Malar. "Bernon here," he said, answering.

"There's a situation. Are you and your crew available to meet with me in let's say 30 minutes?" Malar said.

"Of course," Ty replied. "What's happening?"

"Let's talk about that in person. Please bring Cullen with you."

Ty was mystified. "I will."

She terminated the connection without another word. Ty stared at the comm a moment, wondering what it could be. Did she need them for some kind of mission? Hal wasn't ready for that yet, and he intended on telling her so, but first he had to find out what all this was about.

"Runa, please wake Beryl, Hal and Vivi and ask them to meet me in the galley ASAP."

In a few moments, Vivi and Hal joined him. They had obviously got dressed in a hurry and Hal was a bit bleary. "Cap, what's up?"

"I'm not quite sure. Malar asked that we meet her in her quarters on the double, so grab a ration bar and let's go," Ty said, as Beryl joined them.

. . .

Patrin, Eli and Beall, the latter dressed in Al-Kimian fatigues, were waiting when the *Loshad's* crew arrived. "What's the deal?" Ty asked Beall in a low voice.

"I take it you haven't seen the feeds this morning, then?" Beall asked, an eyebrow raised.

"No," Ty said, reaching for his handheld. Just then, Malar's aide returned. "The general is ready to see you now."

"Cullen. I gotta give you credit. That took some balls," Eli said, looking at Hal and shaking his head.

With a raised eyebrow at Hal, Ty followed Beall and Eli into the room. Malar was standing at her desk, hands clasped behind her back. "Please have a seat," she told them. She waited until everyone was settled before she began.

"Well, there have been some overnight developments," she said, pointedly looking in Hal's direction.

Hal wasn't backing down from Malar's stare.

"General, we haven't seen the feeds this morning. We came directly here. If you could explain..." Ty began.

"So, you were not aware of the vid posted last night, right after the Coalition officially conquered Betald?" she replied, her irritation barely held in check. "Have a look."

She set up her handheld to display a holo and they watched as the *Harbinger* footage played with Hal's narration. "What did you do?" Ty asked, shooting a look to Hal, who said nothing. Other than that, the room was silent until it finished playing.

"I thought we had decided to hold this revelation in reserve," Malar said, once the vid was over.

"I saw what happened to Betald. You're making a mistake by waiting to rally the Edge. It's past time," Hal said.

"I'm not sure you're in the best position to determine that," Malar replied.

Hal stood up abruptly. "With all due respect, General, I've

been a soldier all my life, but I'm not your solider. What happened on that ship happened to vats, and that's not your story to tell. It's time for the Coalition to know that we're gonna fight back, before you lose the war for good. If you can't see that, then you're not the leader you claim to be." With that, Hal turned and left the room.

Beall cracked a smile as he glanced to Ty. "Straight up balls out move." He sobered at the stern expression on Malar's face. "Sorry ma'am."

Ty returned his attention to Malar. "While I wish Hal would have told us first, he's correct. It is his story to tell," he said.

The general sighed. "Very well. There's nothing we can do about it now. The loss of Betald is a blow, and I probably would have given the go ahead to release the vid, but I like to be given the choice myself or at least be informed beforehand," she said with a tight smile. "Either way, we're in the shit now, like it or not. Eli, I need you and Echo to make sure that vid gets maximum play on the feeds. Now that it's out, I want everyone to see it, in and out of the Spiral."

"Yes, ma'am, we've got this." The hacker was on a strong dose of amp, Ty saw. Eli was probably working round the clock coordinating Echo's operations with the Al-Kimians.

"Heard anything from the Anklav?" Ty asked Patrin.

He sighed heavily and shook his head, frustration evident. "There is dissention among them. As you know, I spoke to them, trying to rally them, but they must discuss at a conclave. We're still awaiting their answer."

"Damn," Ty said. "Their answer may come too late."

"It may be that Cullen picked the perfect time to release his message," Malar said grimly. "Beall, we've been asked to reinforce Noea. Will you help lead one of our fleets?"

"Of course," Beall said.

She turned her gaze to Eli. "Do you have assets on Noea?"

"I have assets everywhere," Eli said.

"Can you have them do whatever possible to disrupt an eminent ACAS invasion?"

Eli grinned over at Beall. "It's time for Radiant-Zenith," he said.

"What's that?" Ty asked.

"Contingency plan," Beall said. "Eli's idea in case the Coalition ever caught some of us. Every operative we have will begin fucking up Coalition/ACAS operations as soon as the kid gives the word."

Malar's eyes flashed. "Good."

Ty was reassured watching Malar begin to coordinate. A capable leader, she was secure enough to allow Eli to operate independently, and she obviously trusted Beall a great deal to let the seasoned officer to go assist Noea. If they could help hold Noea, it would go far toward helping Al-Kimia stay independent, but it was a long shot.

She returned her gaze to Ty. "We're going to need every ship out there, doing what they can. I'm sending the military fleet to Noea, but I'll need our civilian friends' ships patrolling and defending our space."

"I need to talk to my crew, but we'll do everything we can, General," Ty said.

"Beall and Patrin please stay behind. We must call a staff meeting."

Ty got up along with Vivi and Beryl and made their way toward the door.

When they were in the hallway outside Malar's office, Ty heaved a sigh of relief. "Well, that could've gone much worse," he muttered, looking around for Hal.

"I didn't know he put that out there. We worked on it

during the trip back from the Mudar, but he hasn't mentioned it since," Vivi said.

"I know. Something's going on with him," he said as they headed back through the crowded hallways in the direction of the main hangar. "Let me try to talk to him alone. Think you can give us a little time?"

"Of course. I'll take the long way back. I've been wanting to try your spicy pe-chai recipe, so I'll pick up the ingredients before I head back to the *Loshad*."

HAL WAS SITTING on the cargo bay bench, disassembling one of the ship's Gpods. It was better than what he wanted to do, which was to go out, get drunk and find a fight. Laying into an opponent in the ring sounded like the thing to ease the anger that had boiled up and over in the meeting with General Malar, however, he'd been told by Ty and Veevs if they found him fighting or pounding a bag before he was healed up, he would regret it, so training was out too.

Telling off Malar had been a mistake, and he knew it, but he couldn't find it in himself to apologize for putting the *Harbinger* vid out there. Plus, being in Malar's office, with her and Beall in uniform...the whole scene was too much like a dressing down in the ACAS, which had brought back Quillon's questioning and a whole host of other bad memories. Now, he was irritable and unable to stay still.

He glanced up briefly when he sensed Ty and Beryl coming up the ramp, then turned his attention back to his work.

"I'll be inside, inventorying the galley," Beryl said.

"So, is she cutting us loose?" Hal asked, carefully not meeting Ty's eyes. He didn't want to see the disappointment that was likely to be there.

"No. She wasn't happy, though."

"Yeah, well, there's a lot of godsdamned unhappy people in the world. She should get used to it." As soon as he said the words, Hal wished he could take them back. He wasn't mad at Ty and he didn't want Ty to think that. He struggled to figure out what to say to walk back his anger as he pulled more parts off the Gpod and tossed them on a nearby tarp he'd set up to keep the work area clean.

Ty was fixing him with that look that Hal found hard to ignore. It was the look that said, *Hey, I care about you, so stop being a fucking idiot.*

"I don't think it's General Malar you're angry at, is it?"

Hal let out a sigh, then dropped his head, looking at the wrench in his hands. "No." There was a long pause before he went on. "Last night, I...I woke up and didn't know where I was," he said. "I was back there in my head, and it made me feel helpless." It all flooded back at his words. The programming drugs, the questioning, the overwhelming fog of confusion and loss. "I think they were trying to erase *me* so that there was only the ACAS left. That feeling...that fear keeps coming back."

"Gods, Hal," Ty said.

"Once my head cleared, I went to the bridge to sit a while by myself," he glanced up as Ty sat beside him. "Sorry, but I finished off your bottle."

"That's understandable," Ty said.

Hal nodded, twisting the wrench between his hands. "The feeds were on, I saw what was happening on Betald, and I had to do something to show that I didn't go down, you know?"

"You were thinking about Quillon."

"Yeah. I think wanted to prove to myself he didn't break me," Hal said, anxiety twisting in the pit of his stomach as he checked Ty's face. There was no hint of anger or frustration there, however. Nor did Ty look disappointed in him. He was proud; Hal realized with surprise.

"We'll, it's obvious he didn't win," Ty said softly, providing reassurance with his calm presence.

"That's all you're going to say? You're not pissed at me?"

"No," Ty said. "I backed you up with Malar, too. She doesn't quite understand everything. I think, though, that we need to keep them in the loop if we make any further statements like that, if it's not too much trouble to ask."

"Sure Ty."

"She's sending the Al-Kimian Defense Force fleet to Noea to reinforce them," Ty began. "We've been asked to stay as part of the civilian force protecting Al-Kimia. It's likely...we could see some action. Are you ready for that?"

"Fuck yeah. I think I'll feel better if I...if I can do something."

"Good." Ty waited long moments, then said in a lower voice. "Look, I know you're struggling a bit. Don't be afraid to tell us what you need. I don't even begin to know what you went through, Hal, but I want you to know that Beryl, Vivi and I ...we're here for you."

Hal blinked the sting out of his eyes as he ran a hand over his cropped hair. "Cap...things aren't right with me yet but having you and Veevs and Beryl near goes a long way toward making it right. I just...I didn't know what good waking you up last night would've done."

"Doesn't matter...wake us up, come get us, whatever. You don't have to explain or say anything. We can just sit there with you so you're not alone. Gods, Hal. Don't try to carry this on your own when we're right here for you."

Hal agreed wordlessly. Like usual, Ty made everything simpler.

"Good. Want some help with this thing?" Ty tapped the Gpod in front of them with one foot.

Hal grinned. "Sure." Then he glanced around. "But hey, where's Veevs?"

"She had a few stops to make at some of the stores on base," Ty said. "I think she intends on making you some Spicy Pe Chai for lunch – the real kind this time, not some ration pack crap. So, let's get this finished before she gets back here."

A DAY AND A HALF LATER, Hal stood in the doorway of his room. Vivi was still asleep. He'd been up for a while. Since being released from the hospital, he'd only hit the rack for a few hours before waking from uneasy dreams. He'd found Ty already up in the galley, watching the feeds as tensions around Noea topped the news. He hadn't had to explain anything; just sitting near Ty's steady presence made everything feel more normal.

Now, a few hours later, he sat down on the bed beside Vivi and placed a hand on her arm.

"Veevs, wake up," he said.

She sat up, eyes wide, pushing her mussed curls away from her face. "I'm awake." She blinked in the dimmed lighting. "Everything alright?"

"Yeah. Beall commed. He's pulling out for Noea with the 3rd in a few minutes. I thought you might want to say goodbye to him with us." It wasn't until after Vivi had described the trip back home from Haleia-6 that Hal had realized how much Beall had done to hold her together. He knew she would want to say goodbye, and Hal realized that he wouldn't mind a second chance to thank Beall either.

"Yes, of course. Let me get dressed," she said.

In about ten minutes, Vivi met him in the common area, wearing a brown pair of cargo pants and a green cropped shirt.

"I don't want to miss him." She told Hal, smoothing down her unruly blond curls.

"Nice case of bed head, Veevs," Hal teased, reaching out to muss her curls further.

"Shut up, you!" She swiped at him gently, mindful of his still healing wounds. Then she caught his hand as he moved away, and he turned back to her.

They locked gazes a moment, then Hal spoke. "Thanks for everything you've done…since I got back."

"Always," she said, wrapping her fingers around his hand more tightly and pulling him toward her. His arm went reflexively around her, and she laid her head on his chest.

They stood there, holding each other until he spoke. "I love you Vivi."

"Love you too," she replied. After a quiet moment, she went on. "Let's go find Beall before he's gone."

Coming down the *Loshad's* ramp, they saw the hurried activity as the transports were being loaded with the last of soldiers and supplies. The small ships would rendezvous with the larger cruisers, already in orbit, then head for Noea.

They found Ty, Beryl, Eli and Beall near the hangar doors. Vivi smiled as Beall turned to meet them.

"There was a time when I never thought I'd see that smile again," Beall said. "It looks good on you, kid," he glanced to Hal, and saw the corresponding happiness there. "On both of you."

Beall held out a hand as if to shake Vivi's hand, but she hugged him instead. "Thank you," she whispered. "For everything."

He returned the hug. "I'm just glad Hal found his way back." Vivi stepped away, and Beall glanced to Hal. "I wanted to tell you the other day that it was damned good to see you up and around." He extended a hand, and Hal shook it.

"Thanks for what you did to get everyone off of Haleia-6," Hal grinned. "I owe you one."

"Not worried about it. I'll cash it in later," Beall replied, clapping him on the back and turning to Eli. "Did you get in touch with all the cells?"

"Yeah. Radiant-Zenith is in play. We're good. You go do what you gotta do."

A soldier came from the nearest transport and approached Beall. "Sir. General Lowell wants you to know we're ready to lift off."

"I'm on my way," Beall said, smoothing his uniform coat. "Well, never thought I'd be doing this again," he said.

"Take care of yourself, Beall," Ty called.

The old man said a last goodbye to everyone and turned to Eli. He clapped a hand on the hacker's shoulder, and they said a few words that were hard to hear with the transports' thrusters powering up for take-off. Then, he turned with his soldier escort and crossed the landing pad to his ship.

Ty, Beryl, Vivi and Hal stood and watched the transports lifting into the still-dark sky. Eli stood a little apart, face turned up in the early morning air. The rain that had fallen all night had paused, and they were able to hear a cool breeze rustling the nearby trees as the transports began to disappear.

"This is it," Hal said, wrapping an arm around Vivi.

"Yeah," Ty replied, as another flash of heat lightning strobed the clouds in golden light.

"Gods watch over them," Vivi whispered as the last transport was swallowed by the uneasy clouds above.

FORTY-FIVE

"Flight, this is the Loshad. We're going to take a wider sweep of the area this time, then head back to base to repair some damage," Ty said.

"Understood on damage but hold position, Loshad and stand by for new orders." The controller's voice was fraught with tension.

Ty watched the blips on the screen denoting the various ships of the Al-Kimian Defense Force's civilian arm. There were a few fleet units closer to Al-Kimia, but the burden of patrolling their space was left up to their friends, as Seren had called them. Terra Malar had continued Seren's tradition of referring to the loose network of civilians as "friends," and they needed all the friends they could get.

And thanks to Hal's vid, they had a few more. He had indeed rallied some on the Edge with his words, which had reached to Jaleeth Station and beyond. The Coalition had offered a sizable reward for information leading to the maker's whereabouts. The vid had had some other effects as well. According to Jaleeth's manager, they were not going to allow the

ACAS to berth or refuel there. For the most part, the Coalition had done some posturing in reply but had largely ignored the station so far. Hal and Ty both thought that they were planning on mopping up there once the battle for the Edge was decided. A few cargo haulers and other ships from Jaleeth had shown up yesterday, running the blockade to offer their assistance to bolster the Al-Kimians' thin reserve forces. Most bore modified weapons and added point defense systems like the *Loshad*.

Meanwhile, the battle for Noea was unfolding. 6 hours ago, The *Loshad* had been informed that an ACAS fleet had appeared in the Noea sector. Since then, they had heard little else. The *Loshad* had been distracted by a skirmish with an ACAS scout ship and had sustained some damage. Eira shored up the hull's superstructure with the nanite skin that lay under the *Loshad's* hull.

"Any word yet?" Hal raised an eyebrow. "Something's had to have happened by now with our fleet and the ACAS in the same system. Gods, I wish I were there."

Eira, who was sitting at the ship's systems station, turned to them, "I have been monitoring the Al-Kimian fleet net. I am getting incomplete data, but it seems a large fleet action is occurring."

Ty and Hal shared a look. They did not need to ask how Eira was monitoring a supposedly classified and scrambled tactical battle net, but they were shocked as Eira piped in the unscrambled feed.

Most of the Al-Kimian ships had apparently been in orbit when the ACAS appeared in the Noea system. The Al-Kimians had been unloading troops and supplies to bolster Noea's defenses. Ty and the *Loshad's* crew could hear the desperation in the snippets of comms traffic.

"Multiple ACAS vessels inbound...now reading two heavy

cruisers and a carrier as well as a force of destroyers," a voice reported.

"Move to intercept. We must protect the transports." Another voice came across the net.

Over the next two hours Ty and the crew of the *Loshad* listened hopelessly as the battle raged – a battle that they were powerless to prevent.

"It must be pure carnage," Ty said as the Al-Kimian ships progressively reported damage on a devastating scale. Eventually, one by one, ships stopped reporting altogether.

Ty, Hal and the rest of the crew stood silently as they listened to one final call across the void, "This is Captain Frazier of the destroyer *Pride*. The *Eclipse, Reckless*, and *Quantum* are gone. The *Retaliation* and *Fury* are wrecked and drifting. I am forced to withdraw with *Tempest* and the remaining transports. We took out three of the ACAS destroyers and the *Eclipse* damaged one of their heavy cruisers, but the enemy's carrier, second heavy cruiser and several smaller ships are still undamaged. They will be taking up orbit around Noea in a matter of hours and could be in Al-Kimian space soon after that..."

"What are our chances now?" Vivi whispered.

"Bad," Hal replied.

"With those losses the Al-Kimian fleet is effectively neutralized except for the few ships they held in reserve," Ty said.

"It doesn't matter," Vivi said. "We're in this until it's done, right?" She linked hands with Hal.

Ty nodded. It was clear to all of them what was at stake after what had happened to Seren and to Hal. He was still struggling not only physically with his healing wounds, but also wounds that couldn't be seen with the eye. Glancing to Beryl and Eira, he saw the same determination there to see this through. "Until it's done," he said.

The comm beeped. "Flight to *Loshad*."

"Go," Ty said as he stepped back to his station.

"Things on Noea haven't gone to plan. The fleet is falling back to Al-Kimia. Report to surface for repairs, then we're going to need you back up there." Command was obviously not aware that the *Loshad's* crew already knew the full extent of the disaster.

"My nanites will hold," Eira said.

"Probably better than the original hull," Hal added.

Ty keyed the comm, "Flight, our damage is not as bad as we initially thought. We'll hold the line."

"Very well, *Loshad*. Good hunting."

"Thanks, Flight." Ty regarded his crew. They were exhausted and Hal was beyond tired. "Get some rest. I'll stay on duty until..."

"Ty, all biologics should rest. I will handle things until everyone is needed on the bridge again," Eira said. "At the first sign of anything, I will call you."

"Eira – I-"

"Ty, I have studied every hostile interaction this ship has had. I can respond more quickly than you can." She held out both her hands. "Allow me to help, amatan."

He agreed and everyone followed Beryl out.

THE DOYEN WAS STILL INCENSED that an apparent fifth column had killed his leading tactician, damaged the fleet's flagship in such a way that it would be months before it was operational and had released that godsdamned vid feed. How did this happen? How did these Al-Kimians continue to be a thorn in his side? His response had been immediate and decisive. He had stripped Rinal Station and several sectors of troops and ships to build a force that would destroy the Noeans, Al-Kimians, and whoever else dared to defy the Coalition. This was a personal affront to him, and he therefore bypassed the usual chain of command. A nat officer came on the comms screen.

"*Warrior* here. Lieutenant Stiles," the man said not looking at the screen. There was hurried activity behind him.

"Get me Admiral Ozvio now!" the doyen yelled.

Startled at the sight of the doyen's red face, he stammered, "Ay...Aye... Sir. At once."

Moments later a sixty-year-old, grey-haired officer appeared on screen: Admiral Felix Ozvio, who until recently had been Quillon's second in command.

"I want to know what's happening on Noea and when you plan to move on Al-Kimia."

Ozvio's response was measured and betrayed no anxiety, "Sir, we have destroyed most of the Al-Kimian fleet and have taken up positions around Noea while preparing our ground assault on Noea's major cities. Our goal is to smother the resistance, which we feel is strong and stiffened by Al-Kimian reinforcements. My plan..."

"I don't want to hear a strategy lesson Admiral; I want you to finish Al-Kimia for good. Strike now, Godsdamn it! If not, I will find someone who will."

Before Ozvio could speak again, the doyen terminated the conversation.

SMUG BASTARD, Ozvio thought. The man had no idea what was really happening out here. Even before the *Vetra* incident the fleet was already responding to riots and insurgencies across the galaxy. Now with the recent vid fiasco there would be more revolts, not to mention that they still had to deal with the ground forces on Noea. The fleet victory had been half the battle, now he was being forced to surge ahead without careful planning to meet the doyen's demand. Damn, why did he not retire when he had the chance? He knew how thinly stretched the ACAS was. For years they had been fighting Anklav pirates who got out of line, protecting merchant shipping and putting down insurgencies across the Edge. He feared that the doyen's reach was now exceeding his grasp. No matter, he was too good a professional to let defeatism creep into his psyche, so he put those thoughts out of his mind, and he called up his force chart. He knew he had inflicted great losses on the Al-Kimians and a quick strike might be the dagger that delivered the coup-de-grace.

He turned to his comms officer, "Lieutenant Stiles, order the fleet to mobilize. I know the *Talent* was damaged in the fight, but reports are it is not enough to count her out. We will leave the *Berserker* here to support the ground forces and protect our troop ships. Inform the fleet we leave for Al-Kimia in 10 hours."

"AMATAN. The remnants of the Al-Kimian fleet arrived in the system shortly after you went to rest. There are two warships which are identified as destroyers, and several transport vessels. Reports coming over the feed say that they are certain ACAS scout ships will not be far behind."

Eira's voice over the feed woke Hal from his uneasy sleep. He sat up in his bunk, struggling to calm his thudding heart.

The same disorienting adrenaline he'd experienced right after they'd come back from the *Harbinger* was coursing through his veins. They were about to engage in battle in the coming hours, something he had done a hundred times before, but this time he had everything and everyone to lose. He turned and saw Vivi watching him with concern.

"I'm good," he said, as he jammed his feet into his boots, trying to keep his anxiety under control.

"Hal." There was a tone to her voice that made him turn to face her. "You don't have to hold it together for me," she reminded him. "It's okay." Her eyes were intently studying his face as she leaned forward, put a hand on his cheek and kissed him.

It had a steadying effect. "This battle doesn't scare you, does it?" he realized.

She shook her head, turning back to her own boots. "I'm not scared of anything anymore. Not as long as you're here, by my side." When she was ready, she stood and turned toward him. "This...this battle means something. What we're doing means something for vats and Edgers. After everything we've been through together, this is the only place I'd want to be."

Hal searched her eyes and saw that she meant what she said, and it made him love her even more, if that was possible. They embraced for a long moment, then headed for the bridge.

Ty was already there. They monitored the traffic around Al-Kimia, quietly waiting for something to change. A few hours in, they all ate a hurried meal in the galley before returning to the bridge for more waiting.

After a few more hours, and another rest period, they had rejoined Eira on the bridge. "Orders are rolling in. An ACAS carrier has appeared on sensors. Flight believes it is carrying about 40-50 Stormhunters. There are also two heavy cruisers and 3 destroyers. Al-Kimia has the cruiser *Independence*, the two destroyers *Pride* and *Tempest* that escaped from Noea, the *Hesperus*, and few light scouts. We also have about a dozen armed cargo freighters and transports," she said looking at the heads-up display that tracked the ships in the system.

"It appears that the ACAS fleet brought nearly everything with them from Noea if the *Pride's* transmissions were correct. That means that Beall and the Al-Kimian forces on Noea might not be facing the full might of the ACAS." Hal surmised aloud. "That's good for Beall."

He met Ty's gaze. They both knew full well how daunting the prospect for Beall's survival was and appreciated the sacrifice those soldiers had made. No matter how this battle went, they were likely going through hell at this very moment, if any of them were still alive at all.

ADMIRAL OZVIO's tactical display pleased him. The over aggressive doyen had committed him to action, but right now it looked like the battle was his for the taking. A few armed transports could be dealt with by committing his Stormhunter attack fighters while he destroyed the remaining Al-Kimian fleet units with a hail of fire from his heavy cruisers and destroyers.

"Helmsman, flank speed. Fire Control, bring weapons online and target the heavy cruiser. Comms, order the *Thornbird* to launch her Stormhunter squadrons to take out the lighter transports and freighters. Have *Talent* and the destroyer squadron concentrate on eliminating the Al-Kimian destroyers."

"Aye, sir, messages sent. We are powering up weapons."

Excellent, Ozvio thought, *a victory here would likely propel him to fleet admiral. After all, someone had to take Quillon's place.*

The battle opened with a few long-range missile salvoes from the heavy cruisers; Ozvio knew that they were unlikely to do any real damage, but they forced the Al-Kimians to concentrate their defenses on shooting down missiles. This allowed the Stormhunters to launch on their deadly mission. It was not long before the reports started coming in, and Ozvio could see the destruction the Stormhunters were wreaking on the lightly armed and defended cargo vessels. These ships had no business being in this battle, and he hated to see brave people sacrifice their lives, but war was war, and it was a dirty business.

"TYCE, we have lost all of our supporting vessels in this sector. I am continuing evasive maneuvers." Eira, with Runa, was fully engaged in flying the *Loshad* to its absolute limits.

Ty and Hal were operating the weapons console and point defense system to try and stop the attacking missiles from getting through, but a few had. The *Loshad*, even with Eira's nanite technology, was beginning to lose integrity in places.

"We've got a breach in the forward cargo bay. I am sealing it now, but that will compromise the med station. Sorry folks, if you get hurt, I can't help you much." Beryl said as she pushed a button on a console to seal a bulkhead door to the cargo bay.

Hal had destroyed four of the attacking fighters, but with the loss of the other cargo ships, the *Loshad* was on her own.

"*Hesperus* this is *Loshad*, we are losing hull integrity and need assistance, can you help?" Ty called into the comms.

"*Hesperus* here. Sorry *Loshad*, but we are neck deep in ACAS destroyers. We got one with the rail gun and put one out of the fight with a missile shot, but we lost our railgun after a blast from one of the heavy cruisers," Patrin said.

"Understood *Hesperus*, gods speed." He glanced to Hal. "I guess we are on our own."

The fighters began to circle their prey like Betaldese vultures. The attack force of forty had been whittled down by determined and largely unexpected resistance from the small cargo vessels, but their speed and maneuverability had outclassed all the ships, save the *Loshad*. The firepower from the *Loshad* had surprised a few of the more aggressive pilots, but now they were systematically wearing down the ship.

"Tyce, I am afraid I cannot make the *Loshad* respond. The engines are crippled, and the damage is such that my nanites are having trouble holding the hull together," Eira said.

Ty knew what that meant. A ship that could not move was doomed.

"Understood." He paused, glancing at Hal. "We can send a surrender message, but I am not sure they will take it. Our other course is even worse."

By the looks on the faces of the crew they knew it was over too. Hal's head fell and Vivi stepped near him to lean in. After a moment, Hal looked up with determination. "If we're gonna go out, let's stick it to these fuckers. We can draw them in and then detonate the Bixby drive to take out a few more of the fighters. It will give Patrin and his crew a chance," Hal said.

Ty swallowed hard. It was grim, but it would make their deaths mean something. He saw Beryl nod. Vivi wrapped an arm around Hal as they stood together. Even Eira's normally serene silver visage showed determination.

"Eira. Go to countdown and detonate the Bixby drive."

Ty watched as Hal and Vivi spoke a few hushed words. He was glad he had lived to see Hal happy, even if it was for all too brief a time. He glanced to Beryl, who reached out a hand for his. Eira stepped up to join them.

"Countdown commencing, 30, 29, 28..."

OZVIO COULD NOT HELP but be pleased. His Stormhunters had taken out the light craft, all save one, and his capital ships had pounded the Al-Kimian fleet into space wreckage. The Al-Kimian cruiser showed no signs of life and the two destroyers were drifting. The battle was his.

"Admiral, we are monitoring a large fleet of ships entering the system," the vat at communications said.

Maybe that fool of a doyen had sent reinforcements. Hardly needed now, Ozvio thought.

"Drive signatures are not ACAS, Admiral, they are not broadcasting transponder codes."

Damn, Ozvio thought, *only freebooters and the Anklav ran ships with no registry.* "How many and what is the composition of the fleet?"

"There are at least six large vessels of cruiser size, what appears to be a carrier of some description, and several smaller vessels," his tactical officer stated.

"Gods help us," Ozvio whispered, "Order the immediate recall of all fighters to the *Thornbird* and *Talent* to break off her attack and rejoin us immediately."

"Sir, we are getting a comms message from Al-Kimia's Defense Force Command."

Ozvio gritted his teeth. "Put them on the viewer."

"22, 21, 20..."

At this point, words weren't needed between any of them as they waited for the inevitable.

"The Stormhunters are breaking off their attack runs and retreating," Eira said interrupting her countdown.

"Wh-What? Abort self-destruct of the drive!" Tyce called quickly.

Hal let go of Vivi and scanned the tactical display that showed the system. There were multiple ships entering the Al-Kimian sector and none of them were using identification recognition codes. "It's...it's the Anklav," he said.

"I am intercepting an uncoded message sent to the ACAS ships. I will put it on speaker," Eira said.

"To the Commander of the ACAS fleet now fighting in the Al-Kimian sector, this is General Terra Malar. You will no doubt realize that you are now outnumbered and outgunned. You have fought for a cause which is unjust and has led to destruction on an unimaginable scale, but my conscience will not allow me to see more bloodshed over a hopeless fight. Should you surrender your vessels, your crews will be humanely treated, and upon terms with the Coalition you will all be released. Those wishing to return to Coalition space will be afforded safe conduct. I give you five minutes to decide."

Hal turned with Vivi, a question in his eyes.

Ty held up a hand. There was a long pause.

"This is Admiral Ozvio. I have called a cease fire, General."

"Very good. You will take a shuttle to the surface. We will send coordinates. There we will talk terms of surrender. I guarantee your safe passage and return to your ship, no matter the outcome of our negotiations."

"I have heard of your reputation, General, so I do not doubt that," Ozvio returned. "We will send a message when we are on the way."

"Affirmative, Ozvio. I look forward to meeting you."

Hal let out a whoop of victory and grabbed Vivi, lifting her up in the air. Ty and Beryl fell back in their chairs, smiling at each other. Eira came to them, a quizzical look on her face. "The battle is over?"

"Yes," Ty said.

"And they will surrender?"

"Most likely," Hal said.

"Ozvio would not meet with her unless he was fairly sure," Ty mused. "But that probably doesn't mean the threat is over."

"We'll have to stay on our guard...and band together," Hal said.

A voice came over comms. "New friends and fellow

soldiers. This is General Malar. We are calling a temporary cease fire. You are to stay ready and hold position until we send further orders."

Acknowledgements came through from the different ships.

"Gods be praised," Beryl said softly.

EPILOGUE

Hal heard them before they approached. He had just finished teaching his normal combatives class in the athletic hangar; every week Al-Kimian recruits kept coming to get their asses handed to them in an attempt to make them better fighters. It had turned out to be something he really enjoyed. He wanted to not only help the soldiers he taught save their own lives but show them that vats and nats had more in common than most thought. It would make the lives of free vats easier if nats began to see them as equals, Hal had realized.

That would be essential if Jacent Seren's dream of a united Edge with both nats and vats would be possible. In the months since the surrender of the ACAS fleet and the overall weakness of the Coalition's forces, more and more worlds were rising against them. Was it possible to completely eject the ACAS from the Edge? After what Hal had seen in such a brief time, anything seemed to be possible – and he wanted to see it happen.

"Ask him," One from the group spoke from behind him.

"I'm not asking. You ask."

"Well, somebody ask," Hal said. "I'm not getting any younger here." He came over, climbed between the ropes and sat on the corner of the ring, unwrapping his hands and examining the group that had come to see him.

The three vats were wearing the Al-Kimian uniform. There were two young ones, a male with Aiza on his fatigues and a female named Destre; both appeared to have been rooks in a vat facility yesterday. The older vat female was named Cantú. She had to be nearing the end of her days, but she still had bright green eyes that sparkled with a hint of humor, despite the fearsome-looking scar running down her right cheek. After examining Hal a moment, she spoke. "You're Cullen, right? Word is you had the treatment."

Hal looked up from the handwrap he was rolling up. He'd been expecting this because he'd told Max to direct anyone with questions about it to him. "Yeah, I had it."

Cantú was talking about Eira's treatment to get rid of the rush. A few months after the last battle for the Edge, three of the Vedik strata had met the *Harbinger* and come back with them. Apparently, the Mudar hadn't yet made a decision to come as a whole, but three of the Vedik, inspired by Eira, had journeyed toward the Spiral. They'd linked up with the *Harbinger* and now, the Vedik, Max and Eira had streamlined the process, and the Al-Kimians were beginning to offer the experimental treatment for adrenaline fatigue to any vat who wanted it. Many of the ACAS vats that had decided to stay on Al-Kimia instead of returning to the Coalition were becoming curious. No one knew about Eira's people yet, although there were a few rumors around base. Only a few vats had taken the treatment...most were suspicious of the motives of nats and hesitant, but more and more were asking every day.

"We...we haven't made up our minds on it or anything," she

said. "But...I'm not getting any younger, either, if you know what I mean."

"Did you fight on Noea or Al-Kimia?" Hal asked. It had taken Noea a bit to push out all the ACAS. Beall had run the resistance there for two months, but now Hal was hearing that most of the ACAS had either surrendered or been taken out of power.

"Al-Kimia." Cantú replied.

"Five-by-five, me too."

"You were on the *Loshad*, right?"

"Yeah."

There was a pause, then Aiza spoke up. "Is it...is it true? That's what I want to know. If we were to get it done...we'll lose the rush?"

Hal glanced to Aiza for long moments before replying. "You will. But I think you'll find that you gain a lot more than you leave behind."

"And you don't die when you normally would?" the other female, Destre, asked, stepping forward.

Hal shrugged. "Can't be sure about that part yet, however, they think the treatment will extend your life. That's more of a guarantee than you have now, isn't it?"

"What's it like?" Destre asked. "Don't you feel...a lot...different?"

"You mean do I feel helpless?"

She nodded at him.

Hal thought long moments. "No." He understood their worries – they'd been his own. For some reason, he thought about the night with Vivi, when he'd finally told her how much she'd meant to him. When he'd had enough courage to tell her he loved her. He wouldn't have had that courage if he'd known his fate was to die in only a few years. "Don't think about what you're going to lose. Ask yourself what you'll gain. The reason you have for wanting to stick around will point you in the right direction."

Aiza gave him a nod. "You've given us something to think about."

"Thanks," Destre said, and they headed for the door. Hal noticed they linked hands on the way out.

"They'll be alright," Hal said.

"Maybe if they can figure it out, there's hope for me," Cantú said. "You sure I can trust this nat I talked to…Dr Parsen?"

"Yeah," Hal said, thinking about Max's dedication to help vats. Starting to give treatments to the vats that wanted it was a dream come true for him. "I'm not shitting you, I'd trust Max with my life."

"I'll do it, then. If it keeps me alive to fight the ACAS the next time they show their ugly faces, it's worth the risk." Cantú said, turning to go. She paused at the door and glanced over her shoulder. "And if I find a good reason for sticking around…that works too. See you around Cullen."

"Yeah," Hal said. He hoped she'd be okay, just like the rooks.

Ty was standing behind the ring when Hal turned to pack his equipment bag.

"Hey, Cap."

Ty came to the ring. "Hi. I got out of the command meeting and came over. I thought I could catch a little of your class." Ty gestured toward the door where the vats had left. "Sorry. I didn't intend to, but I overheard part of your conversation."

"Oh. Think I gave them some good advice?" Hal asked.

"Yeah." Ty nodded as Hal climbed down from the ring. "You sounded pretty damn wise. I'm proud of you, Hal."

"For what?" Hal asked.

"Everything," Ty replied.

Hal had come a long way since they'd gotten him back. He had recovered from the extreme physical stress his body had undergone. The nightmares about his time in ACAS custody were still bothering him, according to Vivi, but they were becoming less and less frequent. His optimism couldn't be wiped out, it seemed. It was like they'd been given a second chance from that moment on the *Loshad's* bridge during the battle of Al-Kimia, and it appeared things were going to work out for the Oppos if they stayed true to the cause.

Hal was looking at him quizzically. "This being proud is one of those nat things I don't get isn't it?" Hal asked as Ty clapped him on the shoulder, and they started walking toward the door.

"Maybe, but I think you understand more than you realize."

"I'm trying. Really trying."

"I know you are." Ty said. "Don't worry, it'll come with time."

"I keep wondering how I got here. I mean a little over a year ago, we were two guys combing the Edge for allenium. Now... here we are. And I wouldn't be here if not for you and Vivi, Beryl and Eira."

As they exited the hangar and made their way to where the *Loshad* was berthed, Ty nodded slowly. "I think we all could say the same about you."

As they entered the hangar, they both saw their ship, highlighted in the sunlight streaming down from the skylights above. It caught Ty and Hal for a moment and they paused. Vivi, Beryl and Eira were waiting for them there. Everything he and Hal cared about – their family – was there. Despite the bare metal from the battle damage, he still thought it was the most beautiful ship he'd ever seen because it was his. His and Hal's.

He saw Vivi step out onto the cargo ramp, gazing out as if she'd been waiting for them.

Ty turned to Hal and saw the same expression of contentment on his face. With a smile, he nudged Hal. "C'mon. Let's go home."

GLOSSARY

Amatan: the Mudar word for friends/family.

Arden: the name of the Mudar worldship.

Blue Rendal: an intensive programming drug that induces an emotionless state in a vat. It is used to toughen up vats that are deemed too sensitive, blunting conscience and emotional connection. Too much Blue Rendal can cause psychopathic traits in a vat.

Borj Gaba: the capital city of Harakat. This city contains many corporation offices and multiple levels.

CASS: Coalition of Allied Systems Ship.

Coren: a vacation planet in the Edge.

Cube: a small hotel room that sleeps two people max.

GLOSSARY

Denar: a Mudar strata specializing in technology and innovation

Drena Base: a major military base on Al-Kimia.

EVA: Extra Vehicular Activity, or a spacewalk.

Exoframe: a light exoskeleton to assist with walking for people with disabilities.

Exomech: an exoskeleton used for loading and unloading ships.

Gpod: a weapons mount on a smaller spacecraft.

Gradites: a Mudar strata devoted to the maintenance and building of new ships

Guardians: a Mudar strata devoted to security of the Mudar world ship.

Haleia Prime: capital of the Coalition.

Harakat: a planet with multiple levels. 235 corporations in the Spiral have offices on Harakat and ACAS influence there is minimal.

Inosu: a series of meditative poses meant to quiet the mind.

Insiders: those nats who don't live near the Edge.

Invern: a forbidding wilderness planet of forests and cliffs.

GLOSSARY

Jhere: a Mudar strata devoted to keeping records of the Mudar's journey across the universe.

Magnapharm: a medical corp that makes amp, Blue Rendal and other programming drugs.

Meliox: a medjet pain reliever for severe wounds.

Mytrite Nanites: the specific nanites required by Mudar for complex tasks and processing. Basically, the brain cells of a mudar brain.

Nova Star: the ACAS's highest honor for vats.

Null: a drug with a tranquilizing and sedative affect, administered by an eyedropper. Vats are particularly susceptible to null, which dulls their programming and allows for a relaxed state.

Nyma: a small wild cat on the planet Delia.

Obis: the Mudar's planet of origin.

Pinete: a beautiful but poisonous shrub with dark strong-smelling flowers. Pinete grows on core planets in the spiral and is sometimes used in assassinations.

Ponea: a spicy meat and rice dish, popular on the planet Celian.

Rationboxes: slang for tiny hotel rooms. Also called cubes.

Sora: a market planet where anything can be purchased for the right amount of scrilla.

GLOSSARY

Specialized Programming: a room on most vat ships and in vat complexes that contains the technology to adjust and reprogram a vat that doesn't meet specs. This intensive programming is done through the interface, using drugs like Blue Rendal.

Spicy Pe-Chai: a spicy vegetable and bi-horn dish.

Stormhunters: an ACAS one-man attack spacecraft.

Task Echo: a condition in which vats perform repetitive behaviors similar to the training they receive from the ACAS through the interface. Task echoes are a particular malfunction, for which there is no treatment. Some vats lash out when startled from a task echo by a stranger.

Template: the living beings on which Mudar were based is their template.

Tranesh: an undeveloped forest moon.

Vac Suit: an EVA suit for spacewalks.

Vedik: a Mudar strata of biologic specialists devoted to cataloging the life the Mudar have found on other planets.

Webmesh: a type of armor for vats and nats in the ACAS. It is also available for civilians from Armacorp.

ACKNOWLEDGMENTS

There are a few people I'd like to thank. First of all, I'm grateful to my husband, Judd, who tirelessly read draft after draft with enthusiasm and gave very helpful comments. He's my first, best critique partner, and none of these books would have existed without him.

I'd like to thank the members of the Transpatial Tavern for their support and encouragement. Thanks to Dan Hanks for the sage advice, Chris Panatier for all the laughs, Rob Greene for being our fearless leader and Halla Williams for your input on the book, plus all the other members who are good friends in countless ways.

Another member of the Transpatial Tavern I'd like to especially thank is author Charlene Newcomb. Without her help, I would not have navigated my way through the forest of self-publishing.

Next, I'd like to thank the editor of *The Rush's Edge*, Gemma Creffield at Angry Robot Books. I learned so much from working with her on the first book, and I hope I have put that to good use in the sequel. Perhaps the fates will have us working together again one day.

Lastly, I'd like to thank Karen Deem of Deem-Loureiro Inc. for designing the fabulous cover that fit the story perfectly.

My final thank you is to the readers. Without you, none of this would have been possible.

ABOUT THE AUTHOR

Ginger Smith became interested in science-fiction/fantasy when reading her father's collection of 1960's-1970's paperbacks as a child. Her writing career started at the age of ten, when she read a fantasy novel that disappointed her with its ending. Soon after, her love of writing stories led to being chosen to participate in the South Carolina Young Writer's Conference. In her early teen years, she wrote her own fantasy novel. In her 20's she played in and ran some tabletop RPG's, and once she DM'ed a game for over 18 hours straight. Ginger holds a master's degree in English from Troy University and has been an English teacher for 20 years. Tabletop gaming and collecting vintage sci-fi toys and novels are just a few of her hobbies. Currently, she lives in the southern USA with her husband and two cats. Her book *The Rush's Edge* was purchased by Angry Robot Books for publication in 2020. *The Rush's Echo* is her second novel.

Links:
Website: https://ginger-smith-author.com/
Twitter: @GSmithauthor

Printed in Great Britain
by Amazon